LOGIC'S END

LOGIC'S END

A Novel about the Origin of Life in the Universe

KEITH A. ROBINSON

Anomalos Publishing House
Crane

Anomalos Publishing House, Crane 65633
 Published 2007
Printed in the United States of America.
07 1

ISBN: 0978845331 (paper)
EAN: 9780978845339 (paper)

Illustrations by Samuel Schlenker

Cover illustration and design by Steve Warner

To Verónica, Mom, and Kevin for helping me with proofreading, editing, and story ideas, and to all of my other family and friends whose support and prayers have helped make this book a reality. I couldn't have done it without you!

Table of Contents

Ka'esch—Southwest Quadrant

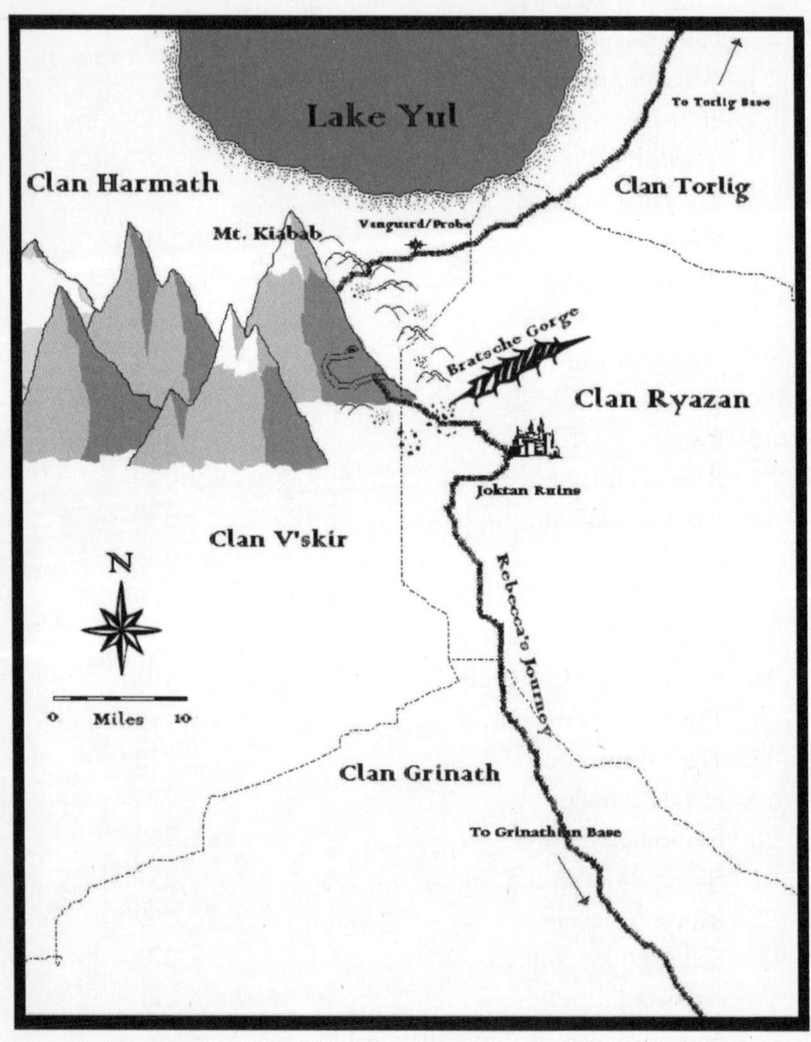

Modir Caverns

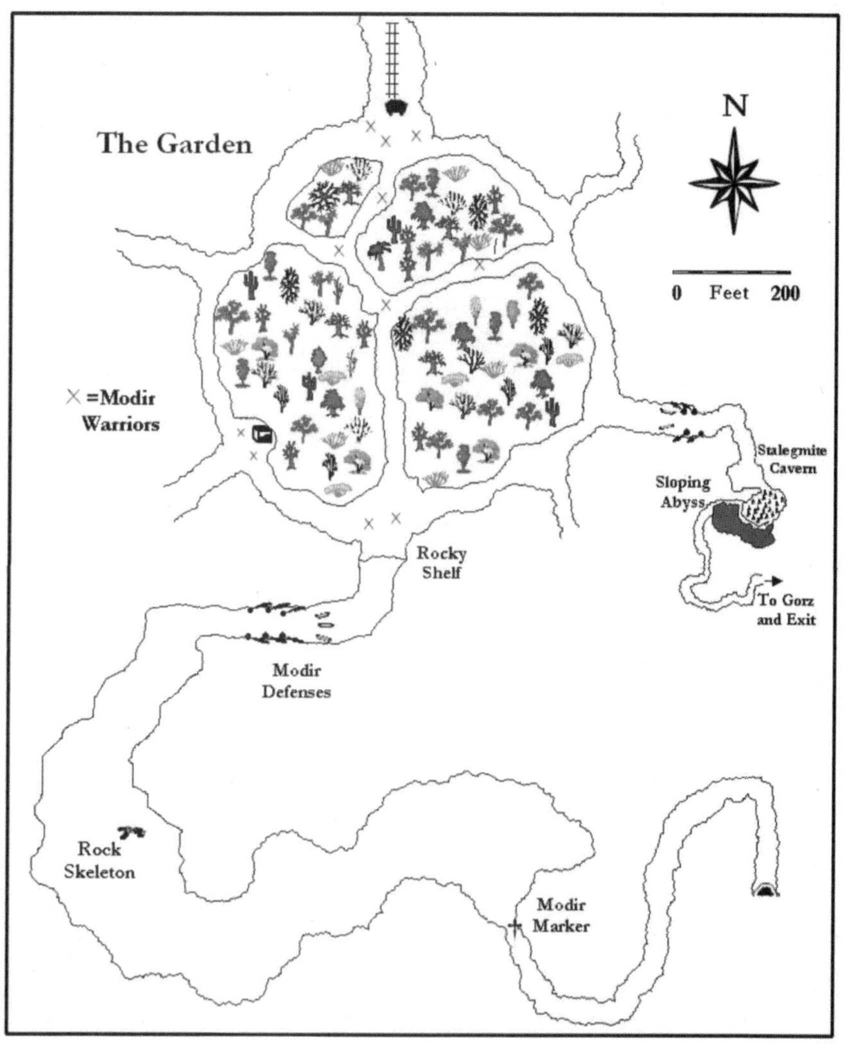

Sikaris Clan: Unknown

Weapons: Sonic roar
Defenses: Speed, gliding ability
Color: Dark brown, gold highlights, black skin folds
Size: 7'

Prin Clan: Diodre

Weapons: Pistol, electric shock, explosives
Defenses: Electric shock, agility, body suit
Color: Yellowish brown with black spots
Size: 5'5"

Rysth-nuul   Clan: Dakkar-nil

Weapons: Two automatic pistols, whiplike tail
Defenses: Quickness and agility, tail
Color: Moss green with dark yellow lines
Size: 6'

Tarrsk Clan: Torlig

Weapons: Shoulder tentacles that shoot projectiles
Defenses: Camouflage, ability to climb smooth surfaces
Color: Dark blue with patches of white, dead scales
Size: 5'

Ch'ran Clan: Harmath

Weapons: Handheld pistol, poisonous tail, claws
Defenses: Armor, jumping ability
Color: Gray
Size: 3'

Jorylk   Clan: Joktan

Weapons: Heavy rifle, spiked body armor
Defenses: Body armor
Color: Dark red and tan
Size: 7'

Kyen'tir Clan: Phaxad

Weapons: Sharp feather projectiles, talons
Defenses: Flight, mist spray
Color: Orange head, black scales/feathers, white torso
Size: 3'

Lohgar **Clan: Cahlah**

Weapons: Three handheld pistols
Defenses: Body armor, agility
Color: Dirty orange
Size: 6'

Druen Clan: Bkor

Weapons: Heavy cannon, horns/tusks
Defenses: Body armor, size
Color: Black and gray
Size: 10'

Breuun Clan: Grinath

Weapons: Automatic pistol, claw projectiles
Defenses: Armor, agility
Color: Dark gray and black
Size: 7'

Lri Errhu Species: Lidrilian

Weapons: Limbs and roots
Defenses: Bark
Color: Dark purple
Size: 10'

Clan: V'skir

Weapons: Guns, stun lights, pincers
Defenses: Hard exoskeleton
Color: Gray and yellow
Size: 5'

Clan: Mrdangam

Weapons: Spit acid, claws, tails
Defenses: Flight; thick, scaly hide
Color: Blood red
Size: 30' wingspan   25' (snout to tip of tail)

Clan: Ryazan

Weapons: Various guns, flammable gel, claws
Defenses: Fire
Color: Gray
Size: 3'

Clan: Modir

Weapons: Breath gas, claws
Defenses: Speed
Color: Dark Brown
Size: 4'

Pronunciation Guide

Bratsche—Br-AHT-sh
Breuun—Bree-OO-uhn
Ch'ran—Chuh-RAHN
Dakkar-nil—Da-KAR-nil
Diodre—Dee-O-druh (the r is a Spanish r, it is rolled slightly, or flipped)
Druen—DREW-en
Grinath—GRIN-ath
Harmath—HAR-math
Joktan—JOE-kten
Jorylk—JOR-ilk
Ka'esch—Kah-ESH
Kyen'tir—Kyen-TEER
Lidrilian—Lih-DRILL-ee-en
Lri Errhu—Luh-ree AIR-hoo
Lohgar—LOH-gar
Lohgur—LOH-ger
Modir—Moe-DEER (the r is soft, almost like a d)
Mrdangam—Mer-DAHN-gahm (the r is a Spanish r, it is rolled slightly, or flipped)
Phaxad—FAX-add
Prin—Prin
Ryazan—RYE-uh-zahn
Rysth-nuul—Risssth-NOOL (rhymes with tool)
Sikaris—Si-KAR-iss (rhymes with miss)
Tarrsk—Tarrrsk (with a rolled r)
Torlig—TORE-lig
V'skir—Vuh-SKEER

LOGIC'S END

1

Mission Approved

DON'T CRACK *your knuckles! Focus on the speech!* Rebecca reminded herself as she grabbed the edges of the podium for reassurance. She hated giving speeches, especially speeches to wealthy, important shareholders and business types. Yet the team had chosen her to be its spokesperson despite her protests, and she couldn't let them down. The whole project would face a major setback if they could not count on the financial support of the hundred-or-so people gathered in this room, and she was determined that she would not let years of study and research go to waste. Forcing herself to shut out the tinkling of glasses and the sounds of the kitchen staff as they removed the last of the dessert cups, she glanced around the large hotel conference room to determine if her speech was having the desired effect. The dim lighting provided by the crystal chandeliers combined with the blinding beam of light from the projector aimed at the screen next to her made it difficult to read the exact facial expressions of her audience beyond the first few round tables directly in front of her. But judging by the looks of those she could see, she took a deep breath and continued, satisfied of their attentiveness.

"In the past, astronomers have located baffling numbers of worlds around other stars. Yet, not even one of these worlds has come close to resembling Earth. These planets are at the extremes of the thermometer, or they are enormous or tiny, or they lack the proper oxygen-rich atmosphere. We have not observed any planets that could possibly support life.

"Until now."

Rebecca paused for emphasis before continuing, her eyes scanning the crowd. "Since NASA launched its Terrestrial Planet Finder space telescope in 2014, my colleagues and I have been scanning the heavens for a planet that would have the characteristics necessary to support life. Our dedication has finally paid off.

"Once this planet, designated 2021 PK, was found, NASA sent a small probe to take photos and readings. As you can see by this next slide, the probe reports confirm our greatest hopes. This planet has many similarities to Earth." Using her fingers to count off the numbers, Rebecca continued. "First, it revolves around a G2V size star. Second, its orbit is only slightly elliptical, unlike most exoplanets we have studied. Third, it is .95 Astronomical Units from its sun, almost exactly the right distance for life to evolve. Fourth, its gravity is only slightly heavier than ours. Fifth, the mean semimajor axis, mean eccentricity, and the mean mass are nearly identical to Earth. And, most importantly, it contains high amounts of liquid water, which would be absolutely necessary for life to have evolved there." She paused and brushed a loose lock of curly black hair behind her ear.

Clicking to the next slide, she continued. "You can see here a photo of the planet showing the dense atmospheric cloud cover, which may be accountable for the disruption in the radio signals and the slight degree of distortion in the photos.

"Although the reports are not conclusive, we believe that there is sufficient evidence to warrant a manned mission to 2021 PK. The primary goal of this mission would be to find proof of other life forms. The team would dig under the surface of the planet to search for fossils, plants, or any other signs of life, as well as collect numerous rock samples and perform various scientific experiments. We at NASA are proposing a partnership with Ionian Laser Technologies to help complete this mission. We believe that your recently completed laser drill, the RSK-320, shown here," she changed the slide to a photo of the sleek machine, "would be ideal for digging through the planet's hard surface. As most of you are aware, the RSK-320 uses radioplasmic technology to cut through dense planetary layers, shutting off within one one-hundredth of a second if it encounters any fossil-bearing materials or any kind of life form."

She leaned forward over the podium, growing excited. "Because of the sheer number of variables that must be in delicate balance for life to arise, we believe that 2021 PK represents the best chance to find other forms of life in our galaxy. For no other planet that we have ever observed even comes close to the perfect harmony of Earth. The discovery of this planet could very well be one of the most profound discoveries in all of human history. But only if we find evidence of life. We must send a team of scientists to scour the surface of the planet if we have any hope of finding the evidence we seek.

"NASA hopes that you will realize the enormous potential for this mission, and support us wholeheartedly. For once the team returns triumphant, it will usher in a new era of scientific study, not to mention a new era of prosperity for ILT. And your generous financial support will have been the driving force that made it all possible. On behalf of all of us at NASA, thank you for your time and consideration." Rebecca took a deep breath, stepped back from the podium and gave a heartfelt smile to the audience, which had begun to clap enthusiastically.

She turned, walked off the platform and continued on to her table in the front of the room as the MC returned to the podium to close out the evening. When she reached the table, her supervisor stood and pulled out a chair for her.

"Way to go, kid!" he said in an excited whisper. "You really made an impact."

Although Rebecca was thirty-two years old and only seven years younger than Dr. Goldsmith, he frequently teased her by calling her "kid." It had bothered her the first year at NASA, but over time she had come to grow fond of it, especially after realizing that that was what he called everyone younger than him. After a few years she reached the conclusion that this was probably due to the fact that his mostly bald head, old-fashioned glasses and very conservative style of suits made him look much older than his thirty-nine years. On top of that, it didn't help that she was an entire foot shorter than him. When they stood next to each other, her thin, athletic stature was dwarfed by his 6 foot 4 inch bulk.

"Thank you, *sir,*" she replied. She smiled lightheartedly at him as she smoothed out the knee-length skirt of her light gray business suit and sat down.

Relaxing into her chair, she took a drink of wine to steady her nerves. *Now's when the real fun begins,* she thought sarcastically, as she unconsciously began cracking her knuckles at the unpleasant thought of the after-dinner "festivities." Although she seemed outgoing and friendly in public, she was, in reality, very uncomfortable meeting new people in unfamiliar surroundings. *Here we go. No rest for the weary,* she thought as the MC finished thanking everyone for coming. Taking out the plain black clip that held her curly mass of hair in place, she pulled her hair back once again and replaced the clip in preparation for the onslaught.

Sure enough, no sooner had the last words left the MC's mouth, than elegantly dressed "well-wishers" immediately surrounded Rebecca. For the next half-hour, she was caught up in a whirlwind of questions, compliments, and congratulations until she felt her face would crack from smiling.

Lost in the flurry, Rebecca didn't notice the slight pressure on her arm until a familiar voice spoke near her right ear. "Excuse me, ladies and gentlemen, but I need to borrow Mrs. Evans for a moment," Dr. Goldsmith said, as he led her by the arm out of the throng of guests.

"My knight in shining armor has finally come to rescue me," she whispered to him after they had turned away from the group.

"You're welcome, fair maiden." He leaned in toward her and, with an air of mystery, said, "There's someone who would like to speak with you."

She pulled away and gave him a look of mock indignation. "Betrayed! Out of the frying pan and into the fire." However, after noticing his expression of excitement, she quickly became curious and began scanning the crowd in an effort to locate Dr. Goldsmith's mysterious guest.

Two distinguished looking men standing near the back of the room immediately captured her gaze. The one on the left was an elderly, gray-haired man wearing thin, wire framed glasses and a navy blue, double-breasted suit. The man on the right looked to be in his mid-forties and was dressed in a shirt and tie underneath a dark blue flight jacket. His hair was cut in typical military style. The insignia on his jacket's left breast caused Rebecca to catch her breath in shock.

*Oh, my God! Is this about...Are they here to...Do they want...*Her thoughts were whirling around at such a dizzying rate that when she found herself standing in front of the two strangers, it took her a moment to realize the elderly man with the glasses was addressing her.

"I said, it is a pleasure to meet you, Gunnery Sergeant Evans," he repeated in a deep, gravelly voice. She looked down, and to her embarrassment, saw that he had his right hand extended toward her. She quickly reigned in her jumble of thoughts and emotions and politely shook his hand.

He continued, "You look even more lovely in person."

Standing under his scrutiny, Rebecca suddenly became self-conscious about her appearance. She had never been considered beautiful as she was growing up. However, she had a plain kind of attractiveness that was brought out further by her bright, intelligent brown eyes and her friendly smile. "Thank you, sir," she managed.

"My name is Henry Bremen, and this is Captain Jonathan Coffner," he said, indicating the man in the flight jacket.

Rebecca shook his hand politely and smiled, her confidence and strength returning. "It is a pleasure to meet you, gentlemen."

"Your presentation was very thorough, and quite impressive. You did a fine job representing NASA. I don't think the board members at ILT will have any problem approving our request. You are clearly very passionate about the search for other life in the galaxy."

Her heart began thudding even harder in her chest. "The question of the origin of life is the greatest question of all time," she responded.

He looked at her and gave her a warm smile. "Yes, I agree; and that is why we're here. Mrs. Evans, as you are probably aware, I am the Mission Coordinator at NASA, and I came here tonight to personally inform you that you have been accepted as Special Mission Science Advisor for the upcoming mission to 2021 PK."

A million thoughts simultaneously assailed her in that instant.

Through it all, one spoke loudest: *It actually happened! I'm going!* When she had first submitted the request to accompany the mission, she never really believed it would be accepted. It was one thing to be a NASA scientist, but quite another to be an astronaut. It seemed like a fairy tale, a dream. And now, it was coming true. Her fantasy was becoming reality.

Dr. Goldsmith brought her back to the present. "I think this is the first time I've ever seen her truly speechless." Rebecca turned to look at him, then looked back at Mr. Bremen, attempting to recover her speech. "Thank you! I…I don't know what to say!" she said, giving a short, awkward laugh.

Mr. Bremen looked to his companion. "Captain Coffner here will be commanding the shuttle *Vanguard* for this mission."

Captain Coffner smiled and extended his hand. "Welcome to the crew. We are all looking forward to working with you. Congratulations."

"Here is your assignment, along with some forms and necessary documents," Mr. Bremen said as he handed her a packet in a manila envelope. "Mission training will begin at the end of the month. Congratulations once again, Gunnery Sergeant Evans. We will see you then."

The two men bowed slightly, then turned to leave.

"Way to go, kid!" Dr. Goldsmith said as they left. "I have to admit, I am quite envious. If I could have passed the physical, I would have jumped at the chance to go myself. When they told me you had been accepted, I thought that tonight would be a great time to break the news. Don't you agree?"

She nodded absentmindedly; her thoughts still a jumbled mess.

"Come on, let's share the news with everyone else and then we'll go celebrate. What do you say?" When she failed to reply, he chuckled to himself and shook his head. "I'll be right back," he said as he walked hurriedly towards the front of the conference room. In the back of her mind, Rebecca could hear him gathering all of their colleagues together.

With shaking hands, she grasped a chair from the nearest table and collapsed into it, one thought breaking through the confusion in her mind. *I'm actually going!*

‡ ‡ ‡

"AAAAAAAAAAAAAA!!!"

Rebecca pulled the cell phone away from her ear as her sister's scream spewed forth from the earpiece. She laughed as she waited for her excitement to die down. "I can't believe it! You're going into outer space! To another planet! I mean, this is like *Star Trek* or something! You're going to be famous! AAAAAAAAAAAAA!"

Her younger sister, Katie, had always been the emotional one; and this time proved to be no exception. "So when do you leave?" Katie asked.

"Well, first we have to go through all sorts of training. Even though my primary assignment will be to operate the drill once we reach the planet, NASA insists that all shuttle personnel be cross-trained in all of the basic shuttle operating procedures, from piloting to navigation." Rebecca sat down on the edge of the bed in her hotel room and kicked off her shoes. "Then, there's the physical training. I've heard it can be pretty tough. It's been awhile since I trained that rigorously."

"Are you kidding? This coming from my sister, the ex-marine? You have always been as tough as nails for as long as I can remember. Remember way back in fourth grade when you beat up Bobby O'Conner?" Katie retorted.

"Hey, that's what he gets for putting a fake spider in my lunch. You know how much I hate those things," Rebecca said, smiling at the memory.

"Yeah, and he sure left you alone after that. Don't worry, Becky. You'll do just fine, especially with all the hours you spend at the gym. But you still haven't answered my question: when do you leave?" her sister asked again.

"Well, the last part of the training is the mission simulators, and those are scheduled for the beginning of next year, so we should probably lift-off about May or June," Rebecca said. Pulling the clip out of her hair, she let it down and brushed her fingers through the tangled knots.

"Wow, that's a lot of training." Katie was silent for a moment. When she finally continued the conversation, her voice was suddenly filled with concern. "Becky, is it safe? I mean, you don't even know what's on this planet. What if there are…I don't know, things out there?"

Rebecca laughed and lay down on the bed, "I sure hope so! That's why we're going—with the hope that we'll find evidence of other life forms."

"You know what I mean. Aliens, or monsters, or . . ."

"Listen to you! You've been watching too many movies. The probe reports don't show any signs of life on the planet's surface in the area in which it landed. But it did find water. The kinds of life forms we're looking for are in the early stages of evolution and are probably buried under the earth. You know, worms, amoebas, stuff like that. I highly doubt there are any *intelligent* creatures out there. And, if there are, we'll be prepared. ILT has developed more than just drills, you know. Each of us on the crew will have one of Ionian's new laser pistols. So if any of your 'monsters' do turn up, we'll blast them to oblivion just like on *Star Trek*," she said with mock bravado.

"Ha, ha, ha," her sister replied dryly, clearly not amused. "Just be careful. You're my only sister, and I need you to come back so that my kids can move in with you when they become teenagers."

"Oh, no. I don't think so, sis," Rebecca said.

"So what's so important about finding a few worms, anyway?" Katie asked.

Rebecca sat up in the bed. "Katie, do you realize that if we find life on another planet, even simple life, that it will prove that evolution is true? It will finally bring unity to science. The problem now is that many scientists spend so much time arguing among themselves about whether or not life evolved, they lose precious time that could have been spent in the pursuit of increasing the quality of life or solving some of the world's problems. If we find life on another planet, it will prove beyond a shadow of a doubt that we truly did evolve. On top of that, it will stop all of this 'Creation Science' religious nonsense."

"I guess I see your point, but just be careful. Religion isn't all bad, you know. It helps to keep my kids in line at times."

"Don't worry. I'm not out to destroy religion. I just think it's about time religion gets its nose out of science."

Her sister let out a slow breath, her amazement still evident in her voice. "Wow, Becky. I envy you so much. I bet Jeffrey's proud, huh? Have you told him yet?"

"No. You're the first one I've called."

"Really? Well, what can I say? I'm honored. Hey, how're you two doing, anyway?"

"Pretty good. We just haven't seen much of each other lately. He's been over in Iraq working on that archeological dig for the university for the last two months," Rebecca commented.

"And let me guess, when he gets back, you'll be down in Florida for training," Katie said.

Rebecca sighed. "Yeah. Distance really tends to put a strain on a relationship. At least I'll be out of these frozen Midwest wastelands and closer to you and Mom and Dad. Speaking of Dad, how is he?"

Katie's voice took on an edge of concern, "The therapist said he is adapting well to the prosthetic, and he will be able to walk with the use of a cane before long. The good news is that his blood sugar has been down near 120, so he seems to be doing better. The bad news is that he is so stubborn that he refuses to change his eating habits."

"Surprise, surprise. Well, what can you do?"

"Hey, hold on a second, Becky. Paul just got home with the kids." Rebecca heard muffled voices in the background, then the phone erupted once again with screams of excitement.

The youthful voice of her eight-year-old nephew suddenly burst from the mouthpiece. "Aunt Becky, is it true? Are you really going to another planet to meet aliens?"

She laughed, "Well, I don't know about aliens, Zach. But I am going to another planet."

"Can I come too? I promise I won't get in the way."

Rebecca smiled into the phone. "Sorry, buddy. They don't have a suit that will fit you. But I'll try to bring back a little alien dirt or rocks for you, okay?"

"Okay. Thanks Aunt Becky. Can we at least come see you blast off?" Zach asked, excitedly.

"Of course you can, Zach. In fact, I'd be upset if you didn't."

"Alright! Thanks again, Aunt Becky. I can't wait to tell my friends at school." There was a slight pause. "Mom wants to talk again. Bye, Aunt Becky." Another pause.

"Paul said 'congratulations.' He's putting Carolyn to bed, and I should go give him a hand. Congratulations, sis. I couldn't be happier for you," Katie said.

"Thanks, Katie. Well, I'll let you go. I've got so many other people to call, one of them being my husband. Take care. I love you guys."

"We love you too. Bye."

Rebecca hung up the cell phone and lay back down on the bed, letting the phone slip from her grasp. *I'm really going to miss them,* she thought as she took a deep breath and let it out with a sigh. Suddenly, unbidden yet familiar tears began to slide down her cheeks. As much as she loved to talk to her sister, each time they spoke together she found herself growing more and more envious. For years, Rebecca had wanted to have children, but for whatever reason, she and Jeffrey were denied the joys of parenthood. With each passing year she grew more and more sensitive to her age, her dreams slipping away with the sands of time. Mixed feelings swirled within her as she remembered the argument they had had right before he left on his trip. Why couldn't he just agree to adopt?

Brushing her tears aside with the back of her hand, she took another deep breath to vanquish her emotions. Once again in control, she picked up the phone and dialed Jeffrey's cell phone number. With each ring, her fears and longings were dispelled by her growing excitement to share her news. After several seconds of anticipation, she finally heard him answer. "Hello. This is Jeff."

"Honey, you'll never guess what happened to me today!"

2

2021 PK

THE VIEWPORT of the sleek shuttle was filled with the image of the space station *Independence*, the sight of which caused Rebecca to marvel at human ingenuity. "Will you look at that," she said in awe.

Lisa Staley, the shuttle technician, looked over to where Rebecca sat several feet away on her right side. "You ain't kidding. We truly are *homo sapien sapien.* Wise WISE man."

The station was by far the largest orbiting space station ever built. Its design was circular and reminded Rebecca of a bicycle wheel with four main spokes stretching in towards the dome-shaped central hub. Reaching out towards empty space through both ends of the hub was a long shaft shaped like a lance with a point on both ends. The station's slow rotation on its axis simulated gravity in the outer sections, offering the eighty-person crew some measure of the comfort of Earth. Rebecca remembered reading in her briefing that due to the lack of gravity in the central spire, it was used mostly for storage and zero gravity experiments. Docked at the farthest tip of the spire sat a short cylindrical ship, which was their destination.

"*Independence*, this is *Vanguard* on final approach. We are preparing to connect to the Cortex Propulsion Drive," Captain Coffner said as the shuttle edged closer to the enormous station.

The Cortex Propulsion Drive consisted of five separate sections that, when linked together, formed a ship that resembled some kind of ancient sword. However, the only section that was currently docked at the station was the "hilt," which housed the bridge, living quarters, and power system, as well as several other vital components. The remainder of the drive awaited them at their destination.

"Isn't it incredible to think that we get to reap the benefit of millions of generations of human knowledge and creativity?" Rebecca commented as their shuttle flew up and over the other ship, aligning itself in preparation for docking.

"Yeah, it is truly amazing what the human mind can do," Lisa replied.

Rebecca turned away from the awe-inspiring view to look at her friend, her face reflecting unease. "Do you have any apprehension about the fact that our fuel for the return trip is waiting for us at the planet? I mean, what if someone made an error and the supply ship is not where it is supposed to be? Our lives depend on so many calculations to be precise. How many times have they used this thing on real missions, anyway?" she asked.

Lisa laughed reassuringly. "Four, but never as far as we're going. Hey, don't worry. The greatest minds on our planet planned this trip. NASA has left nothing to chance."

Rebecca turned back to look out the viewport once again. The docking was almost complete.

Captain Coffner toggled the radio. "Touchdown in 5…4…3…2…1…mark." A thunderous boom enveloped her, accompanied immediately by a violent shake as the shuttle was clamped into place. After a moment, a voice was heard over the intercom. "Welcome to the *Independence*, *Vanguard*. We hope your stay, though short, will be pleasant. Our crew should have all of the connections between you and the CPD double-checked and secure in just under fifteen minutes."

"Thanks for your hospitality, *Independence*," Captain Coffner said. "We'll wait for your green light."

As the minutes ticked by, the excitement of the blast off and docking at the station began to ebb, leaving Rebecca's mind free to dwell on the events of the past month. With the memories also came the feelings of concern and worry.

Noting the change in her friend's countenance, Lisa reached over and placed a comforting hand on her arm. "Hey, Gunny. Are you okay?"

Rebecca shrugged off her thoughts and smiled at the usage of her military nickname, grateful for Lisa's thoughtfulness. "Fine, thanks."

Her best friend had always had a knack for being able to read her mind and her feelings, sometimes to the point of annoyance. Ever since they had met in the marines, they had been like sisters. The hours of training and short combat stint formed an iron bond between them, which had been strengthened further in recent years as they worked together at NASA. In the back of her mind, Rebecca wondered if her friendship with Lisa might not have had something to do with her being assigned to this mission.

Lisa smiled back, but wasn't fooled. "Are you still worried about your father?"

Rebecca smiled ruefully. "I never was a good liar, was I?"

"Nope," Lisa replied simply, trying to lighten the mood.

Sighing, Rebecca turned to look out the window again. "Yeah, I am. He seemed to be doing fine a month ago. He's always had a strong heart. I just don't understand what happened."

"I've heard that diabetes can do that to a person, no matter how strong they are," Lisa added.

Turning to face her friend, Rebecca continued to express her concern. "I just hope he's okay by the time we get back. It's going to eat me up not knowing how he's doing for six months. And being confined to a wheelchair for the rest of his life is going to be hard for him to cope with," she paused, looking uncertain. "Maybe I shouldn't have come."

"I know what you mean," Lisa replied, letting out a sigh of her own. "I miss my girls already. It's bad enough that I won't get to see them for half a year, but I'm going to miss Jenny's ninth birthday on top of that, *and* I'm taking their favorite Aunt Becky with me!"

Rebecca smiled slightly, despite her concern for her father. "At least you won't have to spend three hours trying to get pudding stains out of your couch and make-up off of the neighbor's dog."

Lisa groaned. "Don't remind me!"

They laughed at the shared memory, then lapsed into an uncomfortable silence, each lost in her own thoughts. After several seconds, Rebecca became serious once more. "Lisa, why did you come? I mean, I'm glad you're here, but…but what if something happens to you? What if neither of us comes back? Who will take care of Jenny and Amanda since…since Brad died?"

A momentary flicker of emotion passed over Lisa's face at the mention of her husband's name. "I've told you before, Becky, it's just something I have to do. Since Brad has been gone I have had to really come to grips with who I am. This opportunity came at the perfect time. It was a way for me to move on with my life."

"Yeah, but…what if…I mean, if they were…my daughters, I…" she said, leaving the thought unfinished, her chest constricting painfully.

Lisa, recognizing her friend's emotional struggle, remained silent for a moment before continuing. "Becky, I appreciate your concern. Besides," she commented casually, trying once again to lighten the mood, "it's not like anything is going to happen to us, right? And as for your father, you coming on this mission is probably the best thing you could do for him." Seeing Rebecca's confused look, she explained. "It gives him something to look forward to, something to fight for, kind of like this mission was for me. Not to mention it's a little late to change your mind now anyway, unless you want us to leave you here on the *Independence*," she said wryly. "You could always hitchhike!"

A lopsided grin spread across Rebecca's features. Sighing deeply in an attempt to ward off the remainder of her worries, she turned to face forward once again. "You're right. He's a tough old bird. I'm sure he'll be fine," she said with more confidence than she felt. "Thanks for your concern, Lisa. Anyway, with all of the excitement of the trip, I'm sure the time will just fly by." *At least I hope it will,* she added silently.

The intercom suddenly came alive with the voice of the commander of the *Independence*. "*Vanguard*, you're locked and loaded. Have a safe trip."

"Thank you, *Independence*," Captain Coffner said. "We'll see you in a few months, God willing." He switched off the comm as the pilot, Ricky, reached forward and grabbed the piloting joystick. "Take us to the dish, Ricky."

The thirty-something, dark-skinned Hispanic studied his instrument panel, then responded with a slight accent, "Sure thing, *Capitán.* T-minus 5 minutes."

Rebecca felt her pulse quicken and her stomach knot up. "Stage I complete," Captain Coffner announced. "All stations, report status." Rebecca listened as each member of the eight-person crew responded with an "all clear."

The shuttle and the newly attached CPD module slowly moved away from the *Independence* and headed off towards the moon. Since she was a child, Rebecca had always dreamed of traveling into space and seeing the magnificent, natural satellite up close. All of those years of waiting had been worth it, she now decided. The majesty of it, the sheer immensity, left her feeling small and insignificant. *And to think, without this giant ball floating high in space, there would be no tides to mix the oxygen in the ocean. There would be no life.*

As she pondered its beauty, her excitement grew once more. According to the probe, 2021 PK had a moon as well. Would they really succeed in their mission? Would they really find other life forms? NASA certainly believed it was worth the risk, and the money.

"There she is," Ricky said, pointing to something that was just becoming visible as they came around the dark side of the moon and into the shining radiance of the sun.

The viewport immediately darkened to compensate for the brilliance. After a moment's adjustment, Rebecca could begin to make out five shapes in the distance.

Although dwarfed by the moon, the objects were still immense, particularly the one closest to the sun. Stretching nearly seven thousand miles across but only a fraction of that in thickness, the hexagonal sunlight collector glowed with a bright orange-yellow light, impatient to release its pent-up energy.

Beyond that, three more objects floated motionless in space in close proximity to each other. The cylindrical laser was positioned to receive the focused sunlight, ready to convert it into the high-powered laser beam that, once reflected off of the giant mirror stationed next to it, was channeled through the particle accelerator, which then increased the speed of their laser light to almost fifty times normal, propelling their ship into deep space in record time.

The last of the five objects was their laser sail. The circular, diamond-film disc was a full six hundred miles in diameter. Its clear, crystalline surface refracted the light from the sun, causing rainbows to dance about in all directions. The effect was stunning, causing all within the shuttle to simply stare in wonder.

Several minutes of silence passed uninterrupted, until at last Captain Coffner spoke. "We're coming up on the harness. Take us in nice and easy, Ricky."

The "harness" was a small, eighty-foot wide circle that was attached to the laser sail by several nearly invisible cables. Ricky piloted the Cortex Propulsion Drive through the center of the harness with ease, slowing as they neared the connection point.

"Easy-does-it," the Captain said softly as the ship crawled forward, now moving at a snail's pace. Suddenly there was a loud click and a slight shudder as the connectors locked into place.

The Mission Specialist, Adam, looked up from his console and gave a thumbs up. "All lights are green. Nice job, Ricky."

"*Independence,* this is *Vanguard.* Stage II is complete," Captain Coffner said into the comm. "You may inform NASA that we are ready for Stage III."

"Acknowledged, *Vanguard,*" came the reply.

"It's too bad that we can't take the laser with us," Lisa said as they waited for NASA's signal. Traveling by laser light is so much more efficient than the anti-hydrogen engines used by the CPD."

Rebecca's pulse quickened in anticipation of the coming trip so that she had to swallow hard to even get her voice to work properly. "And quicker, too. If this planet turns out to be all we hope for, maybe they will use the laser to send components to build another laser at the other end so that we can travel both directions instead of having to use fueled rockets. Who knows? Maybe 2021 PK will become a second Earth. The new *New World.*"

The voice from the *Independence* returned, breaking into their conversation. "Hold on, *Vanguard.* We are about to turn up the juice. Have a safe trip."

The viewpoint darkened until it became completely opaque, or so it seemed. Then, the entire world around them became a bright yellow as the laser light was captured by the massive sail. Rebecca was thrown back against her chair as the shuttle and her escort shot forward towards its destination, and its destiny.

The next six weeks passed uneventfully. The laser continually pumped light into the sail, sending their craft hurtling through space faster and faster until they reached their maximum speed of nearly fifty times the speed of light. As the hours turned into days, the crew fell into a routine. They passed their time either conducting scientific experiments, sleeping, or performing various shuttle duties. After nearly a month and a half of travel, the sail reversed, beginning to slow the ship down. Finally, eighty-seven days after launch, they reached their destination.

"Well, ladies and gentlemen, there she is, 2021 PK," Captain Coffner said.

Growing ever larger in front of them loomed a reddish-colored planet with dense cloud cover. The images received by the probe were nothing compared to actually viewing the real thing. Rebecca felt butterflies in her stomach as the excitement of the mission was renewed.

The thousands of questions and doubts that she had wondered about since first learning of the planet's existence bombarded her simultaneously, making her feel lightheaded. *Will we really find life here? What will it look like? What will the soil of the planet feel like? What about the atmosphere? Will it interfere with our equipment? What if there really are intelligent aliens? What if we don't find anything? What if we can't lift-off again? What if...*

As if guessing her next question, the Captain asked, "Now, where are the fuel storage units for the CPD?" Eyes narrowed, he scanned the empty space around them.

"There it is! One o'clock!" Ricky called out as he pointed.

There was an audible sigh of relief as the entire crew relaxed. "NASA, we have arrived and the package is right where you said it would be," Captain Coffner spoke into his comm. "We are preparing for CPD separation and will be entering the atmosphere momentarily. Standby." Without waiting for a reply, which he knew could take several minutes to reach them, he switched off the transmitter and nodded to Ricky to continue.

"Velocity approaching zero," Ricky reported as he grabbed the control stick. "CPD separation on my mark. 3…2…1…mark." As before, a loud metallic bang sounded and the shuttle shook.

"CPD separation complete. Prepare for planetary entry," Captain Coffner said. "Ricky, do you have a solid lock on our probe?"

"It's a bit fuzzy, as expected, but still strong enough to follow."

"Good. Take us down."

As the *Vanguard* penetrated the atmosphere, the clouds swirled around them like spun cotton threads, picking up the red color of the planet here and there. Rebecca had never experienced anything so terrifying in her life. The shuttle shook so violently that she felt it would surely shake apart. Then, abruptly, it was over. Breaking through the blanket of clouds, Rebecca saw a dry barren landscape come into view, which consisted solely of rolling hills of gray dirt. It looked as uninviting as the Mohave Desert.

"Doesn't look like much, does it?" Scott Boland, the shuttle's Payload Commander said, disappointment evident in his voice.

"There doesn't seem to be any vegetation, just a bunch of hills and large boulders," Lisa commented. She turned and looked over at Rebecca. "Do you think the whole planet is like this, or is this just some sort of desert-like area?" Rebecca just shrugged and continued to stare out the viewport, her gaze fixated on the landscape below, desperately searching for…something…anything.

"There it is!" Ricky said triumphantly. "Do you see it? Right there, in front of those mountains. And there's the lake we saw in the reports."

As promised, the probe sat near the edge of a small lake which looked to be about four miles in diameter. Behind it stood a tall range of mountains.

"Put her down over there," Captain Coffner said, indicating a flat area near the probe, about a half of a mile from the edge of the lake. Ricky nodded in acknowledgement and set the shuttle down gently onto the alien soil, the vertical thrusters kicking up clouds of chalky gray dust.

"Well, everyone, welcome to 2021 PK," Ricky said, impersonating the voice of an airline pilot. "And thank you for flying on the *Vanguard.* Enjoy your stay."

Captain Coffner looked at him wryly. "Thank you, stewardess." Clicking his radio, he said, "NASA, we have touched-down. Preparing to disembark." As he began unstrapping himself, he addressed the others, who were already in the process of extricating themselves from their chairs. "Okay, everyone. Remember, although 2021 PK's atmosphere is breathable, there's still a lot of carbon dioxide in the air, so wear your protective breathing gear. Use the hand-held motion detectors until we get the larger perimeter secure with our Motion Detection Units, then we'll unload the laser drill. We don't want anything sneaking up on us while we are working. Joel and I will head to the north by the lake, Jen and Scott will go west, Adam and Dave head to the east, and Lisa and Rebecca go south near the mountains. Ricky will stay with the shuttle and finish post-flight. So far, our readings show nothing moving out there, but keep your blasters ready. Report in once you have your MDUs up and functional. It looks like we arrived at the perfect time. The sun has only been up an hour or so, so we have plenty of daylight left. Let's go, people."

Rebecca checked her jumpsuit to make sure that it was properly sealed. NASA's new astronaut suits were not nearly as bulky as the older ones, tending to look more like thick coveralls than anything else. But despite their appearance, they were much more reliable. Still, she didn't take any chances. Double checking all of her connections and latches, she slipped on her helmet and locked it into place. Once she was satisfied that all was set properly, she moved over to where Lisa and the others were waiting near the shuttle's hatch.

"Are you ready for your first step onto alien soil?" Lisa asked, her voice full of excitement.

"Ready if you are. I still can't believe I'm here."

"Well, believe it. Here we go," she said as Captain Coffner opened the hatch. Immediately, wind blew a fine white dust through the opening as the pressure from the shuttle equalized with the atmosphere of the planet. Weapons in hand, the crew walked cautiously down the shuttle's ramp in pairs.

As Rebecca's booted foot touched the soil, she felt a thrill of excitement lance through her body. She was really here! She stared around her in awe, like a child viewing a rainbow for the first time. *There has to be life here. I can feel it. There's something special about this place.*

"Hey, Becky," Lisa said as she nudged her with her shoulder. "Are you awake?"

"Y...yeah," she stuttered, coming to her senses. "Sorry. It's just..."

"I know. Simply incredible," she finished. "C'mon, let's get this job done so we can do some sightseeing."

Using their short ranged, hand-held motion detectors, they made sure that the immediate area was secure, then split up and headed off in their designated directions. As Lisa and Rebecca walked toward the distant mountains, Rebecca stared in awe at the topography of the alien landscape.

They hadn't traveled far before their headsets crackled to life. Captain Coffner's voice was clear, but the atmospheric distortion was already affecting the equipment. "Be careful out here. Keep an eye on your motion detectors. This wind and dust are reducing visibility, and this distortion may have an unknown effect on our equipment. Report any signs of malfunction immediately."

"Copy, Captain," Lisa said.

Rebecca turned to look back toward the shuttle. "No kidding. It's difficult to see the ship already. How far out are we going?"

"One mile. Any farther and we would be unable to pick up the others with the hand-held motion detectors. Don't worry, although there is some distortion, the equipment is working perfectly," Lisa reassured her.

They kept walking for several more minutes, passing several small mounds of dirty white earth, each reaching no more than fifteen feet tall and about fifty feet in diameter. Finally, Lisa called a halt. Taking the long range MDU off of her shoulder, she set it gently to the ground.

"According to the gauge, this is far enough. If we go any farther, we will run into those large boulders on the skirts of the mountain. Does your motion detector show anything in the vicinity?"

Rebecca studied the screen of the instrument panel for a moment. "It's picking up the others' movements faintly, but nothing else. But this atmospheric interference is really wreaking havoc with the readings."

"Well, let's get this thing unpacked. Once all four are online, we should get a much stronger reading than what we get from those puny, hand-held ones, even with all of the interference." Lisa removed the Motion Detection Unit from the bag and began the process of setting it up. Rebecca began walking around and looking intently at her hand-held unit for any sign of movement.

"These hills give me the creeps," Rebecca said. The tinny sound of her own voice inside the helmet sent an added chill up her spine. "You never know what might be hiding behind one. And these blue jumpsuits will stand out clearly against this grayish dirt."

Lisa's laughter caused her to start as it crackled over the intercom. "Weren't you the one who was laughing because your sister was worried that you would be attacked by monsters or aliens? Relax. If there was anything in the area, we would have picked it up by now." She flipped up the antennae with practiced ease and threw the power switch. The small dish began rotating, accompanied by a flashing light at the tip of the antennae. "All right, that does it. I'm going to check in with the others."

She pressed a button on her wrist commlink, setting it to match her helmet's frequency. "*Vanguard*, this is Team 4 checking in. Our unit is up and running. We're waiting for your signal to initiate link-up. Over."

Static spewed from the comm for a few moments, then Ricky's voice came through, broken but understandable. "Roger, Fo—…—aiting for oth—….teams." There was a short pause. "Uh, standby, Four." After a few seconds, Ricky's voice once again fought its way through the static. "Four, Te—…One is encount—…—ome difficulty. Stay…—osition… until further notice. Over."

"Great," Lisa said. "Well, we might as well get comfortable. We may be here awhile." She clicked off her commlink and sat down next to the

MDU, which was whirring quietly as it scanned the area. Rebecca followed suit. Taking her backpack off her shoulder, she set it down and sat next to it, facing Lisa. She reached down with her gloved hand and picked up a handful of the gray, powdery dirt. "It definitely feels different than Earth soil. The drill should be able to punch through this in no time." She looked up at Lisa. "Do you really think we will find evidence of life here, Lisa?"

"I sure hope so. I didn't spend almost three months in that cramped, tin can for nothing." Just then, Lisa's commlink chirped softly. "Lisa here," she responded reflexively.

"Lisa,…having…problem with…one," Captain Coffner's voice said, frustration evident in his voice. "I need…help over here. Rebecca—ould…able to handle…link-up on that end."

Lisa gave Rebecca a look as if to say, *Great, just what we needed.* "Yes, sir, Captain. I'll be over to give you poor boys a hand in just a few minutes. Over." She stood and shouldered her empty pack.

"Us 'poor boys'…try not…break…–thing until you…here," the Captain replied sarcastically. "Over and out."

Lisa looked at Rebecca and grimaced. "Sorry to leave you, but…"

"Yeah, I know. Duty calls." Rebecca said. "Don't worry. I'm a big girl. I can take care of myself."

"That's more like it. A few minutes ago you didn't sound so sure," Lisa said lightheartedly.

"Well, your confidence is infectious," Rebecca countered. "Besides, this will give me a minute alone to start my audio journal. I promised my sister that I would record all of my thoughts and feelings so that I wouldn't forget anything."

"Just keep an eye on your motion detector. We still have no idea what's out there." Lisa turned and began walking north.

Rebecca laughed and called to her as she walked away, "Now you're the one sounding unsure." Lisa waved back at her and continued walking back toward the ship.

As Lisa's figure retreated into the distance, Rebecca felt her initial fears begin to creep back into her thoughts, this time accompanied by an unexplainable uneasiness. *Come on, Becky. It's just your imagination.* She took a deep breath and shook away her troublesome thoughts. *Maybe my journal will help keep my mind from wandering.* Kneeling next to her pack, she rummaged through it until she found her Verbal Notebook. She removed the hand-held device and set it to the same frequency as her helmet radio. "Testing, testing," she said, watching the small readout screen. As expected, her words appeared in tiny letters. Satisfied that it was functioning properly, she began.

Journal Entry #1

I can't believe it! I'm actually standing on an alien planet! It is difficult to put into words the emotions that I'm feeling right now. This moment is one of the greatest of my life.

Before I go any further, let me first say that the purpose of this journal is threefold: 1) For myself—so that I may always have a record of my feelings and thoughts during this most amazing of times in my life. 2) For my sister and other family members—so that I will be able to tell them everything that happened in detail. And 3) For others—who knows? Maybe I'll write a book someday!

Well, I don't even know where to begin. As I am entering these notes, I am sitting alone next to the Motion Detection Unit about one mile from the ship. Although I understand the importance of all of the security precautions, I must admit that I am quite anxious to begin digging. So far, the probe reports have proved to be 100% accurate. And now that I am actually here, I believe more than ever that we will indeed find life. The planet…

Sudden movement in her peripheral vision caught Rebecca's eye. She immediately stopped speaking, stood, and turned toward the mound on her left. Pulling her blaster from its holster on her right hip, she thumbed off the safety. Seeing no further movement, Rebecca quickly scanned the area, then looked down at the motion detector in her other hand.

Nothing. No movement anywhere. Did I imagine it? Without putting down either the motion detector or the blaster, Rebecca used her right index finger to touch the commlink on her left wrist. "*Vanguard,* this is Rebecca, do you copy? Over." Static. "Team 1, 2, or 3, this is Rebecca. Do you copy? Over." More static. "*Vanguard,* this is..."

Before she could finish her sentence, she saw it again; this time coming from the mound on her right. She whirled around so fast she nearly tripped. Her heart was beating fast and heavy in her ears. "*Vanguard,* do you copy? I sure hope this is a practical joke." She looked down at the motion detector. It still showed all of the other members of the crew, with the exception of Ricky who was aboard the ship.

Rebecca felt her knees weaken. *Something's not right. Why aren't they responding?* Gathering her strength, she began walking back toward the direction of the ship. Drawing on her military training, she fought against the fear that was building within her. Despite her best efforts to remain calm and relaxed, she still found herself gripping the hilt of her blaster so tightly that her joints began to hurt.

Suddenly, there it was again: a dim, but unmistakable moving light. Walking slowly at first, Rebecca began to head toward the ship, her blaster poised and ready. However, the more she moved, the more her fear began to grip her, until finally, giving in to her fear, Rebecca broke into a full run. As she ran, her panic blinded her like a shroud, causing her to stumble and fall, her blaster falling from her grip. Gasping for air, she regained her balance, retrieved her weapon, and began to run once more.

Risking a glance behind her, she noticed the light moving steadily in her direction, as if floating on air. She turned to face forward, panic building in her so much she felt her heart would explode. As she came around one of the small hills, her heart leaped into her throat as the ship suddenly came into view. But before she could take one more step, a light brighter than any she had ever seen flashed before her eyes, instantly blinding her. She felt her body falling and pain exploding in her head, then darkness enveloped her.

3

Rescued?

THE FIRST sensation that assailed Rebecca's senses was not the cold, hard metal beneath her, nor the sound of an old, under-maintained diesel engine, or even the back and forth motion of a vehicle moving over uneven ground, but rather it was the overpowering stench of engine exhaust fumes. It permeated the air. She choked and gasped, her lungs burning. She felt as if she were sucking on the tailpipe of a pickup truck.

Opening her eyes didn't improve the situation much. Her vision was blurred and spotty, and whatever was producing the exhaust fumes seemed to be gleefully belching them in her face. Despite the uneven gait of the vehicle, she managed to get up on her hands and knees and crawl towards her left until her head bumped into a thin, cylindrical piece of metal. Groping the surrounding space, she soon discovered several other cylinders, spaced at even intervals. Although she knew she should recognize the objects, it took her sluggish brain a moment to identify them as the rusted bars of a cage. Thankful that the air was less polluted here, Rebecca propped herself up against the cold metal and took several deep breaths. Her eyes watering, she blinked numerous times in an attempt to clear her vision. After nearly a minute, she could see sufficiently enough to form a general idea of her immediate surroundings.

She was in the back of some sort of moving vehicle; that much was certain. From what she could see with her limited vision, the cage was roughly eight square feet in size and about four feet high. The floor looked like it hadn't been cleaned since it was built, which, judging by the dents and rust, must have been a long time ago. Every inch was covered with dirt, grime, oil, grease, and other fluids that Rebecca didn't care to identify. *What am I doing in the back of a truck? And what's with the cage? Who's truck is this anyway? Where am I going?*

No sooner had the questions flashed through her mind, than the memories of the events after landing on the planet come back to her in a rush. Adrenaline flooded her body like a tidal wave, threatening to drown her in panic. *Oh, my God! I'm still on 2021 PK! But where am I? Where are the others? How long was I out? Oh, God! Am I going blind?*

Feeling more and more like a caged animal, Rebecca grabbed the bars and stared out at the terrain, squinting to try to clear the image before her. What she saw confirmed her fears. The landscape was exactly as she remembered: devoid of vegetation and dotted with rolling hills covered by dull, gray dirt. The sky was blood red and overcast, the dark, luminous clouds threatening to release torrential rains at any moment.

The hot wind suddenly changed directions, sending the carbon dioxide smoke cloud back into her face. Covering her mouth and nose with her gloved hand, she crawled to the other side of the truck bed. *Pull yourself together. Panicking won't do you any good,* she chided herself. *I've gotta think. I still have my gloves and uniform, but my helmet's gone. What else do I have?* After a quick inventory, her hopes diminished as she realized that they took her backpack, weapon, helmet, commlink, and pocket tool. *At least nothing is broken. But how am I going to get out? How much farther are we going?*

As if on cue, the vehicle came to a sudden halt, causing her to lose her balance and fall to the floor. Rebecca quickly got to her knees and crawled to the center of the cage, her body facing toward the rear of the vehicle, her eyes darting frantically from side to side, searching for any movement.

An odd, chittering sound coming from somewhere near the front of the vehicle caused Rebecca to spin around, her every muscle tense with fear. After a few seconds of hunting for the source of the sounds, she finally caught a glimpse of movement to her left, followed by another on her right. Then, to her utmost horror, the indefinable movements took shape. Moving slowly towards her from the front of the vehicle were creatures from out of a nightmare. Their insectoid, bulbous bodies stretched for at least five feet and were as thick as a human torso. The gray and yellow designs on their bloated hides looked almost alive as flashes of lightning splayed across the darkening sky, followed seconds later by menacing rolls of thunder. They crawled ever closer to her on multitudes of small, ten-inch legs that protruded from the underside of nearly their entire bodies. Each creature had a different number of eyes, each of which stared at her from eyestalks positioned on random areas of their heads. But most horrifying of all, however, were the long appendages that stuck out in front of their bodies, each ending with pincers that looked capable of easily snatching unsuspecting prey and shoving it mercilessly toward a gaping maw filled with razor sharp teeth.

All reason fled from Rebecca's mind and was replaced by pure, unadulterated fear. Expecting the things to open the cage and devour her at any second, she curled into a ball and covered her head with her arms, as much to shut out the sight of them as to shut out the sloshing, gurgling, and clacking sounds they produced.

She waited for several terrifying moments, barely daring to breathe, when suddenly the awful sounds ceased. There was a flash of light, followed immediately by thunder. Rain began to fall slowly, but still no other sounds could be heard. Gathering her courage, she lowered her arms and looked towards the creatures. What she saw astonished her so much that she momentarily forgot her fear.

Six of the insect-like aliens stood frozen to the spot, the upper half of their bodies standing erect. They were positioned in a defensive formation around the vehicle: two on each side, one behind, and one on top of the cage. Due to her limited vision, she was unable to tell if there were any more in front. The only parts of their bodies that moved were their eyestalks, which were slowly and methodically scanning the surrounding landscape. Small clusters of the ten-inch legs on the upper segment of their bodies were wrapped around conical, metallic objects, giving Rebecca the distinctive impression of a hand holding a gun. *Could these things be intelligent?*

A sudden flash startled her, causing her to reflexively shield her eyes with her arm. It wasn't until she saw the second and third flashes in quick succession, however, that she realized that they were not the result of lightning, but were actually being produced by the bug-like aliens' bodies! Before she could begin to wonder as to the reason for the light show, the answer presented itself. Appearing suddenly out of the darkness and moving swiftly toward the vehicle came several dark shapes.

The illumination from the alien bodies gave the entire scene an eerie strobe light effect, making it nearly impossible for Rebecca to make out the exact forms of the assailants. Judging by the precision of their attack, however, it seemed that they were completely unhindered by the dancing lights.

The insect-like aliens, realizing this themselves, stopped producing the flashes almost as quickly as they had begun and started firing their cone-shaped weapons. Several of the shadowy figures fell to the ground as the projectiles from the weapons tore through them, but it was apparent that Rebecca's kidnappers were hopelessly outnumbered.

The alien perched atop Rebecca's cage leaped to the ground behind the vehicle, its claw-like appendages snapping at the air. Suddenly, a small figure appeared out of the darkness and landed heavily on top of it. The bug-like alien twisted its pincers around as far as possible in a desperate attempt to crush its assailant, but to no avail. Their quick movements, combined with Rebecca's already weak eyesight and the deepening darkness of the storm made it nearly impossible for her to distinguish what was happening. A moment later, the body of the insect-like alien splashed into a gathering puddle of water, where it lay in the final throes of death.

Deep in her heart, Rebecca had held the hope that the attackers were her crew come to rescue her. But in that instant, her fledgling hope fled, replaced by a numbness that spread quickly through her body. From the spot where the alien had fallen, two slanted, blood-red eyes stared back at her through the curtain of rain. As they fixed upon her, she could feel the blood-lust of the creature emanate towards her.

Still on her hands and knees, she began to slowly back away from the cage door, the sounds of the continuing battle fading from her consciousness. The diminutive form sprang to the cage door, the suddenness of its movements catching Rebecca by surprise.

With her back pressed against the far side of the cage, she watched helplessly as the thing began fumbling with the locking mechanism. Within moments the cage door swung free and the devilish red eyes began moving steadily towards her. The outline of a twisted, impish face slowly coalesced out of the darkness, attached to a body that was armored with thick scales. Although its stature was short enough that it could stand upright in the cage without hitting its head on the four-foot ceiling, Rebecca could tell that this creature was extremely strong and agile. A wicked grin splayed across the mutated face as it approached, its forked tongue moving from side to side causing saliva to drip down its chin. As it drew nearer, Rebecca could hear a maniacal, guttural laugh coming from the lopsided, vicious mouth.

In that moment, with the creature nearly on top of her, Rebecca's survival instincts kicked in. Gathering her strength, she kicked out at her attacker, her foot connecting solidly with its left shoulder, spinning it around and into the side of the cage. Not even daring to see if it was injured, she dove towards the cage door. The upper portion of her body made it through the opening when two incredibly strong arms suddenly grabbed her left ankle in a vice-like grip. Letting out a gasp of pain and surprise, she kicked several more times with her right foot and managed to extricate herself from its grasp, the momentum of her sudden freedom sending her tumbling out of the cage and onto the ground below.

Climbing to her feet as quickly as she could, she stumbled off blindly into the rain, her only thought being to escape those horrid, crooked red eyes. She had barely taken more than three steps, however, when she was knocked off her feet again by a heavy weight slamming into her back. She landed hard on her stomach, her face landing in a shallow pool of dirty water, her arms splayed out in front of her. Raising her head out of the water and gasping for air, she expected to feel the searing pain of razor sharp claws tearing through her flesh at any second.

But the blows never came.

Instead, she heard a quick, harsh growl coming from somewhere in front of her, followed by a gradual easing up of the pressure on her back. She risked a quick glance over her left shoulder and saw the devilish creature standing just behind her. But this time, its cruel red eyes were not focused on her, but on something just beyond where she lay.

Following its gaze, she snapped her head back around to see what new horror awaited her, causing several strands of wet hair to cling to her face. Through the steady downpour of rain, Rebecca could see yet another alien being standing not more than four feet in front of her. But before she could even think or react, she heard its deep voice growl in unmistakable English, "Well, now, what do we have here?"

4

The High Crala

BEFORE REBECCA stood a being that inspired both awe and respect. From her position on the ground, she guessed it to be at least a full seven feet in height. Its arms were crossed and its entire body seemed to be wrapped in a leathery cape. The darkness and rain obscured its face, but Rebecca could nevertheless feel its eyes scrutinizing her from head to toe.

"Stand up," commanded the gravelly voice. "We aren't going to hurt you…yet," it added, almost as an afterthought. Despite her terror and shock, she summoned all of her willpower and forced herself to her feet, even though it felt like the gravity of the planet had suddenly tripled.

Once erect, she could better make out the features of the strange being, and under other circumstances, the sight before her may almost have been amusing. The creature had a clearly feline look about it, yet reptilian scales could be seen under its thin layer of fur. But what caught her attention the most was that its eyes were obscured by an odd pair of dark goggles.

As if reading her thoughts, the being slowly reached up and removed them. The eyes that stared back at her through the rain were such a deep violet and seemed to hold such an unexplainable power and incredible intelligence that Rebecca nearly gasped in awe. She couldn't explain why, but just looking into those velvety depths caused her to feel both terrified and comforted at the same time.

She stared for several seconds, transfixed by the being's eyes, until she noticed them suddenly shift to look at something behind her. "Galkor trrign cu lir kta jonu," it said in a commanding tone. The spell broken, Rebecca looked around her to see that the battle was over and several dark shapes were moving in and around the cage vehicle, obviously searching it for anything that might be of use. The barked command seemed to be directed at the devilish creature that had, just moments ago, been intent on making her its evening meal. The red-eyed monstrosity nodded its oddly shaped head, which seemed to be perpetually cocked to the left, and began to turn away. As it turned, however, it glanced sideways at her and licked its lips. The gesture left Rebecca feeling decidedly uncomfortable, as if the creature was saying, *"Dinner will be delayed, but not for long!"* An involuntary shudder ran down her spine, and as the alien bounded off into the darkness, she once again heard a high, maniacal laugh.

"Now, what do I do with you?"

Rebecca returned her attention to the feline alien that stood before her, all the while attempting to control her frantic breathing and her fluttering heart. The creature uncrossed its massive arms and, to her surprise, the leathery cape revealed itself to be long folds of skin that attached to the being's wrists and ankles.

As the adrenaline began to recede, Rebecca was able to successfully repress her survival instincts and win back control of her rattled mind. "You...you speak English!?!" she managed, her words coming out as both a statement and a question. "But...how?"

The feline-like creature merely stared at her for a moment, its expression unreadable. Then, abruptly, it motioned with its clawed hands, and before she could even comprehend what was happening, three strong arms grabbed her from behind. A blindfold was quickly placed over her head and her wrists were bound securely in front of her with something that felt like spaghetti, but was stronger than rope.

"Wait! I —," she pleaded, but was jostled so roughly that she had to concentrate just to remain on her feet. She was herded off to her right, but soon lost all sense of direction as she stumbled on blindly through the mud and rain. The sounds of alien voices surrounded her, but Rebecca heard no trace of English from any of them, only bizarre growls, slurps, and grunts that were eventually drowned out by the deafening roar of an idling engine. They came to a sudden halt, and the same strong arms that had bound her and pushed her along, grabbed her once again and shoved her unceremoniously into the idling vehicle.

The overpowering stench of oil and gas assailed her as her new captors pushed her onto the hard, metallic floor of the machine. Before she could even rearrange herself into a more comfortable position, the vehicle lurched and began to move.

Rebecca was quickly bruised and battered as the machine made its way over the rough terrain to its unknown destination. Time began to lose all meaning as she was constantly thrown around; the unforgiving, cold metal beneath her doing little to ease her discomfort. Her body ached in every conceivable area, and the aftermath of an extreme adrenaline rush left her exhausted beyond endurance such that she didn't realize they had stopped until all-too-familiar hands dragged her to her feet.

In her current state, Rebecca couldn't react quickly enough to keep her balance and her knees buckled, dropping her hard onto her left knee. Giving out a cry of pain, she grasped her injured leg and lay still, praying that she would suddenly wake up to find that this whole event had been a horrible nightmare.

Instead, she felt as if a sledgehammer had been driven into her stomach by a giant. Sharp stabs of pain lanced through her skull from the blow. She braced herself for the next wave of pain, but was once again saved by the same feline growl.

"Col grrrrrin cha!"

Rebecca heard shuffling near her head, then arms that were almost gentle, yet incredibly strong lifted her and set her once again upon her feet. They held her steady until she regained her breath and strength returned to her legs and sore knee.

Finally, after several minutes, she half walked, and was half carried to what she assumed to be the vehicle's door, based on the sound of it. The jumble of noise around her increased in volume, but before she could even attempt to sort out the sources, her task was made easier by the sudden removal of her blindfold.

It took Rebecca several moments to make sense of her surroundings.

She was in a large, cavern-like room about the size of an airplane hangar. Vehicles of all shapes and sizes were strewn around in no apparent organization. The room's floor, walls, and ceiling were the same dull, off-white color as the surrounding countryside and were rough and uneven, giving Rebecca the impression that this room had been hastily carved out of the rock and never smoothed out to completion. The entire scene was lit by large overhead lamps, the wires of which snaked along the ceiling like long tentacles of some massive sea creature.

As she surveyed the area, she noticed several beings of various species engrossed in their individual tasks. Rebecca looked intently at the odd assortment of aliens, her scientific curiosity temporarily overriding her fear of her current predicament.

The reprieve from fear was short-lived. This time, however, it was interspersed with bewilderment, for moving out from behind a nearby vehicle on her left came an alien shape that caused her knees to grow weak with recognition. Its four misshapen eyestalks didn't give her much more than a casual glance as its multitudinous legs carried its segmented body smoothly through a nearby door. As it departed, her fear slowly receded, giving way to confusion.

Why did they kill the bug-like aliens if they are in league with them?

"Keep moving," her feline-like captor said from behind her, causing her to file that question away with the million others she had gathered thus far. Now that they were under the lights of the cavernous hangar, Rebecca risked a glance behind her to get a better look at the strange alien that was her escort. The room's harsh bright lamps revealed that the creature's coarse, short hair had a dark brown, slightly golden hue, while its cape-like skin folds were almost black, reminding her somewhat of the wings of a bat. Sensing her perusal, it pointed toward a door along the wall and gave her a prodding shove with one of its massive, claw-like hands. Not wishing to provoke the large creature, she readily complied.

She was led through one of the many doors located around the edges of the hangar. The corridor beyond had the same hurried, unfinished look as the previous room; its walls, floor, and ceiling were rough and ran at odd angles, like some kind of odd mine shaft. At the end of the passage, they came to a larger corridor that intersected their current route at a sharp angle. They turned left and followed this new passage up a slight incline towards a large metal door that was guarded by a burly alien of a species that Rebecca had not yet encountered.

The guard was covered nearly from head to foot with spikes that protruded from its muscular, armored hide. Its two, human-like arms were not attached directly at the shoulders. The left arm was nearly at shoulder height, but stuck out from the creature's upper chest, right where a human body would house the heart. The right arm was much lower, sticking out from the enormous alien's side at a weird angle, almost as if it had been broken and never set properly. The guard stood nearly seven feet tall and carried a large weapon similar to a shotgun, which was promptly pointed directly at Rebecca and her captor as they approached.

As they drew near to the being, Rebecca blanched. The creature's face, more than anything she had yet seen on this bizarre planet, unsettled her. Its facial features were arranged asymmetrically. In addition, it had what looked like a second, half-formed nose near its chin, a missing left ear, and a deformed mouth that curled down on one side, making it look like it wore an eternal frown.

"Trea cresc ritran?" it asked her escort mechanically.

She could not be certain, but the guard almost seemed surprised at the feline's response. Lowering its weapon, the massive creature turned, opened the door and stepped aside to allow them entry. Her captor prodded her in the back, but her fear of the giant alien kept her rooted to the spot. When she didn't move, the guard narrowed its mismatched eyes at her, and, clearly drawing pleasure from her discomfort, it lifted the corner of its twisted face in a grotesque grin, revealing several crooked, yellow teeth. Growing impatient, the feline alien placed one clawed hand on each of her shoulders and shoved her toward the open doorway.

The spiked guard was still laughing several moments later as Rebecca picked herself up off of the floor, her captor standing silently in the doorway they had just entered through. The corridor she now found herself in looked to be about ten feet across, but extending forty-five or fifty feet to the right and left in a more-or-less straight line, with doors spaced at various intervals on the inner wall. The ceiling was about twelve feet from the floor, at least at the highest point. Once again, Rebecca noticed that the architects of this cavern seemed either rather careless or very hurried. The ceiling met the walls at odd angles and its height varied from place to place. Similar to the hangar and the corridor, the entire passage was dimly lit by the same open bulbs, with the wiring running down the wall in a haphazard manner.

Looking around at the drab, colorless walls, it suddenly dawned on her that this entire place seemed completely devoid of wall coverings or furniture, giving her the disconcerting impression that she was walking through some kind of medieval dungeon. Ahead of her stood another plain metal door directly across from their entrance.

Stepping fully into the room, her guide shut the door and turned around to face her. Reaching out with lightning-quick speed, it grabbed her firmly with its left claw. With its other hand, it reached into a secret pouch or fold of skin near its body and withdrew a small, metallic device, which it brought up near her head. Panic fueled her imagination as a myriad of violent, painful images of torture and death filled her mind. However, just as she was about to scream from fright at her imagined fate, the reptilian feline spoke.

"Calm yourself. This is only an earpiece for the translation unit. It will cause you no pain." With that, the being quickly inserted it into her left ear before she could struggle further. Although it was not a comfortable fit, as promised, it did not hurt. Reaching into another hidden pouch, the creature brought forth a small black box about the size of a portable radio that was connected to a leather belt. Without hesitation, it wrapped the belt around her waist and adjusted the fit, and as it did so, Rebecca realized for the first time that the creature carried her backpack around its right shoulder. Her fear of immediate pain subsided, causing her rattled mind to come back to awareness.

"Translator? I…I don't understand. Why do I need a translator if you already speak my language?"

The being looked at her with a bemused smile. "The translator is so that you can understand Breuun when he speaks to you."

Rebecca looked puzzled. "Who is Breuun?" she queried.

It looked at her as one looks at an irritating child who just asked a stupid question.

"Breuun is the High Crala and leader of Clan Grinath. Do not speak unless spoken to, and when he does speak, I suggest you answer truthfully and quickly. Breuun is not a patient being."

Rebecca ventured one last question that had been disturbing her since she first encountered this alien. "How is it that you understand English?"

The giant creature looked down at her as if trying to decide the right way to phrase a response. "Let's just say that you are not the first human I have encountered."

As the shock of this statement sent Rebecca's mind reeling, her escort opened the door in front of them and pushed her through.

The forward momentum combined with her injured knee sent her stumbling through the opening off balance. She recovered just in time to avoid knocking over a small creature in front of her, which had turned around at the sound of her not-so-graceful entrance. Rebecca took a step backward, a cry rising in her throat at the haunted expression of hopelessness on its hideous and deformed face. But before any sound could escape her lips, she felt a powerful arm grab her shoulder, tighter this time, as if to remind her of the warning spoken just moments before.

Swallowing her repulsion and horror, she looked away from the creature and instead, focused her attention on her surroundings. She was standing in what looked to be some kind of large audience chamber. The central part of the room was long and rectangular with a high, flat ceiling that reached about sixty feet above the uneven floor. On each of the longest sides of the rectangle were recessed alcoves with a shorter twenty-foot ceiling, each containing an odd-assortment of alien species. It was into one of these alcoves that Rebecca and her captor had entered.

The feline alien forced Rebecca back towards the pathetic creature, and for a moment she thought that she was going to be herded right into the diminutive, rodent-like alien. Yet without a command or sound of any kind, the being, and those next to it, stepped aside to allow them to pass, their eyes downcast in deferential obedience.

For a split second, Rebecca feared that they would walk right out into the center of the large room. Instead, however, the muscular arms holding on to her shoulders halted her at the very edge of the alcove. From this new vantage point, Rebecca could see the entire length of the room. To their right, at the far end, stood a set of double doors that were guarded by two armed and armored aliens. Directly in front of her was an identical pair of guards flanking a middle-sized, powerfully built alien that was bathed in a sickly, yellowish light coming from a large lamp in the ceiling. She could not see the features of the guards due to their heavy, unadorned, metal helmets, but their bodies, like nearly every alien she had thus far encountered, were asymmetrical and looked like some mad scientist's plaything. The features of the alien in the middle, however, were quite clear, and impending doom was written all over its canine-like face. The source of its fear came from a creature that lay perched on a strange, stone slide set up on a dais several feet in front of the unfortunate being.

Breuun, High Crala and leader of Clan Grinath stared down at the prisoner from its odd throne, flanked on both sides by more helmeted and armored guards. Breuun's features were similar to that of the captive, making Rebecca assume that they were of the same species. Although their general appearance resembled that of a canine, with long snouts and pointed ears, their bodies were covered by reptilian scales from which protruded thick, dark colored fur, similar to the feline alien behind her. The way in which Breunn laid on the angled stone slab gave her the distinct impression of a hunting wolf staring down from above at its helpless prey, its powerful claws propping up its torso.

The clan leader may have resembled the other being physically, but its countenance and manner were completely different. Its two largest, crooked eyes were alert and hard, while its smaller eye, located on the left side of its twisted snout shifted constantly, as if expecting danger to appear at any moment. Its face had the look of one who had been in numerous vicious fights and had healed over, leaving permanent disfigurement: its right eye was half-closed, its mouth was missing several teeth, jagged scars crisscrossed its face, and the scaly fur was patched and thin on the left side of its head. As further proof of its battle-hardened nature, the dull gray, metallic armor that covered most of its body from the neck down was dented and worn.

In horrid fascination, Rebecca watched as the clan leader reached over and dipped its right claw into a bowl of thick, dark liquid that was promptly provided by another rodent-like servant standing to the side of the throne. Its claw still dripping, it stood up from the stone slab, stepped down from the dais and strode over to stand within a few feet of the prisoner, its spiked tail dragging on the ground behind it. As it moved, its armor made horrendous scraping sounds that set Rebecca's teeth on edge.

The High Crala growled and snapped its jaws at the captive, its eyes narrowing slightly. A second later, a monotone, metallic voice spoke directly into her left ear, startling her. Caught up in the drama unfolding before her, it took her a moment to realize that the sound was coming from the translator unit that the feline alien had given her.

"You were caught selling Clan Grinath hidden information to Clan V'skir. Do you have things to say in defense?"

The prisoner stood motionless, its limbs trembling visibly in the yellowish light. Its canine-like face had the appearance of one who knows it is doomed, yet is hoping desperately for one last chance. "High Crala, I...please...NO...WAIT..."

Without another word, the clan leader nonchalantly raised its right arm, made a fist and flicked its fingers at the prisoner. For an instant, Rebecca thought this might have been some kind of hand signal for dismissal, had it not been for the quick, reflexive jolt that ran through the body of the traitor. A second later, the being gave a gasp and a shudder, then fell over, its claws clutching at two sharp objects protruding from its chest. Its body twitched convulsively as the poison that Breuun had placed on its claw worked its way through the creature's bloodstream. After several more seconds, the body gave one last spasm, then lay still on the floor before her.

Shocked by the brutal scene, Rebecca took several shuddering breaths and fought to maintain her composure. When she turned her gaze once again back to Breuun, she noticed that two of the long, claw-like nails on its hand were now missing, causing a new sense of dread to settle on her heart. Without a trace of emotion, it turned and began walking back to its throne as the two guards carried the body away. Unable to tear her gaze away from the alien leader, she watched in horror and utter amazement as it strode back up the dais to the throne, a single eye staring at her from the back of its head!

As it lay back down on its triangular throne, it turned its head towards her and snapped its powerful jaws several times, the translation coming a moment later in the same monotone voice. "Sikaris, report," it commanded.

Rebecca's captor urged her forward until they were standing in the same area where the previous captive was murdered, leaving her feeling like a trapped mouse huddled in front of a prowling cat. Awash in the bright ceiling light, she was nearly blind and slightly disoriented, which, she figured, was probably the whole idea. Through the light, she could just make out the vague outline of Breuun, its body leaning heavily on the incline. Next to her, the being named Sikaris began its requested report in the same guttural tongue that the clan leader had used moments before.

"We found and murdered the V'skir patrol that was given the hidden information by the traitor," came the mechanical translation. "The new eye shields helped us to have a great win. No V'skir escaped, and only two Grinathians were murdered."

"Very good," said the voice beyond the light.

"And more," Sikaris continued. "We found this creature in one of their cages."

There was only silence after this proclamation, then a deep, throaty growl that translated as: "What is he?"

"He is not from one of the clans close to us," Sikaris replied. "He may not even be from Ka'esch." At this, murmurs could be heard coming from all corners of the room.

"Can this be a non-lie? How did he come to be here? Are there others?" her translator said in its dry, even tone.

Sikaris stepped forward and stretched out its right claw, offering something to Breuun. "I have made this special language card for your translator so that you may talk to him."

The clan leader made a pleased growl and accepted the offered device. Climbing the dais steps, Sikaris stood on Breuun's right and faced Rebecca, causing an acute loneliness to overshadow her heart. In her darkest of nightmares, she could never have imagined the feeling of standing alone, blinded by a sickly yellow light, in the middle of a large room on an alien planet, surrounded by hundreds of hideous, deformed monsters. She grasped her abdomen and retched several times, nearly losing her balance and falling to the floor. Fortunately, she hadn't eaten for several hours, so her stomach had no contents to disgorge. *Wake up, Rebecca! Oh, God, let this be a dream!* However, no amount of wishing was able to make her stubborn senses relent.

"Stand up," the alien leader snarled.

Calling upon every ounce of will, she wiped her mouth with the back of her hand and forced herself to stand, knowing that her very life hung in the balance.

"What are you," the metallic voice translated in her ear.

For a moment, Rebecca's throat constricted and she nervously began cracking her knuckles. Sikaris stared hard at her in warning. *Come on, Rebecca! Get it together or you're dead!* Behind her she heard the unmistakable sound of two guards approaching to flank her as they had flanked the previous prisoner. She swallowed, took a deep breath and spoke, her voice quavering, but clear.

"My name is Rebecca Evans. I came here from the planet Earth with eight others on a mission of discovery. We...we mean no harm. We... come in peace."

There was silence for a moment as Breuun turned and glanced at Sikaris. "What is 'peace'?" it said, as much to Rebecca as to the feline alien.

What is peace? It doesn't even have a word in its language for peace? Even as these thoughts passed through her mind, Sikaris spoke, silencing her inner questioning. "A truce, High Crala."

Breuun nodded in understanding, then turned its attention back to her. "And what is a 'planet Earth'?"

Rebecca paused for a second to figure out how best to phrase her reply. "It is…another world. A…land far away." The dark shadow that was the clan leader sat motionless, apparently not understanding. "We flew here in a ship…a machine…from beyond the sky." She pointed upward to accentuate her words, hoping desperately that they would believe her.

Breuun turned once again to Sikaris and spoke to it quietly so that Rebecca's translator did not pick it up. After a lengthy conversation, the clan leader turned back to face her.

"Where is this machine?" it growled.

Rebecca hesitated. *Where is the ship? How far away am I from the landing site? I was unconscious during most of the journey.* "I…I don't know," she said truthfully.

Breuun's eyes narrowed. "You lie," it said menacingly, although the translation came out dull and without inflection. "And you lie badly." Even as the translator finished the sentence, the clan leader gestured with its clawed hand and a servant came rushing to its side.

Rebecca felt her knees grow weak, threatening to buckle. In the servant's gnarled hands was an all too familiar bowl of dark liquid.

Oh, God, help me! Rebecca's thoughts became frantic, cluttering her mind and preventing her from thinking clearly. The idea that she had to think of something quickly or die was the very thing that kept her from being able to focus. She stared around nervously, desperate to find some solution, some escape. As she did so, her eyes fell on Sikaris who was lowering her backpack from its shoulder to the ground.

"Wait!" she yelled, causing Breuun to freeze, its left claw dipped into the bowl, while the guards on each side of her twitched nervously. "I know how to find my ship and prove I am not lying." She pointed to the bag at Sikaris' feet. "Inside my pack is a tracker,…um…a device, a machine that will tell me how far my ship is from here. If you let me look at it, I can tell you where it is."

Breuun looked to Sikaris, then nodded as it removed its claw from the bowl and dried it on a towel provided by the servant. Sikaris picked up the backpack, stepped down from the dais and walked slowly up to Rebecca. It stared deeply into her eyes for a brief moment, its expression unreadable, then it gently emptied the contents of her pack onto the floor in front of her. "Which one," it said in English.

"There," she said, indicating the device.

Sikaris bent and picked up the tracker. "Tell me how to work it. When I am sure it is not a weapon, I will show it to you so that you can read it. Attempt to touch it and you will die."

Rebecca swallowed hard and nodded her understanding, her heart pounding against her ribcage. Absentmindedly cracking her knuckles against her thigh, she proceeded to give instructions. After a moment of examining the readout, Sikaris held the unit up for her to read. The same interference that had been disrupting her crew's instruments since they had entered the atmosphere was still present, but Rebecca's heart leaped into her throat with excitement as she saw the unmistakable yellow dot representing the ship. Smiling, she looked up at Breuun. "It is still where we landed, about 150 miles from here. It is on the northeast corner of a mountain range near a lake," she said; hope beginning to swell within her. *If only I can find some way to get back to it.*

Sikaris turned to look at Breuun. "Lake Yul and Mount Kiabab, on the Ryazan/Harmath border," it said, once more reverting to the alien tongue of the clan leader.

Breuun appeared pensive, then suddenly pushed its torso up higher off of the stone slab with its right claw while pointing toward one of the other items from Rebecca's backpack with the left. "What is that? Bring it to me."

Reaching down, Sikaris scooped up the remaining contents and returned them to her pack, with the exception of the small, metallic object that the clan leader had indicated. Walking back up to the slanted throne, it handed Rebecca's laser pistol to the canine-like alien.

"What is this?" it said, turning the weapon over and over in its hand, examining it closely.

"That is my laser pistol. My…weapon," she said.

Breuun snarled. "I can tell it is a weapon. But what is a 'laser'?"

"It is a focused beam of light that is very powerful," she answered.

The clan leader, still staring at the weapon, suddenly barked out, "Prin!" A second later, a smaller shadow emerged on Breuun's left. From what Rebecca could see through the yellowish light, it was thin and wiry, with an almost weasel-like appearance. Most noticeably, however, it had four arms protruding from its sides. When it spoke, its voice was thin and airy. "Yes, High Crala."

"Have you ever seen a weapon like this before?" Breuun asked impatiently.

Prin examined Rebecca's pistol with profound interest. "No. It is not used by any clan that I know of."

"Use it," Breuun commanded.

Without hesitation, Prin pointed the weapon at the floor and pulled the trigger. The red beam that arced out, combined with the sound of the laser's discharge, caused all present in the chamber to start and cry out in surprise simultaneously. Breuun leaped to its feet in amazement. "Give it to me," it demanded excitedly. "Bring me a slave."

The two guards behind Breuun immediately moved over to the alcove and grabbed the rodent-like creature that Rebecca had almost stumbled into and carried it to stand before the throne, just a few feet to the left of where she stood. When the guards released it, the poor creature simply stood there, not showing even the slightest awareness of its predicament. The being slowly turned its deformed head to look at her, the sickly light from above casting an eerie shadow over its face. A profound sadness filled her as she stared at this doomed creature. Yet, the mismatched eyes that stared back at her almost looked relieved, as if a heavy burden were suddenly about to be lifted. The intense sadness became nearly constricting.

A sudden red flash lit the room, accompanied by the same sound of discharged energy. Its eyes still staring into her own, the slave crumpled over onto the floor with a soft thud.

"Bring me another, and put some armor on him," came the gleeful command.

Rebecca turned her head to avoid watching the second, cruel murder, but although she was able to shut out the sight of the gruesome spectacle, the sickening sound of another slave dying near her made her stomach begin to churn. The haunted expression of the rodent-like alien still hung before her eyes as if branded permanently onto her retinas.

After Breuun completed its second test of her weapon, it resumed its perch and returned its attention to her. "Why are you here with strong weapons that can go through armor?"

Rebecca struggled against her rising revulsion of this creature. "As I said before, we are here to discover if there is life on this planet," she said, not even attempting to keep disgust from tainting her voice.

"So you are spies, sent to learn our hidden information."

"No! That's not true."

"Then why do you carry strong weapons? Only warriors carry weapons like this," Breuun stated, its eyes narrowing dangerously.

Rebecca felt her hope beginning to evaporate once again, her voice suddenly losing some of its confidence. "We use them only for defense. We are scientists, not warriors."

Breuun pushed itself up off the stone once again; its stare boring into her. "What did you say?"

"I said 'we are scientists, not warriors,'" she repeated, confusion evident in her voice.

"That would explain your clear weakness of body," it said, almost to itself. The clan leader turned to Sikaris, then to Prin as if seeking some sort of confirmation. The three of them spoke together quietly, as if trying to reach some kind of consensus. Finally, after several minutes, Breuun addressed her again. "Do you have any other weapons like this?"

Just as she was about to answer, a sudden idea struck her, the very implications of which caused her heart to start beating wildly again. "Yes!" she said, a little too loudly, her voice echoing around the room. She paused, forcing calm into her quavering voice. "We have a much more powerful laser drill. And—" *Here we go*— "if you take me to my ship and return me to my…clan unharmed, we will give it to you."

Breuun looked at her cautiously, a muscle twitching in the side of its face. "We do not need you. We can take it ourselves. And how do we know this is not a trap?"

Rebecca felt confidence take root within her and begin to blossom, giving her new strength. *"But you do need me.* You do not know how to use the machine, and my people would not give it to you freely. They all carry weapons like this one. And you know this is not a trap because you freed me from the…the other…clan," she finished.

The clan leader lay back down on the throne, the nails on its left claw clicking on the bare stone, revealing its obvious agitation. "Prin," it said at length, "take this creature to the dungeon until called for."

Prin nodded. As it was about to descend the steps toward Rebecca, Breuun gestured for it to come closer. The two exchanged brief words, and the clan leader handed something to the alien. Prin then stepped down from the dais and stopped in front of her, two of its hands inserting one of the special translation cards into its translator. "Come with me," it said, its voice sounding even higher from this close range. It gestured for her to walk towards a door in the wall of the opposite alcove from which she had entered.

Rebecca began walking, causing the pain in her knee to begin throbbing once again. She barely noticed the pain, however, for her mind was consumed with the hope that she may yet make it out of this alive.

5

Ka'esch

THE ALIEN known as Prin guided Rebecca out of the chamber and through a maze of tunnels, each of which looked exactly the same as the previous one. The only difference she could detect was that each successive corridor sloped farther and farther downward. Finally, after several long minutes of winding passages, they came to a darkened, broken staircase, at the bottom of which sat two muscular aliens.

Although the light here was significantly dimmer, it was sufficient enough for Rebecca to determine that this pair were of the same "kind," or species, as that of the spiked guard she had seen earlier outside the entrance to the throne room. These creatures, however, had features that were twisted and mutated in completely different ways. Where the previous guard had an ear missing, one of these had three ears, and the other had only one, and even that one didn't appear fully formed. Their eyes, noses, and mouths were all in different places, as were the placement of their arms and legs in proportion to the rest of their bodies. It almost seemed to Rebecca that these beings were put together like some sort of bizarre "Mr. Potato Head" toy.

As Rebecca and her alien escort descended the stairs, the two jumped up and eyed them suspiciously, gun-like weapons at the ready. However, as recognition of the ferret-like alien standing beside her dawned on them, their manner relaxed somewhat.

"Prin, thonkla kip sram altri?" the one on the left said, its voice low. A moment later, her translator responded again. "Prin, why are you here?"

Rebecca heard the thin, high voice from behind her respond, and as she listened to the monotonous tone of the translation, she noticed that both of the alien guards wore translator units identical to her own. "The High Crala wants this creature put here for now."

The guards looked curiously at Rebecca with their misaligned, coal-black eyes, then stepped aside. The three-eared alien pointed to the left. "Cell 16." With a nudge in the back from Prin, Rebecca was led down yet another uneven corridor.

After just a few steps, her olfactory senses were ambushed by the most repugnant stenches imaginable. Rebecca began gagging and quickly covered her nose and mouth with her hand. To add to the intensity of the foul smells, the air was dense and stagnant, with no wisp of movement or ventilation.

The corridor they traversed was lined with cells on both sides, the occupants of which could not be seen, as the lighting in this portion of the underground complex was kept to a minimum. Only dark shadows and wisps of movement could be detected lurking on the fringes of the light.

"Stop," Prin said suddenly from behind her, causing her to jump reflexively. "In there," it said, pointing to the dark, foreboding cell on her left—its door open wide as if inviting her to some horrid fate. She was not sure if it was real, or simply the product of her overloaded imagination, but Rebecca was rooted to the uneven ground by what seemed to be movement from within the darkened cell.

Noticing her fear and trepidation, Prin reached over and pressed a switch on the nearby wall, causing the same hazy light that illuminated the corridor to spring to life in the interior of the cell. Her fear subsiding at the sight of the empty chamber, she allowed herself to be guided inside.

The room itself was, in reality, more like a hole. The cell had no corners, but was rounded, bringing to her mind the uncomfortable feeling of being inside an immense egg. Its large size surprised her at first, but after thinking about it, she assumed this was due to the fact that many of the aliens she had seen thus far were nearly twice her size. It was sparsely furnished, with nothing more than a rectangular, granite-like slab that stood about two feet off the ground and was four feet wide and twice that in length. Walking over to her "bed," she sank down onto it, her sore leg grateful for the sudden respite. The loud clang of the metal gate slamming shut jarred her already overwrought nerves.

She sat for several moments in relative silence, as small noises from the adjacent cells filtered into her own, creating an unsettling ambiance. *What have I done? What if they do take me back to the ship? They might attack the others. If they surprise them, they may not be able to defend themselves. After all, we really were not prepared for any kind of combat.* Burying her face in her hands, she felt the despair begin to rise up within her, threatening to overwhelm her mind. Then, with a ferocity that surprised even herself, she hardened her resolve and fought back against the mental tide. *No! I did what I had to do. Maybe when we get closer to the ship I can find some way to escape and warn the others, if they are still alive.*

Sudden footsteps in the corridor interrupted her thoughts. Prin's silhouette framed the doorway; a tray containing some type of food held in its upper two hands, while the lower pair unlocked the gate and swung it aside. Shutting the gate behind itself, the weasel-like alien walked over to where she sat, laid the tray down next to her, then sat on the floor across from the slab, its thin yet muscular legs folded awkwardly beneath it.

Rebecca stared at the being for several moments, unsure what to do. Now that she was able to get a good look at this odd creature, she realized that her initial observation of it having four arms was not entirely accurate. While it only had two arms attached to its torso, each limb had an extra pair of forearms extending out at odd angles from near the elbows. Its lithe, ferret-like body was covered with the same fur and scale combination that she had seen on both Sikaris and Breuun. But whereas their hides had been solid in color, Prin's was yellowish-brown and speckled with flecks of black spots. As she had come to expect, Prin's facial features and body shape were asymmetrical; its slightly protruding snout slanted to the left, its shoulders drooped oddly, and where its nose should have been was a solitary, small hole. Stretched out beside its body was a long tail that was split into two sections near the tip, both of which seemed to twitch impatiently.

"Eat," Prin said, its high, airy voice echoing slightly. Taking her eyes off of the alien sitting before her, Rebecca looked down at the food on the tray. Arranged haphazardly on the circular dish was a large portion of what seemed to be some kind of fruit as well as a bit of raw meat. Upon eyeing the pinkish fruit, her stomach suddenly seemed to realize it was empty and let out a loud rumble. Yet, hungry as she was, she hesitated. *What if it's poisoned, or not digestible by humans? Then again, if they wanted to kill me, they would have done it back in the throne room.* Deciding to take her chances, she grabbed the fruit and hungrily bit off a large mouthful. It was not very juicy and seemed flavorless, although that could have been partly due to the noxious stench around her interfering with her taste buds. Nevertheless, Rebecca was thankful for something to fill her stomach.

"My name is Prin, Clan Diodre. You said you were Rebca Clan Vans, no?" the creature asked, the translator's monotonous voice sounding muffled as she chewed.

Swallowing her latest bite of the tasteless fruit, she corrected it. "Rebecca Evans."

"Reb-ecca Clan Evans, I am very interested in talking with you. Are you really from above the sky?"

"Yes, I am," she said cautiously, still wondering as to the alien's intentions.

It studied her intently. "Yes, yes, you must be. Tell me, what is your land like?"

Rebecca considered the strange being for a moment. *Is this some sort of interrogation or is it merely being curious? Maybe I can learn a little about this place if I can get it talking. I might even be able to find out something that will help me get out of here.* Her mind made up, she asked, "What do you mean? Do you want to know what it looks like, what its inhabitants are like, what its climate is like, or…something else?"

"Yes, yes," it said, its tone inflectionless.

Rebecca thought for a moment how to begin going about describing Earth. "Well, about 71% of my planet is covered with water. The surface of the land differs depending on the climate. The northern and southernmost portions are covered with ice and are extremely cold. Then there are deserts, mountains, valleys, grassy plains, forests—"

Prin interrupted her, confusion showing on its crooked face, "What were those last few words? The translator did not understand."

"Grassy plains are flat stretches of land covered with…small, short…," she struggled to find the right words to explain, "plants. And forests are areas of land covered by tall trees…more plants."

The creature stared at her, sudden comprehension spreading across its features. "Yes, yes. Lidrilian. So your clan lives in the deserts and cold lands, and the Lidrilian live in 'grahs pleens' and 'forsts', yes?"

Rebecca sat confused for a moment. "Are Lid-ir…"

"Lidrilian," it corrected.

"Are Lidrilian plants?" she asked.

"Yes, yes. Pla-hnts."

"Plants on our planet cover the ground where we live," she elaborated further. "We cut down the trees and use them to build houses, for fuel, and for many other things."

"Food, yes?"

"Yes. We eat fruit from trees also."

Prin's arms and tail fidgeted, and its facial features took on some kind of expression that Rebecca couldn't read. "They are your slaves, then, yes? You raise them, eat their offspring, make them serve you, yes, yes? Do any of them roam free in other places on the planet, or has your clan enslaved them all?"

Rebecca was taken aback. *Enslaved? Offspring? Roam free? What in the…?* Then, suddenly, an idea struck her with such force that her mind reeled from the impact. "Do you mean to say that trees…plants… Lidrilian, move, live, are…sentient? Do you mean they can think!?!"

Muscles in different parts of Prin's face creased as if in confusion. "Yes, yes, of course. Do Lidrilian…plahnts, not move and think on your planet?"

"Well, no. I mean…yes, they are alive, but they can't move, or think. And we do eat fruit, but I…we don't consider it offspring…" Her voice trailed off as she finished her sentence, another unsettling thought suddenly occurring to her. She looked down at the plate beside her where sat the remains of the fruit she had ravenously devoured. "Are you telling me that what I ate was…some kind of baby? The baby of a…walking, talking, intelligent tree-thing?"

The ferret-like alien nodded emphatically. "Yes, yes! From our garden."

"Garden?" she said, feeling suddenly ill.

"Yes. Our hunting parties travel to the border of the Lidrilian lands and capture as many of them as possible. We then keep them in our garden for food and other uses. We are lucky to have a large garden."

"Why is that," Rebecca asked dully.

"Because the Lidrilian border is four clan areas away. It is very dangerous to move through them. Do you not have other clans in your land?"

"What do you mean by 'clans'? Do you mean tribes, races, species, gender?"

The alien paused for a moment. "The translator does not know those words. I will try to explain. A clan is a group of beings that have the same parent's, parent's parent. They look alike and fight together to live. Are there others that look like you on your planet?"

"Yes. If I understand your definition, then everyone on my planet is part of my clan."

Prin sat up straight and leaned forward. "Then your clan has conquered all other clans, yes?"

Rebecca shook her head. "Not exactly. We are the only intelligent species, …clan, to evolve on our planet."

The same creased muscles appeared once again on Prin's face. "There are no other intelligent clans? How can that be? How did your clan become intelligent and others did not? Are there no others that speak?"

For a moment, Rebecca couldn't answer. She had never really thought of it that way before. What happened in the early history of the Earth that gave humans alone the ability to speak, develop language, and think? "I don't know," she said aloud, partly in response to Prin's question, and partly in response to her own musings.

The creature's misaligned eyes narrowed, as if it believed she was hiding something. "Yes," it said slowly and deliberately.

"Wait a minute," Rebecca said at length. "When you described clans you said that they look alike and have the same ancestor."

"Yes, yes."

"But all of the creatures I've seen so far on your planet have been very different. And if you took me from those bug-aliens," she shivered involuntarily at the memory, "then why did I see one of them here, in the vehicle hangar?"

Prin leaned back, any possible suspicion forgotten as it became once more firmly engrossed in the conversation. "We call ourselves Clan Grinath, but we are really not a clan at all. Those who do not have a clan come here. Other clans pay us to fight for them."

"Mercenaries," Rebecca said in sudden understanding. "How did you…How does…How do you become a member of Clan Grinath?"

"Most of us become part of this clan when all the rest of our clan are murdered. We come here because there is nowhere else to go. On Ka'esch, if you are clanless, you will die quickly."

"Ka'esch?"

The lithe body inclined slightly, as if nodding. "Yes, yes, that is the name of our land."

"You said 'most' were clanless. What about the rest?"

Prin looked slightly uncomfortable and folded its arms across its chest. "Some want to join because they are not wanted by their clan."

"Not wanted? But isn't a clan stronger the more members it has? Why would a clan kick out one of its own?" Rebecca asked, puzzled.

"Because they broke some law, are sick, or…insane."

The sudden image of the devilish face cackling with laughter in the rain made Rebecca's blood freeze. Unconsciously, she began to crack her knuckles.

"Yes, yes," Prin continued, "but there are many good things about having different clans together: we have learned more than any other clan about our land and the other clans around us. Each new member tells us new hidden information. Many other clans now give us money not to fight, but for information."

All that had happened to her since she landed on the planet began to finally make sense as each new piece of the puzzle fit into place. "That is why you all use translators."

"Yes, yes. A clan like Grinath was not even possible until after the Tarlujian Uprising. After that, these translators were found, and Clan Grinath was formed by groups of clanless ones left from the war."

"What was the 'Tarlujian Uprising'?"

Prin's head bobbed up and down slowly. "Yes, yes, of course. You've never heard the most great story. Do you know any of the history of Ka'esch?"

Rebecca shook her head. "No."

Prin stood and began pacing back and forth in the cell as it spoke; its four arms articulating frequently. "Where to begin, where to begin," it said quietly, thinking aloud.

"No one knows for sure about the history of life on Ka'esch, because no one has the time to spend on it; we are too busy fighting for survival. But from what I have learned from other clans, I think that life began somewhere in the Great Lake to the north. Over millions of years, as life became more complex, basic clans began to form. But since there was very much empty land, fighting was not so bad. The Lidrilian later took the north land; and we, the Hran, lived in the south.

"After some time, all of the land was filled, and the clans began to fight for areas. But about 630 years ago—although as I said, no one know for sure because we didn't write things down until after the war—but about 630 years ago, by Clan Diodre counting of 230 days per cycle, one clan found a large island to live on. This clan, the Tarluj, was left alone because no other clans knew they were there. Clan Tarluj grew in numbers; and, since they were not always fighting to live like all other clans, they spent time making machines.

"Then, after many years of work, they began to murder all the other clans. Their technology gave them such a great help that they could not be stopped. Then, for the first time in known history, many clans made a truce and fought together to destroy Clan Tarluj.

"But the truce was short. Once Clan Tarluj was no more, the other clans began a bitter fight over the Tarlujian technology. Each clan grabbed what they could, then returned to their areas to learn all they could about it. The old law of 'Power to the Strong, Death to the Weak' had to be changed to 'Power to the Strong *and Intelligent*, Death to the Weak *and Stupid*.' Because of this, each clan found their smartest members and kept them from taking their turn at hunting and fighting. They spent all of their time learning about the technology and trying to make new ones. These are the scientists."

Rebecca sat for several moments, her mind still processing all she had just heard. "So that's why your clan leader reacted so much when I said I was a scientist."

"Yes, yes!" Prin said, resuming its seat upon the floor. "We get great respect from the others in the clan, because they know that our technology helps to win fights. In fact, it was my technology that helped Sikaris to beat the V'skir." Two of its hands made circles around its eyes with its fingers. "Goggles. They stop the flashing lights of the V'skir."

But Rebecca was only half listening, her mind still digesting all that Prin had told her. "And this is why your clan leader is so interested in my weapon and drill. They are technologies no one on your planet has."

"Yes, yes. Your weapon would give us a great help. We could learn how it works and sell it to others, or use it to fight. It is a great prize." Prin said, watching her carefully.

Rebecca seemed not to notice. "Is Sikaris a scientist?"

Prin's face changed into an expression that Rebecca was unable to interpret. "No. At least, he does not serve as one here. In his home clan, he may have been one. In Clan Grinath, he is a fighter, but a very intelligent one. He is a leader of fighters."

"How does he know my language? And he said that I am not the first human he has encountered. Have others of my kind ever been here before?" Rebecca asked, curiosity and confusion evident in her voice.

The alien just stared at her, its expression indiscernible. "I do not know. Sikaris is very strange. He is not from any clan in the areas that I know, so he must be from some clan far away. It may be possible that he has met your kind before. He is mostly by himself and does not do activities with others or talk to them much. But the High Crala likes him. He is a great fighter, and he is very smart."

The gradually increasing clicking sound of clawed feet scraping against the floor caused them both to turn towards the entrance of the cell. The golden brown form of Sikaris coalesced from out of the darkness beyond the door.

"Prin, Breuun wants to speak to you," it said in its low, growling voice.

Prin hopped to its feet and began walking toward the door, which Sikaris had now opened. "Well," it said to the tall alien as it passed through the door, "he is either a very great liar or he is insane. Either way, he should fit in here." With that, Prin disappeared down the corridor.

Rebecca sat stunned. *Was it referring to me? And what did it mean by "fit in"? Was this some kind of test?* But before she could come to any conclusions, her attention shifted to an item that was suddenly thrown at her feet. She stared down at her backpack in disbelief. *My equipment! But why…?*

Her question was partially answered a second later when Sikaris looked at her and spoke. "Prepare yourself. We leave soon." Before Rebecca could say a word, it closed the door and was quickly swallowed by the darkness of the hallway.

6

The Journey Begins

ALONE IN her cell, Rebecca picked up her backpack, eager to see what, if anything, still remained inside. She meticulously laid out each piece of equipment onto the slab and began examining them. To her surprise, all of her equipment had been returned to her, with the exception of her laser pistol.

Satisfied that her motion detector, comm, binoculars, and tracker had not been tampered with, she returned them to the bag. Then, reaching down, she picked up a small, multifunction pocket tool and turned it over in her hand. Flipping a small lever on the side of the handle, she cycled through the different settings until she came across the laser drill. Activating the tool, she felt a sudden sense of reassurance as the small blue laser light sprang into existence. After momentarily toying with the idea of using it to melt the lock on her prison cell, she flipped it off and shook her head. *Even if I got out of this cell, there is no way I could make it back to the* Vanguard *without these creatures' help. But this could very well come in handy later.* Closing it back up, she bent down and slipped the tool into a small pocket near the bottom of her left pant leg, then tucked both pant legs into her boots, effectively hiding any trace of the tool.

That accomplished, she picked up the only remaining item: her voice activated journal. With nothing else to occupy her time, she flipped it on and began to record.

Journal Entry #2

I hardly know where to begin. So much has happened since my last entry. I can only hope that this journal will somehow make it back to those who can make use of the information contained within. And if not, then at least it is serving the purpose of keeping my mind from focusing on other unpleasant thoughts. I don't know how much time I have before they come to get me, so I will only briefly relate the events that have occurred.

My last entry was cut short due to a strange light that I saw coming from behind a hill. I quickly grew uneasy when I could not get a response on the commlink from the other crew members, so I began heading for the ship. As I ran, the light followed me and even seemed to draw closer. Suddenly, another light sprang up in front of me that was so intense that it knocked me unconscious.

I woke up a couple of hours later inside of a cage in the back of some kind of truck-like vehicle. I learned later that this vehicle belonged to a group of intelligent, bug-like aliens called the V'skir. It seems that they have an innate ability to produce blinding flashes of light from their bodies; thus the source of the light I had seen near the ship. I shudder to imagine what purpose they had in mind for me. What I still can't figure out is why I didn't pick up their movements on my motion detector.

Furthermore, with all of the life-forms inhabiting this planet, why didn't the probe pick up any of them? All of the other information sent by the probe was accurate, so how could it have missed a planetful of life? It is true that these creatures seem to live below the ground, but they obviously travel on the surface. The only logical explanation I can think of brings with it some frighteningly sinister implications: perhaps one of the aliens deliberately tampered with the probe and sent us only the information that they wanted us to have to lure us here. But to what end?

This is just one of the many puzzling riddles I have encountered. Maybe I will discover the truth as I learn more about these creatures.

But I digress. After I was captured by the bug-like aliens, I was rescued, in a sense, by another group. This "clan," as they call themselves, is made up of aliens of various species. They survive by selling their services in mercenary fashion to other clans. It seems that the inhabitants of this planet, as far as I can tell, are engaged in a never-ending war. They are constantly fighting over territory, food, resources, and most importantly, at least as far as I'm concerned, technology.

This group of mercenaries, who call themselves Clan Grinath, brought me before their leader. After some very intense negotiating, which I will relate later as time permits, I was able to work out a deal with "the High Crala," as they call him. He has agreed to return me to the Vanguard in exchange for the RSK-320 laser drill. I must admit that I am extremely apprehensive about trusting these creatures. However, I don't see that I have any other choice.

I am adding this journal entry while sitting in a cell, waiting for them to come and get me so that we can leave for the ship. According to my watch, it has been nearly seven hours since we arrived on the planet and my tracker indicates that the ship still seems to be where it landed. I only hope it's still there when...um,...please, let them wait for me!

. . .

My emotions are, well, a mess, to say the least. On one hand, I can't believe that I have actually spoken and interacted with intelligent aliens from another planet! And to think that we would have been excited to find bacteria.

Zach will be so excited when I tell…if…I get a chance to tell him. Because, on the other hand, there is a good chance that these same intelligent aliens may yet decide to kill me!

And Jeff will…Oh, Jeff. I'm so sorry. I…

I cannot dwell on those possibilities, for if I do, I will surely be unable to maintain my sanity. Instead, I will use this journal to focus on what I am experiencing and observing. Science and logic will be my salvation.

I am fascinated by what I am learning about the various clans and the history of their planet. I spoke at length with one of their scientists; a ferret-like creature named Prin. It told me that there are two main races: animals and plants. What is most amazing is that both the plants and animals can move and are intelligent!

When I first heard this, it took me by surprise. But now that I've had time to think about it, the more it seems to make an odd kind of sense. Why shouldn't plants have learned to move and develop language? If all of life on Earth evolved from a common ancestor, then that includes plant life. It now seems stranger to me that plants and other animals on Earth did not evolve these abilities. Why were humans the only ones to develop language and intelligence, and why don't plants move on Earth?

Well, at any rate, on Ka'esch, for that is the name of this planet or continent (I'm not sure which), it seems that numerous species of plants and animals can speak. In fact, since this group of mercenaries is composed of many species, they rely on portable, pocket sized translator units to communicate.

Except for one alien. Of all that I have witnessed so far, nothing has perplexed me more than the fact that one of the aliens, a sort of large, reptilian cat with flaps of skin like a flying squirrel between its limbs, actually speaks

English, and it seems, numerous other languages as well. When I asked this Sikaris how it learned English, it simply replied that I was not the first human it had ever met. Does that mean that other humans have visited this planet, or that Sikaris has traveled to Earth somehow? Judging by the technology I have seen, it seems more likely that other humans must have come here. But if so, why did NASA send us? It seems...

Someone is coming. I will have to continue later.

Rebecca switched off the recording unit and hastily shoved it into her backpack. No sooner had she finished securing the bag when Prin's form appeared outside her cell once again.

This time, however, the weasel-like alien wore what resembled ragged pieces of dark green snakeskin strapped together to form armor, which covered various vital areas of its body. Hanging from its right shoulder and crossing its body to its left hip stretched a bandolier that carried small, metallic cylinders about the size of small cans of soup.

"Come, Rebecca Clan Evans," it said as it opened her cell door. "It is time to leave." Prin stepped into her cell and dropped another set of the snake-like armor onto the concrete slab on which she sat. "Since your skin is so weak, we thought this Dakkar-nil skin armor might protect you better."

"Thank you," she said hesitantly as she stood to her feet, being careful not to put too much pressure on her injured knee. Reaching out, she picked up the strange armor. The material felt cold and hard, yet oddly supple. Running her fingers lightly over it, she shuddered inwardly. It felt exactly like some kind of reptilian skin, and judging by what she had seen thus far, its previous owner had probably been a walking, talking alien being. Repressing her revulsion, she unfolded it and began to put it on.

Prin looked at her in surprise. "You will not need that other...skin suit you wear. This will protect you much better, yes, yes."

Rebecca glanced up at Prin as she began attaching the leg sections. "Thank you, but this skin of yours does not cover everything," she said, putting her hand through the hole where the tail should be for emphasis. "So I think I'll keep my other outfit, at least for modesty's sake." Tensing herself, she looked up at the alien, hoping it would not be offended.

Instead, it looked merely confused. "What is that word?" it asked, the translator in her ear robbing the phrase of all inflection.

As she stood there with the belt in hand, it suddenly dawned on her that none of the creatures she had seen thus far wore clothing. "Well," she began, "on my planet we don't like others to see our bodies, so we wear clothes, like this," she said, grabbing a piece of her jumpsuit between her fingers.

"But you wear it for protection and warmth, no?"

"Yes, we do. But we also wear it so that others will not see us naked. We believe that to see someone naked is...wrong," she said, lacking a better explanation.

Prin gave her the same look as it had before, which Rebecca was now beginning to associate with unbelief. "That does not make sense. Are you not all from one clan? Did not all life on your land come from the same parent's parent's parent? Then why hide your body from each other? Do not all of your clan look the same?"

Standing in this cell, in front of this alien, the entire concept of modesty suddenly seemed ludicrous to her. *Where* did *we ever get the idea of modesty? Maybe he's right. What makes us humans different than other animals? Why do we feel ashamed?*

"Come," Prin said finally, interrupting her thoughts "we must go. They are waiting."

Rebecca, still lost in thought, finished buckling the alien armor to fit as well as possible, picked up her bag, and followed the lithe alien out of the cell.

Prin led her past the detention area and back through the maze of corridors. "I am excited," it said dully as they walked. "The High Crala has asked me to go on this important hunt. Yes, yes, it will be good to get out. Scientists do not usually go on hunting parties. But I am ready," it said, pointing to the silver cylinders on its bandolier.

"What are those for?" Rebecca asked

Prin looked at her, its face wearing its typical, expressionless mask. "These are small explosives that have a simple timing mechanism inside. I have made them to work when I *zerng* them."

For a moment, Rebecca wondered if her translator had just experienced some kind of glitch. "When you do what to them?"

"I *zerng* them."

"What is a *zerng*?" she replied

"It is a special ability that my clan has."

"What kind of 'special ability'?"

"Many cycles ago my clan developed the ability to make a mild current of electricity in our bodies." Reaching its arm out, Prin placed a clawed hand over Rebecca's. Immediately she jumped and withdrew her hand as a jolt of energy bolted up her arm. "Since then, this ability has grown stronger," Prin continued. "We now use it as a kind of weapon. I can make enough energy to cause a being to become unconscious. It also comes in very handy with computers and other machines. Yes, yes. By sending a small amount of energy into a machine, I can short it out. In the case of these, however, I have made them so that it sets the timer."

"Do the other clans have abilities like this?" Rebecca asked curiously, her uncertainty and worry about her fate lost in fascination.

"Abilities, yes, but not like this. Not with electricity. Each clan has evolved different kinds of abilities for attack or defense. Sikaris is always careful to choose beings with abilities that work with each other when deciding who will go with him on a hunt."

"How many are going on this…hunt?" Rebecca asked, the images of her friends being killed by dozens of mutated aliens stubbornly pushing their way to the forefront of her thoughts.

"Two full units, led by Sikaris," Prin said.

"How many are in each unit?"

"Eight. The High Crala thinks this is very important. Yes, yes. He is even sending us in two of the new Flyer Transports."

"Flyer Transports?" she said quizzically. "What are those?"

"You will see. Yes, yes, here we are."

Prin opened the door that now stood in front of them and they stepped into a smaller version of the vehicle hangar that Rebecca had first arrived in. Two identical vehicles sat idling several dozen feet in front of them, one behind the other, each surrounded by several aliens engrossed in various tasks. To the right of the door that Prin and Rebecca had just entered through stood an enormous hangar door, stretching nearly the entire eighty foot width of the room. Both transports faced toward the doors, giving Rebecca a profile view of their shape and size.

The transports were immense. They stood about twenty feet high and were nearly as wide. Their box-like shape reminded Rebecca of giant, sixty-foot long mobile homes with treads. The height was divided into three equal sections: the treads, a lower level, and an upper level. Protruding from each of the narrow windows set into the front, middle, and rear of the top level was a weapon that resembled a heavy machine gun. The front and rear guns were mounted on the corners of the vehicle, enabling the gunners to swivel in nearly any direction. With all six guns combined, any approaching enemy would be in the line of fire of at least two of the weapons at any given time.

The lower section, however, seemed devoid of weapons. Judging by the firepower on the top level, Rebecca guessed this was due to the fact that the driver sat below. The tall windows that wrapped around the front and rear of the bottom level further supported this assumption. Standing open in the center of the lower level was a six-foot-long, sliding rectangular door. Leading up to the door was a three rung, metallic ladder that extended down over the treads.

Several moments passed before Rebecca discovered the source of the vehicle's name. Perched on the back of the flat roof of each vehicle sat a small fighter plane, at least, that's what she assumed it to be. In reality, it looked more like a toboggan with wings than any kind of fighter jet. The "flyer" had no protection for its pilot other than a thick, curved window shield that looked like it was made of Plexiglas. Offensively, it carried a missile under each wing and what looked like a single machine gun that stuck out of the nose of the plane.

After giving her several moments to digest everything, Prin motioned her forward. As they walked toward the lead vehicle, the aliens all stopped whatever it was they were doing and stared in the direction of the newcomers. Rebecca felt a lump rise in her throat as a being that looked strikingly similar to a giant snake detached itself from the others and slithered towards them.

The creature stopped just in front of where they stood, then reared up to its full six-foot height as if ready to strike. Its scales were moss green interspersed with dark yellow lines in various places. Four blood-red eyes sized Rebecca up as if deciding how best to devour her, its scrutinizing gaze causing her blood to freeze. She stared helplessly into its multiple, off-centered eyes, unable to look away until a sudden movement from the snake's torso caught her attention. Reaching toward her were two fully developed arms!

Petrified with fear, Rebecca tried to force her body to breathe as one of the deformed claws grabbed her shoulder and the other cupped her face. A mixture of hissing and clicking erupted from the thing's mouth, translated a second later by the monotonous metallic voice of her translator. "So, this is the creature that is leading us to our deaths." It turned Rebecca's head to the right and left, examining her closely. "He looks so weak." Letting her go, its gaze moved down to peruse her recently acquired armor. "I guess that's why you dressed him in this."

Free from its grip, Rebecca quickly took a step back as Prin's high voice responded next to her, its normal confidence gone. "What can I say, Rysth-nuul? Your clan has very strong skin."

It glared at Prin for a moment, then spat, "I do not think even skin from my clan will be able to save him, or us. We are sure to be attacked. We will never make it to this 'weapon,' if it even exists." With that, the snake-like alien turned and headed back to the front vehicle, its lithe body disappearing quickly inside the open hatch.

Rebecca shuddered in revulsion, her eyes drifting toward the protective outfit she was wearing. Several seconds passed before Prin turned to her once again. "That was Rysth-nuul. He is one of our best drivers and pilots. He is very intelligent, but he always thinks bad things are going to happen. I do not think it will be that dangerous. And, if we are attacked, we have two strong vehicles and sixteen of the strongest fighters in Clan Grinath with us."

Suddenly, a maniacal laugh that was disturbingly familiar burst out from behind them, causing Rebecca to jump involuntarily. Turning around in alarm, she looked down into the face of the devilish creature that had attacked her in the cage.

"Nix and I agree with Rysth-nuul." For once, Rebecca was thankful for the inflectionless voice that translated for her, for this creature's speech consisted of shrill grinding and chattering sounds. By focusing on the translation, she was able to somewhat succeed in shutting out the irritating noises. "We are all doomed!" it shouted gleefully, its eyes growing wide and its arms grabbing its neck in mock horror.

In the light of the hangar, Rebecca could see more clearly this thing that had terrified her so much mere hours earlier. It reminded her of a three-foot-tall armadillo, but with powerful hind legs like those of a rabbit or kangaroo. The hard, gray shell covered its back and extended up just past the neck. Two crooked, bat-like ears adorned each side of its head, which seemed to be always slightly tilted to the left.

"Do you think the Torlig will get us first, or the Ryazan? Or maybe… he, he, he…maybe the V'skir will get their revenge. Ooooo," it let out a long howl that rose and fell in pitch as it spun itself in circles. Just as suddenly as it began its mad dance, it stopped and cocked its head as if listening. Its expression, which had just as abruptly become serious, once more beamed with sinister mirth. It fell to the floor and rolled back and forth, its twisted laugh echoing loudly in the hangar. "Yes! You have got it, Nix!" it gasped between fits of laughter. "We are all going to be Mrdangam food for sure!" It rolled once more with laughter, its stinger-like tail writhing like a serpent.

"Ch'ran, that is enough!" came a growl that Rebecca had come to recognize as belonging to Sikaris. Her guess was confirmed a moment later when the brownish-gold creature strode up to them, its wing-like folds of skin flowing behind it like a cape, its face a mask of menace. "Get into the transport, all of you. We are leaving."

The armadillo-like creature stood to its feet and began hopping off towards the front vehicle as if nothing had happened. A sudden command from Sikaris, however, stopped it dead in its tracks.

"Ch'ran, you ride in number two," it said, pointing towards the other transport.

Ch'ran looked crestfallen. "Please, Sikaris. I want to ride with you and with...our new friend," it said in feigned innocence, looking sideways at Rebecca.

There was little on this planet that Rebecca felt sure about; but one thing she did know, she didn't want to be anywhere near this creature, especially not inside an enclosed vehicle.

"No. Now go," Sikaris growled, causing Ch'ran to hop quickly towards the second vehicle and disappear into its interior. Rebecca let out the breath she didn't even realize she had been holding.

"Come, Rebecca Clan Evans," Prin said beside her as it began to walk towards the front vehicle.

Allowing herself a moment to relax, she took several deep breaths to steady her nerves, then followed her guide. As they drew near the sliding door on the right side of the foremost vehicle, Rebecca noticed several large dents in the body of the transport, as well as a cracked window on the lower level. Furthermore, she was surprised by the lack of paint, symbols or any other markings of ownership. In fact, the entire vehicle was caked with mud and grime, as if it hadn't been cleaned in years.

Now that she stood directly next to the immense vehicle, she began to feel both a small sense of comfort and trepidation. Despite its rugged look, the transport appeared tough, which should help them ward off any attackers. On the flip side, however, they would also be more than a match for the *Vanguard* and the rest of her crew, unless she could find some way of evening the odds or escaping. Trying hard to push the nagging doubts back to the recesses of her mind, Rebecca focused on the immediate task at hand.

Climbing up the short ladder, she stepped through the open door and entered the vehicle's lower level, followed immediately by Prin. Hunched over awkwardly to avoid hitting her head on the low, five-foot ceiling,

Rebecca stopped just inside the doorway and studied her surroundings in disgusted surprise. The inside of the transport appeared in worse shape than the exterior. The floor was littered with garbage, dirty rags, and an odd assortment of machine parts. Dirt and grease seemed to cover everything, as it had in the V'skir cage vehicle.

Not only was the entire transport filthy, but it looked like someone had taken it off of the assembly line before it had been completed. Loose wires hung in knotted bundles, wall and floor plates appeared as if they had been installed haphazardly, and the frame of the vehicle was still clearly visible, as if no attempt had been made to cover over it.

To the left of the sliding door that they had entered through, in the rear right of the vehicle, a massive engine was housed. Like some giant, mythological beast, it was belching out a high concentration of black smoke and fumes into the hangar, some of which seeped back into the interior of the transport, causing Rebecca to cover her mouth and nose to keep from gagging. In the rear left corner, opposite the engine, stood a large metal box with what looked like breathing holes in the top and sides. It stood as tall as the ceiling, and seemed about five feet wide and twice as long. Remembering what Prin had said earlier about this being a hunting transport, Rebecca guessed the box to be some sort of cage, similar to what she had been placed in by the V'skir. Lining the walls of the vehicle were several storage compartments of various shapes and sizes. A second door, identical to the one she had just entered through, stood open across from her on the left side. The lower level consisted of nothing else save two pilot stations in the front of the vehicle.

Her former disgust at the condition of the vehicle was momentarily forgotten by what she saw in front of her. Instead of chairs, two, four-foot-long metal benches that looked thoroughly cold and uninviting ran parallel to the walls. Built into the floor directly in front of the benches were the knobs, buttons, and various other controls used to pilot the massive machine.

But what caught her attention most was not the odd configuration of the controls, but the sight of the two aliens that occupied the area. Rysthnuul, lying on the leftmost bench, its body coiled around it like some unfortunate prey, shot Prin and Rebecca an uninterested glance and returned to its work, its gnarled claws punching buttons and turning knobs. Lying belly down on the right bench, was the copilot. Although she was beginning to become used to the strange looks of these beings, Rebecca nevertheless had to suppress her "fight-or-flight" response as a thick, alligator-like alien turned its knobby head to stare at her uncomfortably.

The creature was nearly five feet long from snout to tail, with short, powerful arms and legs. Its dark blue scales were punctuated with flaky, white patches, giving it an almost sickly appearance. Protruding from its lumpy back were two long tentacles that it currently had wrapped around its waist. From what Rebecca could see in the dim light, it had no crease in its head where a mouth should be. Furthermore, it had three thin slits that resembled eyes, but each was placed in random positions on the top of its head.

"Come," Prin said, drawing her attention away from the strange being and towards a ladder that stood against the right wall next to the door. Prin, she now noticed, was not hunching over in an attempt to stand, but was walking on its hands and feet like an animal, pointing up the ladder. "We ride on the second level," it said.

Giving the mutated alligator-like being a final glance, Rebecca climbed up the short ladder and passed through an open hatch, followed closely by Prin. The second floor of the vehicle was a little more spacious and much less noxious. It consisted only of six benches: two in front, two in the middle, and two in the rear. The benches were identical to the ones on the lower level, with the only difference being that these were mounted on some type of pivotal platform. Set into the walls directly in front of the benches were the heavy cannon-like weapons that Rebecca had viewed from outside. This configuration allowed the gunner to rotate the bench in a 90-degree arc in synch with the cannon-like weapon. The control grips for the weapons came up from the floor at the front of the platform in the same fashion as the driver's controls below.

"We lie here," Prin said, pointing to the middle pair of benches. It strode forward on its hands and feet and straddled the left bench, then lay on it, belly down.

You have got to be kidding. Still stooping over so as to avoid bumping her head on the low ceiling, she walked over to the corresponding bench on the right side of the vehicle. As she drew nearer to it, she noticed that, like everything else, it was caked with mud, grease, and grime. Mentally offering thanks for the scale-like protective outfit, she followed suit and lay down on her stomach. "I thought you said the transports were new," she said, as she tried unsuccessfully to get comfortable on the hard metal.

Prin, seeing that she could not touch the floor with her arms, reached over and adjusted the height of the bench with a lever on the side. "They are," it replied. "At least, almost new. This is only their third mission. Why do you ask?"

Rebecca, giving up on her attempt to get comfortable while lying on her stomach, propped herself up on her arms and looked at the ferret-like creature in mild surprise. "It just doesn't look like it was fully finished; what with the wires, loose panels, and lack of paint. And I am surprised at how filthy it is already. No offense, but why doesn't someone clean it?"

Prin looked at her, its expression unreadable. "This is a hunting transport, a working vehicle. Why spend valuable time and energy painting or cleaning it? I don't know about your clan, but our life spans are short. On Ka'esch, we live by the Law of Functionality. Why should we care about how something looks as long as it works?"

Rebecca was silent for a moment, reflecting on this idea. "So you don't value beauty, do you? You don't have art or artists," she stated with new understanding.

"The translator does not know those words. What do they mean?" Prin asked curiously.

"Nothing," she said. "It is too difficult to explain."

Before Prin could inquire further, movement to their left caught their attention. Coming up the ladder from below was Sikaris. Without even so much as a glance in their direction, it moved over and lay down on the rear left bench, directly behind Prin, its body positioned backwards, facing the rear windows. Reaching into a nearby cubby, Sikaris withdrew a translator unit, fit the earpiece into its left ear, and placed the unit into a hidden inner pouch. With its translator/commlink in position, Sikaris switched it on and said in its low, gravelly voice, "Rysth-nuul, are we ready to leave?"

To her surprise, Rebecca heard Rysth-nuul's response through her translator's earpiece even though she could not hear the alien's actual voice. "Everything is in place. Lohgur, Lohgar, and Kyen'tir are entering now, and Druen is standing by and waiting for your signal to climb on."

As if summoned by the mention of their names, three aliens appeared in rapid succession through the two access hatches. From the right hatch came two burly ape-like figures who immediately proceeded to the front two weapon stations. Both wore black, metallic armor plates that covered most of their dirty, orange hair, which stuck up chaotically through their tough, scaly hides. A large hump the size of a softball stuck out from their backs just below the neck. Beneath that, each creature had a long, scrawny third arm that ended in three fingers and two thumbs, which currently hung immobile across their spines and tails.

From the left hatch came a diminutive, bird-like alien. It landed lightly onto the deck and hopped over to the remaining rear weapon station. Upon further examination, Rebecca changed her initial assessment; the being looked more like a three-foot-tall, two-legged dinosaur with wings rather than a bird. Its reddish-orange, reptilian-like head was mounted on a long, curving neck. The thin, asymmetrical body of the creature was covered with black feathers that resembled torn, frayed scales, except on its underbelly, which was a dirty white. Three long, scaly claws stuck out from the tips of the creature's wings, which were composed of the same strange feathers. Its lengthy legs, which seemed more suited to running than flying, ended in razor sharp talons.

As she studied the creature, its head swiveled around to look at her, causing her to pull back in surprise. In addition to the large, round pair of eyes on top of its head, it also had a second set of eyes underneath its beak, centimeters from its throat. As it settled into position onto the bench, its plume–like tail fanned open and closed reflexively to adjust its balance.

"Rysth-nuul," Sikaris' voice growled behind her, "give Druen the signal to climb on, then let's go."

The snake-like alien complied, and a moment later, the entire vehicle shook and groaned from behind as if being crushed by a giant vise. Turning quickly to look over her shoulder out the rear window, Rebecca caught her breath in surprise.

Climbing onto the vehicle was an immense being that looked strikingly similar to a triceratops. However, instead of three horns on its crested head, two long, white horns protruded from each side of its forehead, curving down over its long snout. The left horn was broken at the tip, a trophy of past battles. In addition, two identical tusks rose from its jaw to meet the top horns at their tips to form what looked like a kind of mask. The ten-foot-tall creature, being too large to ride inside the vehicle, was holding onto the back with its stubby, thick claws.

"Katie is never gonna believe this," Rebecca said under her breath as she turned around to face forward once again.

The engine rumbled below as the vehicle lurched to life, sending a particularly strong gust of fumes up through the hatch, causing Rebecca's lungs to burn and her eyes to water. The reddish sunlight streamed through the front windows of the transport and became brighter and brighter as the vehicle moved slowly through the now open doors before them until the entire vehicle was bathed in an eerie glow.

I'm coming, guys. Be there. Please, still be there. Reaching down, she took the tracker out of her bag and set it to her ship's frequency. As before, the ship appeared as a fuzzy blip in the midst of a blizzard of haze and distortion, its location unchanged. Reassured, she returned the device to her bag and attempted once more to get comfortable on the hard, metal bench.

Prin, noticing her discomfort, pointed to a set of eight-inch metal bars imbedded into the floor near the front of the bench. "Try holding onto those with your hands," it offered. "It makes the ride less bumpy."

Rebecca grabbed the handholds, but found it extremely difficult to see where they were going with her chin laying on the seat of the bench. "If I may ask," she said finally, after several minutes of trying to find a suitable position, "why benches? Why don't you just use chairs?"

"A bench fits our natural body position. Most of us can sit, but…," Prin looked down to where the tail hole was on Rebecca's pants, ". . . our tails make it uncomfortable and difficult, yes, yes. Lying down is much better." After a moment of silence, Prin asked tentatively, "How did you lose your tail? Was it cut off, or is that a mutation?"

Rebecca was taken aback. "I…no,…I mean…my clan…no one in my clan has a tail. Our ancestors probably had them, but I guess we lost the need for them thousands of years ago."

A loud, wheezing sound erupted from Prin's mouth as the muscles in its face contorted wildly. "That was a good joke, Rebecca Clan Evans! 'Lost the need for them!' That is funny."

Rebecca stared at it in disbelief. "Why do you find that so funny?"

Prin, suddenly realizing that she was not joking, quickly stifled its laughter and composed itself. "Well, a tail is an extremely useful thing, yes, yes. It is almost like having another arm. In fact, some clans even have mutated hands on their tails. It is used for balance. It can be used as a weapon. It can be used to move things. And, it can help you scratch where you cannot reach." As if to punctuate this last thought, Prin brought its tail up over its back and used its double tips to rub between its shoulder blades. "If your clan really did lose their tails, I do not think it was because they lost the need for them."

Not knowing what else to say in this unsettling conversation, Rebecca looked forward and gazed out the front window, lost in thought. It surprised her that although it was just after sunrise when they landed, the sun was only barely past its zenith. Checking her watch and doing a quick calculation in her head, she realized that over eight hours had already elapsed since their arrival.

Just then, as she was about to ask Prin about the length of the day, the transport began climbing a hill, causing the engine to struggle and emit another blast of noxious fumes. After she had recovered from her latest fit of coughing, Rebecca looked over at Prin once again, all thoughts of her previous question having vanished. "Was the exhaust system damaged on one of its previous missions?" she asked in a raspy voice. "This thing's engine produces more pollution than half of a city."

"The translator does not know that word. But if you mean the gases from the transport, then I would say that we are all used to it," Prin said in its typical matter-of-fact manner. "If you stay on Ka'esch for long, you, or most likely your offspring, will become used to it also."

My offspring? Rebecca thought curiously. Deciding to let the odd comment pass until later, she continued with her current train of thought. "But what about the damage all of this pollution does to the environment?" she replied. "What about *your* children? Don't you care about preserving the environment for their sakes?"

Prin looked at her with that same, strange look. "It is true that the gases from machines will probably make the air unbreathable in a few generations, but why should we care? We will be dead by then. We do what we need to do to survive. And when we are not fighting to survive, we are enjoying other pleasures, not worrying about what will happen in the future. That will be their problem, yes, yes. If they have not mutated enough to breathe the air, then they will die."

Rebecca was shocked at the unabashed, self-gratifying attitude of this creature. *That is so cruel and selfish! How can it…?*

The alien simply stared at her, no malice showing on its features, just hard reality. Disgusted and frustrated, Rebecca turned away from Prin and stared once again out the window, her thoughts a mixture of indignation and confusion.

Several hours passed uneventfully. Whether due to Rysth-nuul's skill as a driver or by pure luck, they had as of yet encountered no hunting parties. After trying numerous different positions, Rebecca gave up on trying to get comfortable on the hard bench. It almost seemed as if the transport itself took some kind of twisted pleasure in bumping and jostling her about.

During this time, Rebecca was asked at various intervals to consult her tracking unit to confirm that the ship hadn't moved. Each time, she grew more and more excited that this horrible nightmare would soon be over.

A sudden screeching alarm caused her to sit up so abruptly that she nearly struck her head against the ceiling.

"What is that?" she asked Prin nervously.

But before it could respond, Rysth-nuul yelled up loudly from below, the translation seeming contradictory in its inflectionless response. "Tarluj's Curse! I knew it! I knew this trip was going too smoothly. Sikaris, you had better see this."

In an instant, the large form of Sikaris sprang to the front of the cabin to stand on all fours in between the two ape-like aliens. "They are coming in fast," it said in a low growl, its attention fixed on a point outside the front left window.

"What is it?" Rebecca asked again, panic beginning to build in her voice. *Not now! Not when we are so close!*

By way of reply, Prin, its face a grim mask of resignation, pointed out the window beside him. "Mrdangam."

Rebecca looked out the window to where Prin indicated and gasped, a terror such as she had never felt before seizing her in an iron fist. Flying towards them over the barren landscape, bathed in the blood-red glow of the sun, were five enormous dragons.

7

Mrdangam Attack

"EVERYONE GET your weapons ready," Sikaris ordered. "Rysth-nuul, take us into the Joktan Ruins. At least we may find some cover there." Turning around, the cat-like alien headed back to its bench. "Lohgur, launch the flyer," Sikaris commanded, its voice strong and firm. Rebecca turned and looked at it and was surprised to find it staring at her in return. Unable to hold the gaze of those intense violet eyes, she quickly looked away.

Immediately and without a word, the ape-like alien on the front right bench leapt up, moved past Rebecca to the back of the vehicle, opened a hatch in the ceiling and disappeared through it. A moment later, a sudden booming sound pushed her already frazzled nerves farther toward their breaking point. Glancing out the window to see if the dragons had somehow already reached them and begun to attack, she was relieved to see that although they were significantly closer, they were still too far away to have been the source of the sound. A second later, she heard the unmistakable sound of rockets firing and watched through the forward window as the toboggan-like flyer launched and banked left toward the oncoming dragons.

"What...," Rebecca choked out, her mouth having gone suddenly dry, "what are they?"

Prin looked at her gravely. "The Mrdangam are very strong fighters with very little intelligence. Because they are so large, they never had the need for it. We will very likely not survive this, Rebecca Clan Evans. A Mrdangam hunting party is not easily killed, especially not one this big. They usually only hunt in pairs."

"But…aren't these transports powerful? And we have the flyers. Shouldn't that…I mean, won't that stop them?" she asked, her hope waning rapidly.

But before Prin could reply, Sikaris' commanding voice came from behind them. "Prin, we do not have any time to waste. Show him how to use the guns."

At once, Prin left its bench and moved over to stand next to Rebecca. Its claw reached down next to her bench and threw a lever, causing her bench to swivel 90 degrees to face the right window and the weapons controls.

"I will explain this quickly, so listen carefully," Prin began, its voice shaking slightly from nervousness. Over the next minute, Rebecca summoned all of her military training to help keep her mind focused on learning the unfamiliar controls and shut out all thoughts of the approaching terror.

"And remember," Prin concluded, "Mrdangam have very strong hides. Our weapons will only hurt them if we hit them in the heads or other weak points, such as their underbellies. So aim there. And if you see one spit acid at your weapon, get off of the bench as quickly as you can."

"Acid?" Rebecca echoed, incredulous.

"Yes, yes. They have the ability to spit acid from their mouths," Prin said downcast.

A low, raspy voiced issued out from the ape-like creature manning the front left gun. "The flyers are almost there."

After glancing over its shoulder to mark the progress of the flyers, Prin looked back at Rebecca, hopelessness clearly evident in its expression. "Good luck." With that, Prin returned to its seat, which now faced directly opposite hers. Since the dragons were approaching from the left side, Rebecca turned around in her seat and watched as the flyers engaged the oncoming threat.

Once they were in range, the two flyers opened up with their machine guns, spraying gunfire at the heads of the flying reptiles in an attempt to divert their attention. They then split off on each side of the five beasts, which were more or less flying in a straight line. The two dragons on the ends of the formation turned to follow, leaving the remaining three free to continue the main attack.

"Well, three is better than five," came the voice of the translator. Since no one on the top floor had spoken, she assumed that either Rysth-nuul or the copilot had made the comment. Her suspicions were confirmed a moment later when a second comment came through the earpiece.

"But still more than enough to fry us all! Now shut up, Tarrsk, and help me figure out how to keep us from becoming lunch."

Rebecca diverted her attention from the approaching dragons to look out the front window at the Joktan Ruins. The small, ruined city still contained many buildings that stood erect in various stages of decay and destruction. Rubble was strewn everywhere from the mud and brick buildings, causing many of the streets to be nearly impassable, at least for conventional vehicles.

"Hold on, Rebecca Clan Evans," Prin called from behind her. "It is about to get very bumpy."

Reaching down, she grabbed the handholds in the floor in a vise-like grip and prepared herself for the worst.

"This is going to be close," the ape-like alien in front of her grunted through clenched teeth.

The ruins loomed ever closer, but to their left, the dragons, which were approaching at a right angle to their current path, were rapidly closing the distance. They were now so close, in fact, that Rebecca could see dark green saliva dripping from their gaping maws. Their blood-red scales, reflecting the hazy sunlight, created a sort of glow that seemed to emanate from them. Massive wings spanning nearly thirty feet propelled their slim, muscular bodies, which were, from head to tail, almost as long as the wings. Like Kyen'tir, each of their wings ended in deformed, claw-like hands, except that unlike Rebecca's alien companion, these looked capable of ripping through even the thickest of hides with ease. Their heads, which Rebecca could now see resembled that of a Pteranadon, were crested with numerous horns and spikes that protruded at various odd angles.

"Fire!" Sikaris shouted. The front and rear guns on the left side erupted with fire; the percussive sounds were so deafening that Rebecca had to fight the urge to momentarily let go of the handholds and cover her ears. Druen, the dinosaur-like alien riding outside on the back of the vehicle, added to the chaos by unloading its heavy cannon several times. Some of the projectiles hit their marks on the approaching beasts, but served only to enrage them.

A sudden, loud hissing sound like that of boiling water could barely be heard over the roar of the gunfire. "Incoming!" yelled the bird-like creature in warning.

Out the left window, Rebecca watched helplessly as a stream of dark green liquid hurled straight towards them. Then, just as the jet of deadly acid was about to strike the window, the outline of a ruined building moved rapidly past their vehicle, blocking her view.

"That was close!" breathed Prin, but a sudden scream from their long-range intercom immediately stole any relief it may have felt.

"We lost our rear left gun!" a voice said in panic.

The dragon-like creatures, having now closed the distance, began circling the vehicles as they sped down the ruined streets. Bracing herself, Rebecca aimed at the airborne beasts and squeezed the trigger of her weapon. The jolt was terrible, and although her ears had begun to adjust to the volume of the others' weapons, the intensity of the sound nevertheless caused her ears to ring painfully. After several wild shots, she became accustomed to the feel of the weapon and her accuracy improved markedly, yet due to the speed of the creatures, she soon became frustrated at her lack of success in hitting her targets.

"What are they waiting for?" asked Rebecca, momentarily ceasing fire. "Why don't they just attack and get it over with?"

Prin, concentrating on firing its weapon, took several moments to respond. "It takes them some time to make enough acid for another attack."

A sudden question from Rysth-nuul crackled through the translator, cutting off any further explanation Prin may have offered. "Tarrsk, have you found the map of this place yet?"

"Yes, it is here," came Tarrsk's reply through Rebecca's earpiece.

"Then what are you waiting for? Find me some place where we can lose these things."

Sikaris' sudden warning caused Rebecca to grab her weapon's grip with renewed fervor. "Incoming!"

In an attempt to avoid the deadly blast, Rysth-nuul jerked the vehicle hard to the left. The bulky transport, however, could not maneuver quickly enough and the toxic liquid struck it with a loud splat. Prin gave out a startled cry and leapt off the gunner's bench just as the acid began to dissolve the controls with a voracious appetite.

Another sudden change of direction threw Prin off balance. Rolling quickly to its hands and feet, it made its way forward to the unoccupied bench in the front of the vehicle, its chest heaving from exertion and fear.

"Tarrsk, I need someplace to go now!" a frustrated Rysth-nuul bellowed.

Tarrsk's translated reply was heard a moment later. "Here. The last scouting report says that there is a mostly undamaged storage building just up ahead. We might be able to lose it in there. Take the next left—LOOK OUT!"

One of the circling dragons had flown slightly ahead and, swooping down, used its lengthy tail to knock over a large corroded wall into the debris filled street directly in their path. Rysth-nuul jerked the cumbersome transport to the right, narrowly avoiding the falling wall.

The sudden evasive maneuver, however, forced the vehicle down a side street in the exact opposite direction they were hoping to take. Rysth-nuul's curse came through Rebecca's earpiece untranslated. The side street was much more narrow then the main street, leaving the wide transports only a few feet of space on each side. Rebecca, her arms protesting from the abuse inflicted on them by the jolting of the gun, ceased fire, thankful that no more of the attackers were in her sights.

Perspiration and fear hung thick in the air. "They're herding us,"

Sikaris said softly, its voice still and calm in defiance of the seemingly hopeless situation. "Get us off of this street," it said more loudly so that the small microphone on the translation device would pick it up, "even if you have to go through a building to do it."

But at the same moment the translation finished, Sikaris observation was proven correct. Perched atop an intact building several dozen yards ahead of them on the right side of the street was a fourth dragon, its massive lungs taking in air in preparation to spew forth its deadly poison.

"Another one? Where did this one come from?" the ape-like alien asked in aggravation.

Rebecca felt a scream rising in her parched throat, demanding release. But just as the beast was about to discharge the attack that was sure to disable their vehicle and leave them helpless, two missiles streaked out of the sky from the left and impacted into the creature's chest. Following in the wake of the missiles came one of the flyers, banking off to the left to circle around for another pass.

The monstrous alien, its attention focused solely on the transport, was taken completely by surprise and therefore received the full force of the explosions, killing it instantly. Even as shouts of triumph and relief were being formed in their throats, a new danger cut off any thought of celebration. The carcass of the giant beast, blackened and smoldering, fell towards the street below.

Rysth-nuul managed to narrowly avoid the majority of the creature's body; its tail slapping hard against the roof of the transport as it passed beneath. The second transport, however, slammed hard into the giant body, causing the vehicle to careen into one of the ruined buildings.

The flyer circled around to get into position for a strafing run in an attempt to aid the trapped vehicle. However, the pilot did not notice that one of the three dragons that had been chasing the transports had maneuvered underneath it. As the fighter was preparing to open fire on the remaining two dragons that were even now disabling the ensnared vehicle with acid blasts from their beaked jaws, a sudden jolt rocked the ship from below, causing the pilot to lose control as the acid began to eat through the rockets that held the craft aloft. The last that the crew of the foremost transport could see was the flyer spinning out of control and diving into the ruined city.

Immediately after the dead dragon's charred carcass had blocked the second transport, Rysth-nuul brought their vehicle to a sudden halt, giving Sikaris and Druen clean shots on the two dragons attacking their comrades.

Frantic cries and a chaotic mixture of sounds came out of the radio transceiver, but Rebecca's translator was unable to sort them out. Suddenly, a deafening roar that would have caused even the bravest of warriors to shrink in fear, rent the air. The dragon that had destroyed the flyer had returned and was headed straight toward them, its fangs still dripping acid.

"Go!" Sikaris bellowed over its shoulder, never ceasing the endless barrage of gunfire.

Rysth-nuul, shaking off the paralyzing fear from the dragon's roar, throttled the engine and turned quickly into the open street on their left, causing the dragon to abort its dive in order to change directions to pursue them. The beast swerved erratically as it followed, keeping the weapons fire from Sikaris and Druen from hitting any of its weak points.

"Tarrsk!" Rysth-nuul spat vehemently at the copilot. "Which way?"

"There." Looking toward the front window, Rebecca saw a building looming up before them as they rounded a corner.

A sudden silence rang loudly in the vehicle as both Druen and Sikaris ceased fire. Rebecca turned to see that the dragon had seemingly given up the chase. "Why did...," she gulped in air, her heart still pounding heavily from adrenaline, "Where...where did it go?"

Prin, still scanning all of the windows frantically for signs of the creature, responded without looking at her. "It most likely returned to the other transport to help its clanmates finish off the others; lucky for us."

Noting that the transport continued on in the opposite direction, Rebecca looked to Prin. "Aren't we going back to help them?" she asked, fully expecting a positive response.

"You really are insane," Prin replied, now turning his mismatched eyes to look over its shoulder at her.

"But...aren't they your clanmates? Aren't you going to at least try to save them?"

The coldness in Prin's eyes caused Rebecca, for the first time, to view it as it truly was: an intelligent, emotionless animal that lacked any kind of concern for others whatsoever. When it spoke, its voice was lower and more feral than Rebecca had ever heard before, causing her to draw back from it in fear. "They served their purpose. 'Power to the strong, death to the weak.' In this case, we are the strong."

"Lucky is more like it," snickered the ape-like alien quietly.

Rebecca stared at Prin, dumbfounded. But before she could even form a thought in response to this statement, her eyes caught movement outside the window behind Prin. "Look out!" she screamed, her hand seemingly moving of its own accord to point over the ferret-like alien's shoulder. The lithe form of the dragon that had been chasing them loomed up suddenly out of the side street they were passing and launched its massive body at the vehicle, catching Druen by surprise and knocking it from its position on the small platform on the back of the transport.

A moment later, a loud hiss burst from the ceiling directly above Rebecca as acid began eating its way through. Even as she recovered her senses and started moving off of the bench, she felt a sudden searing pain on her left forearm. Letting out a cry, she grabbed her burned arm with her right hand and lost her balance, falling hard onto her right hip.

For a split second, she felt her grip on consciousness begin to slip as the acid burned mercilessly through her protective armor and began eating its way through her skin and muscle. The sudden emergence of the dragon's claw through the now weakened ceiling, however, succeeded in snapping her mind back to the present. Its gigantic claw tore large chunks of the ceiling away, leaving the center of the vehicle exposed.

The dragon, perched upon the back of the transport where Druen had once stood, glared maliciously down at Rebecca through the hole it had just created, the fangs in its beaked maw oozing with murderous intent.

Frozen from fear, Rebecca could do nothing but watch helplessly as a claw on the end of the beast's wing descended towards her. Sikaris' body suddenly eclipsed the horrific visage before her as it grabbed her and rolled across the floor of the vehicle, away from the razor sharp claw. In that same instant, Prin pulled a cylinder from its bandolier, charged it with a sudden flash of blue light, and tossed it through the torn ceiling.

The dragon, not realizing the danger of the explosive, ignored it and kept its claw groping about the interior of the vehicle, searching for its intended victim. A second later, a numbing explosion rocked the transport.

At the same moment that the explosion went off, Rysth-nuul changed course once again in an attempt to circle back around to the building that Tarrsk had indicated. The dragon, not expecting either the explosion or the sudden direction change, was thrown off balance and fell from the vehicle, its body reducing a small, nearby building to rubble.

Sikaris eased itself off of Rebecca and calmly returned to its post, almost as if nothing had happened. Although weak from the excruciating pain in her arm as well as still recovering from having the wind knocked out of her, she nonetheless gritted her teeth and forced her body into a sitting position so that she could look out the back window to see what had become of the vile beast that pursued them.

Did we get it? she wondered feebly. In answer to her unspoken question, a violent bellow erupted from the smoke and dust that hung thick in the air over the area where the dragon had fallen. A moment later, portions of the crumbled building were flung aside as the beast emerged from the debris. Stumbling back onto the street, the reptilian creature resumed the pursuit. This time, however, it chased them on the ground; its right wing having been shredded by the explosion, making flight impossible. Rebecca watched in awe as the beast began limping faster and faster towards them on all fours, until the transport turned another corner, removing the creature from sight.

"There!" Tarrsk said. "The entrance should be—"

Before the translator could finish, Rysth-nuul spoke, causing the device to switch focus to its voice instead. "Forget the entrance. I am taking us in here!" With that, Rysth-nuul pressed the accelerator. "Prepare for collision!"

Rebecca crawled back to her bench. However, instead of climbing onto it, she merely wrapped her legs and one good arm around the legs of the bench and held on tightly. Despite her fear, she looked out the front window and watched as the hard, mud and clay building drew ever nearer.

Gunfire from Sikaris' weapon broke the relative silence with jarring suddenness. Leaping from the top of a ruined building onto the rubble-strewn street behind them was the injured dragon, its face contorted in rage.

"Incoming!" Sikaris barely had time to yell before the sickening splat of acid hit the back of the vehicle. The yellowish-green liquid immediately ate through Sikaris weapon, causing it to cease its steady drumming in an instant.

A second later, the vehicle struck the wall of the building full force. Although Prin and the ape-like alien had weakened the wall with gunfire prior to impact, it still retained enough structural integrity to jar the occupants of the vehicle considerably. Prin and the others, having wrapped their tails around the benches tightly, were affected little. Sikaris, however, being in mid leap from its bench to avoid being burned by the acid, was not so lucky. Its body sailed past Rebecca and slammed hard into the front panel between the two benches.

The momentum carried the heavy transport into the building, causing the walls and ceiling of the structure to be torn asunder with abandon. Large chunks of debris fell through the hole in the roof of the transport and landed heavily upon the metal bench above Rebecca, nearly crushing it beneath the weight. After several bone-shattering seconds of destruction, the vehicle entered a larger meeting room of some sort where the vehicle momentarily ceased its demolition. The room looked to be about the size of an average auditorium or conference center, but any furniture or other décor had long since been removed.

Once Rysth-nuul had stopped the vehicle, Sikaris, surprisingly unhurt, regained its feet and strode back to its bench without a word. All eyes in the transport turned to look down the path of destruction to see if the dragon was attempting to follow.

Several intense moments of silence reigned as they stared through the hole behind them, trying to pierce through the haze of dust left in their wake. Suddenly, the building shook around them as if being rocked by an earthquake, sending another layer of dust and debris down upon the transport. Through the hole behind them lumbered the giant creature, bellowing in rage.

"It didn't work," Prin said in defeat as Rebecca rose and resumed her seat on the bench.

"What..." she said slowly, pain, fatigue and exhaustion beginning to take their toll. "What didn't work?"

Prin looked at her in disappointment. "Mrdangam will not usually enter into unknown places that will not let them move freely or fly. That is why we came in here. But," it said, looking out the rear window once more, "my explosive crippled it and made it angry. Now it will not stop until we are dead."

Everyone stood motionless, staring hopelessly down the freshly made entrance, watching as the dragon tore away large chunks of wall, widening the hole as it came.

"Rysth-nuul, go!" Sikaris growled. "Try to outrun it or lose it among the buildings."

The vehicle groaned to life once again, the transport's engine gushing foul exhaust fumes into the tunnel. Gaining speed, Rysth-nuul slammed the vehicle into the opposite wall and opened an exit onto the surrounding streets, which led them to the right and back toward where they had last seen the other transport. A tremendous crash and roar a few seconds later informed them that the dragon-like alien had cleared the building and was once again in hot pursuit.

"Tarrsk, are there any other streets? This one is leading us back," came the translation of Rysth-nuul's exasperated question.

"None that are clear. Most streets around here are blocked by fallen buildings."

As if to accentuate its words, the street they were following turned to the left and ended abruptly where a building had collapsed, preventing them from going any farther.

Rysth-nuul let out a vicious snarl and threw the transport into reverse. But before it could even move the vehicle more than a few feet, the dragon rounded the corner.

Seeing its prey cornered, it gave out a roar of triumph and sprayed its deadly liquid at the vehicle once more. In a moment, the engine died and the back window of the transport had dissolved, leaving them exposed to the air. Grabbing another explosive from its bandolier, Prin prepared to arm it.

Then suddenly, to their utter shock and amazement, another form appeared from behind the dragon. Before the Mrdangam could react, four long horns pierced through the tough hide, skewering it and pinning it to the nearby wall.

Druen, on all fours, quickly withdrew its horns and tusks from the dragon's body. Before it could recover, Druen stood up, unslung its cannon-like weapon from its back, and promptly ended the beast's life.

The occupants of the vehicle, still too stunned from this sudden development, offered no gratitude, but simply stood staring at their companion in disbelief. Its cannon still smoldering, the large, dinosaur-like alien turned and began walking toward the transport.

The sudden sound of leathery wings beating against the air was immediately accompanied by the roar of yet another of the hunting beasts. At the sound of the approaching Mrdangam, Druen quickly scanned the area for cover. Finding none close enough to be of use, it simply dropped into a crouch, its weapon aimed high over the roof of the transport. Giving out its own roar of defiance, Druen began firing, a look of fierce determination on its mismatched features.

Rebecca and the others watched in fascinated horror as a dragon swooped out of the sky from the left and drove Druen's body into the ground with its razor sharp talons. As swiftly as it came, it flew off, the limp form of their giant companion in its clutches. A second later, the dark shadow of another dragon flew low over the top of their vehicle to land next to the carcass of its dead companion. The creature examined it for a moment, then picked it up unceremoniously in its large claws and lifted off to join its two remaining clanmates, leaving the survivors to watch as the Mrdangam flew off toward the mountains, their claws full from a successful hunt.

8

The Aftermath

THE SOFT whisper of the gentle breeze was the only sound that could be heard for several moments. The shock of all that had happened began to ebb, leaving the survivors feeling drained and exhausted. With the weariness also came pain.

Now that the immediate danger was gone, Rebecca slumped on the bench weakly. Closing her eyes tightly, she fought the urge to curl into a ball and weep. As she sat in silence letting the tension drain from her body, her left arm began to throb and burn anew, as if begging for attention. Sitting upright on the bench, she gingerly examined the wound. Reaching up with an unsteady hand, she tenderly pulled the Dakkar-nil skin away from her burned flesh, wincing as pain lanced up her arm.

A sudden grating sound filled the air, caus ing her to jump reflexively, followed by a brief grinding as the engine below struggled to come to life. Swearing and cursing could be heard coming up through the access hatches, accompanied by the sounds of fists slamming against machinery. A moment later, the alligator-like torso of Tarrsk appeared from the left-side hatch. "Sikaris, we have a problem. That last attack seems to have damaged the engine." Rebecca noted that the creature's throaty voice seemed to come from nowhere, as it had no jaw on its head that she could detect.

"How bad is it?" Sikaris said as it dismounted its bench and turned around to face the front of the vehicle.

"We will not know until we look closer at the engine, but it may take some time," Tarrsk replied.

"Very well. You and Rysth-nuul get to work," Sikaris commanded. Immediately, the creature disappeared through the hole. Looking at each of the others, Sikaris began issuing instructions. "Lohgar," it said to the ape-like beast, "you and I are going to secure the perimeter of the area from the ground. Kyen'tir, I want you to do a quick survey from above. We need to make sure that nothing has made this place its home since the last scouting party was here. Prin, take Rebecca below and patch up that arm, then stand guard outside the vehicle." As its fathomless eyes rested on her, Rebecca felt a cold shudder run the length of her spine. "Once Rysth-nuul and Tarrsk finish repairs, we will continue with our mission as planned. If anyone needs to contact me, use the first frequency. Now, go."

Kyen'tir bobbed its scaled, orange head in acknowledgement; and not bothering with the main hatch, flew out the hole in the back of the vehicle created by the last blast of dragon acid. Its armor clacking noisily, Lohgar descended the ladder with ease, followed immediately by Sikaris, leaving only Prin and Rebecca on the top level.

"Come," Prin said simply, gesturing to the hatch.

Rebecca, her body stiff and bruised, rose from the bench and made her way toward the exit, her arm once again demanding attention. Painfully, she descended the short distance to the lower level, where Rysth-nuul and Tarrsk were already hard at work examining the damaged engine. Various arrhythmic noises of metal tools at work filled the room.

Upon reaching the floor, Rebecca waited in silence as Prin climbed down, then walked on all six of its claws over to one of the storage units mounted on the left wall. Opening the door, Prin reached in and withdrew a small, cup-sized container. Returning to where Rebecca stood near the bottom of the ladder, it removed the lid. "Take off the upper parts of your Dakkar-nil skin and sit," Prin said, indicating the driver's bench.

She hesitated, uncertainty etched on her face. "What is that?" she asked, leaning forward to try to peer into the container to view its contents.

"Ager gel," was its reply. "It will ease the pain in your arm and help you heal quickly."

"Aaaaarrrrgh!" came a loud cry from the rear of the vehicle. "Watch what you are doing, slave scum!"

Rebecca looked toward the engine housing to see Rysth-nuul and Tarrsk glaring at one another. For a brief moment, she held her breath, expecting one of the two reptiles to attack the other. Then, just as suddenly as it had begun, Tarrsk averted its gaze and returned to working on the engine.

"Now," Prin said, drawing attention back to the task at hand, "sit."

Obeying Prin's command, Rebecca sat on the edge of the nearby bench. She slowly removed the burned upper sections of armor, careful not to aggravate the injured tissue further. Once they were removed, Prin ripped the sleeve off of her jumpsuit without mercy, causing Rebecca to clench her teeth to keep from crying out. Looking down at her left arm, Rebecca was finally able to see fully the extent of the damage from the acid.

A patch of flesh about three inches in diameter had been eaten away by the deadly liquid, just above the elbow, leaving portions of her triceps exposed. Prin examined the wound carefully, nodding in satisfaction. "You were very lucky. If you had not been wearing the Dakkar-nil skin, the acid would have eaten all the way through your arm."

Rebecca's body went rigid, her muscles tightened into knots as Prin emptied the contents of the container onto her arm. The gel-like substance sent lances of pain shooting through her entire body, threatening to rob her of consciousness. Then, after several excruciating seconds, sudden relief began to flood through her, relaxing her muscles. Prin finished spreading the gel over the remainder of the wound, then began binding her arm with a bandage from the medical kit.

In an attempt to divert her attention from Prin's none-too-gentle ministrations, Rebecca reflected on the recent attack. In her mind, she saw once again the dinosaur-like creature battling with the Mrdangam. "I can't believe that Druen came back to help us, only to sacrifice himself. I thought you said that beings on this planet don't risk their lives for others," she said questioningly.

Without even pausing or looking at her, Prin replied casually. "Druen knew that if our transport was destroyed or if we left him here, chances were he would die before making it back to the base. So he helped us because it was his best chance to live."

Rebecca, who was just beginning to hope that she had found some shred of morality in these creatures, found her opinion reverting to its previous low level.

"Slag it!" came the loud curse from Rysth-nuul. "Sikaris, we have finished our first check. We really have problems."

"I'm on my way," came a reply through Rebecca's translator.

By the time Prin had finished bandaging her arm, Sikaris had arrived and entered through the left door. "What is wrong?" it said to the two mechanics.

Rysth-nuul turned its four mismatched eyes to look at its leader. "See for yourself. It seems that the last acid attack melted much of the wiring on this side of the engine. It also melted the Krin Power Regulator and the main Rif drive, as well as a couple of other small parts."

"Do we have spares to replace them?" Sikaris asked.

"Not all of them. I can replace the wiring, but we do not have the other parts on board."

Sikaris reached into the pouch in which it had placed the translator unit. "Kyen'tir and Lohgar, return to the transport." Sikaris flipped the frequency switch on the unit again, turning the commlink off. "Rysth-nuul, I want you to begin replacing the wires and tubing. Shut all hatches and window shields. Tarrsk, do you know what parts are needed?"

Tarrsk hissed out an affirmative.

"Good," Sikaris continued. "The rest of us are going to go with you to the other vehicle and get what we need."

"What about him?" Prin asked, gesturing towards Rebecca with one of its four arms.

Sikaris gave her a glare that made her feel decidedly uncomfortable. "Bring him along."

Prin stared at it in surprise. "But what if—" It stopped in mid-sentence as Sikaris gave it a look that stifled any further protest.

"I have my reasons," said Sikaris firmly.

A moment later, Lohgar and Kyen'tir returned, entering through the right door. Sikaris turned towards them. "Rysth-nuul needs some parts from the other transport. Kyen'tir, I want you to fly ahead and scout out the area, but not too high. Try to stay as close to the tops of the buildings as possible. We still do not know what is out there."

The reptilian bird bobbed its head in response.

Looking towards the others, it continued with its instructions. "Lohgar, you take point. Tarrsk is second. Prin will be in the middle with Rebecca, and I will come last. Any questions?" It paused. "Then let us leave."

The group began filing quickly out of the transport. On their way out, Rebecca reached down, picked up her bag with her uninjured arm, and slung it over her shoulder. Once on the ground, Sikaris shut the door securely behind them. A second later, a loud clang was heard as Rysth-nuul set the lock in place from the inside. Immediately, large metallic shields lowered over the window in the front and what was left of the rear window, effectively sealing the lower level from intruders.

"Here," Sikaris said in English as it tossed something to Rebecca. She caught the item in her free right hand and was surprised to see that it was a hand-held pistol. "And remember, your only chance of survival is by staying with us. If you try to escape or use this against us, you will die," it said, matter-of-factly. With that, Sikaris turned and motioned for Lohgar to head out.

Prin leaned closer to her and said quietly, "Welcome to Clan Grinath, Rebecca." It stood up on two legs, its crooked features showing just the slightest hint of a smile. "Let us go." Not sure how to respond, she simply followed Prin as it took its place in the group.

As they walked, a thought began working its way into Rebecca's consciousness. *The hand-held motion detector would help tremendously right now. But can I trust it? It didn't pick up the V'skir, but maybe that was due to some special ability they have.* Deciding to at least test it, Rebecca holstered the pistol in one of her pockets, then removed the bag from her shoulder. "Prin, could you help me, please," she said, holding out the bag to the alien. After a few moments, she had the motion detector in her hand and began scanning the area.

"What are you doing?" Prin asked curiously. "What does that machine do?"

Temporarily ignoring the question, Rebecca focused her attention on studying the display screen. *It seems to be working fine despite the atmospheric disturbance.*

Taking a deep breath, Rebecca ventured a comment. "Sikaris," she began, an odd sensation running through her. *My God, I'm on a first name basis with these things!* "I have a device that allows me to detect movement for up to a radius of two miles. Would you…I could use it, if you want."

Sikaris eyed her for a moment, its face unreadable, then said, "Yes. That may help."

"Interesting, yes, yes," Prin said beside her as it lowered its head toward the motion detector to study it closer.

"Is your device picking up any movement?" Sikaris asked.

"No," she replied. "Nothing yet." She felt her confidence growing now that she was at last able to contribute to the success of their mission.

"Kyen'tir?" Sikaris asked through the comm.

"All looks clear from above. I see no movement anywhere," came Kyen'tir's report.

Lohgar, its armor scraping loudly, headed slowly down the street from which they had come, each of its three hands holding a pistol similar to the one given to Rebecca. Tarrsk followed close behind, but carried no weapon that she could detect. Instead, it walked on all fours, its two tentacle-like appendages unfurled and held aloft like two giant serpents prepared to strike. At various times, the reptilian creature stopped, picked up a fist-sized rock, and shoved it underneath its stomach where it instantly disappeared. Although she found this quite odd, Rebecca withheld her curiosity and focused on staying alert.

The team backtracked to the other transport without incident. The body of the dragon that had blocked the street had disappeared, leaving only slightly blackened rubble to indicate that it had ever been there at all. The rear portion of the transport was covered by rubble from a building that it had obviously backed into. On the right side, the treads lay mangled and melted in several places; globs of acid forming small pools on the dusty road. The top level of the vehicle lay torn open, as if giant claws had peeled it back like the skin of a ripe fruit, searching for the sweet nectar inside. The mental image caused Rebecca to shudder involuntarily. The lower level, however, seemed fully intact. In fact, the same kind of protective shields that she had seen Rysth-nuul lower into place on their transport were also covering the windows of this one.

The group moved cautiously up to the right door of the vehicle, careful to avoid the pooling acid, their attention ever focused on their surroundings. Kyen'tir circled above once, then alighted on a rooftop to their left, its bottom pair of eyes scanning the ground even as its upper pair scanned the skies.

Lohgar, Tarrsk, and Prin formed a defensive perimeter around Rebecca and Sikaris, the latter of which strode up to the right door of the transport and knocked twice.

"This is Sikaris. Is anyone in there?"

In reply, the door instantly slid back on its track and a small figure rocketed out of the hatch, causing Sikaris to duck rapidly to avoid being hit. The others immediately spun around and tracked the thing with their weapons. The being slammed hard into the ground about twenty feet from the vehicle and lay motionless for several seconds. Then, leaping to its feet in a sudden burst of energy, it gave out a screech of triumph and began hopping about madly. To everyone's surprise, the armadillo-like creature then threw itself back on the ground and began shoveling large clawfuls of dirt and mud into its mouth, laughing hysterically all the while.

A low, throaty voice turned their attention from the bizarre scene back to the interior of the vehicle. "...next time...pair me up with...thing, Sikaris...swear...going...kill it," came the translation, oddly disjointed.

Emerging from the transport came a giant alien that towered over the group. The seven foot, spiked monstrosity reminded Rebecca of the creature that had stood guard outside of the High Crala's throne room. Like the guard, it was covered from head to foot with spikes of various shapes and sizes, sticking up at odd angles from its thick, armored hide. It had the same lopsided mouth, as well as a second, half-formed nose near its chin, and, if her memory served her, the guard was also missing a left ear, as this one was. If this wasn't the same creature, it must definitely be a close relative.

The bulky alien leapt down from the vehicle to land beside Sikaris, its slightly twisted legs and tail quickly adjusting to its new stance. Up close, its size and wide girth reminded Rebecca of a professional football player.

Sikaris, standing almost eye to eye with the large alien, looked around at the damaged transport, then back at the creature. "It is good you are alive, Jorylk," Sikaris said, matter-of-factly.

"Yes, alive!" came a screeching voice. "Alive, thanks be to Nix!"

Sikaris turned to face the creature, who was still gleefully shoving dirt clods into its mouth. "Silence, Ch'ran! We still do not know if there is anything else out there."

"And stop being such a Bik dugger," added Lohgar with disgust.

Ch'ran, unaffected by the jibe, jumped to its feet and strode over to Sikaris, a broad smile on its mud-caked little face. "But I promised Nix that if he got me out of that attack alive, I would do anything, even eat dirt." It chuckled softly, clearly fighting to control an approaching fit of laughter. "And here I am! Nix saved me!" Ch'ran threw its arms wide in elation.

The corner of Sikaris face revealed a slight grin as it stared down at the diminutive alien. "It is good you are alive too."

"Speak for yourself," Lohgar said under its breath, but loud enough that at least Rebecca's translator could pick it up.

I agree, she thought inwardly.

Whether Sikaris failed to hear Lohgar or simply ignored the comment, it said nothing, but turned to face the spiked alien once more. "What happened?" it asked.

Jorylk began to speak, but, as before, Rebecca's translator cut in and out, catching only a few words here and there. Before long, she completely lost track of the story. Reaching down to the translator unit, she began fidgeting with the device in an attempt to fix it.

Prin, seeing her vain efforts, leaned over and whispered to her, its translation breaking through the other's narrative clearly. "There is nothing wrong with your translator. Jorylk cannot speak good because of his mutated tongue and face muscles." She looked once again at the misaligned face in sudden understanding. Letting go of the translator, she waited with the rest of the group for Jorylk to finish its explanation.

Sikaris reached into its hidden pouch and activated its commlink. "Kyen'tir, circle the area and look for any signs of the others from this transport." Without a word, the winged reptile took flight again and was soon lost from sight.

"Are you going to tell us what he said?" Tarrsk asked.

"He said that once we were cut off from them, he tried backing up, but made a mistake and crashed into the building. The Mrdangam then spat on the treads and melted them. Seeing that they were trapped, Ch'ran and Jorylk closed the hatches and lowered the window shields. The Mrdangam tore open the top level, and the others ran from the transport to try to find cover in the buildings. Jorylk believes that the Mrdangam took all of them, but we should still search the area.

"Prin, Rebecca, and Tarrsk will stay here with me. The rest will search the area and secure the perimeter." Sikaris concluded.

"We can look," Ch'ran commented, "but it will not do any good. Nix tells me the Mrdangam took them all."

"Look anyway," Sikaris shot back, somewhat impatiently.

Shrugging its shoulders, Ch'ran hopped off down the street, the rest of the group following on its heels, leaving the four of them standing next to the open door of the transport. "Prin, stand guard with Rebecca. Tarrsk and I are going to work on the engine parts." Without waiting for a reply, Sikaris and Tarrsk entered the damaged transport.

Prin looked at Rebecca and smiled from its crooked mouth. "It is good that Jorylk and Ch'ran survived. Yes, yes. The more fighters we have, the better chance we have of living."

She returned the ferret-like alien's gaze. "That may be true, but can we trust them? Maybe I didn't understand correctly, but didn't they shut out the others from the lower level, leaving them to die?"

"Trust? On Ka'esch, you can only 'trust' someone if you are useful to them. Once your usefulness is gone, they will likely betray you. Isn't it that way where you come from? Jorylk and Ch'ran were only trying to survive. If they had let the others below, the Mrdangam would have torn the lower level apart also and killed everyone. This way, the Mrdangam forgot about Jorylk and Ch'ran because they were chasing the others, yes, yes."

Power to the Strong, Death to the Weak. The words flashed unbidden through her mind, leaving behind a hollow pit in her stomach.

The sudden monotone voice of the translator interrupted her musings. "Sikaris, this is Kyen'tir. I have found something two blocks west of the transport. It looks like what is left of one of the flyers. Wait...I have found Lohgur, and he is still alive. But,...you need to come, Sikaris."

Sikaris' seven-foot frame appeared a moment later in the doorway of the transport. "We are on our way." It shut the door behind itself and agilely leapt to the ground. "Come with me," it said as it turned to look down at Rebecca, "both of you."

When they arrived at the scene, the others were already gathered and waiting, with the exception of Tarrsk who was still collecting parts from the transport. The street they were standing in was littered with the smoking and charred remains of the flyer. On the right side, lying at the base of a crumbled wall was a still form.

At the sight of it, Rebecca quickly averted her gaze and took a deep breath to collect herself. She had seen worse during her tour in the marines, but it had been many years ago. Steeling herself, she forced her gaze back upon the gruesome scene before her.

Lying beside the twisted metal of the flyer was the body of the other ape-like being that had traveled with them. Its dirty orange fur was blackened and singed in several areas. The heavy, metallic armor it had been wearing lay beside it in a heap, the creature apparently having removed it after crashing. The alien's left arm hung limp across its body at a sharp angle as if broken. But most noticeable of all, where its legs should have been, only two short, bloody stumps remained.

As Sikaris stepped towards the unfortunate being, Lohgur's prominent brows raised as its eyes fluttered open.

"Sit him up," Sikaris said to Lohgar and Prin.

The two reached down and grabbed the downed pilot under the arms, lifted it none-too-gently, and propped its back against the nearby wall. As they moved it, the creature bellowed in pain. Once it was in position, they released it and took a step back. Sikaris dropped down on all fours to be at eye level with the injured alien and walked up to stand within arms reach of it.

The ape-like being looked at Sikaris in fear, its face radiating sheer panic.

"Sik…Sikaris," it managed. "Please. I…I saved your lives. Do not… I can still be of use. There has to be something I can do without legs. Please."

The reptilian feline simply looked at the creature for a moment, then stood to its feet and turned its back on the pilot. "Everyone back to Transport Two. Lohgar," it said, its voice a low growl, "bring the body."

"NO!" came a mad scream from the injured creature. "Lohgar. My offspring! NO—" Before it could finish its sentence, a single shot from Lohgar's gun abruptly ended its life.

Rebecca stood rooted to the spot in shock at what she had just witnessed, until four strong claws grabbed her from behind and started her moving. "Come, Rebecca," Prin said as it released her from its grip. "There is still much to do, yes, yes."

As she numbly followed Prin, she watched as Lohgar stooped down and picked up the now lifeless body of its own parent.

9

Decisions

THEY WALKED for several minutes before Rebecca finally recovered her voice. "Why did Sikaris do that? That being saved our lives and yet he...he murdered him in cold blood!" she exclaimed, anger beginning to build within her.

Prin, seemingly unaffected by her rising emotions, responded as they turned a corner, the second transport coming into view. "If a being is wounded while on a hunt, the commander looks at him and decides if the wound is permanently crippling. If it is, the being is killed."

Rebecca was appalled. "But..." she stammered, her thought jumbled by emotion and her innate morality. "But his wounds were not fatal. He may have lost his legs, but he was still going to live."

The ferret-like creature hunched its shoulders slightly as if shrugging, "That is a non-lie. But he would be helpless, always needing others to do things for him. Also, he would slow us down. He would not be useful to the clan. 'Power to the Strong, Death—'"

She cut it off in mid-sentence, frustration boiling over, "I know, I know. 'Death to the Weak.'" The final cry of the wounded being continued to ring in her ears. "He was Lohgar's father, wasn't he?"

"Yes, yes. Lohgur was Lohgar's parent."

"But how could he...how could he just murder his own father like that?" Rebecca asked in shock.

Prin glanced at her quizzically. "What difference does it make whether he was his parent or not?"

Dumbfounded, Rebecca was silent for a moment. Then she said, "Don't you love your parents, or have any special feelings for them whatsoever?"

"The translator did not translate those words," Prin said casually. "What do you mean?"

For several moments, the question hung in the air without an answer as Rebecca pondered how best to explain the concept of love and emotions. "You know fear and anger, correct?" she began. "Those are feelings."

Prin's face brightened. "Yes, yes. We fear. We have anger. You speak of instincts."

Rebecca paused. "Yes, in a way. But we also have other feelings. *Good* feelings, feelings that make us want to…to do nice things for others. We call this love. Sometimes this feeling is so powerful that it causes people to give up time and money, or even to sacrifice their lives for each other. Don't you have anything like that here?"

This time, it was Prin who was shocked. "No. That makes no sense at all. Instincts are for survival. How could you have instincts that make you less able to survive? Why would anyone spend time and money on someone else, when you could spend it on yourself? And you lie when you say someone would die for someone else. That is insane." Prin looked at her skeptically. "I am beginning to think that you and Ch'ran are similar in your minds.

"Besides," Prin said, noting Rebecca's continued silence, "if such a foolish thing as these good instincts, as you called them, *did* somehow evolve in a being, it would have been wiped out in one generation. It would never have been passed down to its offspring, for a being who gives up his time and money for another makes the other one stronger and himself weaker."

A sudden image invaded Rebecca's mind with such vividness that she immediately stopped in her tracks. Before her, lying in his hospital bed was her father. Her eyes moved down the length of the bed to rest upon the spot where her father's right leg should be. A look of terror suddenly flashed across his face. Then, to her utter horror, she saw her own hand rise up in front of her and level a pistol at her father's head. The image abruptly ended with the loud crack of a gunshot.

Prin turned around and stared at her in confusion. "Why did you stop? Is something wrong?"

A solitary tear slid gently down her cheek at the memory of the vanished image. She quickly wiped away the tear and pushed her thoughts and feelings to the back of her mind so as not to show any sign of weakness to the alien. The more she learned of these creatures and their ways, the more she began to understand that she needed to show more strength and less weakness. It was likely her very survival would depend on it.

"No. Nothing is wrong," she replied firmly. "I thought I may have heard something," she lied. "Let's go."

As they stepped closer to the vehicle, the translator began to pick up snatches of conversation coming from within.

"...have all...parts...power regulator...bent."

"...make it work?"

"...not sure..."

Prin and Rebecca approached the bottom of the left side ladder to see Sikaris and Tarrsk facing each other over a small collection of machine parts laid out neatly on a dirty rag. Sikaris activated its commlink, "We have the parts we need. Everyone head back to Transport #1."

Tarrsk reached down and gently gathered the parts from the floor, placing them carefully into a travel bag. In a few moments, the entire team had gathered and began heading back to their original transport.

Once they arrived, Tarrsk immediately headed inside and began installing the new parts with Rysth-nuul, who had already repaired many of the wires in their absence. The rest of the group, still sitting outside, waited expectantly for instructions.

Sikaris faced the odd assortment of aliens, looking at each in turn as instructions were given. "Ch'ran, go into the transport and give me a report of what food and other undamaged equipment we have. Kyen'tir, continue to keep watch above. Prin and Rebecca, stand guard here on the ground. Lohgar," it said, addressing the ape-like alien who still carried the lifeless body of its parent across its shoulder, "I want you and Jorylk to prepare some food. We may need all of the pre-packaged food for later, so use the fresh meat. If anyone needs me, call. I will be scouting out the area."

Immediately, Kyen'tir returned to its perch atop the nearby building as Ch'ran headed into the vehicle, humming to itself contentedly. Lohgar lowered the body of Lohgur to the ground about ten feet from the rear of the transport as Jorylk entered through the door and returned a moment later with a large box.

Prin and Rebecca settled into their sentry positions just outside the left entrance to the transport. "What is to be done with the body?" she asked, pointing toward where Lohgar was removing what little remained of the metallic armor from the dead alien. "Do you bury your dead? Do you perform any kind of funeral?"

"Bury?" Prin replied. "You mean, bury in the ground?"

"Yes, of course," she said.

Prin shook its head. "But that would be such a waste. Did you not hear what Sikaris said?"

Rebecca scanned her memories, trying to find some part she may have missed regarding the body. Suddenly, an uneasy feeling began stirring in her gut. Something about the way Jorylk and Lohgar were handling the body didn't seem right.

Then she understood. Remembering too late to hide her revulsion, she averted her gaze just as Jorylk pulled out a long, jagged knife from the box and began to slice into the body. Noting her expression of horror, Prin's mutated features twisted disapprovingly.

"Let me guess, you do not eat meat on your planet either," it said. Although the monotone voice removed all inflection from its comment, it seemed to Rebecca that Prin's voice dripped with sarcasm.

Fighting to regain her composure and put up a strong front, Rebecca looked straight at the creature and replied coldly, "Yes, we do. But we don't eat our friends or family. Only livestock."

"What is the difference between them?" Prin asked. "Meat is meat. Are we not all animals?" Prin's face suddenly changed as if remembering something. "Yes, yes. You said that there are no other intelligent beings on your planet, so you do not need to eat your own. Tell me, if all of these other creatures on your planet were intelligent, would you still eat them?"

Once again, Rebecca found herself struck speechless by the strange ways of this alien culture. Even more, she was becoming increasingly uncomfortable with how these ideas were causing her to reevaluate her own beliefs. "I…I don't know. We value human life, but animals are…are different."

Prin continued as another thought occurred to it. "Why do you think the Mrdgangam stopped attacking us after they killed Druen? And why do you think they took the bodies of their dead clanmates? Did you really believe that it was because they wanted to hold some ritual for them? Yes, yes? Or was it because you thought they had some strange insane instinct that made them want to save the bodies?"

Seeing that no response was forthcoming, Prin continued, "It was because the two bodies of their clanmates, plus Druen and the six others from Transport #2, would give them enough meat to last for a week."

Feeling foolish and hurt by the scathing remarks, Rebecca remained silent. Prin shook its head, "You have some very strange ideas, Rebecca." Turning to look at Jorylk and Lohgar working at their gruesome task, it licked its lips in anticipation. "Well, if you do not want your part, you can give it to me, yes, yes!"

"You can have it," she said, quietly, trying carefully to keep any trace of disgust from her voice.

Walking happily over to where dinner was being prepared, Prin took a large portion of raw meat and began eating ravenously.

During the following half-hour, each of the others took turns eating, with the exception of Sikaris, who was still out scouting. To keep her mind off of the revolting food and her own growing hunger, Rebecca took out her journal and began to record.

Journal Entry #3

I apologize in advance if I ramble a bit in this journal entry. So much has happened. Hopefully I can organize some of my thoughts here.

But before I get into all of that, let me briefly relate recent events. Since my last entry, I boarded a transport filled with a number of strange aliens, which I will describe in further detail later. We traveled one hundred and forty three miles without incident, leaving just over fifteen remaining. However, we were suddenly attacked by five enormous dragon-like creatures that damaged our transport. We now wait in a ruined city while two of the aliens I am traveling with attempt to repair the engine.

During the course of the trip, I have had several conversations with Prin that have left me shocked and, to be honest, quite confused. I will now relate some of these conversations here.

First, it seems that these creatures do not wear clothing, except for protective skins and armor. Their genitalia are not visible or are covered by armor and they have no concept of modesty. In fact, after my discussion with Prin, I am wondering why we humans ever evolved such a notion. Is it due to some ancient ritual passed down from Paleolithic man, or simply the result of some kind of religious indoctrination?

Furthermore, their skin seems to be scale-like and hard. They view my soft skin as a sign of physical weakness. They even offered me a suit made out of skin from one of the races here as protection. Upon reflection, I wonder why mammals have soft skin, when scales are much more durable? If we evolved from fish and reptiles, why did we lose the benefit of tough scales? Or why did we humans lose the hair on our bodies? At least those who live in the cold, northern countries should have retained their hair.

Secondly, there seems to be no sense of beauty or artistry here. Prin didn't even understand the concept. Again, the question arises: How is it that we humans spend so much time and energy making beautiful things that often serve no practical purpose? I can imagine how art and music, for example, were used for primitive communication; but how and why would they evolve into anything more than that? Are they just results of our advanced culture? But even so, how could a sense of beauty be developed at all when one who spends time making beauty can spend less time on survival; therefore, natural selection would have weeded that trait out of existence.

Third, these creatures don't care about their environment. Selfishness is the driving force for everything they do. They don't care if the environment gets polluted, as long as it does not affect their existence. The fact that it will affect others after they die does not matter to them. They seem to live only for themselves with no thought whatsoever for the well-being of others, not even their own family. Yet, when I think about it, isn't this exactly what evolution is about? Isn't this at the core of "survival of the fittest"?

Fourth, all of the aliens I have met have tails. Prin thought I was joking when I mentioned that we humans lost ours through lack of need. But is that true? As I have seen here, these animal-like creatures use their tails for many different purposes. Surely an animal with one would have an advantage over an animal without one. What happened with our early ancestors that made it an advantage to not have a tail? I must admit, I cannot think of any scenario that would make sense.

Fifth, trust is not in these creatures' nature. Two aliens betrayed six others to their deaths, and Prin, Sikaris, and the others accepted that as normal. Furthermore, our transport abandoned the second transport that accompanied us while they were under attack. Self-preservation is the ultimate goal here, which, again, makes logical sense. I wonder more and more why humans developed a sense of self-sacrifice at all, for anyone that sacrificed for someone else would be immediately wiped out, thus unable to pass along whatever it was that made him or her act that way.

Sixth, I witnessed one of the aliens murder its own father simply because it had lost its legs in the dragon attack. It seems that on this world, when your usefulness to your clan is gone, you are to be eliminated. If you are a hindrance in any way, you are killed. What is most disturbing to me is that I am beginning to understand these creatures' logic. To them, why spend resources on one who cannot strengthen the clan? Although children drain resources now, they will at least make the clan stronger in the future. But the crippled and infirm...... they are a burden.

Yet, if I apply this logic to myself, then that would mean that my own father should not live! No matter how much I try to rationalize it in other ways, the most logical conclusion, according to my own beliefs, is that he die. How can I reconcile my feelings with logic? Fortunately, we humans have developed a sense of the value of life, even weak life. But how and why did we develop that sense? My thoughts move in circles.

Seventh, the other thing that shocked me about the murder of the crippled being is that it was done by the thing's own offspring. These creatures seem to have no positive feelings at all. As intelligent creatures, they feel fear, anger, and despair, but no love or compassion. To them, love, compassion, and any kind of self-sacrifice is a waste of time and energy. At the risk of sounding redundant, how and why did such emotions ever evolve on

Earth? Surely natural selection would have wiped out any kind of unselfish ideas from the gene pool, for they are, by definition, concepts that put others first.

Finally, these creatures are cannibals. Not only do they kill the weak and infirm, they use them for food. As repulsive as this concept is, I must admit that it makes sense within the context of this civilization. If all life evolved from a common ancestor, then no one creature is any different from another. On Earth, however, we have animals that did not develop intelligence, so we have a different perspective. But what if animals on Earth had evolved intelligence, would we still eat them? And why does intelligence alone change things? How do we define intelligence?

I came to this planet seeking some answers; yet I have more questions now than before.

A sudden, violent curse erupted from the transport, causing Rebecca to look up and stop recording. "You broke it! You idiot, slave scum! Now what are we going to do?"

"Do not blame me, you diseased slime. You damaged it when you took it off the other transport!"

Just as Rebecca had finished returning her journal to its bag, the lengthy form of Rysth-nuul flew out through the door of the transport to land roughly in a jumble of coils barely six feet in front of her. With lightning quick reflexes, the snake-like alien righted itself and began reaching for two pistols that were resting in holsters on each side of its torso. But before it could draw either of its weapons, another form leaped from the vehicle and knocked Rysth-nuul to the ground, landing it hard upon its back.

"Sikaris, come quick," someone said into the commlink.

Rebecca looked around to see if any of the others were going to try to break up the altercation, but, with the exception of Ch'ran who was hopping about and whooping with delight, the rest of the group sat stoically in silence and watched.

"Clan members of all ages, today's main attraction: Tarrsk of Clan Torlig versus Rysth-nuul of Clan Dakkar-nil!" Ch'ran said, its shrill voice echoing slightly off the walls of the nearby buildings as it leaped up to stand on the platform behind the vehicle that Druen had ridden on.

Tarrsk, who was now on top of Rysth-nuul, began digging its fore claws into the tough, scaly hide in an attempt to throttle the snake-like creature. However, as the claws started to pierce the thick flesh, Rysth-nuul's whip-like tail snapped up and grabbed the reptilian creature around the neck. For the first time, Rebecca noticed that Rysth-nuul's tail had three wicked looking, scythe-shaped blades adorning it, which were now beginning to press into the sides of Tarrsk's neck. Suddenly, the alligator-like creature flew backward, propelled by a sharp yank from Rysth-nuul's tail and landed roughly on the rocky ground with a dull thud.

Ch'ran's enthusiastic laughter was shut out of Rebecca's mind as she stared at Tarrsk in surprise. In the brief moment that it was laying on its back, she could clearly distinguish what had to be a large mouth containing several rows of teeth set into the alien's abdomen!

Rysth-nuul, taking advantage of Tarrsk's momentary helplessness, regained its balance and moved deftly into an attack posture. For a split second, it looked to Rebecca as if Rysth-nuul was performing some kind of acrobatic headstand. Using its two arms and underside of its head to form a sort of tripod, Rysth-nuul lashed out over its head with its thin, whip-like tail, scoring several hits on Tarrsk's unprotected flank.

Leaping to its feet, Tarrsk backed away from the writhing tail. Rysth-nuul pressed the attack, causing Tarrsk to back up against a nearby wall. Rebecca held her breath, fully expecting the sharp barbs on Rysth-nuul's tail to begin tearing into the trapped creature at any moment.

But just as Rysth-nuul was prepared to strike out, Tarrsk jumped against the wall and began climbing up it like a spider traversing its web, the two tentacles on its back pointing down towards its enemy. As soon as Tarrsk's claws touched the wall, the color of its scales began to change. Within moments, its body blended in with the wall like that of a chameleon, with one exception. The white, flaky patches of scales never changed, causing Tarrsk's camouflage attempt to be somewhat lessened.

Rysth-nuul somersaulted sideways as a volley of small, rock-like projectiles shot forth from the ends of Tarrsk's tentacles, the maneuver causing the sharp shards to narrowly miss their target. The alligator-like being, now hanging vertically high up on the wall, continued to rain down the deadly pellets for several seconds, keeping Rysth-nuul on the defensive. Finally, its ammunition apparently depleted, Tarrsk ceased fire and leapt to the ground near a pile of rubble. Once there, Rebecca noted in astonishment, it began scooping up fist-sized chunks of rock and shoving them into the mouth on its belly as its scales reverted to their natural dark blue color.

Meanwhile, Rysth-nuul, who was now bleeding from several nasty looking gashes, withdrew its pistols from their holsters and prepared to open fire. Suddenly, movement from up in the sky caught Rebecca's attention, diverting her gaze from the deadly battle.

Gasping in surprise, she watched as Sikaris glided down at them from a nearby rooftop. The feline alien's arms and legs were spread wide so as to catch the wind in the extra folds of skin that stretched from its wrists to its ankles. Landing gracefully just behind the two combatants, Sikaris opened its mouth wide as if to roar. But, to Rebecca's surprise, although no audible sound was produced by the large alien, both Rysth-nuul and Tarrsk, one after the other, suddenly dropped to the ground as if stunned.

Following a moment of hushed silence, both of the downed creatures began to stir, each sitting up slowly, as if awakening from a deep slumber.

"What do you two fools think you are doing?" Sikaris demanded, staring at each of them in turn. "What is the problem?"

Tarrsk stared up at Sikaris groggily, its voice emanating from its stomach. "I told you that the Krin power regulator from the second transport was slightly cracked before I took it off. Well, this Lid dung," it said, pointing a scaly claw at Rysth-nuul, "was not careful and broke it the rest of the way." Rebecca noticed that after it finished speaking, its claw absentmindedly scratched at its side, causing several pieces of flaky white scales to fall to the ground.

"It was so badly cracked, anyone would have broken it," Rysth-nuul spat vehemently in defense. "And how do we know you did not crack it yourself?"

Sikaris growled threateningly to ward off any further arguments. "What is done cannot be changed. Can you fix it?"

Rysth-nuul shook its head. "This part has to be specially made. We do not have the right tools or the right materials to make a new one, and we cannot fix either of the damaged ones."

There was complete silence as the ramifications of this proclamation dawned on each of them. "What are you saying?" Kyen'tir said, breaking the stillness at last with its harsh, squawking voice. "Do you mean that the transport will not run? That we are stuck here?"

"Yes," Rysth-nuul said gravely.

A loud unintelligible grunt erupted from Jorylk as the spiked creature threw its muscled arms up in the air in obvious frustration. Lohgar strode purposefully up to Prin, all three fists clenched tightly. "You filthy scientists. Why do you have to make these things so easy to break? Why do you not do something? You are supposed to be so smart," it said disdainfully.

Prin stood its ground, staring right back at the armored ape-like creature, but not bothering to reply to the accusation. As she watched, Rebecca could see tiny, blue sparks crackling from the tips of Prin's many fingers. Ch'ran, hoping for another duel, jumped from the back platform to land just inside the open door of the vehicle so as to get a better view.

It was disappointed, however, when Lohgar simply grunted and turned away from Prin to seek out easier prey. Its crooked gaze fell upon Rebecca. "It is this one's fault," it said, crossing over to stand in front of her. "Breuun should never have been taken in by your lies. I say we kill him right here for getting us into this."

Rebecca drew her weapon in a flash, but was immediately disarmed by the larger alien. With a malicious grin on its face, it grabbed her by the shoulders, ignoring the wound on her arm, and lifted her over its head where its third arm reached up and began choking her.

She fought to remain conscious as the pain in her freshly bandaged arm burned anew and her lungs began to scream for oxygen. Then, as if piercing through a dense fog, she heard a growl, followed a second later by the seemingly far off translator.

"Lohgar, put him down, now!"

The suddenness of the return of precious air caught her completely by surprise. However, before she could recover her wits, she was dropped unceremoniously onto the ground.

Lohgar, clearly fuming inwardly, turned away without a glance and walked over to lean against the transport, mumbling to itself. Rebecca lay stunned and overwhelmed with pain. *Don't show weakness,* her thoughts screamed at her. Setting her will and gathering all of her strength, she forced herself to stand.

"Now, each of you listen to me," Sikaris said. "It does us no good to fight with each other. If we are going to survive, we have to work together. Think. What options do we have? Can we contact the Grinathian base?"

Prin was the first to speak. "Not unless we can get the engine running. The transmitters use power from the engine."

"What if Kyen'tir flies back for help? We can wait here until he returns with another transport," Tarrsk said, hopefully.

"I cannot fly that far," the feathered reptile replied matter-of-factly.

"Besides, we are in Ryazan territory," Rysth-nuul said with a sneer. "They would probably see him and kill him, and we would be waiting for help that would never come. I would not be surprised if they are on their way here now to see if the Mrdangam left any scraps."

The grating sound of Ch'ran's laughter interrupted the conversation. "Why do we not just put a sign up (he, he, he) on top of (he, he, he) one of the buildings that says, 'FREE FOOD'?"

Jorylk, standing on the ground below the small creature, backhanded Ch'ran and sent it sprawling into the interior of the vehicle, shutting the door behind it. "Idiot Harmath," it said, clearly for once.

Sikaris scanned the group. "Rysth-nuul does have a point. The Ryazan may be on their way here already." Looking up at the sun, it added, "And we only have a few hours of sunlight left. Whatever we decide, we need to decide soon."

A heavy silence descended on the group, broken only briefly by the reappearance of Ch'ran coming around the vehicle after exiting through the opposite door.

"I have an idea," Rebecca said tentatively, causing all eyes to turn towards her. Still fighting against the pain in her arm and the bruise on her throat, she took a steadying breath and continued. "We are very close to my ship. Once we get there, my people will gladly return you to your base."

The aliens exchanged glances with each other as they considered the idea. "And if they do not," Lohgar said with a grin, "then it should not be too hard to kill a bunch of weak-skinned beings and take the ship for ourselves."

Rebecca swallowed hard at the thought, cracking the knuckles on her right hand unconsciously.

Sikaris nodded. "His ship is less than fifteen miles away, just around the corner of the mountains. We can be there before sunset."

"If we do not get killed first," Rysth-nuul said pessimistically.

"Know this, Rebecca," Sikaris said, its gaze piercing through her, "if your ship is not there, you will die. Now, unless anyone else has a better idea, grab some food and other needed items from the transport. We leave in ten minutes."

The creatures all headed towards the broken-down vehicle, leaving Rebecca sitting alone on the rough ground, wondering once again if she had just made the right decision.

10

Ryazan

THE GROUP moved with the efficiency of a well-trained military unit, so that within the ten minute time period given by Sikaris, all needed equipment was packed into backpacks and travel bags and distributed proportionally by size. In addition to Rebecca's own equipment, several small packets of medical supplies were placed in her backpack.

Once everyone was prepared, the motley group of aliens assembled outside the transport. "Jorylk," Sikaris said to the large, spiked being, "Do you think you can find us a quick path to the mountain, or have things changed too much since your clan lived here?"

Before the alien could reply, however, Ch'ran spoke up, a look of cherubic innocence on its devilish face. "If Jorylk cannot remember the way, I am sure that Nix could help."

A spiked fist swung at the small creature, but went wide as Ch'ran leaped to the side, laughing like a child playing a game. This only served to enrage the creature more.

Sikaris intervened in time to keep the situation from deteriorating further. "No, Ch'ran," it said firmly.

Jorylk's chest heaved up and down as it gulped in several breaths of air in an attempt to calm itself down. Finally, having won the inner battle to control its temper, the alien answered Sikaris' original question, "I…find it… keep…Harmath away…." The last portion of its sentence was punctuated by an evil glare at Ch'ran.

"Good," Sikaris said. "Jorylk leads, then Rysth-nuul, Lohgar, Prin,

Rebecca, and Tarrsk. Ch'ran and I will come last. Kyen'tir will continue to keep watch from above. Let us go."

Jorylk led the group through the deserted streets at a brisk pace. At various intervals, they were forced to retrace their steps due to a blocked street or alley. As they traversed the ruined city, Rebecca heard a shrill, grating sound behind her. Turning around, she scanned the area to determine the source of the noise. It took her a moment to realize that the sound she heard came from Ch'ran. The diminutive alien was bounding along as if on a Sunday afternoon stroll, deep in conversation with no one. Facing forward again, she commented to Prin who was walking beside her. "I don't understand why Sikaris brought Ch'ran on this…hunt. He is clearly insane."

"That is a non-lie," Prin responded. "But, Ch'ran is a very good fighter, and his small size can come in useful at times. Although he is insane, he is also very intelligent."

"Intelligent?" Rebecca said, doubtfully. "He talks to himself."

"Yes, yes. You speak of Nix."

"Who, or what, is Nix? Is it a real being?"

Prin looked at her with its mismatched eyes. "Ch'ran believes that he can talk to and hear an invisible being. I do not believe Nix is real. But I must say that there are times when Ch'ran says strange things that make me wonder."

They were both silent for a moment, when Prin asked, "Do you have any creatures on your planet that talk to unseen beings?"

"Yes," Rebecca said softly. "Many." She thought back to her childhood when her parents made her attend church services every Sunday, and how she learned all of those stories about people who talked to God. Shrugging off her memories, and the implications they held, she changed the conversation. "Jorylk seems to really hate Ch'ran. Is it just because he is crazy?"

Prin's crooked face brightened, as if preparing itself to tell a bit of good gossip. "Yes, yes. Jorylk does hate Ch'ran. He hates him because he is crazy, yes. But also because he is from Clan Harmath. Jorylk was captured by Clan Harmath and tortured for many cycles. During that time, Clan

Joktan, Jorylk's clan, was destroyed. When he finally escaped, he returned to find his clan gone, so he joined us.

"When he first met Ch'ran, he nearly killed him. He has learned to control himself better, but I think that Ch'ran enjoys bothering Jorylk. One day, Ch'ran will go too far. Jorylk is not someone you should bother. He loses his temper very easy, yes, yes." Prin's face became serious. "Let me warn you, when Jorylk gets in a fight, get away from him. He often becomes so angry he does not know his companions from his enemies."

Rebecca looked forward and studied the large alien with renewed interest. As she watched, she saw the creature suddenly grab its abdomen and double over slightly as if in pain. Immediately it straightened and continued on as normal, acting as if nothing had happened. Deciding to keep her observation to herself, Rebecca returned to her conversation. "What about Rysth-nuul and Tarrsk? Do they hate each other as well?"

The ferret-like creature gave Rebecca one of its strange shrugs. "Not any more than anyone else, at least as far as I know. But I do know that Kyen'tir's clan," it said, pointing upwards towards the flying alien, "Clan Phaxad, was destroyed by Tarrsk's clan, Clan Torlig."

Thinking of the strange aliens brought to mind the recent skirmish she had witnessed. "Prin, how did Sikaris stop Rysth-nuul and Tarrsk? I didn't see or hear anything come from his mouth, and he used no weapon."

Prin smiled. "Yes, yes. Remember that I told you that each clan has abilities to help it survive? Sikaris can project his voice at a creature, but he focuses it only at its victim, so that others around do not hear. Its voice is so loud that it causes even some of the strongest beings to be stunned for a short time. I have often asked Sikaris to let me study him to see if we could make weapons like that, but he will not let me."

Rebecca felt the familiar tingle of excitement coarse through her body that she always felt when making some new scientific discovery. "Fascinating," she said aloud. "A creature that can focus sound." As she spoke, her scientific training began to take over. "And Tarrsk; am I right that he can eat rocks and change them into projectiles that can be expelled at high velocities from its tentacles? And can it eat metals as well?"

"Yes, yes," Prin said energetically. "He can use both. He contains an extra stomach that grinds up the materials, then sends them through a thin system of tubing that sharpens them, then finally to a holding pouch, which feeds into the tentacles. The whole process takes just under thirty seconds. It is quite amazing."

"And it seems that he also has the ability to change the color of his scales to blend in with his background," she said. "Except for those white patches. What are those?"

Prin cocked its head in some unreadable gesture. "Tarrsk has a skin disease that affects portions of his body. Because those white patches cannot change color, it caused Tarrsk to be a problem to his clan. Yes, yes. The Torlig use their ability to blend in to hide until their prey is close to them, then they attack. Tarrsk's disease would give them away. He was forced to escape from his own clan because they were angry with him for ruining a very important hunt."

"And what about Kyen'tir? Does it have any special abilities other than flight?" she asked curiously.

Prin nodded. "Kyen'tir's feathers not only allow it to fly, but they can also be used as weapons. When he tugs on a feather, it becomes filled with a type of liquid that makes it heavy at the tip, which is very sharp, yes, yes. He then pulls the feather all the way out and can throw it like a knife. The only problem is that it takes a few days for the feathers to grow back, so the numbers that he can use are limited, especially because the more he uses, the more difficult it is for him to fly."

As they walked, their discussion turned towards many of the various species on the planet. Rebecca mentally catalogued everything she was learning, the intellectual exercise keeping her mind from dwelling on other, more unpleasant thoughts.

Before long, the team had left the ruins behind them and was crossing the open plains. The ground was dry and cracked, with large boulders and rocks littering the countryside. Although she had begun to become used to the barren landscape of this planet, she still found it odd to see absolutely no vegetation anywhere. It almost seemed that the soil itself was incapable of supporting life.

After they had traveled about a mile and a half away from the ruined city, Rebecca noticed that their course was changing slightly. After checking her tracker to confirm her suspicions, she looked over at her companion.

"Prin," she asked, "don't we want to go around the east side of the mountain? It looks like we are heading more towards the west. That would take us right into the side of it."

Prin lifted its right arm and pointed off to the northeast toward the mountains with its right set of forearms. "We have to go around Bratsche Gorge. We are going around its western edge, then back to the northeast to go around the mountain. After that, the most dangerous part of our journey will be over, for we can at least find some cover among the rocky cliffs and passages of the mountain if we are attacked. But out here in the open, we are very weak."

Abruptly, her translator switched to the intercom frequency; the dull, flat voice removing all urgency from the words. "Sikaris, Ryazan. Coming quickly from the southeast. From the ruins." Instantly the group halted, all heads whipping around to look in the direction from which they had come. Far in the distance, a dust cloud rose into the air. As they watched, it began to grow steadily larger.

"Kyen'tir, how large is the hunting party?" Sikaris asked calmly, although Rebecca could sense tension in each of the other members of the group as they awaited the reply.

The reptilian bird circled above their heads. "It looks like about twenty Vips and one heavy transport."

Rysth-nuul cursed loudly. "I hate being right all the time."

"What are Vips?" Rebecca asked Prin quickly as she closed her motion detector and slipped it into a pocket.

Without even looking at her, it replied, "Small, one-person vehicles."

Ch'ran chuckled to itself, "The menu is definitely going to be varied tonight! Roast Harmath, Fried Torlig, Joktan with spiced Phaxad legs!"

Sikaris ignored the insane alien and turned to face Prin, its demeanor calm and composed. "Arm several explosives and give them to Kyen'tir." As Sikaris continued speaking, the feathered alien landed on one of the large boulders that dotted the landscape near Prin. "Kyen'tir, I want you to drop them onto the wheels of the transport to see if you can slow it down. That might buy us enough time to reach the mountain. As for the Vips, we will have to try to outrun them."

Prin grabbed three grenade-like explosives from its belt and activated them with a small, blue flash. It then tossed them to Kyen'tir, who caught them easily in its claws on the ends of its wings. "When you are ready to release them," Prin explained, "push the lever up. You have four seconds."

Kyen'tir nodded its orange-colored head once in acknowledgement, and then took flight. No sooner had its claws left the boulder than Sikaris turned to the others. "Now, run! Those who reach the mountain first should lay down covering fire for the others. GO!"

Not knowing what new horror approached, Rebecca began running, spurred on by her imagination of what pursued her. The others secured their bags onto their backs and immediately began running on all fours. In a matter of seconds, they had outdistanced her, causing panic to set in as she realized that she was about to be abandoned. Frantically, she called out to the receding forms in front of her. "Sikaris! Prin!"

Both creatures stopped and stared at her. Prin responded first. "I know your arm was wounded, but you must use it, or die."

Rebecca continued to run towards them, her sore knee beginning to throb once again. "But…I can't…I don't use my arms to run."

Prin looked at Sikaris in disbelief, then turned back to look at her one last time. "Then the Ryazan will get you." With that, the ferret-like creature turned and began running quickly to catch up to the others.

Thoughts of mutated aliens tearing into her flesh with clawed hands and eating her alive flashed through her mind, adding an extra burst of speed to her running. But it would not be nearly enough, she knew.

Sikaris also began to turn away, but was halted by Rebecca's desperate cry. "Sikaris! Please!" she screamed, nearly sobbing. Suddenly Prin's words about being useful came to her mind. Grasping at anything that would convince Sikaris to help her, she shouted, "Please don't leave me! You need me to unlock the ship for you and speak to my people! You need me!"

Sikaris stared at her for a long moment with its unsettling eyes as she ran towards it. Making up its mind, it turned around and began running back towards her.

"Quickly, climb onto my back," it said in English.

Relief flooded over her as she reached the creature's side. Breathing heavily, she mounted the great feline, the short fur protruding from its scale-like hide feeling soft beneath her fingers.

Rebecca had barely situated herself when Sikaris lunged forward, moving quickly over the uneven ground, despite her added weight. She hugged the alien closely, using her one good arm to keep her balance. They had not traveled more than several dozen feet when a large explosion was heard behind them. Turning around to look behind them, she spotted smoke rising from a box-like shape far in the distance.

"Sikaris, this is Kyen'tir. I hit the transport and damaged two of the twelve wheels. That should slow it down enough for you to reach the mountain. However, the Vips have spotted you and are heading your way at full speed. I am on my way back."

Before the translator even finished its translation, Sikaris changed course and began heading straight towards the gorge.

"What...what are you doing? Why aren't you following the others?"

"The Vips will catch us before we reach them," Sikaris said, panting from exertion.

"But you are taking us towards the gorge! I thought it was impassable."

Sikaris did not reply, but simply smiled.

Sudden realization hit her. "Oh my God," she breathed softly to herself. "You have got to be kidding. I'm too heavy. You can't—"

Before she could finish her sentence, the sound of machine gun fire erupted all around her. She ducked her head instinctively and clung desperately to Sikaris' back as the great alien suddenly began weaving back and forth to present a more difficult target to their attackers.

Despite Sikaris' evasive maneuvers, Rebecca managed to turn her head enough to see what chased them. Roughly half of a mile behind them and closing fast were several small vehicles that reminded her of go-carts with giant, balloon-like wheels. The driver's bench was encased in a teardrop shaped frame with no doors, ceiling, or any other type of body. The only other item of notice was the solitary machine gun projecting out of the tip of each vehicle.

"Sikaris," Rebecca yelled to be heard over the constant drumming of gunfire, "it looks like five of them broke off from the main group to chase us. They're coming up fast!"

"Good," came the barely audible reply.

It was then that Rebecca received her first glimpse of Bratsche Gorge. Stretching out in front of them was a magnificent chasm at least a mile deep and several hundred yards across. The massive expanse stretched endlessly to the right, but ended not more than two hundred yards to the left. The opposite side was many feet lower, causing the mainland at the end of the gorge to slope downward to bridge the gap. It was to this slope that the others had headed.

"Sikaris, I sure hope you know what you're doing," she said nervously as she watched the edge of the chasm draw nearer and nearer. The sound of bullets whizzing past her ears intensified as the alien vehicles pursuing them began closing the gap. Rebecca risked another glance backward, once again hoping to gauge the distance between them and the Ryazan. "Sikaris! They are almost upon us!" she shouted. "If you are—"

Her last sentence was cut abruptly by the sudden unpleasant sensation of the world dropping out from under her. Instinctively, she tensed every muscle in her body, her arm clutching the alien beneath her in a vise-like grip. As hard as she tried, she could not help the gasp of fright that escaped her lips. For a split second, it seemed as if they were plunging straight down towards their deaths. Then, just as Rebecca was about to give herself over to her fear, their course leveled out as Sikaris' skin folds between its arms and legs caught the air currents.

It took her several seconds to recover. Slowly, she forced herself to relax her grip on her companion. As she did so, she gazed around them in wonder, her eyes watering from the stinging winds. They were suspended in midair over the gorge, with only the mighty canyon winds keeping them aloft. Rebecca, her fear of her pursuers momentarily forgotten, reveled in the freedom of flight, her body trembling from both the residue of fear and the newfound exhilaration.

"We made it," she breathed, releasing her anxiety and excitement. "You did it, Sikaris!" The stoic being did not reply, its concentration focused fully on maintaining their flight.

Her initial reaction having subsided, she glanced behind her to see that the Vips had ceased firing and stopped at the edge of the gorge. Their prey having eluded them, they headed off in frustration to rejoin the main force at the west end of the chasm.

With her own immediate survival reassured, Rebecca suddenly remembered Prin and the others. Looking off to the western slope, she was surprised to see that they had just reached the far side of the gorge. Since they would have to turn east to go around the edge of the mountain, she and Sikaris were now ahead of them.

The great cat-like alien landed at a run, heading towards the rocky skirts of the mountain, which were now less than eighty yards in front of them. Suddenly, Sikaris stopped, causing Rebecca to nearly tumble off its back.

"What is it?" she asked in alarm, her senses instantly searching for some sign of danger.

Rebecca followed Sikaris' gaze just in time to see a large explosion light the sky near where Prin and the others were. Particles of rock and dust shot into the air, creating a small cloud that hovered over the entire slope. "What happened?" she said, concern evident in her voice.

"Good," Sikaris rumbled deep in its chest. "Prin used one of its weapons to explode some of the nearby rocks on the slope. Not only did that create a dust cloud to cover their escape, but it will also make it harder for the Vips to cross because of all of the debris."

As it spoke, Rebecca could see that several of her companions were heading towards them at full speed. Tarrsk was first, followed closely by Lohgar and Rysth-nuul. Behind them was Jorylk, running oddly and holding its abdomen as if wounded.

Rebecca carefully climbed off of Sikaris' back. Once on the ground, she unshouldered her backpack and took out her binoculars. Holding them before her eyes, she scanned the area. Emerging from the cloud of dust, she could just begin to make out Prin's form. Although its four arms and two legs were pumping hard, it was still far behind the others. Suddenly, the sound of rapid gunfire echoed off the mountain behind her, causing her to flinch involuntarily. The shots were coming from inside the dust cloud, firing wildly in every direction.

She watched helplessly through the binoculars, feeling a twinge of guilt wrenching her gut. Prin was behind the others because it had taken time to respond to her cries for help. *Come on, Prin,* she urged silently.

As the dust began to dissipate, at least a dozen small vehicles lined up in three separate rows came bouncing slowly over the rubble, the drivers being careful to avoid the larger boulders that were strewn about the area.

"It looks like Prin's idea worked," she said to Sikaris, who was now standing beside her. The seven-foot tall alien didn't reply, but stood motionless, watching the battle unfold. Looking back into her binoculars at her approaching companions, she noticed for the first time that Ch'ran was not with them. Scanning the area for signs of the diminutive creature, she finally caught the slight movement of a shadow on top of one of the boulders. She focused in on it with her binoculars just in time to see the armadillo-like creature leap upon one of the foremost Vips passing below.

The vehicle immediately began careening from side to side as the two aliens fought for control. The Ryazan pushed hard against the intruder, causing Ch'ran to nearly lose its grip. Regaining its precarious hold on the vehicle, Ch'ran whipped its tail around and plunged it into the Vip driver. The Ryazan's body convulsed briefly, then ceased all movement. Straightening out the vehicle, Ch'ran gave the dead Ryazan a shove that sent it tumbling out of the vehicle. Then, grabbing the wheel fully, Ch'ran carefully navigated the Vip over the few remaining rocks to the open ground.

In the same instant, the five other Vips in the first row cleared the difficult terrain: four on Ch'ran's left, and one between it and the gorge. The six small crafts shot forth simultaneously as if from the starting gate in a race. Immediately, Ch'ran veered its vehicle to the right, slamming hard into the enemy machine. The driver, not expecting the sudden attack from one of its own, lost control of the vehicle and plummeted over the edge of the gorge.

In her mind's eye, Rebecca envisioned the look of triumph and glee on the mad creature's face. For a moment, she even thought she could hear its wild cackle of excitement in the distance.

The four other Vips began closing fast on Prin, firing wildly. The alien scientist ducked and weaved as it ran, slowing it down further. Suddenly, Prin's body jolted as if hit from behind. The ferret-like creature stumbled several times, trying to keep its balance, but to no avail. It fell onto its left side and skidded several feet in the dirt, raising a small cloud of dust.

Rebecca gasped as she watched from a distance, wishing she could do something for this alien that was the closest thing to a friend that she had in this place. She stood transfixed as the four small vehicles bore down upon their prey. Suddenly, seemingly from out of nowhere, several sharp, knife-like objects fell from the sky like hail upon the attackers. The falling objects sliced through the large, balloon-like tires of two of the vehicles, sending them flipping end-over-end through the air.

Whipping her binoculars up to search the sky, she saw Kyen'tir pulling out of a steep dive. As she watched, the winged alien wobbled slightly in mid-flight as it adjusted to the recent loss of several of its feathers. Its balance stabilized, it circled around for another pass, but Rebecca knew that it would not be soon enough to save Prin from the remaining two Vips.

Just then, Rebecca felt her heart leap into her throat as Ch'ran's stolen craft came into view directly behind the attackers, its single gun ablaze. Attempting to avoid Ch'ran's attack, the Vip on the right swerved quickly towards its companion. Although the maneuver saved it from the gunfire, it also sent it spinning out of control. Clipping the back of the other vehicle, the two of them flipped and rolled sideways numerous times before finally coming to rest upside down several dozen feet off to the side.

To her utter surprise and amazement, the drivers' benches of the crashed vehicles suddenly began rotating clockwise on their axes to place the drivers in upright positions once again. What used to be the tops of the vehicles were now the bottoms. Yet, because of the size of the balloon-like tires and the rotating bench, the two machines were immediately able to resume the chase.

Ch'ran, oblivious to the transformation of the nearby Vips, pulled its vehicle up alongside Prin's fallen form. The wounded alien slowly climbed to its feet, one arm clutching its right side. Even as Prin climbed atop the small vehicle, five more of the swift machines emerged from the dissipating dust cloud at the bottom of the slope. Behind them, Rebecca could see another five still slowly traversing the rough ground. Finally, the five that had chased her and Sikaris were now reaching the top of the slope, preparing to descend.

Not waiting to see if its passenger was secure, Ch'ran accelerated rapidly, almost causing Prin to lose its precarious purchase atop the machine. Before they had gone more than twenty feet, more gunfire spewed forth from the nozzles of the two recovered Vips, now once again hot in pursuit.

The armadillo-like alien swerved and zigzagged evasively, but the Vip drivers doggedly followed its every move. Prin held on tightly with three of its claws, using the fourth free one to grope about on its bandolier. A moment later, a blue flash shot from its claw, activating the small explosive held in its grasp. Loosening its grip on the device, Prin let it fall to the ground, where it bounced several times before finally releasing its deadly energy in a blinding flash.

The explosive shredded the rear tire of the Vip on the left, sending the vehicle into a wild spin, its machine gun tearing into its partner. A moment later, both vehicles sat motionless on the open plain as Ch'ran and Prin headed off towards the mountain in the stolen vehicle.

11

Race to the Cave

ONCE IT became clear that Prin and Ch'ran were going to make it, Rebecca returned her binoculars to her bag. By the time she had finished closing up her backpack, Tarrsk and Lohgar had reached her and Sikaris, followed less than a minute later by Rysth-nuul and Jorylk, who was panting heavily and holding its lower abdomen, pain etched on its abnormal features.

Sikaris looked briefly at the large, spiked alien, who stared back in concern. "Later," was all Sikaris said, the simple word causing a flicker of relief to flash across Jorylk's face. "Do you know of any place we can hide?" Sikaris asked the injured being.

Jorylk nodded affirmative. "Modir cave," it said sluggishly, pointing up the side of the mountain.

Rysth-nuul straightened in alarm. "What!?" it hissed. "Are you crazy? Why do we not just give ourselves to the Ryazan and save a lot of trouble?"

Sikaris shot the snake-like creature a cold glare. "Go ahead, if you want. As for me, I will take my chances in the cave. Unless you have a better idea."

Rysth-nuul backed off, muttering inaudibly, just as the Vip driven by Ch'ran came to a halt next to them. Prin immediately climbed off of the top of the small vehicle, followed by Ch'ran, who virtually leaped on top of Prin in its excitement.

"Whooooo!" it whooped excitedly. "Did you see that? Sikaris, we need to steal some more of these. Of course, you would not be able to fit in one anyway. Too bad. They are great! A little on the bumpy side though. But the speed is—"

"Ch'ran!" Sikaris roared loudly. The small alien immediately ceased its ramblings and looked around as if just waking up from sleepwalking.

"Yes, Sikaris? Did you want something?" it asked innocently.

The feline leader sighed and turned toward Prin, ignoring the devilish grin on Ch'ran's face. "How badly are you injured?"

Prin examined its side. "Not bad. The Dakkar-nil suit took most of the damage."

"Good. Then you, Rebecca, and Jorylk will go first and find the cave. The rest of us will climb up behind you and try to slow down the Ryazan. Kyen'tir, keep them busy as long as you can."

Without any further hesitation, the group began climbing up the steep, rocky slope of the mountain as quickly as possible, being careful of their footing. They had only managed to climb a mere fifty feet up the face of the mountain when the sounds of gunfire erupted from below.

Looking down, Rebecca could see that the remaining fifteen Vips had reached the bottom of the slope, but their guns seemed unable to pivot vertically to reach their escaping prey. For a brief instant, the creatures simply waited inside their vehicles, almost as if they were going to give up the chase. Then, one by one, the small three-foot aliens emerged from the Vips and began climbing the mountain with frightening rapidity and skill.

Her first sight of the strange aliens caused her to halt her ascent momentarily. The creatures resembled giant reptilian rats with scales in varying shades of gray. Although most of the Ryazan had two or three arms and legs, they were oddly positioned in nearly every conceivable location: some had arms in the middle of their chests, some sticking out from their hips, and several of them even had claws on the ends of their tails. Yet despite their many appendages, they appeared to be carrying no weapons. *Which doesn't mean anything on this accursed planet,* she thought dryly.

Prin shoved her hard from behind, cutting into her thoughts. "Why are you stopping? Go! They are almost upon us. Yes, yes!"

Needing no further prompting, she climbed up over the next ridge until she reached a mostly flat path about twenty-five feet wide that wound its way up the mountain.

"...Modir path... lead...cave," Jorylk said, its countenance lifting. The seven-foot alien began heading up the path with renewed vigor, although still oddly clutching its stomach.

"Run! They are almost here!" came Tarrsk's frantic cry as it cleared the edge and landed upon the path. Even as the translation finished, loud shrieks of rage came up from below as Kyen'tir rained down several lethal feathers at the approaching Ryazan.

Rebecca ran on after Jorylk, spurred on by the pandemonium that was suddenly unleashed behind her. Sikaris, Tarrsk, Lohgar, Rysth-nuul, and Ch'ran threw their packs and carry bags onto the ground and turned to face the oncoming attackers. In the same instant, harsh squeals full of blood-lust filled the air as several of the small creatures came up over the lip. Yet, even before they had cleared the edge, a volley of rock pellets and bullets were showered down upon them. But despite the hail of projectiles, only two of the aliens were felled by the attack. The rest of the agile creatures dodged and swerved, advancing slowly toward the group.

Suddenly, a burst of light and heat from behind her caused Rebecca to turn around just in time to see a stream of flame billowing out from one of the creatures closest to the edge of the cliff. But, to her complete bewilderment, it was not aimed at Sikaris and the others, but at the five advancing Ryazan in front of it, totally enveloping them in fire. As the stream ceased, the five attackers burned brightly, their entire bodies covered with dancing tongues of orange flame.

The burning creatures, however, instead of crying out in agony in the throes of death as she would have expected, leapt forward and closed the remaining distance between themselves and their prey, seemingly oblivious to the fire. The battle instantly dissolved into a free-for-all, as each of the defenders broke off the joint ranged attack in favor of the one-on-one melee.

Rysth-nuul dropped to the ground, causing its attacker to miscalculate and leap over its prone form. In the same motion, it snapped its barbed tail at the flaming assailant as it flew passed, catching it squarely around its throat. Using the Ryazan's forward momentum against it, the snake-like alien pulled its tail in the opposite direction, snapping the unfortunate creature's neck. Before the rat-like alien's fiery body had even hit the ground, Rysth-nuul withdrew its tail to avoid being burned further.

Its enemy defeated, Rysth-nuul prepared to rise, but was suddenly forced to throw itself back to the ground as a stream of fire passed over its head. The snake-like alien followed the stream to its source only to find that it was not the intended victim of the attack after all.

Ch'ran and one of the flaming Ryazan were caught in what looked like some sort of acrobatic dance. Both creatures dove and leapt, trying to work their way inside the other's defenses. The burning alien shot jets of flame at its opponent from its outstretched fingertips, narrowly missing each time as Ch'ran dodged skillfully. With every attack, the armadillo-like alien drew one step closer to its opponent, biding its time until just the right moment when it could deal the killing blow with its poison-tipped tail.

Rysth-nuul slithered silently closer to the two, all the while avoiding the wild tongues of fire that shot out in all directions in pursuit of the nimble Ch'ran. When it was finally in range, Rysth-nuul whipped out its long tail towards the Ryazan. At the last instant, the flaming creature sensed the danger and dodged dexterously to the side. But that moment of distraction was all Ch'ran needed. Letting out a screech of triumph, it leapt at its foe. Ignoring the flames, Ch'ran dug its claws into the alien to secure itself, then thrust its razor-sharp tail into its undefended flank. The burning attacker crumpled to the ground, ending its dance and its life.

Meanwhile, Sikaris braced itself as two of the Ryazan charged towards it, claws extended. Waiting until the last moment, the feline alien sprang into action. Leaping to one side to avoid the attack from the first fire-rat, Sikaris dropped the second one unconscious with an ear-splitting sonic roar. The first Ryazan quickly recovered from its failed attack and hurled itself once more at its prey. This time, instead of avoiding the lunge, Sikaris fell backward, kicking out with its legs. The kick connected squarely with the alien's torso, sending it flying over Sikaris' head to smash into the side of the mountain with a bone-crushing thud. Instantly back on all fours, the alien leader finished off its two stunned attackers in a matter of seconds.

Now free of enemies, Sikaris looked around to see how the others were faring. About thirty feet to its right, Tarrsk had climbed the vertical mountain face and was raining deadly pellets down on its enemy below. Yet even as Sikaris watched, flaming liquid sprayed upwards from the rat-like alien's outstretched claws, dislodging Tarrsk from its perch. Running towards the skirmish, Sikaris sent sonic roars in the small creature's direction, hoping to at least distract it long enough for Tarrsk to recover. Although the condensed sound waves did not connect directly with the alien's aural receptors, they did cause the creature to stumble back.

But it wouldn't be enough, Sikaris knew. The rat-like alien was back on its feet, its claws extended once again towards Tarrsk, eager for the kill. Suddenly, three dart-like feathers flew from the sky, slicing through part of the Ryazan's arms and torso, causing the creature to fall backward, howling in pain. As the injured alien glared balefully up at Kyen'tir, Tarrsk recovered and took full advantage of its opponent's distraction.

Not even taking the time to get to its feet, Tarrsk aimed its two tentacles at its attacker and opened fire. The twin spurts of rock-like shrapnel tore into the creature's body like razors, ending its life.

At that moment, a bellow of rage and pain split the air. Several yards farther down the path from where Sikaris now stood, Lohgar lay on its back, a flaming Ryazan sitting atop it. The ape-like alien held the wrists of its attacker as bursts of flaming liquid shot out of the tips of the creature's claws, singeing the fur on Lohgar's face and neck. Up to this point, Lohgar had been successful in keeping the liquid-spewing claws away from its own body, but Sikaris could see that the fire was already beginning to take its toll on the ape-like alien's strength. Lohgar let out another bellow of pain as the flames from the Ryazan began to heat up the metallic armor and burn the scaly flesh beneath it.

Before Sikaris could react, Lohgar managed to move the third arm on its back out from under its body. Raising the pistol held in its claw towards the Ryazan, it pulled the trigger at point-blank range, sending the lifeless body of the rat-like alien flying backward to the ground.

Reaching Lohgar's side, Sikaris helped it to its feet. "Where are the rest?" it said to the remainder of the group. "I thought there were more than this."

Kyen'tir, still aloft and circling, replied first, "I killed two as they were climbing up the side of the mountain, but I do not know what happened to the five that were chasing you and Rebecca."

Sikaris narrowed its eyes. "Kyen'tir, see if you can find them. Let us grab our equipment and go. The transport is almost here. Once it reaches the mountain, we will be greatly outnumbered." As if to punctuate its words, a booming crack echoed off the walls of the mountain, followed a moment later by an explosion not more than fifteen feet over their heads that rained down dirt and rocks on them for several seconds. After the dust had cleared, they looked over the cliff to see several dozen more Ryazan exiting the transport and beginning to climb towards them. The mere sight of the new attackers immediately prodded the motley group of aliens into action. Picking up their supply packs, they began running at full speed up the winding path.

Rebecca, who had been catching glimpses of the battle as she followed Prin and Jorylk up the trail, returned her attention fully to her own predicament as Prin spoke into its commlink. "Sikaris, we found the cave entrance about seventy-five yards up the path from your position. We—"

The ferret-like alien stopped in mid-sentence and reached for its gun, but it was too late. A stream of oily liquid splashed across its chest. An instant later, Rebecca saw four of the small, rat-like aliens leap up from below and land on the path. Igniting themselves on fire, they lunged forward: one throwing itself on Prin, who stood closest to the edge, the other three charging Jorylk.

The leaping creature knocked the alien scientist to the ground, the flames that licked across its body spreading rapidly onto Prin's oil-soaked Dakkar-nil armor. Whether the other three Ryazan had not yet seen her near the cave entrance or were too busy attacking the larger enemy, Rebecca was left unchallenged. Taking advantage of that oversight, she thrust her hand into her pocket and produced her gun. Pausing just long enough to make sure she had an accurate shot, she fired several shots at the flaming alien on top of Prin.

The creature screamed in pain and dropped sideways onto the ground, its body going limp. With its attacker's weight no longer hindering it, Prin began writhing in pain as the fire began eating into its scale-like flesh. After several seconds of struggling, Prin managed to extricate itself from the burning pieces of armor and put out the remaining flames tenaciously clinging to its fur.

A ferocious howl of rage suddenly caused Rebecca to turn her attention away from her wounded companion and towards the spiked giant who was fighting for its life. Jorylk was holding one of the burning creatures by the throat, and with a mighty heave, it sent the creature plummeting down the side of the mountain. A second Ryazan, seeing an opening in its foes defenses, jumped up and landed on Jorylk's chest. But just as the creature was about to spread its burning fluid over the body of its victim, Jorylk did something the alien had not anticipated. Instead of fighting to remove the rat-like alien from its chest, Jorylk threw itself forward onto the ground, using its weight to drive the spikes on its body into its attacker.

Jorylk's abrupt move had an unexpected secondary effect as well: a third Ryazan, standing directly behind the spiked alien, sent a stream of fire shooting forward at the same moment that Jorylk threw itself onto the ground, causing the fire to sail over the now prone form, narrowly missing it. The giant alien, suddenly realizing the new danger, quickly turned its body sideways and began rolling towards the new threat, catching the creature off guard. Like a steamroller, Jorylk rolled its body over its attacker, crushing the life out of it.

Its foes vanquished, Jorylk stood to its feet and let out a feral howl of rage. Then, whirling around in search of new enemies, its gaze fell upon Rebecca standing near Prin's fallen form. Its mind clouded by its berserk rage, it howled once again, its mouth foaming.

Prin, recognizing madness in its companion's eyes, shouted the creature's name in an attempt to halt its attack. "Jorylk! Stop! Jorylk!" Its efforts proved futile, however. The maddened alien lunged forward, intent on their destruction. Prin and Rebecca simultaneously leaped in opposite directions, momentarily confusing it and causing it to miss both of them with its massive spiked arms.

Dropping into a crouch, Rebecca quickly sent several shots towards the creature, deliberately missing. As the enraged being turned her way, she shouted to Prin, "Shock his abdomen. Now." Without hesitation, Prin launched itself towards Jorylk's back. Reaching its double right forearms carefully around the spiked alien's waist, Prin released a jolt of electricity into its stomach. Immediately, the creature doubled over in pain and fell to the ground.

They sat motionless for several seconds, breathing heavily. Finally, Prin ventured to speak to the downed figure. "Jorylk, it is Prin. Do you know me?"

Slowly, the giant alien nodded in affirmation. Satisfied that their companion had returned to its senses, Prin hobbled over to the edge of the cliff to make sure that there were no more Ryazan coming up the side of the mountain.

Suddenly, another loud crack of cannon fire was heard from below followed once again by an accompanying explosion. The missile from the Ryazan transport hit the side of the mountain just below the cave entrance, the resulting impact knocking both Prin and Rebecca from their feet.

"That was close, yes, yes." Prin said, stating the obvious. Regaining its feet, it called out to the others, who were still thirty yards from the cave. "Quickly. The Ryazan are halfway up the mountain!"

"Sikaris, I will try to keep them busy for a little longer, but I have almost used up all of my spare feathers," Kyen'tir said as it began to circle around to head back down the path.

However, just as the winged reptile had finished its aerial maneuver, another shot from the transport shook the mountainside, splitting it and sending chunks of rock hurling down upon them. Kyen'tir, caught in the middle of the explosion, was struck several times by sharp fragments of stone that sent it plummeting toward the ground with the rest of the small avalanche.

Rysth-nuul, Tarrsk, and Ch'ran dove forward and narrowly escaped being entombed with Kyen'tir under the massive pile of earth and stone. Sikaris and Lohgar, being at the rear of the group, were forced to retreat back down the path. Tons of rubble struck the path, shaking the earth beneath them and sending up huge plumes of dust and dirt into the air. It took several minutes for the avalanche to settle enough for the group of aliens to stand.

"Blocked!" Lohgar howled in frustration after observing the damage. "Now what do we do?"

Before Sikaris could reply, a triumphant screech arose from behind. Turning to look, they saw several dozen of the small creatures hurling towards them with reckless abandon.

Rebecca and the others watched helplessly from their vantage point at the cave mouth. After a moment, Tarrsk spoke its thoughts aloud, "They are going to die. Let us go now. We will have more of a head start that way."

"I agree," Rysth-nuul hissed, "But which way? I do not want to face the Modir. I would rather take my chances outside the mountain. The Ryazan are busy with Sikaris and Lohgar, and the path is blocked. I say we go around our original way."

"Yes. I think we can find cover a little farther up—" Tarrsk began.

"Look!" Prin suddenly shouted, abruptly cutting off any further discussion. A lone Ryazan had somehow worked its way up the mountain and now stood directly above Sikaris and Lohgar, poised to strike. Before Prin could call out a warning, the rat-like creature dropped from above, landing directly atop Lohgar. Instantly the ape-like alien was doused in oily liquid from head to toe. A split second later, Lohgar screamed in pain as its body became a living torch.

Sikaris turned quickly to help its burning companion, but Lohgar, desperate to quench the flames, dropped to the ground and rolled madly. Before Sikaris could stop it, Lohgar rolled too close to the precipice and tumbled off the edge, screaming from pain and fear.

As Loghar's cries faded away, Sikaris turned to face the single Ryazan who had sprung to safety on the ledge. Now wreathed in flames, it moved to attack. Sikaris feigned to the left, then dove back to the right, avoiding the creature's stream of burning liquid. Rolling quickly on the ground toward it, Sikaris pivoted its body and kicked out with its muscular legs, sending the Ryazan flying out several feet over the edge before it began to fall to its death.

Even as Sikaris regained its footing, though, several more streams of fire lanced out towards it from the horde of Ryazan, now only a few dozen feet away. The large feline alien backed up towards the side of the mountain, seemingly trapped. Then, with a great heave, Sikaris broke into a run and threw itself off the path, jets of fire shooting after it in its wake.

The Grinathian leader spread its arms and legs wide, catching the air currents in its skin folds. Once its flight was stabilized, it turned back towards the mountain and cave.

"He's lost too much altitude," Rebecca noted with concern. "He's not going to make it."

She had barely finished speaking when Sikaris slammed into the nearly vertical side of the mountain twenty feet below them. The reptilian feline scrambled for purchase as its body began sliding downwards. Finally, its claws grabbed onto a large outcropping, halting its descent.

Prin immediately began rummaging through one of the packs. Producing a length of rope, the alien scientist uncoiled it rapidly.

The attacks from the transport, which had temporarily ceased as the mob of Ryazan grew closer, suddenly began again with renewed fury. Projectiles pounded into the mountainside, threatening to dislodge more of the tough rock and stone.

Prin quickly threw the rope down to Sikaris as rocks fell around them. The Grinathian leader looped the rope over its torso and, with the help of Prin and the others, slowly began to climb up the cliff face.

Then, just as Sikaris cleared the edge, a tremendous roar as of a thousand stampeding horses filled their ears. Looking up, they watched as half of the mountainside seemed to be sliding down towards them. Reacting instantly, the group threw themselves inside the entrance of the cave as the mountain seemed to land on top of them.

12

Jorylk's Condition

REBECCA LOST all sense of time as she lay on the cold, hard stone in the dark recess of the mountain. Finally, after the avalanche had settled, her ears began to pick up a faint, scuffling sound. The darkness, combined with the fear of the unknown, sent her reaching for her pistol. She was about to call out for the others when Sikaris' voice broke through the stillness.

"Say your name if you are conscious."

In turn, each of the other five surviving aliens spoke their names, with Jorylk's sounding more like a painful grunt. Waiting until last, Rebecca offered hers. Not detecting any trace of fear in their voices, Rebecca relaxed and felt the adrenaline slowly ebb from her body, leaving her weak and exhausted.

Suddenly, a blinding shaft of light pierced the darkness. After a moment of adjustment to the newfound luminosity, Rebecca could distinguish the dark forms of the others lying on the ground, one of them holding the flashlight responsible for the brilliance.

A moment later, several more lights shone forth as the others removed flashlights and electronic lanterns from their gear. Soon, the entire area was lit comfortably, with the exception of the back of the cave, which stretched into darkness like a cold, dank well.

"I did not know Ryazan were that persistent," Prin said to the others as it brushed dirt and dust out of its fine yellow-brown fur.

"That is because they are not," Tarrsk replied. "Hunting must be very bad lately for them to become that desperate."

"This is very, very good," Rysth-nuul said, its tone oozing sarcasm. "Look at this. The entire cave entrance is buried. We are as good as dead."

The others stared at the pile of rubble, none offering a counter argument to their companion's observation.

"I am so tired of this!" Rysth-nuul continued, its anger boiling over. "First the Mrdangam, then the Ryazan. Now we are going to end up enslaved or eaten for sure by the Modir or the Gorz. I have had enough. It is over."

As Rebecca watched, Rysth-nuul peeled back a small section of scales on its left wrist and withdrew a tiny vial containing a dark liquid. Popping the attached top off with its thumb, it began to raise the vial towards its lips.

With lightning-fast reflexes, Sikaris' claw shot forward and stopped Rysth-nuul's hand mere centimeters from its destination.

"Do not do this, Rysth-nuul," it said in a low, serious voice. "We need you."

The snake-like alien stood momentarily still like a stone statue, its arm still held firmly by Sikaris. In a throaty rasp, it replied, "I will not be made into a slave again. Not by the Modir, or anyone else. You know we will die. Do not lie to us."

"I agree with Rysth-nuul," Tarrsk said, stepping closer to where the two aliens faced off. "We are trapped. The only way out is down there, inside the mountain, in the heart of Clan Modir! We are going to end up dead like Kyen'tir, Lohgar, and the others." As it spoke, it unconsciously scratched at its torso just below its mouth, causing large flakes of white, diseased scales to fall to the cave floor.

"No, not like the others," Ch'ran's irritating screech rose from behind them. "They were crushed and burned alive. We will probably be gassed by the Modir or eaten alive piece by piece by the Gorz!"

Sikaris shot a searing look at the three-foot alien, causing Ch'ran's expression to become one of feigned hurt.

"What?" Ch'ran asked. "I was only stating a fact. Besides, I am with *you*, Sikaris. Nix has already told me that I will not die inside this mountain, so what are we waiting for?"

Containing its anger, Sikaris simply said, "Since you are uninjured, Ch'ran, scout ahead and stay there as sentry until we join you."

Ch'ran, thrilled at the opportunity to seek out the unknown, set out down the passage at a brisk trot, its flashlight bobbing up and down in a hypnotic rhythm to its jovial gait.

Returning its attention back to the two dissenters, Sikaris attempted to mend the damage done by the departing figure. "You have both hunted with me many times. Every time I have brought us to victory, and I plan to do it again. Remember the ambush by the Kthor? Or the Lidrilian invasion? We can get through this as well."

"And if you are wrong?" hissed Rysth-nuul.

"Then use the toxin. But not now."

"So what is your plan?" Tarrsk said, hesitantly.

"The Modir have several tunnels like this one that lead to the surface," Sikaris said. "We should be able to find one of the other tunnels without going very far into the mountain. We may not even meet any Modir, and the Gorz usually do not come this close to the surface."

Rysth-nuul and Tarrsk looked unconvinced, but reluctantly acquiesced to Sikaris' leadership. The snake-like alien replaced the cap and returned the small vial of toxin to its hiding place, then looked once more at the Grinathian leader. "Even if we do make it out of this mountain, you are betting very much on this thing's ship," it said, its two left eyes turning disconcertingly to look at Rebecca. "I hope you are right." With that, it turned away and began searching through its pack.

Turning towards the others, its face an expressionless mask, Sikaris announced, "We will take a rest here. Bandage your burns and other injuries. I will take care of Jorylk. Once he has recovered, we head out."

Tarrsk and Prin followed Rysth-nuul's example and immediately began opening packages of Ager gel to soothe their blistered scales. Uninjured herself, Rebecca kneeled down in front of Prin. "Would you like some help?" she asked politely.

The ferret-like alien looked at her uncertainly, as if unsure of her motives. "Yes, yes," it replied cautiously.

Rebecca removed her backpack and took out several bandages and packages of gel. Relying on her Marine medical training, she began to dress Prin's wounded side. As she worked, she asked, "Do all of you carry hidden vials of toxin?"

"Yes, yes," Prin said, its concentration focused more on scrutinizing Rebecca's work than on her question. Satisfied that she knew what she was doing, it expounded further. "Each of us carries a small, hidden vial of lethal toxin which we use if captured by other clans."

Aware that her future relations with Prin could be hindered or improved by how well she bandaged its wounds, she slowly worked the bandage into place. "But wouldn't capture be preferable to suicide? If you are a slave, at least you have the hope of rescue or escape."

Prin looked up from watching her work to meet her gaze. "What was the word you said before escape?"

"Rescue?"

"Yes, yes. What is this?"

"Rescue is when others come to free you," she said. *Of course,* she thought. *They would not risk themselves for each other. You've gotta start remembering these things, Becky.* Recovering herself, she rephrased the question. "Well, wouldn't the hope of escape be better than suicide?"

"It all depends on which clan has captured you. Some clans, like the Gorz or V'skir, like to eat their food alive. They eat you limb by limb, until finally eating your torso and head."

Rebecca shuddered involuntarily as the sudden realization of the fate she had been spared when she was rescued by Sikaris and the others struck her full force.

Prin continued, not noticing Rebecca's discomfort. "Other clans, such as the Torlig, use their prisoners for vicious sport and cruel games. And even those clans that do not kill you, like the Modir and Harmath will make your life so full of pain and hard labor that you will want to die. Escape from captivity is rare. And even if you do escape, your own clan may not accept you back, especially if you were crippled in any way. Yes, yes. Do you see now? These vials of toxin are very nice to have when faced with other options. Would you like one?"

The very question sent a cold shiver down her spine. *Should I? What if I don't make it back to the ship? What if the others are dead or the ship is destroyed? What if I am stranded on this planet? Wouldn't it be better to…* Swallowing hard, she said softly, "Yes."

Reaching into its pack, Prin produced one of the small vials and placed it in Rebecca's hand. "Put it somewhere safe and secret. Yes, yes. Clans will take it from you if they know you have it."

Unzipping a small pocket sewn into the inner lining of her jumpsuit, she slipped the toxin inside and sealed it; and with it, sealed in her heart an intense feeling of trepidation and foreboding.

Prin looked down at the completed bandage and nodded approvingly. "Your work is good," it said simply. Its main injury mended, Prin turned its attention to its burns. Suddenly, from the other side of the cave came a ferocious growl, followed immediately by a pain-wracked moan. Turning around, Rebecca saw Sikaris standing next to the prone form of Jorylk, who was curled up on the floor in a fetal position. Leaning back against the wall, she watched Sikaris intently, searching for some clue as to what ailed the large alien.

Withdrawing several tiny objects from one of the medical packs, Sikaris crouched down next to Jorylk. Placing the objects in its mouth, Sikaris held a canteen full of liquid to the disfigured lips of the injured alien. Once Sikaris was certain its patient had swallowed the mysterious medicine, it put away the canteen.

This accomplished, Sikaris reached into another bag and pulled out manacles. With great effort, the feline-like alien pulled Jorylk's muscular arms behind its back and secured them tightly. Satisfied that its patient was securely bound, Sikaris began to treat its burns.

As the alien leader applied the healing gel, Jorylk began to moan more intensely and rock slowly on its side. No sooner had Sikaris finished dressing its wounds then the spiked creature began twisting and contorting its body as stabs of pain wracked it mercilessly.

Rebecca gritted her teeth as she watched the disturbing display, yet found herself strangely mesmerized by the torturous sight. So enthralled was she, that when Prin spoke, she literally jumped with surprise. "Lean back against the wall."

"Why?" she said, suddenly suspicious.

"I am going to change the bandage on your arm."

"Thank you, but that is not necessary," she said, smiling slightly.

A look of mistrust or anger, she wasn't sure which, seemed to cross Prin's lopsided face. "You want me to owe a debt to you, yes, yes," Prin said. "But I will owe debts to no one. I will change the bandage on your arm," it said with a finality that left no room for argument.

Slightly unnerved, Rebecca did as she was told. Leaning back against the wall, she continued to watch Jorylk as Prin went to work on her arm. After a few moments, she could contain her curiosity no longer. "Prin, what is wrong with Jorylk? I didn't see him get injured."

Its attention focused on her arm, Prin responded nonchalantly. "He will be fine soon. He is murdering his offspring."

"What!" Rebecca said a little too loudly as she sat up straight.

Shoving her back against the wall and shooting her a disapproving look, Prin said, "Let me guess, you do not murder your offspring on your planet either."

"Well…I wouldn't put it that way, but…yes, we do abort fetuses, if that is what you mean."

"What are those? The translator did not understand the word."

"Fetuses? Well, I guess you would say they are what we call babies—offspring—before they are born," she said, sucking in her breath as Prin removed the bandage, opening her wound up to the moist, cool air.

Prin shook its head in amusement. "That is strange. Why have a separate word for offspring *before* it is born? Offspring are offspring." Giving her arm an approving look, it continued. "Good. Your arm is responding well to the Ager gel, yes, yes. How does it feel?"

Moving her injured limb tentatively, she found her muscle beginning to respond, albeit painfully. *Still, considering the extent of the damage, that is amazing! I could make a fortune with this stuff,* she thought. Aloud, she said, "That gel works quicker than anything I have ever seen. I'd like to take some back with me when I return to Earth."

The ferret-like alien failed to respond to her comment but simply continued its work. As Prin emptied the contents of another pack of gel onto her arm, Rebecca dwelled on this new revelation. "So Jorylk is a *she*. Fascinating," she said softly to herself. Looking up at Prin, she asked, "Why is Jorylk aborting his—I mean her—fetus—offspring? Is there some complication or problem with the pregnancy?"

Prin seemed momentarily confused by her question, as if trying to make sense of the translation. "No, no problem," it said finally. "But when on a hunt, it is easier to just kill the offspring than have to deal with any pains from the pregnancy. Especially on this hunt. Besides, the offspring would probably not survive anyway."

"Why is that?"

Prin looked at her quizzically, pausing momentarily in its bandaging of her arm. "Because of mutations, of course. Do not your offspring have mutations?"

"Yes, but they are rare. Most children are born healthy and normal, except in poverty stricken areas," she replied in confusion. "Are mutations that common here?"

Prin was silent for a moment, then replied, "Yes, yes. As far as I know, every offspring is born with at least some kind of mutation. Since nearly all mutations are fatal, most of them die before they are born. And many of those that are born alive do not live past the first cycle to maturity."

After a moment of delayed comprehension, Rebecca replied in surprise. "Wow! Do all offspring mature in only one cycle?"

"Yes, yes. Why?"

"And how long are your days, and how many days are in a cycle?

"There are 35 hours in a day, and 421 days in a cycle? Why?" Prin repeated in confusion.

Rebecca was silent for several seconds as she mentally converted the time into Earth years. "Almost two years," she said softly to herself. That is still an incredibly short time."

Its frustration mounting, Prin stared at her firmly. "What are you talking about? How long do offspring take to mature on your planet?"

"Well," she said, wondering if this new bit of information would also make her look foolish somehow, "the typical human…from my clan… doesn't mature until they have reached their tenth or eleventh year—or cycle, and most not until they reach thirteen or fourteen. Even taking into account our 24 hour days and our 365 day cycle, your people still mature in a fraction of the time it takes us to mature."

Prin was taken aback. "Do you mean that your offspring do not become self-sustaining until they reach thirteen or fourteen cycles? You lie," it said incredulously. "What about the other living beings on your planet? Do they also take that long to mature?"

The sudden implications of Prin's question struck her momentarily speechless. Finally recovering her wits, she responded slowly, her confusion plainly evident in her voice. "No, they don't. They mature much quicker."

"How long do they take to mature?"

"Some mature in just over a year or two, like you do here."

Prin shook its head, the muscles on its face wrinkling the skin in odd directions, in what Rebecca assumed to be a frown. "Your lies are even beginning to confuse you. How could your clan be the most highly evolved if they take so much longer to mature? The other clans could produce ten generations in just one of yours. Even if you were more intelligent, they would have conquered you by having more offspring."

Dumbfounded, Rebecca sat motionless. Sensing that no further comments were forthcoming, Prin reverted to an earlier topic. "So tell me then, if mutations are so rare on your planet, how could you have evolved to such complexity? Are all rare mutations beneficial?"

Still musing upon their previous conversation, Rebecca asked Prin to repeat itself before she answered. "No. They are almost all harmful."

Prin's facial features wrinkled oddly once more. "That does not make sense either. If you only have a few mutations and most of those are harmful, then it would take billions upon billions of your cycles to even have the slightest change in a life."

In the light of her companion's logic, Rebecca simply hung her head like a child being scolded by a teacher for making an obvious error.

Giving up on the conversation, Prin went back to working on her bandage. After several more minutes, it nodded. "You are done."

"Thank you," she said halfheartedly. In the same instant, Jorylk let out another painful moan and began writhing toward the opposite cave wall, forcing Rysth-nuul to slither out of the way.

As Prin stood and prepared to return to its equipment, Rebecca grabbed its uninjured forearm. "Prin, one more question. Are you male or female?"

Prin paused, the yellowish-brown fur above its crooked eyes furrowed. "What do those words mean?"

"Females, like Jorylk, can have children. The males only provide the sperm to fertilize the females' eggs," Rebecca explained.

The alien stared at her with a blank expression on its face, clearly not understanding.

"Can you have children?" she asked more directly.

Prin's features changed to reveal intense concentration. "Of course I can. We all can. What kind of question is that? Can you not have children?"

The question cut through her heart like a knife. Fighting to control her emotions, she hesitated and took a deep breath before responding. "Well, I am a female, and females are the ones that carry children. But I must...partner with a male. I cannot have children on my own."

After a moment, its eyes narrowed dangerously and its gaze bored into her. "Are you saying that on your planet it takes *two* of you to create an offspring?"

Suddenly unnerved by her companion's reaction, Rebecca answered tentatively. "Why, yes. The majority of species on my planet have male and female."

Prin's lower right forearm backhanded her so quickly that she had no time to prepare for the blow. Her body swung around and dropped to the floor, her face smacking hard against the cold stone. Stunned, both physically and emotionally, she lay there unmoving for several seconds. She could feel blood running freely down her cheek and lip where Prin's clawed hand had connected with the soft flesh of her face. A moment later, she heard Prin's voice above her, its tone harsh and quivering with rage.

"I have had enough of your lies! At first you really made me believe your strange stories. But the more you tell me about this 'planet' of yours, the more unbelievable it is. And now, you want me to believe that it takes two of your kind to make an offspring? What possible evolutionary advantage could there be in that? You really are insane. And you make me look unintelligent in front of the others."

Rebecca lay still under the scathing rebuke of her companion, not daring to move for fear of another violent backlash.

Prin continued, its voice low and threatening. "I have wasted enough time on you. Rysth-nuul and Tarrsk are right. Even if we make it out of this mountain, we will have no way to get back. We are dead. All because Sikaris believed you." Prin spat on the ground at her feet and strode away, leaving her alone and nursing her bruised face.

As the ferret-like alien crossed the cave floor, Rysth-nuul and Tarrsk began snickering and laughing quietly. "What is wrong, Prin?" Tarrsk taunted. "Is your pet not behaving?"

The tips of Prin's fingers crackled with blue sparks, lighting up the cave wall with dancing shadows. Every muscle in Prin's body went taut as it prepared to pounce on the heckler.

"Prin," Sikaris growled in warning, "no. Let it go."

After a moment of consideration, Prin backed down. Shooting Tarrsk one final look of promised revenge, it turned away. Snatching its bag from the floor, Prin strode toward the back of the tunnel. As it passed Sikaris, it paused. "I do not know why you still believe this…this insane creature, but your belief is going to kill us all." With that, Prin strode off down the tunnel to find Ch'ran.

Picking herself up off the floor, Rebecca proceeded to clean her face and split lip with damp cloths from the med packs, all the while trying to ignore the laughter and snide remarks coming from the other side of the cave. Not knowing what else to do while they waited for Jorylk to recover, and wanting desperately to take her mind off of what the others were saying, she withdrew her journal and began to record.

Journal Entry #4

I didn't believe it could be possible, but I am more confused now then I was when I recorded my last journal entry.

As it turns out, our transport was irreparably damaged by the dragon-like creature mentioned in my last entry. We proceeded on foot to try to reach the Vanguard, but were attacked by a clan of rat-like aliens called the Ryazan. These creatures have the ability to shoot flammable liquid from their fingertips, and are themselves impervious to fire. Two of the aliens accompanying me were killed in the battle, and the rest of us are now trapped inside a cave due to a landslide. Sikaris is hoping we can find another passage that will lead us out, but the others are not as optimistic. I will elaborate on these events further if time permits.

First, however, I will record my thoughts about some of the recent events. After talking with Prin, I have learned that Ch'ran, one of my alien companions, speaks to an unseen being called Nix, who has supposedly been credited with saving Ch'ran's life. Of course, Ch'ran is insane, even by these aliens' standards. However, all of this has brought me to a disturbing realization: if I truly believe that humans evolved by random processes, then isn't it a form of insanity to believe in a supreme, all-powerful being? For by its very definition, evolution is unguided. Yet, all of my life I have been taught by my parents to go to church, and, as my sister said, "Religion isn't all bad." But how do I reconcile my belief in evolution with the faith of my parents? Is it possible that there really is a God, but he or she just used evolution to create mankind? But why would an all-powerful God use such a poor system to design its creation, and why would he or she take so long to do it? Furthermore, aren't the basic tenants of faith based upon a collection of fictitious stories, such as Adam and Eve and Noah's Ark? If those stories are fictitious, then why hold to beliefs that are based upon them, like sin and redemption?

When I return from this awful trip, I will have to discuss this with someone who has thought about it more than I have. For now, let me move on.

During the attack by the Ryazan, we were forced to run for our lives. The others used all of their limbs to run, quickly leaving me behind. They assumed that I could run using both my hands and my feet and were surprised when I explained that I could not.

In college, I remember the question being raised: Why did humans evolve the ability to walk upright? The answer that most of us agreed upon was that it allowed us to be able to carry things and use tools. I still believe this answer to be correct, but the question that none of us ever considered before is: Why did we ever LOSE the ability to run on all fours? It is clear that animals that run on four limbs are much faster then those who run on two. Even if a superior brain allowed us an advantage, surely those with both superior brains and the ability to run on all fours would have an even greater advantage. How can evolution account for the loss of abilities that give an animal such an obvious advantage for survival?

Regardless, I was thankful that Sikaris was able to carry me on its back, or I would not still be alive.

Yet I am beginning to wonder now if I might not be better off dead. The more I learn of this world and its cruel inhabitants, the more I fear the possibility of being stranded here. It seems that even my companions fear capture by other clans so much that they all carry hidden vials of fatal poison. Prin also gave me one, which I hope I will never have to use.

I guess that is what it all comes down to: hope. These

creatures don't have any hope. Even if they survive this hunt (as they call it, although we are now the hunted), they do not have much to look forward to. They have no hope of a brighter future; just a life full of constant war, pain, and suffering. They live from day to day, pleasure to pleasure. I pity them.

I do not know if I will have the courage to take my own life if the time comes, but for now I will not dwell on it. For I, at least, still have hope. The tracker shows that the ship has not moved from its original location, now less then five miles away.

But I digress. Another question that has plagued me is in regards to mutations. According to Prin, nearly every offspring born on this planet is a mutation from its parent. Furthermore, only about ten percent of those born alive actually survive. This is because the majority of mutations are fatal. Prin looked at me incredulously when I told him—it— that mutations are rare on Earth. Now that I am thinking about it, I see why.

On Earth, besides being rare, nearly all mutations that we do observe are negative mutations, causing either harm, such as mental disorders, disease, or death. Very few observable mutations do not affect the survivability of the person or animal one way or another.

Only the smallest fraction of mutations on Earth is helpful in any way. So how did we evolve into such complex organisms when only the smallest number of already rare mutations is beneficial? Add to that the sheer number of mutations required to alter an animal even slightly and it boggles the mind. Could even billions of years account for the complexity of life that we see on Earth?

In addition to the vast number of mutations on this planet, Prin also informed me that offspring here only take the equivalent of two Earth years to mature. This seems like an extremely short amount of time when compared to humans, but when I think about maturation lengths of animals, it does not seem so strange. It also makes sense that a clan with a shorter cycle of maturation would have a definite evolutionary advantage over a clan with a longer one. It would mean more hunters and greater numbers, as well as many generations within a shorter time span. The only thing that doesn't make sense is why we humans take so long to mature when a majority of animals on Earth mature rapidly? I can understand that it might take longer to fully develop our complex brains, but why do we not mature faster physically? It seems so odd to me that we, who are supposed to be more highly evolved, take years to be able to run quickly, when other "less evolved" animals are born running!

As confusing as this is, it still does not puzzle me as much as Prin's last revelation. Prin him—itself—was so shocked by what I said that it now firmly believes that everything I have told it about Earth has been a lie. It seems that every creature on this planet is asexual. There is no male and female. No sexual intercourse or mating practices. According to my observations, these creatures simply produce offspring at various, random times throughout their adult lives. It is not something they have any control or choice about. Because of this, and combined with the high mortality rate, abortion is common.

At first, I was completely nonplussed by Prin's reaction. Why is it so unbelievable to have two sexes? But I think I am beginning to understand its reaction.

If evolution occurred as we believe, then all life began from chemicals mixing in Earth's primordial oceans. This simple life then reproduced itself, creating another life form just like it, but possibly slightly altered by mutations. If this scenario is correct, then asexual reproduction is absolutely imperative to life. How, when, and why did life suddenly diverge into two separate sexes, neither of which could produce offspring by itself? This is compounded by the fact that the female body is far more complex than the male body, which means the male body would have evolved first. But how could that be? What possible survivability advantage would a male have without a female?

After analyzing all I have learned so far on this nightmare of a world, I am beginning to believe that the theory of evolution, as I have been taught, cannot account for life on Earth. There must be some other, logical explanation for all of the inconsistencies I have thus far recorded in this journal. However, as of yet, a feasible theory continues to elude me.

For now, I must sign off. Jorylk has recovered from his—her— its—abortion and Sikaris is rousing the others. May I live long enough to record another entry.

13

Discoveries

ONCE JORYLK had recovered enough strength to walk, they set out again, moving deeper into the bowels of Mount Kiabab, their lights casting disturbing shadows on the cave walls. With Prin still farther ahead of them, Rebecca found herself walking in silence beside the ever-stoic Sikaris, lost in her thoughts.

Their surroundings did nothing to alleviate the depression caused by her turbulent emotions. The dank, humid cave grew narrower and more claustrophobic the farther they traversed.

Before long, they came upon Prin, who fell into place at the back of the group without uttering a word. As she passed the ferret-like alien, she felt her cheeks begin to burn in remembrance. She used to take pride in her education and knowledge, often inwardly reveling at the level of success she had achieved. Yet every time she spoke to this mutated, asymmetrical alien, she felt like a grade-school kid who had just failed a test.

Thankfully, Rysth-nuul and Tarrsk refrained from any further ridicule as they walked, moving silently through the underdark. In the oppressive silence, Rebecca clenched her teeth together and berated herself mentally every time her pack would scrape the wall or she would trip lightly over the uneven ground. In her mind's eye she could picture formless, shapeless creatures coming out of the inky blackness towards them, alerted by her clumsiness.

With these dark thoughts taunting her maliciously, she nearly fulfilled her own vision when a soft, yet shrill screech floated out of the darkness mere inches from her right ear. Only by biting her lower lip until it bled did she keep from crying out.

"No, Nix. I know she looks tasty, but Sikaris said 'no,' so stop tempting me!" came the monotone voice of her translator.

In her fright, Rebecca had stumbled and fallen backwards against the wall. As she stared into the darkness from where the sound had originated, a rock began to move. A second later, Ch'ran's beady, devilish eyes and cocked head appeared before her, its small form perched on top of a boulder that rested near the side of the passage.

"How much farther did you go?" Sikaris asked.

"Not far," the small alien replied, turning to face the hunting party's leader. "Just ahead, the tunnel opens into a wide corridor. It is very dark. This seemed like the best place to wait. Nix thought so too."

"Good work. Rysth-nuul, you have the best vision in dark places. You take the lead."

The snake-like alien's body twisted in some unknown gesture, its moss green scales catching the dim light from the lanterns. "I may be able to see better than the rest of you, but the Modir will see us long before I see them, so what does it matter who goes first?"

"I know," Sikaris replied. "But we have no other choice. Just stay close to the walls and give us as much warning as you can before they attack."

Reluctantly, Rysth-nuul slithered on ahead, followed by Jorylk, Sikaris, Rebecca, Tarrsk, Ch'ran, and Prin. They walked on for several long minutes before they reached the corridor which Ch'ran had mentioned. They paused for a moment as Rysth-nuul scanned the area, searching for any signs of movement.

As they waited, Rebecca stared at the walls surrounding them and was surprised to find some markings a few feet from the floor. "Sikaris," she called softly, pointing to her discovery, "I think I may have found some kind of written message."

The alien leader followed her gaze, then moved closer to examine it.

"What is it?" Tarrsk whispered from behind.

Sikaris raised its flashlight to illuminate the odd scratches. "It is Modir writing. It marks the outer border of Modir territory. Rysth-nuul, do you see anything?"

"Nothing at all. But I would not be surprised if they have some kind of ambush or defenses just waiting for us," it said pessimistically.

"Everyone on your guard. Let us go," Sikaris said with finality.

They stepped out into a large, cavernous tunnel, the size of which caused their feeble lights to be swallowed instantly in the enveloping blackness. If she focused hard, Rebecca could just make out the cavern ceiling high above them.

The walls and floor of the huge, underground passage were surprisingly smooth, making their going easy. However, they still traveled very slowly, always wary of any recesses in the walls or possible ambush points along their route.

After more than a half-hour of traveling with her every sense in a heightened state of alertness, her nerves began to wear down. Only her military training allowed her to endure the crushing weight of stress. Drawing upon her former discipline, she fought to keep her mind sharp and not dwell on the possibilities that some unspeakable terror may be lurking just beyond the lantern's reach.

Then, suddenly, she remembered her motion detector. Chiding herself inwardly for being a fool, she quickly withdrew the device from her pack. Activating it, she was instantly rewarded with the knowledge that nothing moved anywhere within the limit of its range, which was considerable given the openness of the cavern. Furthermore, the motion detector gave her the exact distance to the far wall and ceiling, taking away much of her fear of the unknown. *Assuming, of course, that it is working correctly,* she thought, her mind flashing back to the floating light from the V'skir that was the cause of her current predicament.

Deciding that the readings from the device were indeed accurate and reliable, she called out softly to Sikaris. The others immediately halted, their lanterns continually scanning the immediate area as the feline-like alien turned towards her. She quickly related her findings from the motion detector, once again thankful to be of some use to the group.

"Very good," Sikaris said, a rare smile spreading across its proud features. "Come closer to the front and continue monitoring at all times."

A sudden, wheezing gasp from Prin caused all of them to whirl immediately around, weapons at the ready. They were caught by surprise, not by attacking Modir, but by the bizarre behavior of their normally calm companion. The alien scientist was crouched over something imbedded in the floor of the cavern, three of its claws brushing and digging at the dirt excitedly while the other shined the beam of the flashlight at the object.

"This is very, very good! I cannot believe it! We found one, yes, yes!" it whispered, the excitement evident in its voice despite the muted volume. "I never thought I would be lucky enough to actually see a real one."

"A real what?" Ch'ran said, its innate curiosity instantly aroused.

"This," Prin said as it continued to remove more of the dirt and debris that covered parts of the object that seemed to be buried just under the surface of the cave floor. Sikaris, Tarrsk, Ch'ran, and Rebecca gathered around Prin as it finished its task, while Rysth-nuul and Jorylk continued to search the surrounding darkness for signs of movement. Standing up proudly, Prin backed away so that the others could have a closer look at its discovery.

On the floor in front of them lay the partially revealed skeleton of some large, aquatic animal. What was visible of the remains was roughly five feet long from the points of its toothy jaw to the tip of its spiked tail. Clearly discernable were six, oddly shaped appendages: two on its back and four on its underbelly. The latter were in the shape of fins, yet with definite separations for fingers and toes. The two on its back, while also resembling fins, were more elongated and tubular in shape.

"That is it?" Tarrsk asked incredulously. "That is what made you so excited? A dead being? Aagh!" it said in frustration. "With all of the excitement, you would have thought he had found a way out," it mumbled to no one in particular.

"But you do not understand," Prin countered, its enthusiasm undiminished. "These are extremely rare!"

"But what is it?" Ch'ran asked in confusion. "I have never seen one of these before."

"Very few have. This being has been dead for probably millions of years!" Prin pronounced, trying with difficulty to contain itself.

"But if it has been dead for millions of years, then why have the bones not turned to dust by now?" Tarrsk asked skeptically.

Prin didn't seem to even notice the other's disdain. "Because this being's body was buried quickly, probably by a mud slide or flood. Yes, yes, a flood! Look," Prin indicated, pointing one of its many fingers at the lower appendages, "its fins show clearly that it was in the first stages of coming out of the water. It could probably breathe air already. Yes, yes."

Moving away from the fossil, the alien scientist raised its arms in an all-encompassing gesture. "And this whole cavern was probably some big river under the mountain." As Prin spoke, it became caught up in its own tale and began acting out the entire story like an actor on a stage. "Then, a part of the tunnel fell down, knocking the being into the water. Large rocks broke the dirt from the tunnel into small pieces that mixed with the water to make mud. Yes, yes. The mud caught this being as it tried to escape. It struggled to survive, but the mud dragged it under the water. Once it was dead, the mud pulled the body to the bottom where it was buried. Yes, yes. Then, after millions of years, the minerals slowly replaced the bones, turning them to rock, as we see now. The river ran dry, and the Modir tunneling has brought it to the surface.

"This being is probably one of our earliest parent's parent's parent!"

The others, thoroughly taken aback by their companion's ravings, merely stood silent and still as Prin continued in hushed exhilaration. "Look at how the tail is spiked, just like Ch'ran and Rysth-nuul. And see how the top fins are becoming long and round? They probably evolved into Tarrsk's tentacles."

Tarrsk narrowed its eyes at Prin, its expression one of mockery. "Really? And how do you know all of this? Did you see it get buried? How do you even know it lived here? Were you there?"

"Well, no, of course not. But it is clear that it was buried, because that is the only way it can become rock like this," Prin said in defense. "And the smooth surface of the ground could be the result of an underground river."

"*Could* be. But you do not know for sure. And tell me, how do you know it lived millions of years ago? Did it tell you? And what makes you think it was one of our parent's parent's parent?"

Prin faced its challenger head on. "As a scientist, I make guesses based on what makes sense from what I see. Here I see a being that has many similarities with the clans in this area. Therefore, it is reasonable to believe that it was our parent's parent's parent."

Tarrsk was not daunted by Prin's response. "But there could be other explanations that fit what we see. For all we know, it was a slave that was captured in a hunt far from here. We do not even know if it had any off-spring. All we know for sure is that it died! You cannot *know* anything. All you can do is guess."

Prin's demeanor changed at the criticism. Tiny blue sparks from its fingertips shone brightly in the dim passage as it fought with itself to contain its anger and frustration. "What do you know of science? Why do you think we scientists do not go on hunts? It is because our brains are more evolved than yours."

The alligator-like alien did not back down at the insult, but rather broadened its chest and leaned toward the smaller creature. "I do not think it is because you have a more evolved brain, but because you are a better liar and storyteller. Do not try to trick us with your stupid stories. Any fool could tell that you just made up that whole thing."

"That is enough, Tarrsk," Sikaris said firmly as it stepped in between the two of them.

"You do not understand, Griben Guts," Prin continued, ignoring the feline-like alien. "This is a link to our past!"

Ch'ran covered its mouth to keep from howling with laughter. "Griben Guts! That was a good one, Prin!"

"So? What good does that do us now?" Tarrsk countered. At Sikaris' warning growl, it backed away slightly. "Just one more thing. Is it going to help us get out of here? No. So it is useless. A waste of time. Let us go." Ending the confrontation, the alligator-like alien turned away and began heading off down the tunnel.

"He is right, Prin," Sikaris said, with finality. "We have already lost too much time. Come."

"I thought at least you would understand, but you are just as stupid as they are," it growled in disgust.

Sikaris merely looked at the ferret-like creature, its face showing no sign of anger. "Think what you want. We do not have time for this now." Turning away, it moved to join the others.

As much as Rebecca wanted to defend Prin, she knew that her help would probably not be welcome. Most of them already believed she was crazy, so anything she said would only make matters worse. In addition, like so many other things that had happened since her arrival, she found this fossil and Tarrsk's accusations disturbing. Tucking away her questions for further contemplation, she followed the others as they continued their quest, leaving Prin alone to say goodbye to its priceless treasure.

Angry and dejected, Prin followed behind as they continued down the passage. Rebecca once again walked on in silence, staring down constantly at her motion detector as they went. The machine eased her tension some, allowing her to lower her sense of alertness to bearable levels.

Then, just as she had begun to relax slightly, the readout on the display screen began to twitch. She froze instantly, her heart beating madly. *Oh God, what now?* She forced herself to calm down and called out softly to the others. "Stop! Wait! I have picked up something."

The alien hunters froze instantly as the translation came through their earpieces. After a quick visual scan of the area, Sikaris moved closer to her while the rest remained motionless and alert.

"What is it?" Sikaris asked quietly.

"I don't know," she replied as she worked with the controls on the tiny hand-held unit. "I am not getting actual movement, but there is definitely some kind of electronic signal bouncing off of the walls. It seems to be originating from around that corner up ahead of us."

Sikaris motioned to Prin with a wave of its claw. In a moment, the alien scientist joined them. After repeating her findings to Prin, it sat silently for a moment, deep in thought.

"We know these tunnels belong to the Modir, but we have never sent a hunting party this far into their territory," Prin said. "We do not know what kind of defenses they may have in place. We do know that their technology is based upon their physical abilities, so this could be some kind of weapon to defend their territory. Yes, yes. What kind of signal is it?"

Rebecca checked her display screen, glad to be on speaking terms with Prin again. "An electronic pulse set to a very high frequency."

Prin nodded its head. "Yes, yes, that makes sense." Looking to Rebecca, it explained. "Modir do not have eyes. They do not even have a head. Instead, they have a membrane that makes high frequency sound waves. These waves bounce off of objects and are then picked up again by the Modir's sensitive antennae. This allows them to 'see.'"

"Like a radar, similar to bats," Rebecca said quietly in understanding.

The alien scientist only shrugged. "From what we know of their technology, it uses the same methods, yes, yes."

By this time the others had begun to grow restless, their eyes straining as they stared into the darkness for any whisper of movement. Tarrsk, its concentration focused on the enveloping blackness around them, sidled slowly to where the three of them stood in hushed conversation. "Why have we stopped?"

Sikaris responded without so much as a glance at the lanky reptile. "We may have found the Modir's outer defenses."

"So what are we waiting for? Let us kill them and move on."

"It is not that easy," Prin interjected. "We are not even sure what the defenses are."

"So let us go look. What is the problem?" Tarrsk sneered at Prin in derision.

Sikaris put a restraining claw on Tarrsk's shoulder. "The problem is that if Prin is correct, any movement around that corner will be immediately 'seen' by their machines without light, even though we would not be able to see them."

The alligator-like alien was silent for a moment before offering a suggested course of action. "If I blend in with the wall, I could climb onto the ceiling and drop down on it from above. Even though my disease does not let me blend in totally, maybe the darkness will help hide me."

Finding its chance, Prin unleashed some of its pent-up anger and frustration that had been building since the beginning of the hunt. "You Drak slime! Go back to watching for the Modir and leave the thinking to those of us with larger brains, yes, yes!" Ignoring Tarrsk's threatening growl, the alien scientist continued. "This machine 'sees' with sound, not by light. Your ability to blend in would not help, neither would walking on the ceiling."

Tarrsk's eyes revealed that it had made a mistake even while the mouth on its stomach formed a nasty snarl, revealing its broken, yellow teeth. "Then maybe Sikaris' roar could destroy its ability to hear. Have you thought of that?"

Sikaris answered before Prin could think up a retort. "I have to see what I am aiming at. Also, we do not even know what is out there or how far away it is. It could alert the Modir and kill me before I even see it."

Feeling foolish in front of Prin, Tarrsk became frustrated. "Then what are we going to do? We have not found any other passages."

"If you would leave us alone and stop asking stupid questions, we could think of a solution," Prin snapped, barely keeping its voice to a whisper.

Even as Tarrsk's muscular body tensed in preparation to strike, Rebecca suddenly spoke, diffusing the conflict.

"I think I have a solution," she said excitedly. Seeing that she had their attention, she expounded. "My motion detector operates similarly to the way Prin described the Modir's ability. It should be able to determine the frequency of the Modir device. Then, I can set the motion detector to emit a cloaking signal at the same frequency, effectively making the person who carries it invisible. Since the Modir do not use light, that person could use a flashlight to locate whatever is creating the signal and destroy it, allowing the rest of us to follow later."

The three aliens stared at her momentarily in silence. Then, slowly, a grin formed on Sikaris' strong features. As its violet eyes reflected the light from the electric lanterns, Rebecca noticed for the first time how symmetrical its features were. Every other creature she had seen on this planet had eyes, noses, arms, mouths, and other physical structures in odd places. Yet Sikaris' entire body showed no sign whatsoever of asymmetry. Her curiosity about this formidable alien deepened, even as the number of questions about it increased.

"Good," Sikaris said, its low voice growling deep in its chest. "Prepare the device. I will carry it with me and destroy whatever defenses they have."

"What?" Rysth-nuul said in shock as the translation came through its earpiece. Slithering across the cavern, it stopped in front of the alien leader. "You are going to put our survival in the hands of this crazy being that thinks it is from another planet? What is wrong with you? You gamble too much with our lives. And why do you always defend this…this…weak creature?"

"What do *you* think we should do, Rysth-nuul? Go charging around the corner, announcing to the entire mountain that we are here?" Sikaris shot back. "We have no other choice. The way behind us is blocked, and there are no other passages. Besides, what is the worst that will happen? I fail and the Modir know we are here. That will happen anyway if we do not try something. Now let Rebecca work and just be ready to charge in case he is wrong."

Listening to Sikaris' explanation of what would occur if she miscalculated or erred caused her heart to leap into her throat. Mustering her courage, she set to work on the motion detector, being sure to triple check every step.

As she worked, she saw out of the corner of her eye that Prin was watching her intently. She resisted the temptation to look at the alien scientist, but instead pretended to keep working. Although she was getting better at reading Prin's facial expressions, she still wasn't sure if it was looking at her approvingly, or with pity.

Focus, Becky! she chided herself. Shutting out everything around her, as well as all thoughts of the future, she concentrated on the task at hand.

After several long minutes, she completed her work, confident that she had calibrated the machine properly. *Here goes nothing.*

Walking towards Sikaris, she handed it the device. The Grinathian leader stared at her as it accepted the motion detector, its eyes succeeding once again in making her feel uncomfortably weak and powerless, yet strangely comforted. Without so much as a 'thank you' or 'good-bye,' it secured the makeshift stealth device around its waist with a length of rope and set off.

The creature's fluidity and grace were incredible. Within moments, Sikaris had reached the bend in the passage without making a single sound.

Rebecca and the others stood alert and intent upon the retreating figure, their muscles taut and ready to spring into action, for they knew that their continued existence would be decided in the next several seconds. As they stood transfixed, Rebecca caught movement out of the corner of her left eye. Tearing her gaze from Sikaris, she saw Prin move up beside her, its eyes not even glancing her way.

Turning her attention forward once again, she watched in consuming fear and excitement as Sikaris' form disappeared around the bend.

In her mind she could plainly hear a blaring alarm that shook the very ground beneath them. She was about to begin running for her life when the realization hit her that the others were not reacting at all. For a brief instant, she thought that they had been paralyzed by the sound. But when she saw Prin exhale and smile, she realized that the sound of the alarm was only a product of her overworked imagination.

"It seems to have worked, yes, yes! Good work, Rebecca Clan Evans."

Before she could recover enough of her faculties to respond to the compliment, Rysth-nuul hissed quietly behind them. "You fools! We have no idea if it worked or not. For all we know, the Modir may already be on their way here, while we sit by quietly like tied-up Cronlets."

Prin turned and gave the pessimistic alien a disapproving glare. "But we probably would have heard an alarm."

"Probably," it said, edging closer. The smooth manner in which its muscles propelled its body forward sent shivers of queasiness down Rebecca's spine. "But what if the alarm sounds somewhere else? Or what if it makes a sound that only Modir can hear? We will not know for sure until they attack, and by then it will be too late."

Rebecca found herself hating Rysth-nuul more and more each time the creature spoke. She hated it not only for being so pessimistic, but for having the uncanny knack for being right. *Even if Sikaris returns, we can't be 100% sure he was successful,* she thought in frustration.

Even as this thought crossed her mind, they all tensed in unison as they detected movement from near the bend. A moment later they released their collective breath as Sikaris emerged from the darkness.

"The way is clear," the feline alien said as it neared the group. "There were three machines guarding the corridor. I was able to deactivate them without being detected."

"How can you be so sure?" Rysth-nuul said, repeating its previous argument.

Sikaris did not seem the slightest bit affected by Rysth-nuul's doubt. "Because the six guns placed around the walls of the corridor and controlled by the three machines did not shred me to pieces."

The others stood in silence for a moment as they digested this latest bit of news. Finally, Tarrsk's guttural curse broke the stillness. "Kraktcha! If we had gone any farther…"

Sikaris nodded at Tarrsk's unfinished thought. Then, turning to Rebecca, it handed the motion detector back to her. "Reset the machine and continue monitoring. Let us go. The longer we wait, the more chance there is of being found."

Without delay, they began to follow Sikaris. Rebecca had just finished situating her pack on her shoulder when she was suddenly shoved hard from behind. Throwing her arms out in front of her, she managed to prevent herself from smashing face first into the floor. Jumping quickly back to her feet, she turned around to face the perpetrator. She immediately swallowed her pride and anger at the sight of the spiked alien towering over her. It did not offer any explanation, but merely looked at her, then headed off down the passage.

Dumbfounded, Rebecca simply stared after it. Suddenly, the annoying voice of Ch'ran spoke beside her. "That is how Joktan's say 'good job.'"

Calling upon every ounce of willpower, she didn't shy away from the leering face that was staring up at her. "Nix and I say 'good job' also. Maybe I will not eat you after all."

Not sure how to respond, Rebecca refrained from commenting and proceeded to brush herself off. Resituating her equipment, she headed after the others.

They rounded the corner that Sikaris had traversed minutes prior, their lights illuminating the path in front of them. After walking for several yards, they came upon the death trap that Sikaris had deactivated. The sight of the ominous weapons pointing threateningly at them caused the hackles to rise on her neck, despite the knowledge that Sikaris had successfully disabled them. *This part of the cavern is so narrow, and so far from the entrance, we would have been torn to bits,* she thought dismally.

Breathing more easily once they had moved passed the deadly machines and into the passage beyond, they traveled several more minutes before encountering yet another bend, from around which a pale red glow seemed to emanate. Upon receiving a questioning look from Sikaris, Rebecca consulted the motion detector. Seeing nothing out of the ordinary in the display screen, she shook her head negatively. With a wave of its claw, Sikaris motioned to Jorylk, who proceeded to peer slowly around the corner. After a moment of intense silence, it signaled for them to continue. Once around the corner, they found themselves facing a seven-foot rocky shelf.

Tarrsk climbed the shelf with practiced ease and looked over the edge. After a quick perusal of the surroundings, the agile alien gestured for the others to join it. They spread out and climbed up enough to see over the edge the scene that lay before them. Nestled in a type of underground valley, bathed in hazy red sunlight that shone through a hole in the cavern ceiling, lay a Modir outpost.

14

The Garden

REBECCA'S MIND frantically sought to make sense of the odd sight in front of her. The outpost, for that is what her limited knowledge assumed it to be, stretched out across the area, the near edge of which sat roughly one hundred feet downhill from where she and the others were hidden. The high, circular cavern that housed the outpost reminded her of a small, domed coliseum.

Encircling the entire camp was an open pathway that was roughly twenty feet wide on average. Six other passages identical to their own led from the outer path into the mountain.

In the entrance of the passageway on the side of the valley directly opposite from their position, several stocky aliens were loading items into what looked like a type of mining car. Although the reddish-light provided by the hole in the ceiling was an improvement over their flashlights and lanterns, it still did not afford them enough light to make out many details.

What Rebecca could see, however, made the bile rise in her throat. Although the Modir had necks, they were not used to support heads. Instead, their necks ended in stumps that had a kind of vibrating membrane stretched over the top, similar to a drum. The rest of their broad, barrel-like bodies reminded her of moles. But unlike the furry rodents from Earth, these creatures had no hair to cover their twisted, mutated bodies. Instead, their skin seemed to be similar to that of the Ryazan: dark and scale-like.

Looking away from the bizarre aliens, she gazed at the surrounding area. It took her a moment to comprehend what it was that covered the majority of the cavern. Jumbled together in groups throughout the area were numerous twisted pillars of various heights, shapes, and sizes, each of which had crooked beams protruding from odd places with no apparent purpose or pattern. Rebecca was further confused by the fact that the pillars seemed to be made of a material that resembled the reptilian skin of her companions. Moving around slowly underneath the strange pillars were the outlines of several different species of aliens, each shuffling along as if in a daze.

In sudden recognition, Rebecca inhaled sharply. "An underground forest," she whispered aloud to herself.

Sikaris, its large feline-shaped head peering over the edge of the rocky shelf next to her, corrected her assessment. "No. A garden."

Finally her mind fitted the remaining pieces together, the truth filling her with a mixture of awe and disgust. "You mean, those are plants…I mean, Lirid…Lidr…"

"Lidrilian," Ch'ran offered, coming up closer on her other side. "And very tasty, too!" Ch'ran's forked tongue flicked out of its twisted mouth and licked its dry, crusty lips. "This is good! Not only did we find a way out, but we found some food, too! Rebecca, you have to try the offspring of the short, purple ones. Ooooooh!" it squinted and crinkled its face into an expression of ecstasy as it squealed softly.

"Prin, what do you think?" Sikaris asked, returning the groups attention to their immediate circumstances. "Can we sneak by without being seen?"

"Why sneak by," Tarrsk interjected, "when we can take them? I see only about ten or twelve Modir. The few Hran slaves they have harvesting the Lid offspring might help us, too."

Prin responded before Sikaris could answer, thoroughly enjoying getting the intellectual upper hand on one of its antagonists. "The main Modir clan may not have found out that their machines are broken, so they will not come looking for us if they do not know we are here. But if we kill some of them and destroy their garden, they will probably not be very happy, yes, yes."

The alligator-like head swiveled to glare at Prin, but if Tarrsk was sneering at it, Rebecca couldn't tell, as its lithe torso was pressed up against the side of the raised floor, covering its mouth. But even if Tarrsk had a comeback, Prin didn't allow it the chance to speak. "However, to answer Sikaris' question, no, I do not think it is possible. If even one of the Modir points its vibrating sound producer in our direction, the Modir will know we are here. I think we have no choice but to attack them."

Tarrsk, surprised by Prin having agreed with it, remained silent. Rysth-nuul, however, took up the argument in its stead. "I agree. But the problem is, how do we murder all of the Modir without any of them escaping or calling for help?"

The group was silent as they pondered the question and studied the layout of the cavern. At first, Rebecca did not understand Rysth-nuul's concern. Then, as she surveyed the area more carefully, she caught sight of three distinct groups of the odd looking Modir.

Besides the group at the far end of the tunnel loading the mining car, there were several of the headless, mole-like creatures on the left side of the cavern huddled around what looked to be some type of computer or machine. Finally, interspersed throughout the pathways within the garden were several more of the aliens.

As Rebecca was observing this last group, she saw a Modir swivel its neck towards one of the bizarre, tree-like aliens that comprised the garden. Suddenly, a gnarled and twisted branch began to move towards the mole-like being as if in slow motion. The Modir slave master, detecting the attack through its internal radar system, quickly held up some sort of device in its claw. Instantly, the tree-like slave made a cacophony of sound with its branches as it began to wilt and withdraw them towards its trunk at the same sluggish pace.

Rebecca was so transfixed by the drama before her that she forgot her surroundings, until the sudden monotonous tone of her translation unit brought her focus back to bear on Sikaris as it gave commands to the group. "The Modir must point their sound producer in our direction in order to detect us. Therefore, Tarrsk should be able to climb across the ceiling of the cavern without the Modir knowing. Tarrsk, can you carry Ch'ran while upside down?"

"Yes, he is small enough," it replied while unconsciously scratching a particularly white patch of scales on its chest.

"Good. When you and Ch'ran have reached the far side, wait for the signal and see to it that the Modir loading the cart do not escape."

Ch'ran was nearly exploding from pent-up excitement at the prospect of the coming battle. "Nix will help too, right Sikaris?"

"Sure," Rysth-nuul hissed. "Maybe it could make the wind blow away from you to save us from your bad stench. That would help."

The little creature's mood was not affected in the least by the snide remark. "We are going to murder! We are going to murder!" it chanted in a shrill, sing-song voice, although the straight tone of the translator caused it to lose some of its macabre jollity.

"As soon as Ch'ran and Tarrsk attack," Sikaris continued, "I will jump towards the machines with Prin on my back. Prin will make sure the Modir do not use the machines to call for help while I stop the others from escaping.

"Once the remaining Modir are distracted by the attacks, Jorylk will attack the Modir in the garden. Rysth-nuul and Rebecca will remain here and cover Jorylk's charge with gunfire."

The great, spiked alien said nothing, as usual, but simply twisted its already crooked mouth into a grotesque grin.

"Any questions?" Sikaris asked.

Rebecca was slightly taken aback at the blood-lust she now saw in the eyes of her companions. Each one of them, including Prin, seemed eager to begin killing. These were not mere animals hunting for food or defending themselves, these were malicious, intelligent beings who desired to kill simply for pleasure.

Except Sikaris, she noted mentally. Although darkness obscured much of its features, it almost seemed to Rebecca that she detected a trace of sadness on its face. She immediately dismissed the notion, reminding herself that these creatures do not feel those types of emotions.

With nothing further to be said, Tarrsk and Ch'ran moved towards the wall to begin their treacherous climb. "Watch that tail of yours," Tarrsk hissed as the diminutive armadillo-like alien climbed up its back, giggling madly.

The rest of the group watched in silence as Tarrsk began slowly ascending the cavern wall. In a matter of minutes, Rebecca lost sight of the two aliens among the dark crevasses of the ceiling. After several minutes of anxious waiting with no visible sign of them, Rebecca was beginning to wonder how they were to know when the pair reached their ready position. However, before she could venture the question, Sikaris inadvertently answered it with a question of its own.

"How is their progress, Rysth-nuul?"

The alien's four misaligned eyes were fixed upon a point far above on the ceiling. "They are almost halfway there."

"What about the number of Modir? Have you made an exact count?"

Rysth-nuul shifted its gaze down to inspect the area. "I count two by the machines on the left, three in the back by the cart, and another seven within the garden."

Sikaris nodded in agreement. "Twelve."

Suddenly, Prin's two right hands grasped Sikaris' arm in alarm. Look!" it whispered urgently, its left hands pointing towards the machine station.

Two large Modir from within the garden began walking towards the machines at the beckon of the operators stationed there. The four aliens huddled briefly over the devices, then one of them pointed towards the cave entrance where Rebecca and her companions were hidden.

"This does not look good," Rysth-nuul stated.

As they watched with trepidation, their fears were confirmed. The two gardeners broke off from the others and began heading straight for them.

"Blast it!" Rysth-nuul spat. "They must have found out that their machines are broken. Now what do we do?"

"Everyone down," Sikaris ordered. The group immediately obeyed and ducked behind the rocky shelf. "We stay with the plan." Reaching inside its skin folds, the feline-like alien switched its translator to commlink. "Tarrsk, Ch'ran—we may have to attack sooner than planned. We have two Modir coming towards us, so we will have to attack first. Tarrsk, as soon as we attack, use your tentacles and try to stop them from escaping. Ch'ran, if you are low enough to the ground, drop and attack."

Not expecting a verbal reply due to their precarious position, Sikaris switched off its commlink and turned to look at the others. "We will wait as long as we can. When the Modir come over the ledge, we attack."

They all nodded agreement, then moved to the sides of the cavern and placed their backs against the cold cave walls. Silence reigned heavily around them until the pounding of Rebecca's heart became a roar in her ears. Then, after nearly a minute of strained listening, she began to detect a slight clacking sound of claws striking hard rock and dirt.

Sikaris held its claw up, gesturing for the others to wait. Then, the clacking noise, which had been slowly growing louder, inexplicably ceased. For a split second she saw Sikaris' eyes go wide in sudden realization, then it leapt to its feet, its jaws gaping open. This time, however, Rebecca was momentarily stunned by the sheer volume of sound that was produced by her alien companion. The effect on the two approaching Modir was even more profound. Standing directly in the path of the roar, and being extremely sensitive to sound, the Modir were immediately rendered unconscious.

The reverberation of Sikaris' attack echoed throughout the cavern for several seconds. As if choreographed, every creature in the expansive underground area turned towards them in the same instant.

"What are you doing?" Rysth-nuul hissed in frustration.

Sikaris, ignoring the snake-like alien, barked out a command. "Attack now!"

Several things happened simultaneously, leaving Rebecca breathless. First, Sikaris jumped the seven-foot shelf and headed off towards the left side of the cavern. Prin, instantly discerning Sikaris' intentions, matched the great alien's stride, then leapt onto its back with the finesse of an acrobat. A second later, Sikaris' mighty muscles surged and launched the two beings into the air.

At the same time, Jorylk lurched up and forward, its deformed mouth letting out a wild battle cry as it charged towards the garden, its heavy rifle spewing forth death to all in its path.

In tandem with Jorylk's attack, Rysth-nuul let out a barrage of gunfire from its twin hand-held pistols. Rebecca, following Sikaris' instructions, popped up over the edge of the shelf and added her weapon's harmony to the discordant melody of her companions' attacks. In the midst of the commotion, Rebecca barely took note of the shadowy form that dropped from the ceiling at the far side of the garden near the mining cart.

The Modir, although startled by the sudden burst of sound, recovered quickly. The machine operators, detecting the large, cat-like alien hurtling through the air toward them, abandoned their post and began running on two legs towards the nearest passageway while simultaneously attempting to extract pistol-like weapons from pouches on their hips.

This proved to be their undoing; for had they simply run on all fours, they may have escaped into the nooks and crannies of familiar territory. But by running slower, they gave Sikaris the extra few seconds it needed to reach them.

Altering its flight path to intercept the fleeing aliens, the Grinathian leader crashed full force into them. The weight of Sikaris' massive frame, combined with the momentum of the leap, snapped the first creature's neck, ending its desperate flight.

The second Modir, although thrown from its feet, quickly regained its balance and continued running towards the exit. Sikaris recovered rapidly from the collision, but momentarily lost sight of its foe as gunfire from the direction of the garden caused it to dive for cover behind a stack of crates. A second later, the gunner suddenly changed targets to focus on Prin, who had leapt to the ground just before the initial impact with the Modir.

Taking advantage of Prin's diversion, Sikaris bolted from its protective cover and chased after the fleeing Modir. As the Grinathian leader reached the cave entrance, it could see the frantic alien turning around and beginning to take aim, the barrel of its weapon pointed directly at Sikaris' head.

However, even as it prepared to fire, it continued to retreat farther into the passage. Suddenly, light exploded from every direction as the Modir outer defenses snuffed out the light of one of those it was designed to protect.

The moment Prin's six limbs reached the moist earth, it ran swiftly towards the tech station. The ferret-like alien had barely reached its destination when several hard, metallic projectiles slammed into the machine, sending Prin diving to the ground for cover. Pulling an explosive from its bandolier, the alien scientist armed it with a flash of blue. Venturing a quick glance over the top of the machine, it located the Modir attacker standing not more than forty feet away on the nearby garden pathway. Pausing for a moment to aim, Prin launched the grenade at its opponent, then ducked back down behind the tech station. An instant later, the sound of a violent explosion rocked the area. After a few moments of silence, it peered around the side of its makeshift bunker to inspect its handiwork. Next to the bodies of several of the Hran and Lidrilian slaves, the mole-like alien lay motionless on its back, each of its shovel-like appendages bent at odd angles.

Prin simply smiled.

The instant Sikaris had roared, Tarrsk, still hanging upside down on the ceiling, sent forth a barrage of sharp pellets from its tentacles towards the startled Modir below. However, since it had not yet reached its intended position of attack, it was too far away to be accurate. Even with this disadvantage, Tarrsk's volley still managed to kill one of the three Modir, as well as injure a second.

The third, uninjured alien stood up from behind the cart which it had used for cover and began running on all fours down the tunnel, ignoring the pleas for help from its companion.

Ch'ran let out a loud "whoop" as it released its grip on Tarrsk and fell towards the floor some fifty feet below. The insane creature somersaulted in midair and grabbed onto one of the upper branches of a surprised

Lidrilian. The plant-like being reacted by smashing its limbs together in an effort to shake off the intruder. However, the agile alien had leapt to the ground, shrieking with glee, long before the garden-dweller could attack.

As soon as its rabbit-like hind limbs touched the ground, Ch'ran bounded off in hot pursuit of the fleeing Modir. Without even slowing its pace, it finished off the wounded alien as it passed with a quick thrust from its poisonous tail, even as the creature drew its weapon to defend itself.

Drawing its own pistol from its waist pouch, Ch'ran entered the dark cave. Flipping on its flashlight, it searched the area for its prey. The beam of light fell upon a small, but rapidly expanding cloud of mist near the wall. Taking a deep breath, Ch'ran plunged head first into it. Reaching the wall, the armadillo-like being reached out and grabbed the hind leg of the headless alien just before it could disappear inside the newly dug exit.

The panicked being kicked loose dirt in Ch'ran's face, trying desperately to dislodge its pursuer and seal up the exit. But the insane alien ducked its head beneath its hard, shell-like cowl for protection, then, with its free claw, thrust its pistol into the small hole and fired. Immediately the kicking stopped as the leg in Ch'ran's claw slackened and went limp. Leaping back out of the mist, Ch'ran took a deep breath and cackled maniacally, its laughter echoing throughout the underground cavern.

Meanwhile, on the opposite side of the cave, Rebecca, Rysth-nuul, and Jorylk pounded the edge of the garden with gunfire. Two Modir just inside the borders of the garden were mowed down instantly. Rebecca, seeing no more of the mole-like slavers, ceased firing, her gaze scanning the area for new targets. Rysth-nuul and Jorylk, however, seemed not to notice the lack of primary enemies, but continued to eliminate both Lidrilian and the animal-like Hran slaves that harvested the garden.

Jorylk reached the pathway unchallenged. The spiked alien, now enraged with blood-lust, continued down the path in search of more of the underground dwellers. Its search ended when it reached the center of the garden; for huddled together in the small circular clearing were the three remaining Modir.

Detecting the monstrous alien bearing down on them, they immediately opened fire, hitting Jorylk's armored hide several times. However, instead of stopping, or even slowing the giant down, it merely served to enrage it further.

Throwing its heavy rifle aside in favor of hand-to-hand combat, Jorylk launched itself at the group. Two of the Modir succeeded in dodging the wild attack, but the third was crushed beneath the hulking body of the seven-foot being.

Jorylk stood on all fours, turned its head to face its victims, and snarled viciously, blood oozing from the wounds inflicted by the Modir's initial attack. The two surviving aliens simply held their weapons up and aimed directly at Jorylk's deformed head, certain of victory.

Suddenly, branch-like arms wrapped around the mole-like creatures from behind, causing them to lose their grips on their weapons. The plant-like Lidrilian held the squirming Modir tightly in its grasp, crushing the breath from its four-foot frame.

One of the slavers managed to twist itself free from the death-like grip, only to stumble directly into the waiting arms of Jorylk. The incensed member of Clan Grinath held its victim in a crushing embrace, thrashing from side to side, driving the spikes adorning its armored hide into the scale-like flesh of the Modir.

In a last-ditch effort to prolong its life, the doomed alien extended a thin proboscis from the side of its headless neck and released a thin mist into Jorylk's face. Coughing and sputtering, the spiked reptilian alien dropped the Modir and stumbled backward. Both creatures collapsed in a heap on the garden floor; one mortally wounded, the other unconscious from the toxic gas.

With both combatants down, the Lidrilian that had saved Jorylk began to move. Ripping up huge clods of dirt, it slowly extracted its massive roots from the dark, underground soil. Once its entire network of roots was free, it used them to propel itself slowly towards the giant creature's body. Hovering over the motionless form, the creature raised its thick, branch-like limbs menacingly.

15

Revelations

THE TALL Lidrilian suddenly reeled back in pain, its thick limbs pulling away from Jorylk's motionless body.

Rebecca stood on the path beside Rysth-nuul, who was holding the slaver's control device pointed directly at the encroaching alien. "Get away from him, Lid scum," Rysth-nuul commanded.

Rebecca stared in wonder at the creature as it shuffled away. All around her were living, moving, intelligent plants! Although they did not resemble any particular species of plants on Earth, they did share similar characteristics. Most had a cylindrical, trunk-like torso supported by a network of roots, which dug into the ground, anchoring them in place. Yet, unlike any plants she had ever seen, these could uproot themselves and move about like some multi-legged insect. Their upper bodies contained anywhere between two and fifteen arm-like limbs, depending on the clan.

Judging by the variety of colors, shapes, and sizes surrounding them, Rebecca guessed that this particular garden contained a wide selection of Lidrilian clans.

The creature that stood before them reached a height of almost ten feet. Its thick, dark purple trunk, which was spotted throughout with bumps and knobs of all kinds, split into three twisted, arm-like branches. On the tips of each branch were several long, flexible tendrils that appeared to serve as fingers. Rebecca could see no mouth or head on this particular specimen, or any of the other Lidrilian that inhabited the garden for that matter. *I will have to ask Prin about that, if he will even speak to me,* she thought.

As they watched, the tendrils on the ends of the branches began to move, a whistling sound emanating from their tips. "I will not hurt him. I would not want to make you angry with me."

The sudden translation caused Rebecca to spin around, her eyes seeking out the speaker. It wasn't until Rysth-nuul responded to the tree-like creature that the truth dawned on her.

"You lie. You probably have not had a good meal for a long time, and you are not going to get one from him, so back off!"

The sound of approaching footsteps silenced any further conversation. Rebecca and Rysth-nuul were soon joined by Sikaris and the others as they each returned from their separate skirmishes. They quickly compared notes, eager to ascertain if any of the underground dwellers had escaped to alert the main Modir force.

"Luck seems to be with us," Sikaris said finally. "Ch'ran, go back to the cave we entered from and finish off the two unconscious Modir before they wake up."

The small creature nodded and smiled wickedly. "Sure. Just do not start eating the Lid offspring without me and Nix," it said as it bounded off down the path.

"Prin, check on Jorylk," Sikaris said as Ch'ran quickly disappeared. "If he is still alive, see what you can do to help him."

Prin nodded, then moved over to where the large alien lay facedown on the hard, stone pathway.

With the immediate concerns taken care of, Rysth-nuul narrowed its eyes and shot an accusatory glare at Sikaris. "Luck is right. What is the matter with you? Why did you attack early? We were VERY lucky none of us were killed."

Sikaris returned the creature's hard gaze without flinching. "If I had not attacked early, we would all be slaves of the Modir by now."

"What?" Rysth-nuul said skeptically. "How?"

"When I heard the Modir footsteps stop as they were approaching our hiding place, I realized that they were going to gas the whole cave. They must have thought that since the defenses were down, they should be extra careful. When I attacked them, they already had their gas sprayers out."

The others, realizing how close they had come to being captured, sat in stunned silence. Rysth-nuul, once again embarrassed in front of the rest of the group, decided to change topics. "So, what is your next brilliant plan," it said sarcastically.

Without answering, Sikaris turned and surveyed the carnage around them. In addition to the Modir, all of the Hran slaves, as well as a good number of Lidrilian, lay dead. Only a dozen or so of the plant-like aliens remained. "Do any of you understand me?" the Grinathian leader asked the odd assortment of slaves. Sikaris repeated the question several times in different languages, causing Rebecca to ponder anew how it was that this strange being understood English. And not only did it speak English fluently, but with no accent. Try as she might, she simply couldn't come up with a plausible explanation to account for it.

Suddenly, the Lidrilian slave that had saved Jorylk whistled a response. "Yes. I understand."

Ignoring the others and focusing its attention on the speaker, Sikaris asked, "Do you know a way to the surface?"

"Yes. There are many ways. I have lived here a long time. I know the best ways."

Rysth-nuul shook its head. "I do not like this, Sikaris. I do not think we should trust a Lid."

The cat-like alien turned its gaze towards Rysth-nuul. "It is our best choice. We need a guide through these caves."

The snake-like alien hissed in disapproval, yet it could not deny Sikaris' logic. As they spoke, the tree-like being shuffled towards them, causing Rysth-nuul to raise the slaver device warningly. Fearing further pain, the creature stopped immediately.

"I want to speak," it said.

Sikaris looked toward the slave. "What do you want?"

"I, Lri Errhu, promise to help you. But you must help me, too. When we are out, you will frcc me."

Hissing vilely, Rysth-nuul pressed the button on the device in its wicked claws, sending bolts of electrical pain through the slave's trunk-like body. "You are a slave. We make the deals, not you. And if we want to know your name, we will ask for it!"

"That is enough," Sikaris said calmly. "It does not understand you anyway, so save your energy."

Giving the plant-like alien one last burst of pain just out of sheer spite, Rysth-nuul released the button and relaxed.

"We agree," Sikaris said in the same odd language. "If you lead us out, we will free you."

Prin stood up from where it had been examining Jorylk's body and crossed back over to join the rest of the group. "Jorylk is unconscious from Modir gas. His wounds are not very bad. I gave him a shot that should wake him up in about fifteen minutes."

Sikaris nodded in acknowledgement of Prin's report as Ch'ran came bouncing down the path, its vile task accomplished. Addressing the group, Sikaris instructed them on their next coarse of action. "Ch'ran, you and Rysth-nuul will feed this Lidrilian. Use the Modir. Tarrsk, check out the opening in the ceiling to see if we can somehow get out that way. Prin and Rebecca, watch Jorylk and make sure no other slaves bother him."

"Here, you might need this," Rysth-nuul said, still clearly not happy about the situation. It tossed the slave controlling device to Prin, who caught it deftly in one of its four claws.

"I will be searching the area," Sikaris continued. "Once Jorylk is awake and the Lidrilian is fed, we leave."

They immediately set off to accomplish their assigned tasks. Rysth-nuul fuming as it went. Rebecca watched it go, her unease growing. *How much more will it take?* she wondered. What would she do if Rysth-nuul decided it had had enough? This entire group was only held together with the thin strand of Sikaris' leadership. She knew that Sikaris was stronger, but what if Rysth-nuul caught it by surprise? Tarrsk would probably side with Rysth-nuul. And Ch'ran and Jorylk couldn't care less, it seemed. That only left Prin, and even it seemed ready to side against Sikaris because of her.

Let it not come to that, she prayed. For the first time in her life she wished she actually believed there was some kind of supreme being that was guiding her. She now fully understood one of the reasons that religion appealed to so many: it gives them purpose, direction, security, and adds meaning to life. *"Wishful thinking,"* she had always said. *"Religion is a crutch for those who can't face the cold hard facts of life. We are the masters of our own destinies!"* Her own words seemed to taunt her now. *But what happens when you lose control? What happens when your destiny controls you? That is when belief in God really comes in handy.* Her own beliefs and convictions, by contrast, left her feeling hollow, empty, and alone.

"Rebecca," Prin called to her as it was walking over to where Jorylk lay. "Come here."

She forced back her disturbing thoughts and switched mental gears. Following Prin over to the side of the garden, she came up alongside the alien scientist, whose attention was now focused on the purplish tree-like alien.

"Have you ever seen a Lidrilian feed?" Prin asked. Before she could answer, it answered its own question. "No, of course not."

Unsure as to whether Prin was ridiculing her or simply stating a fact, she remained silent.

"Go ahead, yes, yes," Prin called to Errhu. "Eat."

The strange alien, determining Prin's meaning by its hand gestures, shuffled over to one of the dead Modir lying on the pathway. As she watched in fascinated horror, the creature lifted up several of its foremost roots and plunged the sharp tips into the lifeless corpse. Immediately the roots began to pulsate as blood was pumped through them into the torso of the living tree. As the seconds passed, the creature seemed to expand, growing stronger before their eyes. Lifting its three twisted limbs into the air in ecstasy, it waved them about, its movements noticeably quicker.

Suddenly, the other Lidrilian slaves, having figured out what was happening, began to wave their mangled branches and limbs, their tendrils whistling in their peculiar speech. Rebecca's translator tried to keep up, but was overwhelmed by the numerous voices speaking simultaneously. "Free me—I…help—Do… leave— Give… blood…blood…feed!"

Prin was instantaneously on its feet, using the slaver's device to shock them all into silent submission. After a moment, the commotion died down, returning the garden to its former state of eerie tranquility.

Errhu, completely absorbed in its feeding frenzy, continued without pause. Once the first Modir body was drained, it shuffled over to the second body and repeated the process.

With no further disturbances forthcoming, Prin resumed its discussion with Rebecca, all the while wary of the garden slaves. "It is taking all the minerals from the body. The more blood it drinks, the quicker it becomes, yes, yes," Prin explained. "By the time Jorylk wakes up, it should be fast enough to run with us, or away from us. But, that is what this is for," it said, holding the device it had just employed moments ago.

Disgusted by both its choice of food and its method of consuming it, Rebecca was nevertheless enthralled by the blood-sucking alien. As she watched in scientific fascination, a sudden thought struck her. "If blood makes them stronger and quicker, what happens if they don't drink any?" she asked. "Do they die from starvation?"

"No. They can feed off of the minerals they get through digging in the ground. But it makes them very slow and weak." Prin studied her for a moment as she digested this bit of news. "You believe that is what happened to the Lidrilian on your planet, yes, yes?"

Suddenly defensive, she looked at her companion, her face a mixture of frustration and pleading. "I know you do not believe me, but I am not lying to you. I admit, your questions about how my people, my clan, could have evolved confuse me too. But it happened." When Prin did not react harshly to her initial outburst, she grew bolder and continued to vent her feelings. "I don't know all of the details on how it happened, but I do know that it happened. The fact that I am alive is proof enough."

She half-expected Prin to lash out at her as it had previously done, or at least chide her or call her a fool. However, the ferret-like alien's reaction to her statements caught her completely off guard: it smiled.

"I believe you."

Rebecca was taken aback. "What? You…you do?"

"Yes, yes. At least, in part."

"What made you change your mind?"

Prin let out a staccato wheeze that Rebecca took for a chuckle. "It was actually something that Tarrsk said, believe it or not, back by the rock skeleton of the dead being. But first, let me ask you: do you have rock skeletons like that on your planet?"

Unsure whether Prin was being sincere or setting her up for further humiliation, she hesitated. Finally, deciding that there was no point in Prin insulting her again, especially considering the fact that the others were not around, she answered honestly. "Yes, we do. In fact, we have millions of them."

Prin paused for a moment in confusion. "I think the translator misunderstood you. It said 'millions of them,' but that cannot possibly be what you said, is it?"

Rebecca eyed the alien scientist suspiciously. "Yes, that is what I said. Why is that so hard to believe?"

"Well, because rock-skeletons are extremely rare," it replied. "If you really have millions of them, then something must have happened in the past to bury so many so quickly, otherwise they would not have become rock, yes, yes."

After a brief silence, Rebecca took a breath and prepared to reply, but then decided against it. The weasel-like alien simply stared at her with its crooked eyes, then shook its head in dismissal.

"But that is not important. That is not what I wanted to talk about," it said. "So, tell me, with all of those skeletons, you must have a clear record of how each clan evolved."

Again Rebecca hesitated, wondering where Prin's thoughts were leading. "Yes, and no. We have found many fossils, but it is difficult to be sure how they link together."

Prin looked at her curiously, its eyes bright and inquisitive. "But with millions of rock skeletons, why can you not understand? All you need to do is look at how one transitions into another."

"It's not quite that easy," she explained. "We have found many fossils, but not that many transitional ones. Most of our scientists believe that we evolved rapidly in spurts, leaving very little record of transition."

"Transitional ones?" Prin repeated. "But how can a rock skeleton *not* be transitional? Because of mutations, we are all in transition into something else. My offspring's offspring's offspring will be different from me. We are never complete. Evolution is always continuing."

Heat filled Rebecca's cheeks as her frustration level rose. "If you are not going to believe me, then why do you ask questions about my world?"

Prin shook its head. "No, no. You do not understand. I do believe you. In fact, what you are saying fits with my idea."

Rebecca, still on her emotional guard, looked at her companion skeptically. "What idea?"

"Well," it began, its posture resembling that of a school teacher explaining a new concept to a class, "you have said many things that do not make logical sense, such as: You *forgot* how to run on four legs; beings on your planet do not mutate often; you do not eat others in your clan; your offspring take a long time to mature; and, most unbelievably, it takes two of you to even make an offspring.

"So, I am left with two choices, yes, yes: either what you tell me is a lie, or it is a non-lie. If it is a lie, then I am left with two more choices: either you know you are lying, or you really think you are telling a non-lie."

A slight movement from Jorylk caused Prin to momentarily pause in its discourse. Making sure that their large companion was fine, Prin continued. "At first I believed you were telling a non-lie, but the more you told me about your planet, the more it seemed that it had to be a lie. Then, I thought that you might be insane, yes, yes, like Ch'ran. Maybe you really believed what you said about these strange things. But then I realized that you always say the same things; your stories do not change, and, as you showed with the Modir defenses, you are very intelligent, yes, yes.

"Even more, your body does not show any of the signs of evolution, at least not compared with the rest of us on Ka'esch. This made me think that maybe you really were telling a non-lie after all."

Rebecca's heart swelled with vindication. "So you do believe me, then?"

Prin smiled. "Yes, and no."

Her budding hope deflated like a balloon; confusion flooding her mind. So intent was her focus on Prin that she didn't even pay any attention to Ch'ran and Rysth-nuul as they returned, fed several more Modir to the Lidrilian slave, and departed once more. "What do you mean?" she asked.

The alien scientist stared at Rebecca with its typical blank expression. "Yes, yes, I do believe you are telling a non-lie. When we were looking at the rock skeleton, that brainless, under-evolved, diseased scum Tarrsk said something interesting. Although what he said was very, very wrong about the rock skeleton, it did make me think about you."

Rebecca rapidly searched through her memory of the incident, trying to pinpoint what the alligator-like alien had said. Finally, with no success, Rebecca prompted Prin to continue. "And? What did he say?"

"He said that there might be another explanation. Maybe you are telling a non-lie, but you do not even understand your own history correctly."

A strange, disturbing feeling began to take possession of her. *Another explanation? My own history? What is it talking about?* "An explanation for what? What history?" she asked, suddenly afraid to hear the answer.

Prin, as nonchalantly as reciting a simple math formula, said, "An explanation of how life began on your planet, yes, yes. Based on everything you have told me, the only theory that makes logical sense is that you did not evolve at all. You must have been made."

The ferret-like alien's words caught her completely off guard. *Made?* The very idea struck her as so outrageous and preposterous that she almost laughed out loud. However, Prin's ever-serious demeanor immediately stifled any mirth. *Is it serious?* "Made? As in, 'created'?" she said, trying to cover her reaction lest Prin take offense. "By whom, or what?"

"By beings from other worlds, yes, yes."

"You mean aliens? You think I was created by some clan here on Ka'esch?" she prompted.

"Not from here maybe. And I do not think they created *you.* They probably developed life on your planet, then left."

Created by aliens? Rebecca was silent for a moment, her brows furrowed and her eyes drifting off toward the ceiling of the cave as her mind sifted through her memories. She had heard of that theory before. "Directed panspermia," she said at last, looking back at Prin.

"What?" it asked, looking at her quizzically.

"Several of our scientists have proposed versions of that theory, but I never gave it serious consideration. But why do you say this is the most logical explanation?" she asked.

Prin looked at her with its dark, calculating eyes. "First, it would explain all of the strange things you have told me about your clan and your planet, yes, yes. And it also fits with an idea I have had for some time about Sikaris," it continued. "As I told you back at the Grinathian base, Sikaris is not from any clan that I know of. And, he knows many languages, including yours. How is that possible?" it asked, letting the question hang in the air for a moment before supplying a possible solution. "If you are from another planet, maybe Sikaris is also."

Rebecca remained quiet, her mind slowly digesting Prin's words. "Are you suggesting that Sikaris, or his clan, created life on my planet?"

Prin moved its body in what Rebecca had come to take as a shrug. "Maybe. Or maybe his clan and your clan were made by the same beings, yes, yes?" it replied. "You do have some similarities. You both are very symmetrical. I have seen some beings that are almost symmetrical, but none as perfect as Sikaris or you."

On the garden pathway beside them, Jorylk began to twitch, the spiked head turning back and forth as if caught in the grasp of some dark nightmare.

"Jorylk is beginning to wake up, yes, yes," Prin stated.

Rebecca, her mind engulfed in the depths of Prin's theory, barely heard the comment. Cracking her knuckles as she went, she began pacing the area, her mind mulling over the implications of this revelation.

The very concept that life on Earth was created or designed by intelligent beings was ludicrous. Hadn't she always derided and scoffed at those who believed that? Yet, she had never really believed in intelligent alien life forms either, and here she was surrounded by them. If aliens really did exist, then was it so illogical to think that some highly advanced species might not have created life on Earth? And what about Sikaris? Is it somehow connected to her?

The more she thought about it, the more her mind reeled from the possibilities. It was as if Pandora's Box had burst open in her head.

By this time, Rysth-nuul and Ch'ran had completed their gruesome task. Errhu, having finished its meal, was nearly exploding with new-found energy. Prin, noting the change, was now closely monitoring the slave, the control device readied in its clawed hand.

Jorylk's eyes suddenly popped open, as if cold water had just been thrown in its face. Leaping to its feet, its eyes darted back and forth, searching for enemies. For a moment, Rebecca feared they would have a repeat of the incident that occurred at the mouth of the cave.

However, the sight of the pile of dead Modir surrounded by its companions had a calming effect on the great brute.

"Do not worry, Jorylk," Ch'ran said in jest. "We finished off the Modir while you had your little nap."

The short-tempered beast did not find any humor in the small creature's statement. If it had not been for the lingering effects of the toxic gas, Rebecca was certain that Jorylk would have torn the little fiend to pieces. Instead, the spiked alien only sneered groggily.

Strolling over to Rebecca, Ch'ran tossed a purplish piece of alien fruit to her. She caught it reflexively, as her mind was still preoccupied.

"Try it," the impish figure said. "You will like it. It is Nix's favorite."

Although she did not feel like eating, her stomach was crying out in protest at the recent neglect. Not knowing when she might get her next chance to eat, she swallowed her revulsion at the thought of what it was she was ingesting and took a bite. *At least it is not raw meat,* she decided. Whether from her knowledge of her meal's origin, her current mental distraction, or the food itself, the "fruit" seemed tasteless. Forcing herself to eat, she slowly finished the entire serving, feeling the hunger pangs in the pit of her stomach begin to subside.

"It is good, right?" Ch'ran chirped. "See, I told you." Munching on one of its own, Ch'ran hummed contentedly to itself, reveling in each bite.

All at once, Ch'ran's jovial mood evaporated as Sikaris came bounding into the center of the garden, its eyes boring holes through the armadillo-like creature.

Tarrsk, who had just returned from its scouting mission near the hole in the ceiling, reported its findings, oblivious to Sikaris' baleful glare. "We cannot get out that way. Even if we could somehow get everyone up there, we would not fit through the metal grating."

Sikaris, ignoring the alligator-like creature entirely, strode purposefully up to Ch'ran, its face a mask of rage. "I thought you said you murdered the Modir that Tarrsk wounded?"

Ch'ran stood rooted to the garden floor, Lidrilian juice sliding down its mutated chin. "I stabbed it with my tail as I chased after the other one."

Sikaris' eyes narrowed. "I just checked. There are only two dead Modir by that passage; one filled with Tarrsk's rocks, and the other half buried in the hole. And," it paused, adding weight to its next statement, "the cart they were loading is missing."

A blanket of dread settled over the group. Slowly, each head turned to glare at Ch'ran accusingly.

Rysth-nuul was the first to vocalize its current opinion of the insane alien. "You idiot! Why did you not check to see that it was dead?"

Ch'ran stared up at them, a look of child-like innocence on its twisted features. "Because I asked Nix to do that."

After that pronouncement, Rebecca was sure that Ch'ran would end up as garden fertilizer. That may have been the case, too, had a sound heard far off in the distance not diverted attention away from the armadillo-like alien.

All those present in the underground garden froze instantly, their ears straining to identify the distant sound. Immediately the Lidrilian slaves began to wave their branches and rock back and forth in fear.

"What is that?" Tarrsk said, giving voice to the question on all of their minds. "It sounds like a waterfall, or someone pouring sand."

Errhu's tendrils began to whistle rapidly. "We must leave. Now!"

Sikaris stepped towards the plant-like slave. "Why? What is making that sound?"

"The Modir are coming!"

16

Escape From Mt. Kiabab

THE CLATTER of the approaching Modir sent the remaining Lidrilian slaves into a panicked frenzy. Prin shocked several, causing them to pause momentarily, but the majority of the creatures began shuffling off to siphon any blood they could find from the dead garden slaves and slavers, hoping to gain enough energy to flee from the coming horde.

"Prin, let them go," Sikaris called. "They may cause the Modir to split up, giving us a better chance to escape." Turning towards Errhu, Sikaris yelled, "Which way?"

"The Modir are blocking the best way. We must use the longer way. It is more dangerous," it whistled in reply.

"We do not care!" shouted Rysth-nuul impatiently, forgetting that the plant-like alien could not understand it. "Just shut-up and lead."

The slave, however, guessing at Rysth-nuul's meaning, shot off towards the passageway on the eastern side of the cavern, its speed rivaling that of its animal-like counterparts. Rebecca and the others quickly fell into line behind it, the gradually increasing volume of the approaching aliens spurring them on. Once again Rebecca felt the familiar fear of being left behind well up within her as they ran. This time, much to her relief, her companions did not drop to all fours as they had done previously, but instead chose to remain on two feet, maintaining their grips on their weapons.

Just as they reached the tunnel entrance, the northernmost passageway burst forth, releasing a veritable flood of angry Modir, each one emitting a high-pitched screech that reminded Rebecca of nails being scraped across a chalkboard.

The sight of their pursuers sent a jolt of renewed energy into the already frenetic party, urging them on to even greater speed. They paused in the entranceway for what seemed like an eternity as Tarrsk sliced through the wires connecting the motion detectors to the guns, deactivating the Modir outer defenses. Once completed, they continued forward, casting frequent glances over their shoulders as if expecting to see the entire army of Modir bearing down on them at any moment.

The tree-like Errhu led them from the narrow passageway into a much wider cavern that was roughly fifty feet across. Their flashlights and lanterns produced just enough light for them to see that the entire place was littered about from floor to ceiling with stalactites and stalagmites. The low, fifteen-foot ceiling and pock-marked uneven floor caused their Lidrilian guide to have to slow its pace slightly as it weaved and ducked the innumerable protrusions.

Even at their current reckless pace, Rebecca feared that they would not make it to the cavern's far exit before the Modir would be within firing range. As she glanced at Prin running beside her, she found confirmation for her assessment. Pulling several explosive devices from its dwindling supply, it began arming them with flashes of blue from its fingertips. Reaching into her pocket, she extracted her own weapon and braced herself for the inevitable gunfight, hoping that her already throbbing knee would hold out.

Suddenly, the darkness around them exploded with the shrieking of the Modir, magnified by the natural acoustics of the cavern. A second later, shards of rock and stone flew in all directions as Modir projectiles tore into the pointed formations.

The Grinathians tried desperately to return fire as they continued to flee. However, the layout of the cavern was such that they had to shine their lights in front of them or risk a twisted ankle or sprained knee, thus rendering their attempts at defense nearly useless.

Their only advantages were the distance between them and the

Modir, and the stalactites themselves. Rebecca knew that it wouldn't be long, however, before the mole-like aliens closed the gap.

"Stand and fight!" Sikaris called out, its gravelly voice seeming to come from everywhere at once, making it impossible for her to discern the being's location. Immediately, the lights from Rebecca's companions halted and reversed direction as they sought refuge behind the towering rocks and prepared to at least slow down the horde's advance.

Before she managed to secure her own position, the others opened fire. The already loud weapons were intensified to a nearly unbearable level in the confined space of the cavern, causing Rebecca to cover her ears momentarily.

Had she not done so, she would for sure have been knocked unconscious by the concussive explosion that suddenly sent everyone sprawling to the cavern floor. Beneath her, she could feel the ground tremble from the force. Closing her eyes and holding her breath, she prayed inwardly that the cave would not collapse upon them.

"Run for the exit," the inflectionless translator said in her ear, its calm voice completely out of place amid the chaotic cries and screams of the battle. On each side of her, the dark shapes that were her companions, left the cover of the stalagmites and began heading towards the far side of the cavern once again, their flashlights and lanterns bobbing up and down as they ran.

Without even checking to see the outcome of the explosion, Rebecca made a mad dash towards the exit, the sounds of frustrated and enraged Modir assailing her. Suddenly, the rock next to her split apart as it was struck by a stray bullet. Crying out in pain as fragments of stone cut into her face, Rebecca stumbled and nearly fell onto the uneven cave floor. Regaining her balance, she forced herself on, using the back of her hand to wipe away the small streaks of blood from her face.

Time seemed to stretch on interminably as she ran through the darkness, the ever present sounds of the vicious creatures suppressing all conscious thought and leaving only the instinct for survival to guide her.

Finally, before she even realized it, she was through the archway leading out of the cavern and into a much narrower passageway.

"Prin," she heard Sikaris call somewhere just behind her, "we are all through. Bring down the ceiling."

Just as Rebecca turned a corner in the narrow tunnel, an explosion rocked the mountain and sent her tumbling forward. Her body hit the floor and rolled several times before she suddenly felt herself sliding head-first on her stomach into pitch darkness.

Reaching out in panic, she let go of her gun and flashlight and clawed at the stone slope in a desperate attempt to arrest her descent. Her fingers were scraped and bleeding before her frantic efforts succeeded. Grabbing onto a small, rocky ledge with her right hand, she winced as her body weight pulled at her arm. She tried several times to climb the steep incline, but her efforts proved futile.

Even as her fingers screamed for permission to release the outcropping, she found her voice and called out to the others for help. Looking upwards, she saw beams of light shining down the slope, searching for her whereabouts.

"Come on, let us go," came the monotonous voice of the translator in her ear. "It will not take the Modir long to tunnel through the collapsed rock."

"No. We should save him," came a second voice, which Rebecca was surprised to recognize as belonging to Tarrsk.

"Rysth-nuul," Sikaris said, its unmistakable growl filtering down from above, "we may need his help. Lower your tail."

Her arms began to ache from the strain, causing Rebecca to call upon every ounce of willpower to override her body's cry for respite. Reaching up with her wounded left arm, she struggled to find another handhold to bring relief to her taxed right arm. Finding nothing, she brought it back to the same ledge and felt the wounded muscle from her encounter with the Mrdangam burn with renewed fury at the strain. "Hurry, please," she called feebly.

Her reservoirs of strength were all but depleted when Rysth-nuul's uncoiled tail finally wrapped itself around her. The lengthy appendage squeezed her so tightly that it made her wonder if the creature wasn't taking advantage of the opportunity to inflict a little pain.

"We must not stop," her translator chirped once again, relaying Errhu's urgent suggestion with typical apathy. "The Modir are digging. They are coming through the walls."

With Rysth-nuul's assistance, Rebecca dragged herself up until she reached the safety of the path that led around the dangerous slope. No sooner had her upper body reached the level ground then Rysth-nuul released her abruptly and headed off down the treacherous path after the others, who had already resumed their flight. Only Sikaris remained beside her. Hauling her up to her feet, the feline-like being urged her forward with a gentle shove.

She stumbled on, still weak from her exertion, her arms and fingers aching. Now that she was on her feet, she could see that the pathway they were traversing was merely three feet wide before it began its angular descent into the abysmal pit. Above, the cavern stretched on indefinitely, the ceiling hidden by a thick cloak of blackness.

Rebecca found it extremely difficult to strike a delicate balance between haste and caution, especially without the aid of her lost flashlight. Several times she misstepped, causing her to have to hug the stone wall on her right to keep from plunging to her death.

Fortunately, she was not alone in her struggles. Several of the others, particularly Jorylk and their plant-like guide, were having difficulty navigating the narrow walkway. Since they were the vanguard of the group, they slowed the progress of everyone, except Tarrsk, who climbed the vertical wall and was now waiting at the mouth of another cave nearly forty yards in front of them.

Still shaken from her brush with death, Rebecca was keeping as close to the wall as she could. As she pressed her hand against it for support, the hard surface beneath her fingers shifted. Startled, she quickly withdrew her hand just in time to see a six-inch diameter portion of the formerly solid rock give way. Before she could react, Rysth-nuul shoved its pistol into the new opening and fired off several rounds.

"They are coming through the walls!" it yelled out in warning.

Throwing caution to the wind, the group moved forward with renewed urgency. Ahead of her, Rebecca could see dirt and rock begin to come loose from the wall, indicating where the tunneling Modir were about to break through.

By the light of Sikaris' lantern, she could begin to see shovel-like claws protrude through the wall in front of her. Weaponless, she was forced to duck under the groping claws, or step out briefly onto the deadly slope to evade the outstretched arms.

The cries of the mole-like creatures, combined with the scraping sounds of their digging, pushed Rebecca's already fragile nerves to their breaking point. Her breathing had become so rapid that she began to hyperventilate. She fixed her eyes on Rysth-nuul, who was fighting the emerging aliens several paces in front of her. Thus distracted, she was sent tumbling to the ground by the sharp claw of a Modir that had managed to snag her ankle as she passed.

Letting out a blood-curdling scream of fright, she kicked out with her other leg and succeeded in freeing herself. Suddenly, she heard a loud hissing noise from behind her. Looking over her shoulder, she saw tendrils of dense fog reaching for her out of the darkness, beckoning her to embrace it and rest in blissful sleep…

From seemingly out of nowhere, two muscular arms reached out and lifted Rebecca into the air with one fluid motion, then carried her the few remaining feet to the cavern exit.

"Run!" Sikaris yelled in English as it set her upon her feet just inside the entrance to the new cave.

The forcefulness of the creature's command brought Rebecca back to her senses. Nodding her head dumbly, she took off running as fast as her sore knee allowed her. The passage they now found themselves in was much smaller then any other they had traveled thus far, reviving old fears of claustrophobia she had once thought conquered. The ceiling, in stark contrast to the lofty heights of the previous cavern, was just over ten feet high, with walls merely half as wide.

Glancing behind her, she saw the large form of Sikaris hurling sonic blasts at the pursuing Modir as they extricated themselves from the numerous holes in the cavern wall. Although the cat-like alien was facing backwards as it ran on its two legs, it still managed to keep pace with Rebecca.

On they ran, farther and farther through a maze of passages, the Modir always just one step behind them. Rebecca pushed herself to the limit, ever aware that if she failed to keep up with the others in front of her, she would become hopelessly lost in the underground labyrinth with no source of light.

Suddenly, she heard shouts of surprise, mingled with cries of pain and sounds of melee coming from up ahead where Jorylk and Errhu were leading the way. Her mind preoccupied with what was happening farther up the tunnel, she failed to notice that Rysth-nuul had stopped in front of her. Slamming full force into the back of the alien, she nearly collapsed from the jarring impact.

Rysth-nuul whirled around and shoved her backwards. For a split second, she thought it was due to her clumsiness, but the moment she heard the translator speak, she realized the terrible truth.

"Gorz! Go back!"

Disoriented, Rebecca froze in place as Rysth-nuul and Ch'ran both pushed past her, heading back towards the Modir. Looking ahead, she could just make out the forms of Jorylk, Tarrsk, and Errhu heading straight for her. As they ran, their limbs flailed frantically in an attempt to ward off the attacks of a host of Gorz.

The sight of the bloated, worm-like aliens left Rebecca feeling numb. In her mind she could hear Ch'ran's words echoing, *"We will probably be gassed by the Modir or eaten alive piece by piece by the Gorz!"* For a single heartbeat, her mind flashed with images of the worm-like Gorz pinning her to the cave floor with their twisted arms while their gaping, toothy maws began to devour her bit by bit.

No! she shouted mentally. *I'm not going to die on this blasted planet!* Reaching deep within, she gathered her courage and focused her mind on one thought: survival. Ignoring the pain in her leg, she took off back down the tunnel.

It took the group several precious seconds to backtrack to the last intersection. With the Modir closing on one side and the Gorz on the other, the side passage became their only option. As Rebecca neared the juncture, she could see the silhouette of Sikaris as it grappled with several of the mole-like aliens on the outskirts of a cloud of Modir gas not more than a dozen yards away.

Although it struck her as odd that Sikaris did not seem to be affected by the mist, she had no time to reflect on it further, for just as she reached the new tunnel, Tarrsk and Errhu caught up with her and practically launched her into the opening.

No sooner had they cleared the entrance then Sikaris came bounding in behind them. Suddenly, a deafening roar broke through the chaotic sounds of the battle. A second later, Jorylk's massive form appeared, its body mostly obscured by four of the three-foot, worm-like Gorz.

As Jorylk thrashed about in the mouth of the cave in an attempt to dislodge the clinging attackers, several Modir sprang into the fight. Upon seeing their longstanding foes, the remainder of the Gorz forgot about their prey and set upon the horde of Modir with a blind fury.

"Go!" Sikaris commanded.

As she headed off down the tunnel with the others, she risked one final look behind her. The last thing she saw before the Modir mist clouded the area was Jorylk's giant frame being dragged to the floor by a mass of mutated arms and legs.

17

The Price of Freedom

HOW LONG they ran down the musty corridor, Rebecca could not tell. The whole of her mental faculties were spent on simply placing one foot in front of the other. In some far-off place in her mind, she could see her parents and sister laughing and calling to her. She instantly recognized the scene from her childhood. They were on vacation in Florida, enjoying a sunny day at the beach. She was running along the shore, waving to her parents, her curly locks blowing freely in the hot, salty breeze.

The water felt cool as she splashed into it, the wet sand squishing through her toes. Suddenly, she screamed as something grabbed her leg. Looking down in horror, she saw several deformed and mutated arms reach out from the shallows and begin to drag her down. She twisted and struggled, but to no avail. It was then that she understood that although the surroundings had not changed, she had. Her body was no longer that of a child, but of an adult.

Calling out for help, she looked towards the beach where her parents and sister still stood waving. However, their smiles were now replaced by looks of intense sadness. They continued to wave, but not in good humor. Instead, they waved good-bye.

She wanted to call out, to say something, but her voice refused to cooperate. As the water began to close over her head, she watched as her family turned and began walking slowly away.

"Stop."

Rebecca jerked as her mind caught up with her weary body. Sikaris called to the others to regroup. Once they had all gathered around, the cat-like alien addressed their Lidrilian guide. "How much farther?"

"It is still far," Errhu replied. "But there should be no danger."

"Then we will rest for a moment," Sikaris said, setting its lantern down on the cavern floor. "It has been a while since we have heard any sounds of pursuit."

Their exhaustion was such that no one muttered so much as a single comment, even the normally vocal Ch'ran. Instead, they either found a small niche in the dank, oval cavern in which to rest, or they simply dropped where they stood.

Rebecca, weak, tired, and in pain, barely had enough energy to remove her backpack before slumping to the hard rock floor. In moments, her mind had drifted off into the deep sleep of the fatigued…

She slept fitfully, dark shadows moving in and out of her dreams, leaving an ominous sense of impending dread in their wake. Then, like a beacon of light shining in the darkness, a familiar beeping sound rang out.

Rebecca opened her eyes slowly, setting aside the heaviness of sleep like a thick blanket. Something was making that noise; a noise that she recognized, but could not place.

As her brain fully awakened, it brought with it the memories of recent events. Still groggy from sleep, she sluggishly took in her surroundings. She had a vague recollection of stopping in this particular cavern, but she remembered little else.

Suddenly, the beeping ceased, causing her to resume her search for the direction that the now absent sound had originated from. It was then that she spied the dark form hovering over her pack, which now lay several feet to her right.

Coming instantly awake at the sight of the figure, she nevertheless remained motionless so as not to alert it, her eyes straining in the dark to try to make out the details. However, the only light in the cavern came from Sikaris' lantern, which happened to be on the opposite side of their camp.

The being finished whatever it was doing, then stood completely erect. Even through half-closed eyelids, Rebecca could clearly see the outline of two sets of forearms. Feigning sleep, she continued to watch as it silently slunk back to where it had left its own belongings.

What was Prin doing? she wondered. *Why was it looking through my pack?* Even as the questions flashed through her mind, she remembered the beeping sound that had awakened her moments ago. *But why would Prin want to mess with my journal? Could it have put something dangerous in with my equipment? Or did it take something? But what could I have that would be of use to it?*

Lest she give away the fact that she knew about Prin's snooping around, Rebecca refrained from getting up and checking her equipment. Instead, she lay still for many long minutes, her mind whirling with possibilities while her eyes examined every shadow for possible movement.

The others seemed to be asleep, except for the infatigable Sikaris, who stood vigil over them, making sure that they were not attacked by other denizens of the mountain, as well as making sure their Lidrilian guide did not decide to desert them.

She lay there for what seemed like an eternity, physically spent, but afraid to sleep for fear of another intrusion by Prin.

"Everyone up," Sikaris said at last. "It is time to move out."

Her body stiff and unresponsive, she nevertheless forced herself to stand. Although seemingly asleep, the others were on their feet and ready with surprising quickness, leaving Rebecca rushing to catch up.

With the threat of pursuit abated, their pace slackened considerably. Taking advantage of the fact that Tarrsk was in between her and Prin, Rebecca risked opening her pack as they walked, doing her best to appear casual. After a cursory inventory of her equipment, she spent several seconds checking her journal for tampering. Finding nothing out of the ordinary, she examined her other items. Picking up her ship's tracker and turning it over in her hand, her heart sank, sending her spirit plummeting until it matched the gloomy air around them. The device in her hand was clearly damaged beyond repair. The display screen was cracked from top to bottom, and several of the padded controls were bent or missing.

Did Prin do this? she wondered as she resealed her backpack and placed it back upon her shoulder as if nothing were amiss. *But why? What could it gain? Maybe it was damaged during the battle. That is a definite possibility. Oh, it doesn't matter. When the others find out… I only hope we are close enough to the ship that we can find it without the tracker. Otherwise…*

She left the thought unfinished, not even allowing her mind to consider any other possibility. They walked on for more than an hour longer without incident. Finally, Rysth-nuul and Errhu, who were at the forefront of the group, turned a corner and stopped abruptly.

"Daylight," Rysth-nuul announced. "We made it. I cannot believe it. We actually made it."

"See, I told you," Ch'ran said jovially. "Nix told me I would not die in the mountain."

"Shut up!" the snake-like alien spat vehemently. "I am sick of hearing about 'Nix.' Because of your stupid belief in a being that does not exist, we were almost murdered."

Ch'ran was about to respond when Sikaris cut if off. "No more talk. We do not know where we are or who may be outside the cave."

Rysth-nuul sneered one last time at its small companion, then turned away. Ch'ran merely smiled back with its devilish grin.

"Wait here, all of you," Sikaris said quietly. Putting down its lantern, the Grinathian leader dropped to all fours and padded silently toward the hazy red afternoon sunlight at the far end of the tunnel. After several minutes it returned and waved them forward.

"There are no signs of anyone," it reported. "We will take a short rest inside the mouth of the cave while Rebecca uses her machine to find out which direction his ship is. We are very close to Lake Yul, so it must be close."

Rebecca felt a lump settle in her throat. Drumming up her courage, she delivered the bad news. "I…I can't use my tracker. It is…damaged."

"What?" Rysth-nuul and Tarrsk both said simultaneously. Sidling up to her, the snake-like alien shot daggers at her from its mutated eyes. "What do you mean, 'damaged'?"

Something snapped within her. Her hatred for this being had been building since she had met it, until it now reached the boiling point. *How dare it blame me!*

For the first time since her arrival, Rebecca moved closer to the creature, facing its challenge head on. "Do you think I did it on purpose? Do you think I want to stay on this dump of a planet, constantly running for my life? It was probably damaged during the battle, although for all I know one of *you* might have done it!" As she spat the accusation, she looked around to see if any of them reacted, particularly the ferret-like scientist. Prin, however, remained expressionless. Turning her attention back to Rysth-nuul, she reached into her bag, grabbed the broken device, and tossed it at the alien. "Here. See for yourself."

The creature's four mismatched eyes stared at her as a smile slowly spread across its reptilian face. "So he does have some guts after all," it said slyly. Narrowing its eyes at her, it continued, "And you may be right, but that does not mean I will not murder you anyway."

"Fine," she growled, her anger still fueling her bravado. "But if you do, you'll never make it back to your territory alive. You know as well as I do that my ship is your only hope."

"If it is even real," it hissed in reply. "And what good does it do us if we cannot find it? Or was that your goal all along: to lead us here by pretending there is a ship?" Switching its gaze to look at Sikaris, it added, "I still think we should have murdered him long ago."

The cat-like alien strode over to stand next to Rysth-nuul and Rebecca. As it spoke, its violet, oddly symmetrical eyes seemed to bore into her. "If we cannot find her ship, you may yet get your chance."

Although she maintained a calm front, inside her the fear was building like floodwaters behind a dam.

"But enough," Sikaris said as it turned away. "Let us waste no more time. Ch'ran, you will search to the east, Tarrsk to the west. Search only up to two miles. If you have not found anything by then, return here. If you do find it, use your commlink to let us know, and we will meet you. Everyone else will wait here."

"What about the Lid?" Tarrsk snorted, looking sideways at their plant-like guide.

Errhu, sensing the turn in the conversation, finally spoke. "Lri Errhu has kept his promise. Now I will go free."

The entire group stood facing the creature in a semicircular pattern. There was a sudden tension in the air that was almost palpable. A second later, the tendrils on the tips of Errhu's three, branch-like arms whistled in agony. Surprised, Rebecca looked over to see Rysth-nuul holding the slaver's device in its claw.

"Yes," it said wickedly, "we will set you free."

The stunned creature recovered from the initial attack and tried to make a dash towards the cave opening. It had barely moved two feet when its body was wracked by another round of intense pain delivered by Rysth-nuul. Errhu's movement, combined with the painful shock, put the creature off balance, sending its large, trunk-like body crashing to the cave floor.

Ch'ran let out a malevolent whoop of delight and leapt on top of the enslaved alien. Driving its razor sharp tail into the trunk of the tree, the devilish creature cackled viciously. "That should slow it down. Well, Nix, are you ready for some fun?"

Rebecca sat frozen in horror at the brutal display that followed. Once the creature was down, both Tarrsk and Prin joined in, each using its unique abilities to deliver blow after blow. Tarrsk unleashed several jagged rocks from the tips of its tentacles at point blank range while blue sparks shot from the tips of Prin's four hands, sending convulsive spasms of pain lancing through the tree-like alien's body. Rysth-nuul had abandoned the slaver device and was using its whip-like tail to slash and cut the downed alien.

In agony, the helpless creature writhed and twisted its poisoned body back and forth as each successive blow fell, the cave filling with the weakening whistling sounds of the Lidrilian's tendrils as it cried out. "NO! Lri Errhu helped…can…still…help," her translator offered, its monotonous tone seeming to mock the alien's dying pleas.

"Shut up, slave scum," Rysth-nuul spat as it grabbed several of the tendrils in its mangled claws and severed the ends. It continued to do so until all of the tendrils lay strewn about the cave floor as a testimony to the snake-like alien's cruelty.

Rebecca flinched in sympathetic pain as Tarrsk began snapping the root-like legs, each "crack" causing the creature to jerk in excruciating pain. Ch'ran, still laughing maniacally, continued to leap about and use its tail to stab and slash its victim. Gradually, a dark pool of sap-like blood began to form on the floor of the cave as it oozed from the plant-like alien's numerous wounds. At last, whether from Ch'ran's poisonous tail or from losing consciousness from pain, the Lidrilian slave soon ceased its struggles.

Unable to endure any more, Rebecca turned sharply towards Sikaris. "Why don't you stop them? They are going to kill it!"

The feline-like alien merely looked at her, its expression one of boredom or unconcern. "So," it replied in English. "Why should I stop them from having a little fun?"

"Fun? But...but you promised to set it free," she said accusingly.

Sikaris' piercing eyes simply stared at her. "Have you learned nothing yet about Ka'esch? There is not even a word on this planet for 'truth.'"

Indignation flooded her. "It kept its promise. It told a 'non-lie,'" she said sarcastically. "What did that poor creature ever do to us to deserve this?"

"Deserve? It is a Lidrilian; that is reason enough. The race of Lidrilian are not as evolved as the Hran. They are only useful as slaves, food, and entertainment."

"But...isn't all life related? This...brutality is just...just wrong," she sputtered.

"Wrong?" Sikaris said curiously. "By whose standard? Who says it is wrong, *you*?"

She remained silent under the creature's scrutiny.

"On Ka'esch, those who hold the power determine what is right or wrong. And right now, we hold the power. Maybe I think it is right to let my tired group have a little fun."

"But it is a life," she said softly.

"So. Life is but an accident, the mixing of uncaring, impersonal, unintelligent chemicals. What is one lifetime when compared to the billion-year history of the universe? Life is worthless. Disposable. 'Power to the Strong and Intelligent, Death to the Weak and Stupid.'"

What could she say to explain the feeling within her that cried out for justice, the feeling that told her that the murder of this innocent creature was wrong? Yet, she could find no flaws in Sikaris' logic. So where did these feelings come from? Was it simply the residue of her religious upbringing or her cultural heritage?

Turning back around, her heart nearly burst with pity for the Lidrilian slave. The plant-like creature's hard, bark-like skin had been flayed in several areas, its roots hung limply or had been torn off, and nothing remained of its tendrils but mangled stumps.

Ch'ran, Tarrsk, Rysth-nuul, and Prin finally ceased their activities, their pent-up frustration and anger from the last day released. Standing over the lifeless form, they howled and congratulated each other. Rebecca found it sickeningly ironic that for once, Prin fit in easily with the others.

"Eat what you want, then throw the remains farther back down the cave," Sikaris said, once their celebration had ended. "Ch'ran and Tarrsk, grab something to eat, then leave. When you are outside, make sure you are not seen."

As Rysth-nuul and Prin began to eat what remained of the Lidrilian, Tarrsk and Ch'ran each grabbed several slices of food and headed through the cave opening out into the reddish sunlight beyond. Moving off to a secluded corner, Rebecca withdrew her journal from her pack. After a quick check to make sure it still functioned properly, she began recording, her voice low to prevent the others' translators from picking it up.

Journal Entry #5

I have to get away.

The only reason I am still alive is because I have convinced them that they need me to find the ship and negotiate with my crewmates. But after seeing these creatures in action and knowing more about how they think, I am certain that once we find the ship, they will dispose of me and attack Captain Coffner, Lisa, and the others. I have to warn them, but either my commlink is not working properly, or…or they cannot respond for some reason. Either way, things will be decided soon enough.

For now, we wait. More then anything, I am tired of waiting. At this point I would almost prefer any outcome to this…this infernal wondering and waiting. Just let it be over!

Oh, God! I just want to get off this rock. I want to get away from these monsters. But it seems more and more like I won't make it. I only wish I had a chance to see Jeff one more time. If only I could tell him…If only I could say I'm sorry.

NO! I can't start thinking about that now. I WON'T think about that now. I have to keep my head clear, not get lost in self-pity.

. . .

Okay. Let me start over.

Since my last entry, we have traveled many miles through an underground maze of tunnels and caverns. We were able to successfully bypass the outer defenses of a clan of headless, underground dwellers called the Modir. We then surprised them and managed to take control of one of their gardens (as I explained in one of my previous entries, gardens on this planet contain living, moving, intelligent plant-like creatures). It was one of these Lidrilian—as they are called—who guided us out of the mountain, at the cost of its own life.

I must admit that my companions continually find new ways to shock me with their brutality. The tree-like alien promised to lead us out in exchange for freedom. Yet, once we had reached the surface, Rysth-nuul and the others proceeded to torture and murder the innocent creature.

What shocks me even more than the act itself is that I now understand the reasoning behind it. I am amazed that in all of my secondary schooling, I never really comprehended the ramifications of the theory of evolution. For, if it is true, then there are no moral absolutes. How does one determine what is right or wrong? Is it determined by consensus? Does the majority decide? Yet, human history is full of instances where the majority has been 'wrong,' at least by modern standards.

That brings me to another point: values and morals differ from culture to culture, and from generation to generation. Which values are 'right'? Whose morals are the 'right' ones? It all depends on your personal beliefs, which of course means that there is no one right answer. So how, then, can you say that even the vilest of acts is 'wrong,' or the most benevolent of gifts 'right'? With evolution, everything is relative.

Therefore, within this framework, one cannot say that Hitler was 'wrong' or that Mother Theresa was 'right,' for they both sincerely lived out their beliefs. It is odd that here, on a planet billions of miles from Earth, I hear the echoes of the philosophy and logic that caused World War II. For in addition to relative morals, evolution also provides strong support for racism. Sikaris said that Lidrilian are not as highly evolved, and therefore their lives were worth less than those of the animal-like Hran. Isn't that what Hitler believed? His extermination of the Jews and Africans was based on the belief that they were not as evolved as the white races and that he was purifying the gene pool.

How drastic is the contrast between evolution, which supports slavery and moral relativism, and the beliefs of a woman who, one could argue, wasted her life serving the poor. Mother Theresa was a woman who could have been very successful in life, but because of her beliefs, she lived a life of poverty. Yet, I must admit, her beliefs at least provide a foundation for the value of life and for an unchanging right and wrong. For if there is a God, then he, or she, being the creator of humans, would also hold the position of determining morals.

Even the idea of liberty and freedom depends upon a moral foundation. The framers of the Declaration of Independence and the Constitution understood this. "All men are created equal" and "endowed by their creator with certain unalienable rights" are foolish statements from the standpoint of evolution. If evolution is our worldview, then it should read "all men are not equal, some are more highly evolved" and "you have no rights other then what you can take for yourselves."

It almost makes me wish I believed God exists.

One other thing puzzles me about this issue: why do humans seem to have an innate sense of morality? Why did the ideas or feelings of morality evolve? What possible survivability advantage did it offer to our ancestors. I have always been told that it was because of our desire to see the human race survive and continue to be the dominant species. But where did that desire come from? The beings on this planet do not even care about their own offspring, much less the common good of others. Evolution, at its core, is a selfish philosophy. It seems difficult to think how morality could have ever evolved. Of course, maybe the real question is not how did it evolve, but rather, did it even evolve at all?

Prin has presented me with a very interesting, and somewhat frightening, explanation about the origin of life on Earth. While its theory at first seems far-fetched, it makes more and more sense to me as time goes by. Prin believes that life on Earth was created by extraterrestrials.

While this is not the first time I have heard of the theory of directed panspermia, I must say it has become much more plausible since I arrived on this planet. I always ridiculed those who held this belief, but that was because I never believed in aliens. Obviously, I was wrong about that. Is it possible, then, that I was wrong about the origin of life on Earth as well?

And Prin's reasoning is very intriguing. It came up with this theory because of the many physical differences between me and the inhabitants of this planet, as well as the "odd" things I have told it about Earth (which I have related in this journal).

Now that the idea has had time to sink in, I find that it answers many questions. And after getting a really close look at the evolved life on this planet, I am starting to agree with Prin.

If its theory is right, it would seem that some…thing or things created at least the basic species of animals, fully formed with male and female. This would account for the symmetry of life on Earth, and the stark differences between humans and all other animal life. I am certain that natural selection has changed things somewhat since the beginning, but obviously not enough time has passed to allow for many mutations to alter the original design too much.

The biggest question that remains, though, is who is the creator or creators? Prin's answer to that question brings with it more questions. It believes that Sikaris is somehow connected. According to Prin, Sikaris is not from any clan it has ever seen, its body is symmetrical, it has no visible mutations, and, as I well know, it speaks English.

Furthermore, Sikaris acts differently. It has defended and saved me several times, it was immune to the Modir gas, and there have been a couple of instances when I could have sworn I saw emotions in its eyes. And, now that I think of it, it did not join in the torture of the Lidrilian.

Prin guesses that either Sikaris, or its people, are the creators, or that Sikaris was created by the same intelligent beings that formed life on Earth. But where are they now? For what purpose did they create us? Are we just some great biology experiment? Or did they have other, more sinister designs for us? How long ago were we created? What do they want from us?

I may never find the answer to these questions, as I don't intend to stick around to chat once we find the ship. But I know that I will never look at life the same way again.

There is also the question of—

Rebecca instantly stopped recording, her mouth suddenly gone dry and her pulse quickened. Had she heard correctly? She waited silently for a moment longer, when she heard it again, her translator unmistakable this time.

"Sikaris, I found it. Nix and I found the ship!"

18

The Vanguard

REBECCA NEARLY leapt with excitement. They were still there! Her hope of escaping this horrible planet, which had at times been fleeting, broke into full bloom. She was going to make it!

"Very good, Ch'ran," Sikaris said into its intercom. "Are there any signs of other clans?"

"No," came the terse reply. "There is not even any sign of Rebecca's clan."

Her spirit deflating like a punctured balloon, she drew in a sharp breath. "What?" she said quietly to herself.

"Ch'ran, give us your location."

After a brief pause, her translator relayed the distant creature's reply. "I am about a quarter of a mile east of the cave. Just follow the curve of the mountain. Nix and I will contact you when we see you and guide you to our location."

Sikaris nodded. "Good. Stay there and watch. Let us know if you see anything. We are on our way. Tarrsk, did you hear?"

"Yes. I am on my way," came the slightly distorted response.

As Sikaris turned off its commlink, Rysth-nuul tilted its sinewy neck in Rebecca's direction. "Well, I will be a V'skir's gribok. He was telling a non-lie after all." Moving its four-eyed gaze to the cat-like alien, it nodded once. "You are a lucky being, Sikaris." With that, it slithered over to its belongings and began preparations to leave.

With her thoughts focused on creating possible scenarios to explain the absence of her crewmates, Rebecca's mind barely registered the creature's comment. *Where are they? Could they have gone out looking for me? Were they captured also? If they are gone, then Rysth-nuul and the others are sure to take the ship. They will probably force me to show them how to get inside and operate it. Then, once my usefulness is gone… I have to find the others.*

Seeing that the rest of the group was preparing to leave, she reigned in her thoughts and focused on the present. As she looked around the cave, her eyes fell upon Sikaris. Her skin crawled as she locked gazes with the large alien, its features revealing nothing of its thoughts, yet leaving her with the odd impression that Sikaris somehow knew what they would find when they reached the ship.

Unnerved, she broke its gaze and turned away to retrieve her pack. Just as she was about to place her journal inside, she remembered Prin's unexplained interest in her journal. Glancing around to make certain the others were not looking, she deftly slid the small, hand-held instrument into the inside pocket of her jumpsuit. Shouldering her pack, she strode purposefully towards the cave entrance.

The side of the mountain upon which they now stood was littered with large, gray boulders and enormous rock formations scattered haphazardly around the area, as if deposited there from some giant avalanche a millennium ago. Although the topography made travel difficult, it brought with it the added benefit of providing the group ample cover and protection from prying eyes.

Rebecca grew more and more anxious with each step, her mind frantically developing, then discarding, possible means of escape. As time passed, the pressure of her impending flight weighed upon her mind, further inhibiting her ability to focus. With her mind thus in frantic disarray, she was startled when her intercom translator came to life. "I see you. You are almost here. Follow the line of rocks to your right. I am behind the large boulder on the ledge."

Immediately, Rebecca's eyes looked out over the terrain, seeking for any sign of the *Vanguard.* As she and the others traversed the last short distance to where Ch'ran was hidden, Rebecca couldn't take her eyes off of the horizon so much so that she stumbled several times over the uneven ground.

Then, finally, as they neared the rocky outcropping on which sat an enormous rectangular boulder, she saw it. The hazy light of the late afternoon sun reflected brilliantly off of the pristine silver hull of the T-shaped ship. Nearly collapsing in relief at the sight of it, Rebecca reached out to a nearby rock for support, her eyes moist with brimming tears. Her joy quickly evaporated, to be replaced by astonishment, as the rock beneath her hand suddenly sprouted a lopsided grin.

"Ooooh, ooooh! A little to the left. I have an itch!"

Leaping back, she watched as Ch'ran's wicked-looking tail came from out of nowhere and began scratching, gently, between its shoulder blades where Rebecca's hand had rested moments before.

Rising from its disguised posture, Ch'ran stretched and yawned, revealing a mouth full of brown, crooked teeth in various stages of decay.

"Nix, you won again," the insane creature said, its mismatched eyes focused on an empty patch of ground on Rebecca's left. "I was sure they would take longer to get here. When we get back to the base, the first round of krizzle juice is on me."

If any of the others had even heard the little alien's ramblings, they showed no sign of it, for before them, not more than a mile away, sat a ship unlike anything native to the planet.

"Yes, yes," purred Prin. "Very interesting. Look at how clean it is. I could probably spend half of my life studying it," it said as it looked over at Sikaris.

"I wonder what kinds of weapons it has," Rysth-nuul remarked, its tail twitching involuntarily. "Do you think the V'skir found the ship when they captured Rebecca? Maybe they murdered the rest of Rebecca's clan, but could not get inside the ship."

Sikaris scanned the area, and then nodded in agreement. "Yes, we must be careful. They may have left a hunting party here to protect it until they could return with more clanmates."

Rebecca listened numbly to the conversation around her. The sight of the *Vanguard* and the rolling hills and rocks surrounding it brought with it the sense that this was indeed really happening. Since her abduction, it had seemed that she was merely drifting along in some hellish nightmare. But to see an Earth-made ship resting in the center of this alien landscape that she had become so familiar with, made her shudder.

From their vantage point, she could see that they were southwest of the ship, with the dark waters of the lake to the north of them, and the peaks of the mountain to the south. To the east, she recognized the area where she and Lisa had set up the MDU, amid the maze of rolling gray hills.

"Rysth-nuul, move down the slope to the left and position yourself there," Sikaris said. "Prin, you do the same to the right. Ch'ran, climb up the slope a little higher and make sure no one is heading our way. All of you, be alert. When Tarrsk arrives, I will decide what our next move will be."

"What about Rebecca?" Rysth-nuul said. As it spoke, its eyes slowly moved toward her and its tail twitched slightly, giving its simple question a sinister air.

Sikaris looked over at her, then back to its snake-like companion. "He stays here with me. Now get into position and be careful. We do not know who may be out there."

As Prin, Rysth-nuul, and Ch'ran moved silently away, Rebecca's mind worked furiously. She could not believe her sudden good fortune. Her chances of slipping away unnoticed with an entire team of seasoned alien hunters standing next to her would have been nearly impossible. But with only Sikaris around, her chances were improved markedly.

If she could somehow get away from it, she might be able to lose them in the little valleys created by the small hills. The most dangerous part would be crossing the open clearing between the end of the hills and the ship. *But if I could contact the others, they might be able to lay down some cover fire long enough for me to... if they are even inside the ship, that is. But how can I get away from Sikaris without it seeing me? It doesn't miss anything. Well, Becky, whatever you are going to do, you had better do it quick.*

Trying to appear casual, she walked around the rocky outcropping upon which they stood, her roving eyes searching for the best route of escape. As she walked, her calm demeanor was betrayed by her incessant cracking of knuckles. Out of the corner of her eye, she could see the piercingly violet eyes watching her every move.

Forget it, Becky. There's no way. I might as well just—She stopped mid-thought. Several feet away, on the other side of a medium-sized boulder, the final slope of the mountain gave way to the hilly area below. But this particular little path was hidden between two rows of boulders and looked just wide enough for her to fit between comfortably. If she could manage to climb over the one boulder and into the hidden path, she might just make it.

She had found her escape route, but she still hadn't figured out how to avoid being seen by Sikaris. Barring some miracle, it seemed impossible that she could escape from a creature whose whole existence was dependent on its ability to be alert. If only she could find a way to…

Sudden movement from her left caught her attention, bringing her thoughts of escape to a temporary halt. Tarrsk came rushing up the path to the rocky shelf, its body heaving from the exertion of a long-distance run. As it drew nearer, it slowed its pace and began to relax noticeably.

Turning toward the newcomer, Sikaris regarded the alien with interest. "Is something wrong?"

Tarrsk seemed slightly caught off guard by the question. "No. I…it is just that I did not want to be left behind," it stammered, its arm unconsciously scratching flaky white scales from its neck. Then, as its gaze fell upon the *Vanguard*, it paused mid-scratch. At the sight of the craft, the alligator-like creature's abdominal mouth fell open in awe and wonder. "I have never seen anything like it. Have you, Sikaris?" When the Grinathian leader failed to respond, Tarrsk continued. "So, what are we waiting for? Let us go take the ship and get out of here."

"No," Sikaris said finally. "We wait, and watch."

"What?" Tarrsk said anxiously. "But the longer we wait, the more chance there is of somebody else finding it."

"Yes, but it is also not smart to just run into unknown territory without first scouting the area," Sikaris retorted. "Remember the mistake Cl'ingar made with the Bkor?"

What was said next, Rebecca didn't hear. For all sound was drowned out by the sudden drumming of her heart in her ears as she realized that her miracle had come. Since Tarrsk's arrival, Sikaris had not given her the slightest glance. And the way things were escalating, hopefully Sikaris would be too occupied to notice her absence.

Realizing that her window of opportunity would be very narrow, she immediately began moving slowly toward the hidden path. Tarrsk was still deep in its heated conversation with Sikaris by the time Rebecca had reached the rock. Keeping her eyes fixed upon the two aliens, she climbed up onto the rock.

Slowly, so as not to draw the attention of either of the aliens, she swung her legs over the rock and down into the crevasse, all the while keeping her eyes fixed upon the disputing creatures. Finally, she inhaled deeply as if preparing to dive underwater, and slid off the rock. As she landed on the hard, sloping ground between the two giant boulders, she froze as several small pebbles went skipping down the incline. Her terror of discovery mingled with adrenaline, causing her to shake and breathe rapidly.

"I do not want to just sit out here and wait to be captured!" she heard Tarrsk whisper loudly.

They are still arguing! she thought, relief washing over her. *There's no turning back now.* Half sliding, half running, she made her way down the path, using the boulders on each side of her for support.

Before long, she was out of earshot of the two arguing creatures. She knew that it was now a race. The only question was how much of a head start she would have before the others set off in search for her.

In a matter of moments, she had reached the end of her narrow escape route. Although there were plenty of large rocks to use for cover, she would still be vulnerable as she moved from rock to rock, especially since any sudden movements in the dead and dormant landscape would surely alert the wary hunters.

Pausing at the end of the crevasse, she pulled out her commlink from her pack and fastened it to her wrist. Even with all of the atmospheric distortion, surely she was close enough for anyone aboard the ship to hear her. "*Vanguard*, come in…This is…Rebecca," she said brokenly between nervous gulps of air. "Do you copy?"

...static...

"Do you copy? Anyone? Lisa? Captain Coffner?" she whispered forcefully into the device.

...static...

Growling in frustration, she closed down the commlink. Slowly, she peered around the corner of the rock she was hiding behind and glanced up the slope toward the rocky shelf where Sikaris and Tarrsk were stationed.

The hidden path had taken her down the skirt of the mountain about sixty feet and a dozen more to the east. Just as she was about to risk a sprint to the nearest rock, Sikaris and Tarrsk suddenly appeared above her on the rocky shelf, both staring hard at each other, neither speaking. At first this struck her as odd, until she remembered the location of Tarrsk's mouth.

So far so good. She watched them closely, waiting to time her dash to the next rock. Suddenly and inexplicably, Sikaris turned and looked out towards the ship. Flattening herself back against the rock, she held her breath in fear. For the briefest of seconds, she was almost certain that Sikaris had looked directly at her, its eyes alert. She clung to the cold surface of the rock, afraid to move, her heart beating painfully beneath her breast.

After several excruciatingly long moments, with no sign of discovery forthcoming, she ventured to look up once more toward their location. To her immense relief, Sikaris and Tarrsk were still visible, both still seemingly engrossed in their argument.

It didn't see me! she thought in amazement. As she watched, both creatures turned away from her, their arms gesticulating angrily. Immediately seizing the opportunity, she dashed toward the nearby rock and continued running, not even turning to look to see if they were pursuing her.

She weaved in and out amongst the boulders and hills, always keeping a hill or boulder between her and her former companions. She couldn't be exactly sure where the ship was, but she knew if she kept running away from the mountain, she would sooner or later make it to the clearing in which the ship rested.

After several minutes of frantic running, her translator suddenly crackled to life, scaring her so much as to nearly cause her to stumble. The monotonous voice spoke, relaying its cryptic message with calm matter-of-factness.

"Run, Rebecca Clan Evans. We are coming for you."

The simple message succeeded in driving the last vestiges of conscious thought from her mind. Resolutely setting her will upon the task of reaching the ship, she ran on. She knew she had to be close, for the small hills were diminishing in size, affording her less and less cover the farther on she went. At any rate, she would have to find it soon, for her wounded knee was beginning to throb once again, and her battered and bruised body was nearly spent from prolonged anxiety and sheer exhaustion.

Then, as she rounded the latest hill, her strength was instantly renewed. For in front of her, not more than a hundred yards away was the *Vanguard*, sitting dormant on its landing skids. Knowing that she would be visible as she sprinted across the clearing, she gathered everything within her and urged her body on. As she ran, she opened a channel from her commlink.

"Open the hatch! Please! This is Rebecca. Open the hatch!"

…static…

Behind her, she could hear sounds of the others as they pursued her with abandon, all thoughts of caution having been tossed aside. *Don't look, Rebecca. Just keep running,* she thought, knowing that if she turned to look, she may lose all remaining courage. Instead, she kept her gaze fixed upon the control panel next to the ramp that was even now only twenty yards away. *Code #482-48-736*, she repeated to herself. *482-48-73–*

Suddenly, from underneath the ship, the sinewy form of the Grinathian leader emerged, its piercing eyes narrowed dangerously. Backpedaling in horror, Rebecca tried to turn and run back towards the hills, only to find Ch'ran's small form bounding towards her with giant leaps, its shrill voice cackling with pure exhilaration.

Then, before she even had a chance to react, she felt a thin, rope-like object wrap itself tightly around her waist. An instant later, her breath escaped from her body as she was yanked violently off her feet from behind. She doubled over in pain as she hit the cracked surface of the planet, her lungs screaming for oxygen.

"A very good try. You almost made it, Rebecca Clan Evans," Rysth-nuul hissed as it uncoiled its tail from about her waist.

Oh, God, let it be over quick, she thought, her eyes closed tightly to ward off the image of the mutated aliens around her. Yet, she found that the images conjured in her mind were worse than those facing her in reality. For in her mind's eye, the memory of Errhu's torture and death came unbidden to the forefront of her thoughts.

"NO!" she shouted aloud, her body shaking from terror both within and from without.

"Do not worry," Rysth-nuul said, its voice oozing sarcasm. "We will not torture you as much as we did the Lid."

"Wait, Rysth-nuul," Sikaris said. As it strode over to where she lay, its gaze darted warily back and forth, as if expecting the hills to erupt with alien attackers at any moment. "Rebecca, how do we enter your ship? Tell us that, and we will still let you live."

Emotional numbness had begun to override her fear and rational thought processes, causing her to chuckle derisively. "Right. Like you promised the Lidrilian? No, Sikaris. I have learned how things work on Ka'esch. 'Power to the Strong and *Intelligent,* Death to the Weak and *Stupid.*' But this time, I hold the power, and I will never give it to you, so you might as well kill me now!"

For a moment, no one moved. Then, almost imperceptibly, Sikaris nodded at Rysth-nuul. Grinning wickedly, the snake-like alien raised its double-tipped tail in preparation to strike. All of the blood immediately drained from Rebecca's face as realization struck. They were going to do it! They were calling her bluff!

"Wait! I…I…I'm sure we can work something out," she cried, panic causing her voice to quaver uncontrollably. "Prin, tell them…" She looked pleadingly at the ferret-like alien that had become closest to a friend, but the alien just stared at her blankly.

From behind her, she heard Ch'ran laugh hysterically. "Two dinners in one day! I want the thigh!"

"Wait," Tarrsk said, striding forward and placing a claw on Sikaris shoulder. "I think that we should—"

Suddenly, from seemingly out of nowhere, several sharp bullet-like objects slammed into Rysth-nuul's body, sending the alien crashing to the ground beside Rebecca. Immediately, Sikaris and the others spun around in search of the attacker.

They didn't have to look very hard, for they now found themselves surrounded on all sides by what Rebecca assumed to be Tarrsk's clanmates. Each of the mutated, alligator-like beings had either hand-held weapons, or projectile spewing tentacles pointed in their direction.

"Torlig," Prin cursed as more and more of the aliens seemed to materialize from out of thin air.

Rebecca sat up slowly, sudden comprehension dawning on her. Her mind flashed back to the times she had seen Tarrsk attempt to blend in with its background like a chameleon, only to be given away by its diseased patches of dead, white skin. These creatures obviously had no such hindrances.

"Do not touch the strange being." The speaker was a particularly large specimen who had three tentacles protruding from its back: two long, thin ones similar to Tarrsk's, and one shorter, wide one. As it spoke, the creature took several steps towards their group, its three disfigured eyes resting upon Tarrsk. "Congratulations, Diseased One. You actually did it. The being still lives."

Rysth-nuul stirred beside her. Although clearly wounded in several places from the attack, its thick Dakkar-nil hide had absorbed the brunt of the damage, protecting its body from serious injury. Slowly raising itself up so as not to startle its edgy captors, Rysth-nuul cursed loudly at its former companion. "You traitorous scum. You sold us out."

Tarrsk turned and regarded Rysth-nuul coldly. "Yes, I did. And you are jealous that you did not figure out a way to profit from this alien first. My clan had already captured this ship when I contacted them, but it seems that the hunting party that found it made the mistake of murdering all of Rebecca's clanmates before they realized what they had found."

The large Torlig leader narrowed its eyes at Tarrsk, clearly not happy with its criticism. At the same time, Rebecca sat up straight, startling the nearby hunters with her sudden movement as the translation reached her ears. "What? What…did you say?"

"That is right, I forgot," Tarrsk sneered, moving closer to her until its foul, mouthless face was mere inches from her own. "You still hoped they were alive."

Rebecca felt as if all life had suddenly drained from her body, leaving her nothing but an empty void. *Dead? No, they couldn't be. It has to be lying.* Yet, despite all efforts to convince herself otherwise, she knew it had to be true. She was now, truly, all alone.

Tarrsk continued, enjoying the spotlight. "However, before they died, your clanmates managed to lock up your ship. Barraca was very mad. But when he found out that I could bring you to him, he was willing to offer me whatever I wanted."

Sikaris narrowed its eyes in fury. "And what was the payment you were promised?"

"Can you not guess?" Tarrsk said smugly. "My clan has agreed to allow me to rejoin them. I am clan-less no more."

At this statement, the Torlig leader gestured towards them with one of its massive claws. "Enough of this. Bind them all."

"WHAT!?!" Tarrsk shouted in dismay as it spun around to look at the larger clan member.

Without expression of any kind, the creature spoke. "I am tired of your talking. You have been very useful, but you are a fool to believe that Clan Torlig would allow such a worthless, sickened being like yourself to return."

"NO!!!" Tarrsk cried as its fellow Torlig threw netting over its body and began pinning the struggling creature to the hard, cracked plain floor. Ch'ran's hysterical laughter at its companion's misfortune was suddenly drowned out by a cry of fury as Rysth-nuul lashed out at the nearby captors with its whip-like tail. "I will not be a slave again!"

The tense scene immediately dissolved into chaos. In the split second of distraction afforded by Rysth-nuul's outburst, Sikaris vaulted into action. Striking out at the nearest attacker, the great cat-like alien felled its opponent in one single swipe of its mighty claw. Without hesitation, it sent a blast of sonically charged particles toward the Torlig that had nearly enveloped Prin in a tangle of netting, knocking the alligator-like creature senseless.

Once it had extricated itself from the net, Prin leapt to the side, narrowly avoiding an onslaught of sharpened projectiles. Rolling to its feet, it grabbed the last of its explosives from its bandolier and prepared to launch it.

Ch'ran, meanwhile, laughing like a child playing tag, jumped about, shooting madly at anything and everything with its small, hand-held pistol. Weaving and bobbing as it went, the insane creature found itself heading straight towards the Torlig leader. "Fifty points for killing the leader, Nix! I will win for sure!" it cackled loudly.

Weaponless, Rebecca knew her only hope for survival was to make it to the ship. Climbing to her feet, she dashed towards the *Vanguard*. She had barely taken a dozen strides, however, when one of the Torlig swept her legs out from under her with a well placed throw of its net.

A low, throaty laugh emanated from the creature's torso as it prepared to secure its prize. Suddenly, an explosion erupted behind it, sending the mutated alien sprawling forward to land on Rebecca's legs, pinning her helplessly to the ground.

Summoning every ounce of strength in her body, she pushed hard upon the body of the unconscious alien, but despite her efforts, she was unable to free her legs. Trapped, she watched as a now grenade-less Prin fought desperately against three Torlig as they proceeded to ensnare it in one of their nets.

Nearby, Rysth-nuul was quickly losing ground. Then, letting out one final scream of frustration, the snake-like alien collapsed under a barrage of fists and tentacles that rendered it unconscious. In her mind, the remainder of the battle seemed to move in slow motion as, one by one, she watched each of her former comrades fall.

A shrill, high-pitched cackle drew her attention. Ch'ran, leaping through the air, landed squarely upon the back of the large Torlig leader. The muscular alien twisted its torso and flailed its three tentacles about wildly in an attempt to dislodge the mad attacker. Ch'ran's face was a mask of devilish delight as it lifted its tail high, ready to plunge it deep into the unprotected flesh of its victim.

Then, unexpectedly, the impish creature's features contorted horribly as the large, third tentacle found its mark. The razor sharp teeth that protruded from the end of the tentacle sunk firmly into Ch'ran's underside. After a brief instant, they withdrew, allowing Ch'ran's body to fall limply to the ground.

Although she would never have considered these creatures friends, it nonetheless made her feel an even deeper sense of loneliness to see them fall. Looking up from Ch'ran's body, she saw Sikaris, surrounded by wounded or dead Torlig, fighting its way slowly back toward the hills.

But deep down inside, Rebecca knew the feline-like alien would not make it. Even as it ran, its limp became more pronounced and its fatigue more apparent. The Torlig surrounding it seemed to be almost toying with the great hunter, feigning attacks from all directions, keeping Sikaris off balance. Finally they struck. Its attention divided between many foes, Sikaris did not notice the heavy, club-like tentacle slipping in under its defenses. Even as far away as she was, Rebecca could still hear the sickening thud as the tentacle connected with Sikaris' head.

As quickly as it had begun, it was over. Each of the five remaining members of the Grinathian hunting party lay motionless, either unconscious or dead.

Struck dumfounded by the rush of events, Rebecca didn't even struggle as a group of Torlig hauled her to her feet. The remainder of the alligator-like creatures were dragging her companions back towards the large alien commander, who was staring down at the now bound and helpless Tarrsk.

The large creature sneered in disdain. "You stupid, worthless being. You do not deserve to live. You do not even understand the depth of your stupidity. Did you really think we would trust you to bring us the last of these creatures? We knew that your deal with the Mrdangam would fail, so we made one of our own. But since the rest of them did not attack your transport, it seems that the stupid being who made the deal with us must have been greedy and not shared our offer with its clanmates."

Moving even closer to Tarrsk, it grabbed it by the throat and held it in a vise-like grip. "And the Ryazan, you fool, attacked because you were not careful with your transmission to us. They overheard and found you before we could, hoping to capture the strange being and sell him to us. We learned this after torturing several of the ones who survived when our hunting party surprised them, right after the avalanche buried you in the Modir cave." Releasing Tarrsk, it took several steps back, then motioned for its clanmates to bring Rebecca towards it.

She was dragged before the large Torlig hunter without resisting, her mind still in shock. The creature sized her up with a critical gaze. "Barraca will be pleased." Turning to one of the others standing nearby, it pointed towards the *Vanguard*. "Bring the Wryll and tow this vehicle back to the base. And bring this slave fodder for the games."

Looking at her once more, its abdominal mouth split into a wide grin. "Yes, Barraca will be pleased indeed."

As they began marching her away from the field of carnage, she heard a soft, yet high-pitched whisper being carried by the hot wind. Looking down, she saw Ch'ran's body lying in a pool of its own blood, its face turned upward. Rebecca was surprised to see a look of peace on the creature's face as its twisted lips moved slightly.

"I will be there soon, Nix..."

19

Hope Rekindled

THE CELL door shut with the grating sound of rusted metal that rang loudly in the dank cellar which served as the Torlig prison. The fetid air around her reeked with the smells of dead and dying creatures, and the steady pulse of dripping water could be heard echoing down the ancient corridors, mingling with the moans and cries of the other prison occupants.

But all of this escaped Rebecca's notice. For in her defeated and stunned brain, only one thought was present, caught forever in a cycle of numb repetition, like a scratched and broken record: *They are all dead.*

Even the trip from the *Vanguard's* landing sight to the Torlig base seemed nothing more than a blur. Did it matter that Sikaris, Prin, Rysthnuul, and even Tarrsk still lived and were prisoners like her? Or did it even matter that the Torlig had managed to tow the *Vanguard* to this base? As far as she was concerned, what difference did any of that make? It was all over now, for Lisa and the others were dead. She would never return to Earth. She was going to die, alone, on this cruel planet millions of miles from home. She would never see her parents, her sister, or her husband ever again.

Jeffrey. Would he even miss her? He had been so wrapped up in his archaeological excavations on the other side of the world that they rarely saw each other. She was amazed that he had even shown up to see her off. Maybe it was best that they could never have children. At least that way they wouldn't be left without their mother like…like…

Overcome with grief, Rebecca began to weep. In her mind's eye she could see Jenny and Amanda, their innocent faces suddenly marred by sorrow, their childhood forever robbed by the news that their mother would never be coming back. First Brad, now Lisa. Why hadn't she listened? Why had she been so set on leaving her children? Now they were left to face life without both of their parents.

"Where's Mommy? Why isn't Mommy coming home?"

Letting out a groan of pain, Rebecca fell to her knees and doubled over, her shoulders wracking with sobs as the words echoed in her mind.

Physically and emotionally spent, she kneeled on the cold stone floor for many long minutes without moving. Finally, the soreness in her knees began to draw her mind out of hibernation and focus it upon her present condition. Shifting positions, she sat down cross-legged on the floor and stared blankly at her surroundings.

What little she could see from the dim light that filtered through a grate in the ceiling revealed a small, dank chamber about ten feet square with a single rectangular gate made of rusting bars bent in a type of criss-cross pattern. The typical slipshod workmanship of the creatures of this planet was once again apparent in the uneven walls and floor, as well as the open wiring that led to the now darkened lighting system in the corridor.

Shivering in the cold, she crossed her arms over her chest, wishing she still had the Dakkar-nil armor. As her hands hugged her sides, she felt a bulge on the inside of her jumpsuit that made her pause, realization striking her. They had taken her protective outfit that Prin had given her, but they had left her with her jumpsuit, as well as her translator unit. Reaching into the inside pocket, she withdrew the object.

Why didn't they search my jumpsuit? she thought numbly, turning her journal over in her hand. Staring down at the it, she punched in the code and, for lack of anything better to do, began listening to her previous entries. It was so odd to see how her thought processes had changed since having landed here merely a day ago. So much had happened. And now…

Flipping the switch to record, she began speaking, her voice sounding hollow in the small chamber.

Journal Entry #6

I was wrong.

In my last entry I said that waiting was worse than any fate. But that was because I failed to imagine that my situation could become more horrible than death. Yet, here I am. Lisa, Captain Coffner, and the others are dead, the ship is locked away in some secure hangar, and I am alone in a cell. Escape is impossible. And even if I could manage to get out of the Torlig base, what would be the point? I can never return home. I will never see my family again. Why should I want to go on living?

I no longer fear death, for to live in this God-forsaken planet would be a far more terrible fate. Yet, with death so close, I cannot help but wonder: is this life all there is? Is there life after death? If all life in the universe evolved from the big bang, then life itself is nothing more than a cosmic accident. So even if Prin is right and life on Earth was created by some intelligent race, the question still remains: did they evolve, or were they created? Eventually, you must face the question of how did the first life, or for that matter, all of the matter in the universe, come into existence?

If there is no God, no Great Planner or Universal Force that designed everything, then why should we believe there to be anything beyond this material world? And if that is the case, then I should...no, I must, seek a quick end to this physical suffering.

But...

What if I am wrong? What if there really is a life after death? What if there is some sort of Higher Power that created everything? What is he, or she, or it—like? Is he a kind of big Santa Claus who answers the prayers of the faithful? Or is she a vengeful goddess who takes delight in causing suffering. Maybe it is asexual, like these creatures.

And does this god require anything from me to enter into paradise? Is there even a real paradise? Is there something one must do or believe before death? If there is, and I miss it, or fail to do it, then death should indeed be something to fear, for my existence after death would be worse than life here.

Why is it that we humans have a tendency to overlook the most important questions in life until it is too late? For surely the most important question one can ever ask is: what will happen to me when I die? All of the choices we make in this life are determined by the answer to that one question. If we believe in evolution, then there is no life after death, so we should seek a life of physical pleasure. If we believe in reincarnation, then we should do as many good deeds as possible to build up good karma. If we believe in God, then we seek to follow his or her rules, whatever we believe those to be.

But is there even a way to know for certain what is true? What if that which I believe to be true is not really true? I may believe it sincerely, but I might be sincerely wrong. What if one of the many "gods" that men claim to have spoken to actually turned out to be real? How could we know for sure? The only way would be for the real god to somehow reveal himself/herself/itself to us. To prove beyond a shadow of a doubt that it is the real god by a display of power and knowledge that no one else could duplicate.

Then, if one could know for sure that God was real, one could have hope. For only then would we have a reason to believe that life has any meaning or purpose, and we could know what requirements to meet before we die to be able to go to heaven. For if we believe we will go to a real heaven, then this world is as bad as our eternal existence is going to get. Even Ch'ran, as insane as he was, had hope that when he died he would go to be with Nix and live on in another, better life. In this case, ignorance truly was bliss.

But, I do not have the luxury to enjoy such ignorance. Science has ruined my "happy ending." For I believe that it has explained the origin of life apart from any divine interference. The harsh reality is that we are all just dust in the wind. And as painful and horrifying as this universe is, there is nothing else. As hard and cruel as it is to accept, now that I face death, I must believe it. This is as good as my existence is ever going to get.

Rebecca clicked off the recorder and sat motionless for several seconds, her thoughts dwelling on recent events. Listening to her journal had reminded her that she still had the vial of poison Prin had given her stashed away in the inside pocket of her jumpsuit.

Should I do it? It would be so simple, her thoughts seemed to taunt her. *The Torlig are going to torture me until I tell them everything about our technology, then they will simply dispose of me, or make me some kind of slave. Better to die here and now.*

Her mind made up, she slowly slid her hand into her pocket and removed the vial. She thought that once she had made the decision to go through with it, the actual act would be easy. Yet she fought to keep her hands from shaking as she pried the top off.

NO! Somewhere within her, a voice broke through her subconsciousness to the surface of her mind. *I don't want to die. I want to live! Don't give up now. There has to be hope.*

Suddenly, the loud creak of rusted metal hinges being forced open echoed like a thunderclap in the stillness of the prison. In the split second she had to make her choice, she gave in to the new voice inside and replaced the cap. Returning the vial to its hidden pocket, she turned to face her cell door just as the lights in the corridor brightened.

The sounds of numerous claws clicking on stone reached her ears long before the party responsible came into view. Three wounded and battered prisoners were being led past her cell by eight burly Torlig. As they passed, Rebecca caught sight of two violet colored eyes staring in her direction, one nearly swollen shut from some recent abuse.

Sikaris!

The sight of the familiar face, despite all of the recent experiences, lifted her spirits. She almost called out to the alien, but quickly decided against it. Moving a little closer to the prison door for a better view, Rebecca watched in silence as Rysth-nuul and Prin were paraded in front of her.

The change in the snake-like alien's countenance was striking. Where its long, whip-like tail had once been, now only a stump remained. Its moss-green scales were now blackened with streaks of dried blood that crossed over the alien's yellow body markings like smeared paint.

Most remarkable, however, were the creature's eyes. Not only had one of them been lost in the fight, but the other three showed that Rysth-nuul had lost something else as well. She now saw the same look she had seen in the eyes of the rodent-like creature back in Breuun's throne room: defeat.

The same look you have in your eyes.

As the dark thought whispered through her consciousness, she swallowed hard, recognizing it to be the truth.

"Move it, Diodre scum," one of the guards spat as it shoved Prin from behind. Stumbling, the ferret-like creature pressed its two right forearms against the opposite wall for support. As Prin recovered its balance, Rebecca noticed that one of its right hands was curled in upon itself, clearly crippled from some injury during the battle. In addition, all four of its wrists were encircled by some kind of metal bracelet. She would have assumed it to be handcuffs, except there was no chain linking them together.

The procession stopped just past her door, where one of the lead guards opened the gate to the cell that was diagonal to her own and herded the three prisoners inside. Slamming the door shut behind the dejected beings, the Torlig guards traipsed back down the corridor and disappeared into the darkness, followed immediately by another thunderous creak and the dousing of the hallway lights.

She sat in silence for several long moments, wondering if she should call out to Sikaris or Prin. *Why should I? They were going to kill me. Serves them right.* Yet, deep inside of her, that same voice rose up again with a thought that both surprised and disturbed her at the same time. *They were only following their instincts. How can they be expected to show kindness when they have never seen it before?* She paused, confused by her own thoughts. *If evil breeds evil, and good breeds good, then how could good ever evolve in a world of selfish evil? In the battle of good vs. evil, good must be taught, but evil comes naturally.*

"Rebecca."

The sound of her name being called brought her back from her reflections.

"Rebecca," again came the call, yet she did not immediately respond, for the voice did not sound like it belonged to any of her former companions.

The raspy, hoarse-sounding voice called a third time, speaking in perfect English. "Rebecca, it is Sikaris. Can you hear me?"

Sikaris? "Yes, I can hear you," she responded, her voice inflectionless. "What happened to you?"

The feline alien coughed several times, then gathered in a rattling breath and continued. "Tarrsk must have told his clanmates about all of our abilities. Once we had reached the prison, they made sure we would not be using them against our captors."

After another bout of coughing, it expounded further. "They injected me with something that has affected my throat, they cut off Rysth-nuul's tail, and they put some kind of binders on Prin that are supposed to turn his electrical current back upon himself, if he tries to use it."

Rebecca did not respond. What was there to say? After a moment, Sikaris spoke again, apparently preferring even a one-sided conversation to the stillness of the prison. "If that was not bad enough, Tarrsk must also have told them where we kept our hidden vials of toxin, for they took them from us."

So Rysth-nuul's worst nightmare has come true, she thought cynically. *It is a slave again, and it can't commit suicide.* In her mind, she envisioned the snake-like alien doing different kinds of menial tasks for its new masters. *It is nothing less than it deserves. May it rot here.*

The loud creak of long-neglected hinges and the sudden lighting of the hallway lights abruptly ended the conversation, as another group of Torlig guards dragged a cursing and struggling prisoner down the corridor. Once her eyes had adjusted to the light, she realized that the captive was none other than a bruised and beaten Tarrsk.

"No! They will murder me! Do not…Please! I can still be of use to Barraca."

Laughing sadistically, the guards opened the door to the same cell that Sikaris, Prin, and Rysth-nuul occupied, and roughly threw the traitor inside. The sight of their former companion roused Rysth-nuul and Prin from their lethargic, defeated state of mind. Even before the rectangular cell door was shut, the snake-like alien sprang forward and pounced on Tarrsk, driving its diseased body into the cold, unyielding stones of the floor. The prison guards laughed uproariously as Prin and Rysth-nuul began to pummel Tarrsk with their fists.

Rebecca found herself caught between her curiosity of what kind of revenge Sikaris, Rysth-nuul, and Prin would exact from the traitor and her knowledge that it would probably not be something she would want to witness. For the moment, her curiosity won out. As Rysth-nuul and Prin reigned down blow after blow upon the flaky, scaly flesh of the alligator-like being, she actually found herself wishing she was in the same cell so she could help deliver a few well-placed kicks of her own.

The prison guards began cheering and crowding closer to the door of the cell, obscuring her vision of what was transpiring inside. Inwardly cursing the creatures for blocking her view, she stepped back from the cell door, contenting herself with just listening to the screams of the traitorous creature.

What am I thinking? I can't believe I am actually upset that I can't see what's going on! One day on this planet and I am beginning to think like these things. Disgusted by her own bloodthirstiness, she sat down on the floor and listened as the guards hollered and hooted as each blow fell.

Then, after one final shout from the spectators, it was over. The Torlig guards remained for a few moments longer, hoping for more entertainment. When none seemed to present itself, they headed back down the corridor, laughing and talking to each other in excited tones about the beating they had just witnessed, as if it were some sporting event. Several seconds later, the outer door shut noisily and the lights flashed off, returning the prison to its previous state of eerie, black calmness.

Once her eyes had readjusted to the darkness, Rebecca looked across the hall to see if she could discern what had become of Tarrsk. The dim glow filtering down from the grate above afforded her just enough light to make out the traitorous alien's body lying sprawled on the floor in the back of the cell, its already disfigured and mutated face made even more revolting with the addition of blood and swelling. It appeared dead, but she could not see clearly enough to make an exact diagnosis.

No one moved or spoke for several minutes, leaving Rebecca to wonder what, if anything, Sikaris and the others were thinking. The only sounds that could be heard were the incessant dripping of water and the far-off moans of other prison occupants. Then, breaking through the silence, Rebecca's translator picked up the harsh, grating sound of Rysth-nuul as it cursed.

"Stupid, diseased, screel infested Torlig. I cannot believe that he was allowed to join Clan Grinath. Breuun should have known better. And then to let him come with us as the technician. That was just stupid. I bet it was part of his plan to break the piece we needed for our transport, too."

"Does that make any sense?" Sikaris shot back in the dark, fighting to keep from lapsing into another fit of coughing. "He said himself that he didn't want the Mrdangam to disable our transport. Why would he then break the part we needed to fix it?"

"I do not know," Rysth-nuul sneered in frustration, "but I still think it was too much of a coincidence, and a Krin power regulator does not crack easily."

Before the snake-like alien could say more, a soft moan rose up from the floor where Tarrsk lay.

"Well," Rysth-nuul said viciously, "it sounds like he is waking up. Maybe I should just ask him myself."

Rysth-nuul's shadowy form reached down and grabbed Tarrsk by the throat and hauled the creature to its feet. Several more groans escaped from the battered creature's abdominal mouth. Then, as Tarrsk became fully conscious, it rapidly sucked in a panicked breath.

"No! Please, wait! Do not hit me again!" it cried.

"Sikaris," Rysth-nuul said, "ask him why he broke the part we needed for the transport."

Prin stood and walked over to where the three of them stood, its eyes lighting up in interest. Sikaris stared at the traitor sternly and relayed the question, indicating to Rebecca that although the Torlig had not taken her translator, they obviously must have removed them from the others. Immediately Tarrsk began to gasp and choke. "I…I did not want our transport to be broken. But when I contacted my clan from the Joktan ruins, they told me it may be better if we were on foot, because there was a hunting party of Torlig on the edge of the mountain waiting for us."

"So you *did* break it, you slime," Rysth-nuul spat, after hearing the translation from Sikaris. Lashing out in anger, it threw the alligator-like being into the wall. "I told you, Sikaris. I knew it. We should just murder him now and be done with it."

"What is going on?" Prin asked, to which Sikaris quickly recounted the situation.

"Yes, yes," Prin remarked evilly. "I agree with Rysth-nuul. Let us murder him."

"Wait! Wait!" Tarrsk pleaded. "I know a way that we can escape!"

This last statement caught Rebecca's attention. Coming closer to the door of her cell until her face was pressed up against the cold metal bars, she made sure her translator was able to pick up every word.

Prin and Rysth-nuul, however, having not understood, were preparing to follow through with their suggestion when Sikaris stopped them. "Wait."

Crouching down next to the beaten Torlig, Sikaris ceased translating for Prin and Rysth-nuul and instead spoke directly to Tarrsk. "How?"

"Rebecca's weapon," it said in desperation. "We can use it to escape from the prison. Once we are out, we can steal a transport or something. I know many secret ways around the base from when I used to live here, before my disease."

Leaning into the crooked bars, Rebecca called out, "What 'weapon'? What are you talking about? I lost my gun in the caves, remember?"

By this time, Rysth-nuul and Prin had become impatient, sensing that something important was being discussed. "What is it? What are you talking about?" they each said in their own language.

Frantically trying to plead its case, Tarrsk ignored them and spoke directly to Rebecca. "I was afraid this might happen. I thought it would be good to have another plan in case my clan might betray me, so I lied to them and told them that you would die if they took your protective suit off. I did this so they would not find the weapon in your lower pocket, tucked inside your boot."

For a moment, Rebecca didn't move, her mind completely perplexed. Then, suddenly, the truth rushed over her like a wave. *My tool! I had completely forgotten about it. I hid it there back in the Grinathian base when I was...*

"Wait a minute," she said aloud. "How did you know I had it hidden there?"

"We figured that the easiest way to find out what your various items were used for was to give them to you and watch what you did with them," Sikaris replied nonchalantly, the last words dissolving into a fit of wheezing.

"Someone had better tell me what is going on!" Rysth-nuul demanded impatiently.

While Sikaris translated for Prin and Rysth-nuul, Rebecca sat in her cell, thankful that the darkness hid the flush in her cheeks. *Rebecca you fool! You should have known. They don't trust anybody. Of course they were watching. Well, in this case it was a good thing.* Having finished chiding herself, she extracted the small tool from its hiding place and opened it to the laser cutter. However, before lighting it, a thought suddenly struck her.

"Sikaris, ask Tarrsk if his clanmates have any hidden cameras set up in here." *Let's not make the same mistake twice, shall we?*

Once she received a negative confirmation from Tarrsk, she pressed the button and activated the laser. The tiny, reddish-orange beam nearly brought tears to her eyes as new hope rose up within her. Satisfied that it was fully functional, she turned it off again.

"So, what's the plan?"

20

Desperate Measures

AS MUCH as Rebecca hated to admit it, she was going to be forced to trust these creatures once again. She thought about the possibility of opening her cell and leaving them, but she quickly discarded the idea, for she knew she wouldn't get very far without their help. But once they were free, she would need something to keep them dependent on her.

"You want to trust this diseased Torlig scum again?" Rysth-nuul commented, after hearing Sikaris' translation of the previous conversation between Tarrsk and Rebecca.

"We have no choice," Sikaris said gruffly. "Besides, Tarrsk would not betray us again. Our escape is his only hope now."

"We must hurry," Tarrsk said worriedly. "I heard the guards saying that the games will be starting soon, and we are sure to be the main attraction. It will not be long before they come for us."

Rebecca knew that if she was going to guarantee their cooperation, it had to be now, while she still had leverage. "How do I know that you will not leave me behind or kill me after I free you?" she asked, putting more confidence into her voice then she actually felt.

Without bothering to translate, Sikaris merely stared at her for several moments with its deep, probing eyes. "You do not know. You will just have to trust us."

"That is not good enough, Sikaris," she countered. "You have to give me a reason to trust you."

"You will never make it on your own," the feline-like alien stated matter-of-factly, the distortion in its voice making it difficult to understand.

Rebecca did not back down. "And you know we don't have much of a chance anyway."

Sikaris was again silent, as if measuring her sincerity. Finally, the Grinathian leader responded, its simple statement catching Rebecca completely off guard.

"If you help us escape, I will tell you who created you and your people."

For several seconds, Rebecca was paralyzed with shock. *Could he really know? No. It has to be a trick. But still, what if...*Rebecca took her time collecting her thoughts. The others, growing tired of waiting, had begun to prod Sikaris for an explanation as to the delay.

Just as Sikaris had begun to translate, she called back to it, breaking into its conversation midstream. "Nice try, Sikaris. But it still doesn't give me any way to hold you to your promise. If I help you escape, you must help me get my ship back."

The large, cat-like alien stared at her through the curtain of darkness that separated their cells. In the dim light that filtered down from the grates in the ceiling, Rebecca thought she saw the slightest hint of a smile cross Sikaris' features. Turning towards the others, it translated her demands.

"What?" Tarrsk said in exasperation. "We cannot. His ship would be in the main hangar. It will be heavily guarded. It would be much easier for us to try to steal a transport."

"But they would catch us in a transport. My ship could fly us to your base much quicker. Also, its advanced weapons technology could fend off any attack," she lied. "And," she continued, baiting her trap further, "Breuun would reward you for returning with such a prize."

It took several minutes for Sikaris to translate and for the four aliens to discuss her plan, leaving Rebecca time to formulate one of her own. *Once we are off the ground, I will pilot the ship out of the atmosphere. They will then either have to kill me and try to fly an unknown ship through an atmospheric entry, or they can return to Earth with me. Even with all of the scientific community wanting a piece of them, I should be able to convince them that their lives would be better off on Earth than here.* And although her conscious mind did not admit it, deep down inside, she thought of how she would become a world-wide celebrity and hero.

"Alright, we will try to escape in your ship," Sikaris said at last. "Tarrsk says that he knows a way we can access the hangar that your ship is in without being noticed."

"Good," she replied simply, although within her she fought to contain her excitement. "Let's get out of here." Igniting the small laser cutter, she set to work on the locking mechanism of her cell door. Within thirty seconds she had severed the lock, allowing the door to swing freely. Gritting her teeth in anticipation, she quickly opened her rusted cell door just enough to squeeze through, wincing at the blaring sound of the neglected hinges.

"Quickly!" Tarrsk whispered anxiously. "They may have heard."

"Shut up!" she snapped back, nervously cracking her right knuckles on her leg as she prepared to work on their cell door. Breathing deeply to calm her shaking hands, she set to work on the lock.

Each second that passed saw her tension build exponentially, until she felt the muscles in her body begin to ache from constant use. "Come on, come on," she urged the machine quietly.

Finally, she felt the telltale release of the cutting blade as it sliced through the last centimeter of metal. Stepping away from the door, she shut off the laser as the others opened the cell door and quickly filed out.

"Now what?" Rebecca whispered to Sikaris.

Without hesitation, Sikaris took a deep, rattling breath and resumed its command of the small party of hunters. "Cut Prin's binders off."

Being careful not to slash open Prin's wrists in the process, Rebecca made several surgical slices that allowed the ferret-like creature to remove the bracelets. Flexing its three good hands to revive the circulation, it smiled as tiny blue sparks shot forth from the tips of its fingers, like small firecrackers ready to explode.

The sudden sound of the outer prison door opening sent Rebecca's heart into her throat. Sikaris reacted instantly by grabbing Rebecca's laser cutter as the lights in the corridor flared to life. Igniting the tool, Sikaris reached up and sliced open a deep gash in the piping that ran over their heads. Immediately, a torrent of water fell onto the floor in front of them.

"Everyone, back inside," Sikaris shouted hoarsely.

They had barely managed to reenter the cells when eight Torlig guards burst through the inner prison door and spilled into the hallway, weapons at the ready. Upon seeing the broken pipe, the guards paused in confusion.

Their hesitation cost them their lives. Extending its hands between the bars, Prin touched to water-soaked floor. Suddenly, blue sparks lit up the prison hallway as Prin sent a blast of high voltage energy into the rapidly expanding puddle. The Torlig guards began to convulse violently as the energy was transported through the water and into their bodies. Within seconds, the entire group of guards lay unmoving on the hallway floor.

"Quickly now," Sikaris coughed, "grab their weapons."

Rebecca picked up a large pistol from the nearest alien and smiled. It felt good to be armed again.

Tarrsk led the way through the outer prison door and into the guard room, where they encountered several more Torlig. Caught by surprise by the liberated prisoners, they were quickly mowed down by the Grinathians' newly acquired weapons.

Moving fully into the room, Tarrsk ran quickly towards the center table where several objects lay in a clutter. "Good. They have not yet moved our translators." Passing out the devices, the group paused long enough to put them on and power them up.

Prin, however, seemed to be perturbed, looking around the room as if in search of some important, lost artifact. Finally, it looked toward Sikaris. "Where is the rest of our equipment? Our packs, weapons, and…other items?"

Tarrsk gave an odd shrug. "The scientists are probably studying them. Who cares about that now, anyway?"

Prin looked concerned. "Sikaris," it said, placing a clawed hand on the tall creature's arm, "Rebecca's recording device had much information about Clan Grinath. Breuun will be mad to hear that the Torlig now have it."

The cat-like alien stared down at the Grinathian scientist. "We cannot worry about that now. Besides, Breuun will not find out about it, will he?"

Reaching up to brush the pocket of her jumpsuit that contained her journal, Rebecca mind flashed back to the Modir caves, the image of Prin's shadowy form hovering over her bag suddenly taking on new meaning. Now that she knew why the alien scientist was interested in her journal, it made her all the more thankful that she had hidden it when she did. It would become invaluable if she managed to make it back home.

"This way," Tarrsk called as it disappeared through a doorway to her right. Sikaris was next to follow, then Rebecca, Prin, and finally Rysthnuul.

They moved as quickly and quietly as possible down the featureless, stone hallway until they came to a flight of stairs that ascended to a metal door. "Wait here," Tarrsk said. Opening the door, their guide slipped silently through the portal. After a brief inspection of the area beyond, Tarrsk waved them through.

"We are lucky. Most of my clan are in the arena, so we should not meet anyone," Rebecca overheard Tarrsk tell Sikaris as it led them down the corridor.

They had not gone far when Tarrsk stopped outside a nondescript door. Signaling that they should wait, it slipped inside. As they stood nervously in the hallway, half expecting a contingent of Torlig to round the corner at any moment, they could hear the sounds of a brief struggle coming from the other side of the door. A second later, Tarrsk reappeared and waved them inside.

They stepped into what looked to Rebecca like some sort of boiler room or utility closet. Several large cylindrical machines were spread out in rows around the area, thick pipes extending from their tops to form a maze over the heads of those standing on the floor. Steam and hot gases escaped from valves and hatches in various locations, causing the temperature and humidity in the room to escalate to stifling levels.

On the floor, just inside the doorway, two dead slaves lay in a heap, obviously the result of Tarrsk's handiwork.

"This way," their alligator-like guide said as it began a rapid ascent up a ladder mounted against the wall. Rebecca stared at the rickety ladder with trepidation. It was clearly overused and in desperate need of repair. Rysth-nuul was inclined to agree. "You want us to climb *that* thing? It looks like it could collapse at any minute."

Sikaris, halfway up the ladder, barked down at its pessimistic companion. "Have it your way. Good luck finding another way to the hangar."

Rebecca cracked her knuckles, then grabbed the first rung. *If it will hold Sikaris…*, she thought. Taking a deep breath, she hauled herself up. When she reached the thin catwalk, which hung nearly forty feet above the floor and ran the length of the room, Sikaris and Tarrsk were already deep in discussion.

"Yes," Tarrsk was saying. "I used to repair these pipes. This access way follows the entire piping network under the floors of the base."

Rebecca followed Tarrsk's gaze toward the far wall, where the catwalk upon which they stood ended. The pipes, however, continued on through the wall with enough space between them and the ceiling for a single being to crawl.

"Let us go, then. We do not know how much longer it will take them to find that we are missing."

Leaping onto the nearest pipe, Tarrsk began crawling expertly into the maintenance hole. Sikaris was quick to follow, its broad shoulders nearly brushing the sides of the narrow passage. Rysth-nuul had finally reached the top of the ladder as Rebecca was preparing to mount the pipe.

Suddenly, over the roar of the hissing steam and rumbling machinery, the unmistakable sound of a door opening could be heard. Freezing in her tracks, Rebecca looked down towards the room's entrance to see a small group of three slaves huddled together over the bodies of their dead comrades. The sight of blood on the floor sent them into a frenzy. Looking around the room nervously like caged animals, they turned and quickly fled through the door, disappearing into the hallway beyond.

"Go!" Rysth-nuul said, spurring Rebecca on. "It will not be long now before they come looking for us."

Needing no further prompting, Rebecca mounted the pipe and set off into the darkness of the access tunnel.

Once they were through the wall, the serviceway opened up wider, allowing any Torlig repair workers the freedom to climb underneath any of the pipes to affect repairs. For Rebecca and the others who lacked the ability to cling to smooth surfaces, the prospect of falling off the large pipe onto the tangles of wires, hoses, and conduits containing who knew what, was an ever present concern. Nevertheless, they crawled on in near darkness until Rebecca had lost all track of time. Finally, Tarrsk brought them to a halt beneath a three-foot square hatch.

"We are here," Tarrsk said as it performed a 180-degree turn on the pipe to face them. It waited until Rysth-nuul and Prin had caught up, then began its description of what awaited them above. "This will take us into the southwest corner of the hangar that Rebecca's ship should be in. The main hangar door leading outside is on the north wall, but the controls to open it are among the machines along the western wall. In the center of the south wall are the main entrance doors that connect the hangar to the base. There will be guards posted outside them, so we must try to lock them manually before the scientists inside the hangar raise the alarm."

"Rysth-nuul and Prin, you will lock the doors," Sikaris said in its raspy voice. "Tarrsk and I will fight the scientists and open the hangar doors. Rebecca, get your ship ready to fly."

"I…I cannot do it by myself," she stammered. "I need at least one of you to help with all of the pre-launch procedures. It isn't difficult, but it would take me much longer to do it by myself."

Sikaris considered for a moment, then replied, "Rysth-nuul, you are more familiar with piloting machines, so you will help Rebecca." Sikaris coughed into its shoulder to muffle the sound, then continued. "Prin, you will have to lock the doors by yourself. Are there any questions?"

If there had been any, there was no time to ask them, for suddenly the blaring sound of alarms could be heard throughout the base.

"They have discovered our escape!" Tarrsk said nervously.

With one mighty kick from its powerful legs, Sikaris sent the hatch above their heads flying into the hangar. Leaping up out of the serviceway, they found the Torlig scientists looking around in confusion at the sound of the alarm. Upon spying the intruders suddenly standing between them and the exit doors, they immediately bolted towards the main control consoles on the western walls. Sikaris and Tarrsk, being the first out of the crawlspace, set off in hot pursuit.

Rebecca waited as Prin leapt out before her, then she and Rysth-nuul quickly climbed out. Pausing momentarily to take in her surroundings, Rebecca's heart swelled with excitement at the sight of the *Vanguard*, sitting majestically on its wheeled landing gear in the center of the large hangar, its sleek nose pointed towards the eastern wall. In front of the ship, almost out of view from their rear-side vantage point, sat some kind of crane-like vehicle. Scattered throughout the rest of the hangar were what Rebecca assumed to be various equipment storage containers and diagnostic tools.

"Where is the entrance hatch?" Rysth-nuul asked beside her, its voice strained with tension.

"On the right side," she said, pointing towards the hatch even as she began sprinting in that direction. A moment later, she stood before the access panel, breathing heavily from excitement. She had finally made it! With trembling fingers, she punched in the code. As she waited for the boarding ramp to lower sufficiently enough for her to enter, she scanned the outer hull of the ship for signs of intrusion or damage.

Her heart stopped suddenly as she examined more closely the crane-like vehicle in front of the ship. "Tarrsk! Sikaris! It's still connected!" she shouted toward the pair of aliens who were engaged in battle with the scientists who had turned to fight them. Sikaris glanced briefly in her direction and nodded in confirmation.

"Let us go," Rysth-nuul urged. "Let them worry about it."

Heeding the snake-like alien's advice, Rebecca led the way into the ship. Had it not been for the desperateness of the situation, she would surely have broken into sobs at the familiar sight and sounds of the vessel.

However, with her mind focused only on the task of getting the ship into the air, she brushed aside all feelings and thoughts of home.

Making their way into the cockpit, Rebecca began issuing instructions to Rysth-nuul. With some difficulty, she struggled to remember everything she had learned in her cross-training piloting classes taken seemingly ages ago. Praying that she wouldn't forget some crucial step, she began flipping switches and priming the engines for flight, while at the same time attempting to instruct her alien copilot in the basics of piloting the unfamiliar spacecraft.

"Come on, come on," she repeated to herself, cracking her knuckles nervously as the hum of the engines warming up slowly grew in volume and intensity. Looking out the window, she saw that Tarrsk was running rapidly toward the rear of the *Vanguard* while Prin, who had successfully locked the hangar's main entrance, had returned to help Sikaris finish off the last of the scientists, many of whom surrendered rather than try to fight off the attackers without weapons.

An enormous thud echoed throughout the hangar as the Torlig guards attempted to break through the main doors. Almost simultaneously, the floor beneath her rocked back and forth, nearly sending her tumbling over one of the command chairs. After a brief moment of panic, she realized that the sudden motion must have been due to Tarrsk releasing them from the grip of the crane-like vehicle. *We might actually make it! Now if only Prin and Sikaris would hurry up and—*

Her translator sprung to life, interrupting her thoughts. "Tarrsk, the scientists managed to damage the controls. We cannot open the hangar door. Do you know if—"

The transmission was abruptly cut short by a mighty explosion that erupted on the southern wall. Before the smoke had even cleared, several Torlig warriors poured through the opening like water bursting forth from a crack in a dam.

"What are you waiting for?" Rysth-nuul shouted. "Use the weapons from the ship!"

"I...I lied. It doesn't have weapons," she yelled back in exasperation. Picking up her stolen pistol, she ran back towards the open hatch.

"What?" Rysth-nuul hissed. "Where are you going?"

Once she reached the entrance ramp, she opened fire at the Torlig guards with her pistol, drawing some of their attention and giving the trapped Prin and Sikaris a much needed reprieve. Rebecca noted with despair, however, that with each passing second, another Torlig hunter would slip through the breach formed by the explosion, further diminishing their chances of escape.

Sikaris and Prin, coming to the same conclusion, rushed out from behind the console and made a desperate dash for the ramp of the *Vanguard*, hoping that Rebecca's covering fire would provide enough distraction for the ever increasing number of Torlig.

Rebecca's arm ached from the constant jolting of the large weapon built for a Torlig claw, not a human hand. Ignoring her pain, she sprayed fire relentlessly, trying unsuccessfully to stem the advance of the hunters, like a fisherman plugging a leak in his boat, only to have two more open beneath him.

Her clip depleted, she quickly slammed her last stolen supply of ammunition into place as Prin and Sikaris ducked behind a storage container, almost halfway to the ship. She resumed firing, noting as she did so that the number of Torlig fighters had grown to nearly a dozen. As much as she wanted to help Prin and Sikaris, she knew that if they did not make it in the next few seconds, she would be forced to leave without them. *If Tarrsk manages to get that blasted door open!* she added.

Glancing toward them, Rebecca locked eyes briefly with Sikaris, its deep orbs reflecting calm resolve. In that instant, she could see that Sikaris new that time was up. It was now or never. Leaping from their concealment, the two Grinathians made one final desperate sprint for the ship.

Rebecca resumed her fire when suddenly a loud squealing of metal on metal filled the hangar and the deep red of the setting sun flooded in through the hangar door that was opening rapidly.

"Yeaaaahhhh!" Rebecca yelled in triumph. *Tarrsk did it!* "Rysth-nuul, the door is open! As soon as the others are in, we—"

Out of the corner of her eye she saw Rysth-nuul's twisted arms lunging for her. "We are leaving NOW!" it hissed.

Her reflexes taking over, she sidestepped the attack and spun her body around to avoid the alien's grasp. However, in doing so, Rebecca miscalculated her step and her foot slipped off the platform. Losing her balance, she fell sideways, struck the edge of the ramp, and tumbled to the hangar floor, her pistol flying from her hand as she landed.

For a brief instant, the impact caused her to lose consciousness. She awoke a second later to the thunderous roar of the *Vanguard's* engines. Dazed, she stared around her in bewilderment. Off to her left, both Sikaris and Prin lay unmoving on the floor. With the two of them out of the fight, the Torlig guards were now focused solely on stopping the *Vanguard*, which was slowly and awkwardly turning towards the open hangar door.

Rising painfully to her feet, she cried out in despair as the vehicle's entrance ramp closed tightly, sealing her fate. "No!" she gasped. "NO!"

With her mind consumed with catching the departing ship, she didn't notice the Torlig hunters until they had tackled her to the floor. As she lay on the cold, hard surface of the hangar, she watched in shock as her last hope of escape passed through the wide doors and into the open.

Time seemed to slow down to a crawl as she watched Tarrsk leap from the wall above the hangar door to land on the ship as it passed beneath. Once clear of the hangar, Rysth-nuul began to accelerate, seemingly unsure of how to lift-off from the ground. The snake-like alien's unfamiliarity with the controls gave the Torlig outer defenses enough time to acquire their target. Just as Rysth-nuul rotated the vertical lift engines into place and had managed to raise the ship twenty feet into the air, several rockets streaked into the sky, exploding into the belly of the *Vanguard* with fury.

The resulting explosion rocked the base and sent large chunks of flaming debris hurling out in all directions, mirroring the shattering of Rebecca's hopes within her.

21

Sikaris' Promise

AS THE last piece of burning metal settled onto the dry and cracked ground, Rebecca was hauled to her feet by two Torlig guards. Her face was completely devoid of expression or emotion, for the shock of the destruction of the *Vanguard* had caused her mind to turn inward, replaying the last minutes' events in a never ending loop.

They had tried and failed. Now, escape was impossible. She would die on this planet, and probably soon, for any usefulness she had was destroyed along with the ship. The only hope she had now was that her death would be swift and painless.

The Torlig hunters began to half-carry her by her arms across the hangar floor towards the main entrance. Still in a dazed state, she stared down at the bodies of Sikaris and Prin. A hollow sadness filled her at the sight of the scientist's sightless eyes staring at the ceiling, its heart pumping the last of its blood through the numerous wounds in its body.

Next to Prin, Rebecca was surprised to see several Torlig lifting Sikaris to its clawed feet, its right leg covered with blood, and its arm hanging useless at its side. In addition, she noticed a dozen or so holes in the creature's leathery skin folds on its right side.

"Barraca will not like this," a harsh voice said in front of her. Slowly turning her attention toward the speaker, she recognized the Torlig commander that had been in charge of the hunting party that had captured them and killed Ch'ran. "No," it continued, staring hard at Rebecca as though it was contemplating various methods of torture it wished to inflict upon her, "he will not be happy at all. Take him to the arena holding cell."

Rebecca offered no resistance and allowed the Torlig guards to lead her away. Taking one last glance towards the open hangar door, she watched as the last vestiges of reddish sunlight slipped beyond the horizon, plunging the world into darkness.

An indeterminable amount of time passed, as they led her through the passageways of the Torlig base and into a cell that was nearly identical to the one she had just left, with the exception being that instead of eerie silence broken by moaning prisoners, this cell was filled with the far-off sounds of the roaring mob of bloodthirsty Torlig.

The guards shoved her into the cell, followed a moment later by Sikaris, who instantly collapsed to the floor without the support of the guards. Slamming the door shut, four of the Torlig hunters took up positions outside their cell, their eyes alert and suspicious, as if daring Rebecca to try something.

In numb despair, she leaned her back against the wall and slowly slid down it until her knees were pulled up against her chest. Hugging her legs tightly, Rebecca wept softly.

After several long seconds, Sikaris hoarse voice spoke quietly next to her, cutting through her emotion.

"I am ready to fulfill my promise."

"What?" she said, looking up, her red-rimmed eyes wet with tears.

Sikaris was sitting next to her, its violet eyes piercing through the darkness of the cell. Even with one eye almost swollen shut, there could be no mistaking the expression etched into the creature's face: Sikaris' eyes shown brilliantly with a compassion she had never seen from anyone before, a compassion that, despite all odds, filled her with hope and infused her with strength.

Had it not been for the depth of emotion conveyed by Sikaris' eyes, Rebecca would have lashed out at the alien leader for wanting to discuss some silly promise after what had just happened. Instead, she simply said, "What promise?"

Sikaris shifted its position until it was directly in front of her. "I promised that if you helped us escape, then I would tell you who created you."

Rebecca chuckled sarcastically. "In case you hadn't noticed, we didn't escape."

"Nevertheless, you kept to your end of the bargain. It is time for the truth to be revealed to you."

Within her, Rebecca felt that same, odd, almost frightening sensation she had felt before when looking at Sikaris. Yet, at the same time, she felt an equally strong feeling of excited expectation, despite her grief and despair.

Staring deep into her eyes, Sikaris spoke. "You and Prin talked often about many things. What did he say to you about how life began on your planet?"

"He...he said that he believed we were created, and he thought that...that you might know something about it. Do you...did your... people create life on my planet?" she asked, unconsciously holding her breath in anticipation.

"No." Sikaris said. "I was created, like you."

So Prin was right, she thought in wonder. *It's too bad he—it—never learned the truth.* "So, then...who did create my people? And why? Did they create you as well? What planet are they from?"

Sikaris shook its head from side to side, as if Rebecca's questions were sapping its patience. "You have much knowledge, yet you lack wisdom. Do you not yet see? Do you not yet understand?"

See what? Understand what? Rebecca, confused by Sikaris' questions, simply stared back at the alien, when it suddenly dawned on her that Sikaris' voice sounded stronger, and its coughing and rasping were gone.

But before she could verbalize her thoughts, Sikaris continued. "Do you remember how Tarrsk disabled our transport by breaking one piece? All of the rest of the vehicle was dependent on the correct operation of that one small piece, and thousands of other pieces just like it. Each part is vital and necessary for the vehicle to function. If even one piece is damaged, the entire machine becomes useless. And yet, one single cell in your body is far more complex than that transport. It is even more complex than the ship that brought you to this planet.

"In the caves, you recognized the Modir boundary marker. You knew it was some kind of written message, even though you had never seen those symbols before. How? How did you know? Because you recognized a pattern to the marks. You saw the symmetry in the letters, and you knew that natural causes could not account for such precision. You knew it had to be written by an intelligent being, for information can only be created by intelligence, not by chance.

"Yet when you look at living things, you suddenly change your thinking. You believe that DNA, which is the most efficient information storage system in the universe, could be the result of non-thinking, random processes!

"Even more," Sikaris continued as it stood to its feet, "stored information is useless without some way to read it and translate the coded symbols into meaning. You recognized that the Modir marker contained a message, but you had no way of understanding it. In the same way, life not only contains information, but it has a means to translate that information, and microscopic, biological machines to carry out the instructions."

As Rebecca sat dumbfounded, trying to follow Sikaris' impassioned speech, it suddenly occurred to her that the feline-like creature was standing on its injured leg, and its right arm no longer hung limply at its side. However, Sikaris continued before she could comment.

"Remember your conversation with Prin in the cave regarding mutations? Don't you realize that mutations are mistakes in DNA? They never add new information in the genes of a being. Therefore, even if you had an eternity of time, mutations will never cause one animal to become another, because the possibility of new genetic information to create new structures is simply not there!"

The cell door behind Sikaris opened abruptly, cutting off anything further it might have said. Several guards entered swiftly and grabbed the Grinathian leader from behind. With Sikaris' voice returning to normal and its body miraculously healed, Rebecca expected it to launch into a last-ditch attack, and prepared herself for that eventuality. However, the cat-like alien merely allowed the guards to lead it out of the cell, without the slightest bit of resistance.

Resigning herself to her fate, Rebecca followed suit. The Torlig guards led her through the hallway and into the domed arena. The frenzied multitude of spectators broke into howls and screams that brought her back to the reality of this waking nightmare.

Her boots sank into the soft sand beneath her feet, causing her knee to throb once again from the stress of walking on the shifting surface. Sikaris' words a few moments before were instantly forgotten as paralyzing fear crept into her heart and body, heightened by the smell of dried blood and death that permeated the entire area.

As they approached a set of chains anchored in the ground near the center of the circular arena, uncontrollable panic began to invade her mind. Twisting and contorting her body in every conceivable way, she fought against her captors, who easily restrained her and kept her moving inexorably forward.

"Sikaris!" she screamed. "Do something! Oh, God! Oh, God, please help me!"

The guards locked manacles of rusted iron onto her wrists and stepped away. Pulling immediately on the chains connected to them, she quickly discovered the other end to be firmly attached to a metal ring, which was cemented into the ground beneath the sand, like a dog leashed to a stake in the yard. She could run, but not far.

Falling to her knees, she buried her face in her hands as the throng cheered around her. Softly, almost imperceptibly, Rebecca did the only thing she had left to do. Like a child curled in her father's lap, she called out softly.

"God, if you are real, please help me. Have mercy on me."

Shoulders heaving, she began to weep, her tears mingling with the dust and sand beneath her.

The sudden touch of two gentle hands upon her shoulders startled her. Looking up, her eyes met Sikaris', who was kneeling before her on one knee.

"Rebecca, time is short. You must listen and understand."

The roar of the cheering crowd seemed to fade into the background as Sikaris spoke. "You do not yet comprehend the truth because you have been blinded by what others have told you. You have discarded the truth as an answer before you ever asked the question. You have become willingly ignorant, choosing to believe the lie because you do not like the ramifications of the only other option."

Suddenly, the grating sound of rusted metal being forced into motion reverberated throughout the arena. Taking her eyes off of Sikaris, she looked over its shoulder and froze in sheer horror. The Torlig spectators howled in anticipation as a creature out of Rebecca's darkest dreams emerged from a holding cell on the opposite end of the arena.

The spindly-legged monstrosity was nearly eight feet tall walking on all seven of its mangled limbs. As she watched, it reared up on its three hindmost legs, nearly doubling its height. Its bulbous, segmented body looked like a cross between a large, multi-armed Torlig and the insect-like V'skir. To Rebecca, however, its resemblance to some freakish spider was what caused her to begin backing away in panic.

Somewhere in the back of her mind, her irrational childhood fear of spiders surged to the forefront, causing her to begin crawling backward on her elbows, her back carving a trench into the sand, her eyes riveted to the grotesque creature before her. Panting heavily, Rebecca began to gasp and cry, her fortitude spent, her resolve and composure evaporated.

The creature, seeing its prey's feeble attempts to flee, seemed to draw strength from Rebecca's fear. Letting out a shrill, high pitched shriek, it lumbered forward, the pincers in front of its mouth opening and closing in expectation.

Suddenly, Sikaris was standing over her, blocking her line of sight with its body. "Rebecca, look at me!" it commanded. "REBECCA!"

Half out of her mind with fear, she shifted her gaze to stare at her companion.

"You must listen to me," Sikaris said calmly, its voice gentle, yet firm. The longer she looked into the alien being's fathomless eyes, the more the sound of the crowd diminished, along with her fear.

"You now believe that you were created, but do you not see that the same logic that convinced you that you had to be created, is the same logic that proves that all life in the universe must have been created? Evolution did not occur on Earth, nor did it occur here on Ka'esch, or anywhere else in the universe, for evolution is not possible. It is a lie formulated by the enemy."

"Who…who are you?" Rebecca muttered.

"I am a messenger. I have been sent by the One who has created all of life. The Great Designer of the Universe."

Suddenly, Sikaris' features began to alter subtly. The fur-covered scales dissolved to reveal beneath it tanned skin, so smooth it almost seemed like glass. Gone were the claw-like hands and feet, replaced instead by human hands and feet that were strong and masculine. Instead of folds of skin stretching between its limbs, a robe of purest white surrounded its body. Its face shone like a hot, white star, its light washing away the arena, the spider-like creature, and even the ground they stood upon.

Rebecca covered her face with her arms like a child attempting to hide in plain sight from an adult, then, overwhelmed by awe, she rolled over and lay face down in the sand before Sikaris as if dead.

Gently cupping her face in its powerful hands, Sikaris slowly lifted Rebecca's head. "Do not be afraid," he said, his voice low and comforting.

Although the being kneeling before her looked nothing like the creature that had been her companion, its violet, depthless eyes were unmistakable. She knew that until the day she drew her last breath, the image of those deep orbs would be indelibly burned into her memory.

"The Almighty Lord of the Universe has brought you here to show you many things. Never forget what you were shown and all that you have learned. You are the chosen vessel. Chosen to deliver the message to those who will listen.

"Return now, and remember."

The light surrounding them intensified until all Rebecca could see were Sikaris' eyes fixed upon her. Then, a moment later, even they faded away as her entire being succumbed to the shining radiance.

22

Rebecca's Calling

"SHE'S COMING around!"

The voice seemed to be coming from far off in the distance. Rebecca could faintly hear someone or something moving near her, but her mind seemed sluggish, as if her senses and brain were not communicating properly with each other. She opened her eyes, yet all she could see was whiteness, like standing in the center of a blizzard.

Then, gradually, the whiteness began to fade away and images started to coalesce before her.

"Rebecca, can you hear me?"

The words were clearer this time, and the voice sounded vaguely familiar, but her mind just couldn't make the connection. She tried to speak, but, like everything else, her vocal chords refused to respond to her mental prodding.

"I will go and inform the others."

She sensed more movement, then the sound of a door opening and closing. She continued to struggle to make sense of the swirling images before her eyes until they became clearer and took on a definite form. Finally, after what seemed like an eternity, the pieces of the puzzle clicked together, and she recognized that the shape before her was the smiling face of her friend.

"Welcome back to the land of the living. You gave us quite a scare."

"Lissha?" Rebecca managed to say, with much effort. Her entire mouth felt as though it was coated with peanut butter.

"In the flesh," Lisa said jovially.

"But, you…you died."

Lisa raised one eyebrow, then smirked. "I feel pretty good for a dead person. Here, drink this."

Rebecca drank mechanically from the offered straw, the cool liquid washing away the stickiness in her mouth and throat. Even the small drink seemed to revive her and bring her strength.

Experimentally, Rebecca attempted to sit up, only to be gently held down by Lisa. "Whoa, easy does it. You need to give your body a chance to recuperate."

"Recuperate?" she said, her brows knitting together. "From what?"

"You have been in a coma for two weeks, since shortly after we arrived."

"Arrived? Where are we?" Rebecca asked.

"2021 PK."

The memories returned with such force that Rebecca sat up and gasped for breath like a drowning person breaking through to the surface. "What?!? We have to get out of here! The Torlig—the Torlig might be blending…waiting in disguise…we…we have to take off, now!"

Startled, Lisa jumped back, then immediately put her hands on Rebecca's shoulders in an effort to steady her friend's shaking body.

"What are you talking about? Relax. Everything is okay."

She could see it all vividly: her capture, the "rescue" by Sikaris, the trial before Breuun, the Mrdangam, the Ryazan, the caves, the destruction of the *Vanguard*…

"The *Vanguard*!" she cried in amazement. "We are inside the *Vanguard*!"

"Yes," Lisa said, worry etched on her face. "Of course we are."

"But I saw…it was destroyed! How did you…they told me you were dead. What about the others?" she said as she brushed aside Lisa's hands and tried getting out of bed.

"Oh, no you don't," Lisa countered, pushing Rebecca back down. "The others are fine. Now—"

"YOU DON'T UNDERSTAND!" Rebecca suddenly shouted, shoving Lisa away from her, her hysteria fueling her strength. "THEY ARE OUT THERE! WE MUST—"

The door suddenly opened behind her and two men rushed in. Rebecca froze in mid-sentence at the sight of them. "Captain Coffner? Ricky?" she breathed in surprise. Shaking her head as if to ward off her shock, she continued her urgent ranting. "Quick. We may yet escape. Me must take off now before—"

"Calm down, Rebecca. You need to rest," the Captain said, attempting to help Lisa keep her patient from leaping out of bed.

Struggling against the three of them, Rebecca fought like a caged lioness. "LET GO OF ME! YOU...MUST...LISTEN!"

In her panic, Rebecca did not hear Captain Coffner's command to Lisa, nor did she notice as Lisa picked up the tranquilizer and administered the dosage. All she remembered was a blackness that grew and enveloped her until she fell unconscious.

Rebecca slowly regained consciousness to find that her entire body ached as if she had been run over by a rampaging elephant. Even the slightest movement of her arm caused her to groan in pain. Opening her eyes, she saw two familiar faces leaning over her.

"Try to relax, Rebecca. You overdid it last time. Your muscles were weak from not being used, and you pushed them to their limits," Captain Coffner said with concern.

Still groggy from the aftereffects of the tranquilizer, Rebecca remained silent.

"Your family sends their greetings," he continued. "They were extremely relieved to hear that you have come out of your coma. Mission Command also sends their regards."

As the effects of the drug began to wear off, the captain's words began to penetrate her muddled mind. "Cap...captain...Lisa...we need to..." she said weakly.

"Now, now. Let's not start with that again," Lisa said warningly. "I'm sorry we had to sedate you, but your body was not ready for the strain, and we were afraid you would hurt yourself."

Rebecca shook her head slowly. "No. You don't...understand. There are...creatures...out there."

Captain Coffner laid his hand gently on Rebecca's arm. "We have searched the entire area during the two weeks that you have been in a coma. We even flew to different locations around the planet, hoping for some signs of life. Trust us, there is nothing out there. I'm sorry to break the news to you, but our primary mission has failed, Rebecca. This planet is an inhospitable, lifeless rock. No aliens, no animals, no vegetation, not even any microbes."

"But...I have seen them. They can blend in...you can't see them. They captured me...I...was trying to escape. We went under the mountain."

Lisa leaned closer to Rebecca, her voice comforting. "Rebecca, when I left to help Team One repair their MDU, you were fine. After we brought the units on-line, we returned to find you unconscious, laying face down just inside the clearing around the ship. You were only by yourself for about forty-five minutes.

"We got you back to the ship and did a medical check on you. Your vital signs were normal, and you seemed perfectly fine in all other areas," Lisa continued. "Although you appeared to be in some sort of coma, you had an unusual amount of brain activity, almost as if you were still awake. It sounds like you had a very vivid dream."

A dream? Rebecca closed her eyes momentarily. *Could it really have been just a dream?*

"*Return now, and remember.*" The words echoed in her mind as she saw Sikaris' eyes staring out at her from behind a veil of whiteness. *No. It was too real. There has to be more to it than that.*

Opening her eyes, she looked at her friends and shook her head in confusion. "No. I was there. I remember everything. The name of this planet is Ka'esch. There is a group of aliens called the Grinathians. They were helping me." As she spoke, the memories cleared away the residue of the sedative, focusing her mind. "Sikaris, Prin, Rysth-nuul—I can tell you all of their names, what they looked like, even how they smelled."

Captain Coffner and Lisa exchanged concerned glances.

"I'm not crazy! I know what I saw!"

"Rebecca, think for a moment," Lisa said intently. "You told me that I had died. Do I look dead to you?"

"They *told* me you were dead, but I never saw any proof," she responded, her voice rising in pitch. "Maybe they lied to me. Maybe..."

"But you also said that you saw the *Vanguard* destroyed. Yet here we are inside of it."

Rebecca crinkled her forehead in concentration and closed her eyes tightly, trying to make sense of everything. "I don't know. Maybe they... had another one." Looking up at them, she pleaded, "We must get off of this planet! Please!"

"Calm down, Rebecca. The others are loading the probe into the hold as we speak," Captain Coffner said. "Once it is secure, we will be ready for lift-off. If all goes as planned, we should be leaving in another hour or two."

"And the MDU grid? Is it still functioning?"

"Yes, yes," the captain said, beginning to lose patience. "In the meantime, you need to rest. I am glad to see you are feeling better. Lisa, may I speak to you for a moment please."

As the two of them stepped over to stand near the door, Rebecca leaned back, her emotions simmering between nervousness and controlled panic. *An hour or two. Will that be quick enough? Will the Torlig, or V'skir, or some other clan find us before we can liftoff? How can I make them understand?*

Once Lisa and Captain Coffner finished their conversation, the captain excused himself and left the room. Walking back over to where her patient lay, Lisa smiled. "Now, before we let you out of bed, let's check your vital signs."

Rebecca tried to force herself to relax, letting Lisa perform the needed tests. Staring blankly at the wall, her thoughts began to wander, reflecting on what Lisa and the captain had said. *Am I going crazy? If it wasn't a dream, then how did I get away from the Torlig arena, and how could the Torlig have copied the* Vanguard *so quickly? But it all seemed so real. I can still smell the burning fuel from the destruction of the ship and the taste of the sand from the arena. Could it all really have been nothing more than a coma-induced hallucination? And what put me into the coma in the first place? Was it some kind of shock brought on by my fear of an imagined moving light?*

Lisa's voice halted her train of thought. Turning her head to look at her friend, she said, "I'm sorry. What did you say?"

Her attention focused on reading the blood pressure gauge in her hand, Lisa merely repeated her question without looking at Rebecca. "I was just wondering how you got that scar on your arm. I didn't remember seeing it before we left Earth. Did this happen on the trip here?"

Rebecca turned her head even further to look at her left arm as Lisa removed the blood pressure gauge. What she saw made her heart stop suddenly with alarm and astonishment. Just above the elbow was a nasty burn scar that was almost three inches in diameter. She almost cried out in pain as the memory of the Mrdangam's acid searing through her flesh flooded over her like a torrent of rushing water.

Lisa, seeing Rebecca's distress became instantly concerned. "What is it? Becky, are you hurt?"

Her barely controlled fear broke through its thin leash and burst out like a caged animal suddenly released. "It…it *WAS* real! Oh, my…oh… we…we have to…"

"Rebecca, look at me!" Lisa commanded, grabbing her by the shoulders. "We are safe here, nothing is going to—"

"But you don't understand!" Rebecca said, cutting her off. "It *WAS* real! I can prove it. This scar is from a wound I received when a Mrdangam spit acid on my arm."

"A what?" Lisa said in bewilderment.

"A Mrdangam. It is a dragon-like alien that spits acid. They live on the mountain. That is why we must leave quickly!"

"Rebecca, listen to yourself. A dragon? Spitting acid? Do you really believe you saw these things?"

"Yes! How else do you explain this?" she shot back, pointing at her arm. "You may not believe me, but I know these things are out there. If you are not going to...wait. What are you doing? Stop it. Lisa, I'm... not...crazy."

The last thing she remembered before the sedative took effect was the look of profound sadness on Lisa's face.

Before she was even fully conscious, Rebecca could feel and hear the rumble of the *Vanguard*'s engines firing, creating a steady background hum. Opening her eyes, she stared around at the familiar surroundings of her makeshift hospital room. The lights were turned down low and music played softly in the background. The overall effect was soothing, and Rebecca, not yet fully awake, drifted peacefully in the calming ambiance.

The sound of the door opening and closing softly behind her dispelled the relaxing atmosphere and brought her mind closer to full alertness. Turning her head, she saw a shadowy form approach her bed. Before she could inquire about the person's identity, the visitor spoke.

"It's me, Lisa. I'm glad to see you are waking up again."

"What...what happened?" Rebecca said, still groggy.

Lisa sat down in a chair near the bed and situated it so she could see Rebecca easily. "Before I tell you that, I want to let you know that we are on our way home. We left 2021 PK an hour ago."

Rebecca came fully awake now, but this time, Lisa's news lifted a great weight from her shoulders. "You mean...we actually made it? We...we were not attacked?"

Lisa smiled and shook her head. "Everything went smoothly. No problems."

Sinking comfortably into her bed, Rebecca closed her eyes and sighed deeply. *Home.*

"I am sorry I had to knock you out again, but...well, with your state of mind being what it was, I thought it would be best if you were unconscious until we were safely on our way," Lisa said apologetically.

With her eyes still closed, she merely nodded to her friend in understanding.

"Also, I wanted to tell you that all of your vital signs look normal, so, once you feel up to it, we can get you up and about. Until then, I'll leave you alone and let you rest. If you need anything, just give me a buzz," she said as she handed Rebecca a commlink.

"Thank you, Lisa," Rebecca said with an appreciative smile. "Thank you for taking care of me."

"Hey, no sweat, Gunny."

Rebecca watched Lisa turn and prepare to leave when a sudden though struck her. Reaching out, Rebecca grabbed her arm. "Lisa, have you seen my journal?"

"Yeah. It's right here, along with some of your other stuff," she said, indicating a drawer built into the wall near the bed.

"Thanks," Rebecca said softly, trying not to let any of her suddenly turbulent emotions reveal themselves, lest Lisa decide to sedate her again.

As the door slid shut, Rebecca sat motionless, staring intently at the drawer as if she could pierce its metal exterior by merely gazing at it. *Could it be possible?* Stretching out a trembling hand, she slowly opened the drawer and removed the device. Cradling it gently in her hands as if it were an armed explosive, she held her breath and turned it on. The machine sprang to life as usual. Entering the access code, she cycled through the menu with shaking hands, looking for the list of previous entries.

With each passing second of searching, her heart beat more rapidly. Finally, finding what she was looking for, Rebecca inhaled sharply as the screen displayed the number of entries contained in the machines memory: six. She nearly dropped it in shock. With trembling fingers, she opened the last entry and heard her own voice speaking words of despair from within the Torlig prison. Her thoughts scattered and confused, she shut off the recording. *Oh, my God! It's all here! All of the entries I made while on 2021 PK—Ka'esch. I was right! It wasn't a dream!*

I have to show this to the others. This is proof that...She stopped mid-thought, her body halfway out of bed. Slowly, she sank back down. *No. They still wouldn't believe me. They would probably end up sedating me again. Not to mention I need to think this through and figure out for myself exactly what I believe happened before I start trying to convince others.*

As she sat in deep reflection, the soft music played continuously in the background, completely unnoticed by the room's lone occupant.

Rebecca stared out the viewport at the distant stars as they passed silently by the rapidly moving vessel, the ever present rumble of the engines beneath her feet comforting her like a soothing massage. Her mind at peace for the first time in recent memory, she sighed contentedly. Pressing the record button on the device in the palm of her hand, she began to speak.

Journal Entry #7

I knew this trip to 2021 PK would be life changing, I just never understood how deep that change would go. The very foundation of everything I have believed and built my life upon has been shattered. What I once thought was true has proven false, and what I once thought impossible, I now believe possible.

Even though the Cortex Propulsion Drive has been running at full speed, it still cannot match the speed of the laser sail. It has been almost four months since we left 2021 PK, the world that I will forever refer to as Ka'esch. We should be arriving at Earth within the next couple of days. I cannot wait to see my husband and family, yet I am also somewhat apprehensive. I have so much to tell them, and I have changed so much. I pray they will understand. But before we arrive, I want to record my thoughts about my experience on Ka'esch, for I believe that I finally comprehend what happened to me there.

Growing up in church, I remember hearing many stories of people having visions and meeting angels. As I matured, I came to the conclusion that they were just that: stories. Stories made up by imaginative people to get across some moral idea. A fable. But now, after what I have experienced, I am forced to reevaluate my own beliefs, for my experience has direct similarities and parallels to those supposedly fictional accounts.

I have never believed in the existence of a Creator God. Yet now, how can I deny it? I could have written off the whole thing as a delusion or hallucination, but how can I write off a physical scar, or the recordings in my journal? Are they just figments of my imagination? Even if I could dismiss them, even if it was just a dream, the arguments made by Prin and Sikaris against evolution are still valid.

It seems that I have based my life on a lie. Evolution is a bankrupt theory that fails to account for all of the complexity we see around us. Logic demands a Creator, and the evidence, when examined objectively, points to His handiwork.

And for some reason, He has chosen me to tell others. I am thankful that He has left me with my journal recordings. For not only are they proof that I am not crazy, but they will also provide me with a starting point for my new research.

So, where do I go from here? Should I let the others listen to the journal? Would they believe me? No. I don't think so. I know I wouldn't believe me. Maybe my family will understand, but I doubt anyone else will.

Sikaris said, "The Almighty Lord of the Universe has brought you here to show you many things. Never forget what you were shown and all that you have learned. You are the chosen vessel. Chosen to deliver the message to those who will listen." My calling seems clear: I must study and refine my understanding of the scientific and logical arguments for creation and against evolution, then share that knowledge. I know it will not be easy, and it may even cost me my job. But when the God of the Universe marks you and interrupts your life, it is bound to make an impact.

But before I begin, I have one thing I must do first. In order to tell others about the Creator's work, I must find out who He is. There are so many religions and opinions as to who God is, will I even be able to know for certain which idea or theology is the correct one?

It is one thing to believe that God exists and that He created everything, but it is quite another to find out who He is and what His purpose is for your life. But no matter what the outcome, this much I know: He has personally called me, and I must respond.

Epilogue

REBECCA GRABBED the sides of the podium with confidence, her posture relaxed, and her mind alert. Scanning the crowd gathered in the hotel conference room, she locked gazes with as many of the attendees as she could. Taking a deep breath, she clicked the remote in her hand to switch the screen to her final slide.

"Ladies and gentlemen, what we must understand is that we can firmly say that evolution is impossible, not because of what we *don't* know, but because of what we *do* know. Because of our modern understanding of chemicals, it would be foolish to continue to pursue ways of transmuting lead into gold. In the same sense, we *know* that information cannot be created randomly, we *know* that complex organs cannot be put together step by step, and we *know* that mutations cannot create genetic material, yet some scientists spend countless hours and billions of dollars every year trying to do just that.

"Instead, we should simply face the cold, hard facts: the universe, and all life, must have been created.

"But many do not like that conclusion because of the implications. If we were created, then we are no longer the highest authority. We no longer set the rules of morality. They would prefer to believe in the impossible.

"People who believe in God are often painted as naïve or foolish by the die-hard defenders of evolution. Some have even gone so far as to equate it with a mental disorder. The famous 20th century evolutionist, Richard Dawkins, said, 'It is absolutely safe to say that if you meet somebody who claims not to believe in evolution, that person is ignorant, stupid, or insane (or wicked, but I'd rather not consider that).' If evolution was truly supported by science, then I might agree that to believe in God would be a form of insanity." The hint of a smile formed on Rebecca's face as the memory of a cackling laugh echoed in her mind. "But in reality," she continued, "it is the other way around: to deny the existence of God in the face of all of the supporting evidence is the height of foolishness.

"When we examine the facts and follow them to their logical end, without letting our preconceived ideas, our biases, get in the way, we must conclude that we were designed.

"Thank you for inviting me to speak tonight, and may God bless you."

The conference hall erupted with applause as Rebecca collected her notes from the podium and stepped down from the stage. As she approached her table, the smiling faces of her family greeted her. She silently thanked God for their support, for it had taken most of the six years since her return from 2021 PK for them to accept the changes that had happened to her.

Everyone except her husband.

Their already strained marriage had suffered even further. Jeffrey had difficulty accepting her true account of what had happened. Rebecca knew it was a risk to tell him, so she had waited several months before revealing her vision to him, or anyone else in her family. Even after he had accepted the fact that she had experienced some sort of "realistic dream," he still struggled to come to grips with Rebecca's newfound beliefs, putting further tension in their marriage.

Her parents had very different reactions. Upon her return they were extremely concerned for her health and wanted her to check herself into the hospital for tests of all kinds. Her refusal to do so only served to worry them more. In an effort to assuage their fears, as well as check on her father's diabetes, Rebecca made it a priority to visit with them at least once a month. When she finally told them the truth about what had happened on 2021 PK, her parents actually responded with relief, thankful that the coma was God's doing, and not the result of some unknown space sickness.

Out of all of her family, her sister was the one who really supported her immediately. Although she expressed some initial concern when Rebecca first told her about the vision, her trust for her older sister quickly over-rode any apprehension. Katie even jumped on board to help out as a kind of secretary as the speaking engagements started to roll in.

And roll in they did. Although they had failed to find any signs of life on 2021 PK, the scientific data they had collected had made the overall mission a success. For a short time, the entire crew attained instant celebrity status. Although she was thrilled at the attention and excitement that came with the interviews and news stories, she was also deeply engrossed in her own personal research, using every moment of free time to devour books, articles, and websites about the scientific arguments supporting creation and intelligent design.

After the initial media frenzy died down, Rebecca spent several years trying to work on her struggling marriage and rebuild her relationships with her family, as well as adjusting to her new beliefs. Eventually, she received a call to speak at a science convention, which she accepted. For the first time, Rebecca shared the results of her research into the scientific proofs for creation and the flaws of evolution. Although the general audience was not enthusiastic about her views, there were many in attendance who asked her afterward if she would be willing to speak at other venues about her findings. After several months of conferences and private functions, it became clear to her that she would have to resign from NASA in order to meet the increasing demand for speaking engagements.

Although Lisa understood why she had decided to leave NASA, it nevertheless saddened her to lose daily contact with her best friend. As Rebecca traveled across the country to speak, she made it a point to always stop in to see Lisa, Jenny, and Amanda whenever she was in their area.

"Great job, Becky!" Katie said, her voice bringing Rebecca's thoughts back to the present. Rising from her chair, she gave her sister a quick hug as the applause in the room slowly died down.

"Thanks," she said as she slid into the chair that Jeffrey had pulled out for her. *At least he stayed for the whole speech. Lord, maybe this time…* She smiled at him, her eyes searching for some sign of his feelings. Yet despite her probing, his thoughts proved unreadable, locked up tight like a vault.

Once she was seated, she brushed aside her concern for her husband and forced herself to relax, allowing her mind to wander. It seemed ironic that this was the very conference room in which she had given her speech about the need for a manned mission to 2021 PK so long ago. *So much has changed since then.* As the conference session ended, people began to stand and head directly for her table. *Then again, some things never change,* she thought wryly.

"I'll be waiting in the car," Jeffrey said abruptly as he stood up from the table and immediately headed for the exit.

As she watched her husband depart, the ache within her seemed to deepen and swell. *Lord, how I love him. Please help him to see.*

"I…uh…I think I'll join him," Paul said noting Rebecca's concern. Giving Katie a quick kiss, he stood and followed in Jeffrey's footsteps.

Eager to gloss over her son-in-law's rapid departure, Rebecca's mother stood and patted her daughter on the arm. "You get better each time, dear. Keep it up."

"Yes, we are both very proud of you," her father chimed in as his wife maneuvered his wheelchair closer to where Rebecca sat. After a quick kiss on the cheek, the two of them wound their way through the conference hall, leaving Rebecca and her sister standing alone.

"Don't worry, sis," Katie whispered into her ear. "He'll come around. Maybe Paul can help him see what a gem he has for a wife."

Grasping her sister's hand tightly for reassurance, she forced her thoughts aside. "Thanks. I don't know what I would do without your support."

"Hey, I'm only in it for the money and fame," she said with a grin.

For the next several minutes, a crowd gathered around the table, eager to ask questions on one subject or another. Rebecca politely responded time and again, thankful for the opportunity to share her knowledge with those who were hungry to learn.

Then, just as she was about to answer the latest question, her gaze fell upon a familiar looking dark complexioned gentleman dressed in a navy blue, pinstriped suit standing near the back of the room. For a moment, she simply stared at him, trying to determine where she had seen him before. Then, recognition hit her like a lightning strike, causing her to gasp aloud. *The eyes! Could it really be...* Without taking her focus off of the stranger, she excused herself from the group of conference attendees and headed off in his direction.

She had not taken more than two steps when he turned and began heading towards the main set of double doors that led from the conference hall into the foyer beyond. Fighting her way through the crowd, she headed toward the exit as quickly as possible without being impolite. In the back of her mind she could barely hear the voice of her sister calling after her with concern.

Rebecca was about to call out to the stranger when he walked through the doorway and disappeared from sight. Several seconds later, she finally managed to push her way past the last of the crowd and made it through the doors. Breathing heavily, she stopped just beyond the entrance and stared around in all directions in search of the pinstriped suit.

Where did he go? All around her, people milled about, moving slowly due to the crowded foyer and hallways. *He couldn't have gotten far. He must have—*

"Mrs. Evans? Mrs. Evans!"

Turning towards the voice calling to her, she saw a young man approaching, wearing a nametag bearing the insignia of the hotel. In his hand, he carried a small, folded piece of paper. Disappointed, she resumed her visual search of the area as she replied, "I'm sorry, but I can't give an autograph right now. I am trying to find someone."

"I'm not here for an autograph, ma'am. I was told to give this to you."

"What?" Rebecca said, suddenly giving the young man her full attention. Taking the offered piece of paper, she glanced at it, then stared at him, her nerves on end. "Who...who told you to give this to me?"

"He just passed this way a moment ago," he replied, suddenly taken aback by the intensity of Rebecca's mannerisms. "He was a tall man with black hair and brown skin, dressed in a dark blue suit with white pinstripes."

"Thank you," she said, her voice shaking with excitement. As the young man turned away, she unfolded the paper and began to read.

Rebecca Clan Evans,

You have done well. I am encouraged to see that you are fulfilling the calling that the Master has placed on your life. Always remember what you learned during your time on Ka'esch. Keep it in the forefront of your mind so that your faith will not waiver during the difficult times that lie ahead.

May the Eternal Creator continue to light your path and guide your steps.

Sikaris

Rebecca reread the letter two more times before slowly refolding it and looking once more around the foyer in the fleeting hopes of catching a glimpse of the pinstriped suit. As she stood there in silence, her sister came jogging through the doors of the conference hall. Upon seeing Rebecca, she immediately walked up and placed her hand on Rebecca's shoulder, concern etched on her handsome features.

"Are you okay? Is something wrong?"

"No," she said, shaking her head slowly, her eyes still staring off at nothing in particular. Handing her sister the folded note, she reflected upon the message. "*Difficult times that lie ahead." What did he mean?*

As Katie read the letter in shock, Rebecca simply smiled. There was once a point in her life where the thought of difficult times would have caused her to worry. But now she knew that no matter what came at her, her faith would see her through. For her life was now based upon an unchanging foundation.

Afterword

WHERE DID we come from? How did life begin? The answers to these two questions form the foundation on which all other questions in life are based. And, when broken down, there are really only two possible answers: either the universe and all matter in existence sprang into being on its own, or it was created by some eternal entity that exists apart from time and space.

Although there are some who propose a third explanation—that we were created by aliens—this is, in reality, the same as the first argument. For if we were created by aliens, then how did the aliens come to be? Eventually, if you go back far enough, you end up at the previous two possible answers: special creation or random evolution.

The question of origins, whether we realize it consciously or not, is the driving force behind every decision we make. For if evolution is true, then man is the ultimate authority; there is no one higher. Therefore, all things are permissible, all behaviors and choices are acceptable. There is no objective basis for morality.

However, if there is a Creator, a Designer of the Universe, then we must find out who He is, and why He created us. Morality then becomes based upon His rules.

Because of this, all of our modern social issues—abortion, euthanasia, homosexuality, racial prejudice, etc.—have their roots in the question of how life began. This is why the debate over creation and evolution is of utmost importance. If we as a society cannot agree upon this foundational issue, then it is nearly impossible to reconcile our opinions about the other issues.

Unfortunately, when attempting to answer this most fundamental question, many scientists rule out one answer before they even begin looking at the evidence. Without verbalizing it, many often have the mentality that says, "There is no god, now how did life begin?" This would be akin to a math teacher telling the class that the number four does not exist, then asking, "What is two plus two?"

Part of this mentality is due to the fact that many believe that religion deals with things about God, and science deals with things that we can see, feel, and touch. While science *does* deal with the material universe, it does not mean that we must automatically rule out a supernatural *origin* of the universe.

Furthermore, it is important to understand that the science that deals with the origin of life is different from laboratory science. If an experiment can be repeated in a laboratory, it is called operational science. This is the type of science that put man on the moon and allows us to see distant stars.

Forensic science, on the other hand, is using scientific methods to examine evidence in an effort to understand a past event. Detectives, archaeologists, and pathologists are examples of professionals who utilize this type of science. In forensics, it is important to note that interpretation is critical. If a detective misinterprets a vital piece of evidence, it could completely throw off the final conclusion. It is also possible to have several interpretations of the same evidence.

Origin science falls into this category. No human was alive at the dawn of time. Therefore, we study the evidence around us, such as fossils, rock layers, and living creatures, and we draw conclusions based on what we find.

To many scientists, the theory of evolution best explains the evidence. However, there are a large and growing number of scientists who believe that the creation model offers a more complete explanation. (For a list of over 600 scientists who hold this conviction, visit the website:www.

discovery.org, keyword: doubt) Both sides have the same evidence, what differs is the interpretation. Often the media, activist groups, and others try to convince the general populace that the battle is between religion and science, but that is simply not true. The real debate is within the academies of science themselves.

Since it is a matter of interpretation, how do we tell which one is correct? We must apply logical reasoning and carefully examine both theories to search for areas where the interpretation is not logically supported by the evidence. After spending several years researching both theories, I am convinced that the theory of evolution is based on several assumptions that are not simply a matter of interpretation, but they are scientifically unsound.

(If you are interested in learning more about how the creation scientists counter evolutionary arguments about things like ape-men, dinosaurs, or rock layers in the Grand Canyon, I encourage you to check out the materials listed on my reference page.)

Due to space constraints, I will only focus on those areas of scientific impossibilities within the theory of evolution. I have broken them down into four main categories: Biological Information, Irreducible Complexity, Mathematical Probability, and Random Mutations.

Biological Information

If you were walking along the beach and found a message written in the sand that said, "John loves Mary," you would immediately recognize that it must have been written by an intelligent being. Or if you saw a message written in the clouds that said, "Eat at Joe's," you would not confuse the skywriting with natural shapes formed randomly. But why? How do we define information anyway?

Webster's Dictionary defines information as: "the communication or reception of knowledge or intelligence." Information is conveyed when a series of symbols are combined into certain patterns, and those patterns are assigned specific meanings. The letters themselves mean nothing. It is the combinations of the letters that are important. In addition, when certain words are combined, you get sentences, and sentences can be combined to make paragraphs.

Now by randomly combining letters, you may form a few words. But if you randomly combine words, you get gibberish. Again, over an extremely long time, you may get lucky and form a few simple sentences like, "he sat down", but you would never get any meaningful paragraphs, much less an entire cohesive book.

The only way to get meaningful combinations of letters and words is to have an intelligence manipulating them and placing them in the proper patterns and sequences. Therefore, when we find information in living things, the only logical conclusion is that it must have been placed there by an intelligent being.

DNA is the most incredible storage system in the known universe. It is so complex, it has taken generations of scientists building on each other's work to map it out. By using a system of four different proteins called nucleotides, DNA encodes all kinds of instructions that tell the various parts of the cell how to perform a variety of tasks. It is very similar to the software needed to run a computer. And the amount of information contained in the DNA molecule boggles the mind. Although the entire DNA of a human could fit in a tablespoon, it contains enough information to fill 1000, five hundred-page books of very small print (3 billion letters long)![1]

By contrast, a bacterium contains enough information to fill only one book of five hundred pages. Therefore, two questions come to mind: 1. How did this supposedly "simple" life form get so much information to begin with? and 2. How did life go from one book of information to one thousand books?

Furthermore, information stored in DNA would be useless without a method of retrieving it. What good is a computer program stored on a compact disc without the computer to read it? In life, it is the RNA that translates the stored information in DNA and instructs the various biological machines on what to do. And, it is the RNA that tells the cell how to construct DNA! So you can't have one without the other. It is the typical "chicken and egg" situation. It defies logic to think that one could somehow evolve independent of the other.

Irreducible Complexity

All complex machines must have a minimum number of parts to function. In the early 1990s, Michael Behe coined the phrase, "Irreducible Complexity." The main point of his book, *Darwin's Black Box,* was that complex organs could not have evolved bit by bit because in order to function at all, all parts must be present and in the correct order.[2]

His famous example is that of an old-fashioned mousetrap. In order to catch any mice at all, you must have all five pieces—the hammer, the platform, the spring, etc.—in the right position at the same time. If you were missing any one part, such as the spring, or if a part were positioned incorrectly, the mousetrap would be useless.

The same holds true for biological machines. Take birds, for example. It has often been theorized that dinosaurs evolved into birds, yet birds must have a combination of complex structures to fly. For the sake of argument, I will mention just three: hollow bones, a digestive system built for flight, and feathers. (And the complexity of the feather alone could fill an entire book or more—visit the Answers in Genesis website for more information.) [3] Now imagine a dinosaur born with hollow bones, but no feathers. Would it be better able to survive? No. The hollow bones would actually make it more likely to die without offspring. Or what if, miraculously, the creature evolved wings with feathers and hollow bones, but its digestive system was not suited for flight. Again, it would not survive.

Or, for another example, look at the different systems in the body. How could the first single-celled creature survive without an immune system? How many generations did it take to evolve a reproductive system, much less a male/female reproductive system? Or how could a nervous system, or the respiratory system evolve step by step? All of these systems are complex. It is impossible for them to evolve slowly.

Now, it might be believable that an ape might evolve into a human, because they both have arms, legs, hearts, lungs, etc., just like modern cars have more efficient tires and engines than their predecessors. But even the first car ever built was irreducibly complex. Imagine if a car was missing even one of its major components, like wheels, a fuel source, a method of steering, or a source of power? It wouldn't function at all. Along the same lines, what good would a heart be with only one chamber, or no valves or arteries?

Modern science has now determined that one single cell of the human body is like a miniature factory more complex than a space shuttle. But when Darwin first formulated his theory, he thought the cell was simple, like a blob of protoplasm. From his perspective, the theory of evolution was perhaps believable. But with our current knowledge, it is not only unbelievable, but impossible.

Another way to understand irreducible complexity is to consider a stereo system. One may ask: "How do you play a CD?" The response? "Simple. Just put the CD in the player and press play." But is it really that simple? At the most basic level, you need a CD player to read the stored information, an amplifier to boost the signal, and a set of speakers to translate the electronic impulses into sound. Yet, each one of these larger components is incredibly complex. The CD player has a laser, a motor to spin the disc, a power supply, and numerous amounts of wires and circuits all carefully placed in the precise location. And if even one of them is damaged, no sound will be produced.

If logic dictates that this complex device must have been designed, then why do we say that the human body, which is infinitely more complex, could have evolved randomly?

"But, if given enough time, it could happen," some will say. Well, when you understand the complexity of DNA and the cell, and you combine that with a basic knowledge of probability, you realize that no matter how much time you have, a complex structure like a cell could never evolve by random processes.

Mathematical Probability

Imagine you have a ten-sided die. Your chances of rolling the number one would be 1 out of 10. If you add a second ten-sided die, the chances of rolling a one, then a two in succession would be 1 out of 100. For each additional die you add, you multiply by ten. Therefore, to get a sequence of numbers from 1 to 10 in a row, the chances would be 1 out of a billion. You will be rolling dice for a long time before you get even a simple sequence.

Now imagine the probability of getting a specific sequence of information that would fill a five hundred-page book. The probability is so small, we cannot even fathom it. Sir Fred Hoyle, a famous astronomer, once calculated that the chance of life arising by random processes was $10^{40,000}$. This would be comparable to lining up 10^{50} (which is ten followed by fifty zeros) blind people, giving each one a scrambled Rubik's Cube, and finding that they all solve the cube at the same moment.[4] Or to put it another way, imagine rolling an ordinary six-sided die and getting the same number five million times in a row!

Dr. Emile Borel, who discovered the laws of probability, has said:

> The occurrence of any event where the chances are beyond one in ten followed by 50 zeros is an event which we can state with certainty will never happen, no matter how much time is allotted and no matter how many conceivable opportunities could exist for the event to take place.[5]

Furthermore, if we were created by unguided forces, then we, with our intelligence, should be able to duplicate the process, for randomness can easily be copied by intelligence.

In the example given earlier, to get the numbers 1 through 10 in the correct order would require one chance out of a billion, yet a five-year-old child could line up the same numbers very quickly. So why can't we, with all of our advanced technology, reproduce something that was supposedly formed randomly? It simply doesn't make any logical sense.

And even if this were not sufficient to put the nail in the coffin of evolution, there is still the matter of mutations. As I mentioned previously, there is enough information in the DNA of a bacterium to fill a five hundred-page book, and a human DNA would fill 1000 books of the same length. So even if a bacterium somehow arose by natural processes, how did humans accumulate 999 more books worth of information? Where did it all come from?

Random Mutations

The most common answer given to the above question is: mutations. However, there has never been a single observed instance of a mutation adding genetic information to a living organism.[6] Even the extremely rare, so-called "helpful" mutations, such as bacteria becoming resistant to pesticides, when studied closely, have been shown to be due to a *loss* of genetic information.

Mutations are mistakes in gene sequences, causing diseases or deformations, not new, complex structures. You may find a mutated chicken with an extra leg, or a snake with two heads, or a person who was born with an extra finger or toe. But this is nothing new. In each instance, the genetic information already existed within them to create a leg, a head, or a finger, it just got mixed-up and put in the wrong spot. What we would never find, however, is a mutation that gives a dog gills, or a pig wings. It just doesn't happen.

Genes can be compared to a deck of playing cards. You can shuffle them and get millions of combinations, which accounts for all the various types of dogs we see in the world, or the different sizes of beaks on Darwin's finches. But how long would you have to shuffle a deck of cards to create a new card?

The answer, of course, is that you could never do it, even if you were given all of eternity, because the possibility is just not there. Instead, what you find is that the longer you shuffle, the more the cards get bent and damaged.

So when it comes down to it, mutations *cannot* account for evolutionary changes. Yet, that is what the entire theory of evolution is based upon. Natural selection alone cannot do it, for it only preserves changes in gene combinations, it is not the source of new genes.

As Rebecca said in the Epilogue, we can firmly say that evolution is impossible, not because of what we *don't* know, but because of what we *do* know. The more we learn about biology and the unseen structures of life—DNA, cells, genes—the more we realize that creation is the only theory that makes logical sense.

Theistic Evolution

Before I conclude, I would like to very briefly address the issue of theistic evolution. Due to the sheer volume of propaganda produced by the proponents of evolution, many average citizens are caught with a dilemma: they believe evolution is true, but they also believe that God is real. So, they often try to fit the two together. Thus, we get theistic evolution, where God guided evolution to create all of life, including humans. This compromised position is held by many people of faith, and even by some of its greatest leaders. However, there are numerous theological problems with this stance, and a plethora of articles and books have been written about this issue.

But I have found that the majority of people of faith who hold this position have simply not looked into the flaws in the evolutionary theory. They try to make it fit with creationism because they believe both to be true. However, as I have shown, evolution is not based on observable science, thus, to try to make it fit with the theory of special creation by God would be like trying to make the theory that the Earth is flat mix with the scientific fact that the Earth is round! There is no reason to try to make a proven fact fit with a false theory.

So where does this leave us? I have thus far shown that a Creator must exist, but the question remains: who is He? For what purposes were we created? It is beyond the scope of these notes to deal with this issue, as it is even more complex than the issue of creation and evolution. However, the answer to this question is of infinite more importance.

For me, after having done the research, I can confidently say that I believe that Jesus is the Son of God, and that the Bible is indeed the Word of God. Space does not permit me to present you with all of the arguments supporting my belief, but there are many books available which do.

I *strongly* encourage you to research this question for yourself. Do not just believe something because someone told you it is true. Question the logic, scrutinize the arguments, and make a decision based upon research, study, and logic, and pray that God will reveal Himself to you. "Real gold fears no fire." If a belief is true, it will withstand scrutiny. A great place to start would be the Answers in Genesis or Institute for Creation Research websites, or the book *The Case for Christ* by former atheist, Lee Strobel. Good luck in your journey. May God guide your steps.

Keith A. Robinson

Appendix: Suggested Informational Material

Websites

www.AnswersInGenesis.org—The official website of Answers in Genesis, one of the largest creation ministries in the world.

www.discovery.org—The official website of the Discovery Institute, the "think tank" for the intelligent design movement.

www.icr.org—The official website of the Institute for Creation Research.

www.creationscience.com—This website contains the complete, FREE, online edition of *In the Beginning: Compelling Evidence for Creation and the Flood* (7th Edition) by Dr. Walt Brown.

www.evolution-facts.org—This website contains the complete, FREE, online edition of *Evolution Cruncher* by Vance Ferrell. This paperback is based on the 1,326-page, three-volume Evolution Disproved Series.

www.christiananswers.net/creation—This website has lots or great material, including the entire video *A Question of Origins* available to view for FREE online.

http://www.leestrobel.com/—Lee Strobel was a former atheist and has now written several books investigating the Christian faith, including *The Case for the Creator.*

Books

Darwin's Demise: Why Evolution Can't Take the Heat by Joe White and Nicholas Comninellis

Darwin's Black Box: The Biochemical Challenge to Evolution by Michael Behe

Darwin on Trial by Phillip E. Johnson

The Design Revolution: Answering the Toughest Questions about Intelligent Design by William A. Dembski

Icons of Evolution: Science or Myth? Why Much of What We Teach about Evolution is Wrong by Jonathan Wells

Evolution: A Theory in Crisis by Michael Denton

The Answers Book by Don Batten, Ken Ham, Jonathan Sarfati, and Carl Wieland

The Case for the Creator by Lee Strobel

DVDs and Videos

Incredible Creatures that Defy Evolution, Vol. 1, 2, 3 *with Dr. Jobe Martin*—Exploration Films

Unlocking the Mystery of Life—Illustra Media

Icons of Evolution—Illustra Media

The Priviledged Planet—Illustra Media

The Case for the Creator—Illustra Media

A Question of Origins—Eternal Productions. This entire video can be viewed online for FREE at www.christiananswers.net/creation.

For other products, visit the Answers in Genesis or Institute for Creation Research websites mentioned above.

Notes

1. Joe White and Nicholas Comninellis, *Darwin's Demise: Why Evolution Can't Take the Heat* (Green Forest, AR: Master Books, 2002), 29.

2. Michael Behe, *Darwin's Black Box: The Biochemical Challenge to Evolution* (New York, NY: The Free Press, 1996).

3. Jerry Bergman, "The Evolution of Feathers: A Major Problem for Darwinism," *Creation Ex Nihilo Technical Journal,* 17(1):33-41 (April 2003).

4. Fred Hoyle, "Hoyle on Evolution," *Nature,* vol. 294 (November 12, 1981): 148.

5. Emile Borel, *Probabilities and Life* (New York, NY: Dover Publications, 1962).

6. L. Spetner, *Not by Chance* (Brooklyn, NY: The Judaica Press, Inc.) See review in *Creation Ex Nihilo,* 20(1):50-51 (December 1997/February 1998).